# *On Ashover Hill*

# On Ashover Hill

ANTHONY SCOTT

Matador
9 Priory Business Park
Kibworth Beauchamp
Leicestershire LE8 0RX, UK
Tel: (+44) 116 279 2299
Fax: (+44) 116 279 2277
Email: books@troubador.co.uk
Web: www.troubador.co.uk/matador

ISBN 978 1780883 052

British Library Cataloguing in Publication Data.
A catalogue record for this book is available from the British Library.

Typeset in Palatino by Troubador Publishing Ltd
Printed and bound in the UK by TJ International, Padstow, Cornwall

**Matador** is an imprint of Troubador Publishing Ltd

*"Eppur si muove"*
*Galileo Galilei 1633*

*Chapter 1. Discovery. February 12th 2046. Ashover, Derbyshire, England*          *1*

*Chapter 2. William. November 1943. Naples, Italy*          *10*

*Chapter 3. Francesca. March 1948. Florence, Italy*          *36*

*Chapter 4. William and Francesca. May 1952. Florence, Italy*          *40*

*Chapter 5. Robert. July 1st 1963. Edinburgh, Scotland*          *59*

*Chapter 6. Angus. July 1977. Edinburgh, Scotland*          *60*

*Chapter 7. Robert. May 1982. Sheffield, England*          *74*

*Chapter 8. Alison. July 1982. Sheffield, England*          *92*

*Chapter 9. Robert. Summer 1982. Edinburgh, Scotland*          *103*

*Chapter 10. Robert. October 1982. Sheffield, England*          *116*

*Chapter 11. Building the Business. June 1985. Sheffield, England*          *124*

*Chapter 12. A Visit Home. April 1989. Edinburgh, England*          *137*

*Chapter 13. The Birthday Party. Summer 1989. Ashover, Derbyshire, England*   *152*

*Chapter 14. Desolation. September 1992. Edinburgh, Scotland*          *178*

*Chapter 15. Holiday. 1st July 1993. Bourg, France*          *188*

*Chapter 16. William. May 1994. Port Isaac, Cornwall, England*          *203*

*Chapter 17. Back to Business. June 2000. Sheffield, England*          *221*

*Chapter 18. Taylor. Winter 2010. Spain*          *237*

*Chapter 19. Jasmine. April 2019. London, England*          *274*

*Chapter 20. Angus. 1st July 2023. Thoresby Hall, Nottinghamshire, England*   *296*

*Chapter 21. Edith. Autumn 2031. London, England*          *312*

*Chapter 22. The Gift. July 2034. Florence, Italy*          *341*

*Chapter 23. The End. June 1994. Port Isaac, Cornwall, England*          *371*

# Chapter 1

# Discovery

February 12th 2046. Ashover, Derbyshire, England

Henry is making his third of the night security check, walking around the dark and brooding perimeter of the building site. As always he struggles with the nagging thought that he would be far better off in his warm and welcoming site cabin, a mug of far too sweet tea in one hand and a chocolate biscuit in the other. Things are normally fine out on site anyway, and Henry can count on one hand the number of times over the 15 years of him doing this mind numbing job that something had been seriously amiss. Sure enough, one of those resulted in him having an arm badly broken by two unruly youths bent on trouble, but the company were good and the damages paid for his new car. He could do with another new car now so maybe something being amiss tonight wouldn't be such a bad call after all. Mind you his old friend Dan, who did the same job as Henry for the same firm, had got attacked the other year and it had changed him. Fearful, he was now, a different man. Henry would not want that. Fear killed a man slowly, ate him up from the inside. You could see the light fade from the eyes, the burning to live gradually being watered down to a near nothingness save for regret and terror. That wouldn't do for Henry, no sir, he had too much to live for. He considered himself a man with many bright years ahead of him, a man who still had a bright future to live, something to offer the masses and much joy to experience.

All in all Henry likes his job. It gives him plenty of time, highly valuable time, to read extensively and become more knowledgeable about national and world events. Education had never really been Henry's thing as a young lad with so many other things that seemed to fill the time but now, later in life, he is playing catching up. He reads *The Times* every day without fail, and he does so in absolute and complete detail. Every word is soaked up like the worlds best blotting paper, and he has found he can replay such a selection of facts that his envious friends are blown away by the new, all knowing, Henry. He likes that. He likes that very much indeed.

The job pays the bills and leaves a little left over and these days that is not to be sniffed at. After all how many people have virtually nothing, no money, no hope, no future. Not Henry. He is sorted.

And the best bit of the job? Well the best bit is that it keeps Henry away from his wife, Fay, who he seriously hates. The feeling is very much mutual and the wealth of loathing they both feel for one another is the only sign of actual passion left in their relationship, well that and their joint love for their dog Bowser. Things went wrong between them as soon as the children left home and were no longer there to fill the huge gap of boredom that was all that was left between them. The fact that he was made redundant at the same time from his long-term job in the bank, along with thousands of others during yet another recession, probably saved the marriage as it had meant Henry needed a new job and he took this one. It had the grand title of Senior Security Guard for 'Be Safe Security' and it suited him down to the ground. His family had sneered a little at the drop in status from bank clerk to security guard, but it had never bothered Henry. He was fed up with the bank anyway, had been for years. That job had been just plain boredom from start to finish, whereas this job was boredom mixed with lots of free time and Henry uses this to the full to fill his mind with matters of interest. It was a much better combination that suited him totally and was moving him forward in the world. He was becoming an academic genius. Turns out he is a natural for storing information that just fits comfortably in his head.

So the new job had kept the two erstwhile lovers apart, and therefore kept them from constantly repeating the otherwise endless arguments they would have had. You could say 'Be Safe Security' saved the marriage and you would not be far wrong. Being a security guard filled the majority of Henry's nights, which meant he slept most days. This was a perfect result for Fay who was able to fulfil her life long ambition of ballroom dancing in the now blessed privacy of her days. She loved to foxtrot with Mr Jones, the early-retired local butcher and neighbour, who she had always had more than a soft spot for. He was so good with his hands! Yes, this was an arrangement that suited them both just fine and dandy.

39 years of marriage and the big ruby wedding anniversary was looming like a bad dark dream on the fast advancing horizon. Divorce would have been a kindness but each was not prepared to give the other the pleasure. Besides, with legal fees and divorce settlements being one of the strongest areas of the national economy, Henry had no intention of letting some eager little spotty faced lawyer get their greedy soiled fat fingers on any of his hard earned cash. No sir, the lady would just have to cope with being Mrs Pearson for many more years to come. That made him smile, just the very thought of what it was doing to her.

Oddly then, Henry and Fay had settled into a steady routine, a way of avoiding each other as often as possible, and only coming together for curtain calls with family and friends. On these occasions they became a glowing unit again, happy to proudly lord over others the glory and the longevity of their marriage to anyone and everyone, hiding rather successfully the chasm that was now between them. Henry had always had a feeling he could have been an actor. Had been great at school taking the one of the leads once in the musical Grease. Now he acted every day for anyone who cared to watch his marriage.

As Henry paces around the site, he tries to amuse himself with little mind stories that take his brain off the fact that the majority of the fence is looking out into total darkness. There, in the shadowy surroundings, rest the departed souls of those lost to eternal peace and they seem intent on torturing Henry as he just does his job. He often feels their stare, the eyes of the night, looking directly at him, asking him to feel the fear that he has never managed to shake off despite the years of doing this.

Having spent the early years of walking a building site in the dead of night trying to fight the anxiety he constantly felt, he now tries a new concept to accept the darkness for what it is to his mind, and in turn to try and relax with the rhythms that face him and go with the flow of his walk. This is something he had read only recently and had taken to heart from the middle pages of The Times weekend health supplement under a whole section on relaxation techniques. He had always been a man to avoid anything relating to health, but, having lost 2 friends in quick succession, one to heart failure and one to suicide, he had found his eyes wandering to such articles. In fact this one on relaxation had been a godsend and he had pretty much taken the whole article as a wake up call as to how he should live his life. And so, several months later, Henry continues his quest to master the words of the highly esteemed Dr John D. McDermott, Senior Consultant in Human Behaviour at the cutting edge Nottingham University Hospital.

Henry had now reached the very positive stage where he is often getting back to his cabin without having caused himself to sweat too much with fear. He is so proud of himself and knew the good doctor would be too. Maybe he should send in a letter, under an alluring alias maybe, such as Floyd J. McTaggen of Edinburgh, thanking the intelligent Doctor for his wise words and exhorting others to take heed. Maybe not. He would think about that some more. Getting his actual name in the letters section of The Times would be one of the proudest moments of his life and would be a matter of hot topic for all his friends to hear. Yes, maybe not a bad idea after all.

The night is clear and cooler than normal. Henry wears his firm's dark blue jacket, covered in the bright luminous corporate logo, on top of his thick black jumper, which is something he has not had to do for some weeks. Unlike many of his friends who yearn for the winters of years ago when cold seasons brought snow and frosts, thick winter coats and log fires, Henry thanks God every night for a warmer climate. Sure in summer the heat is beyond unbearable, but he is lucky. He sees the cooler hours on the night shift and is able to sleep during the hot hours of the day with the blessing of an air-cooling unit to keep him comfortable. It costs him the earth to run it, but in summer it is an essential luxury.

This new site has been on the go now for 6 months. It is an exclusive building development on the edge of Ashover in Derbyshire, one of the UK's preserved heritage villages. Called 'Ashover Hill,' the site has beautiful aspects and is therefore a much-desired place to live. It is a highly unusual site because it is open to fields on three of its sides, something that rarely happens now with planning stipulating building up and not building out. As a result, high rises now dominate every city and town, with even the smaller towns having bitten the inevitable high-rise construction to accommodate its people. The effect has been, Henry believes, to the detriment of the way his country looks. Tall buildings of the mini skyscraper variety cast more shadows and are ultimately pretty much faceless. After all one high rise looks pretty much like another no matter how much glass and fancy shapes and snazzy lights they want to disguise it with. It makes Henry bristle with annoyance to think of how much money so called architects earn to come up with such nothingness. They should give him a piece of paper and let him plan! Maybe he should buy a book on how to become an architect. Yes, Henry would consider that some more.

Population growth had caused these issues and Henry feels very strongly that action should have been taken sooner. Still at least something had happened in the end, and at last you felt like Britain was again in control. Well maybe not in control, but at least not so damned to failure and the inevitable anarchy that had been breeding like a dark undetected illness.

On this particular evening of the 12th of February 2046, the moonlight had the sky free from its adversary of clouds that hid its wonders. It used this blessed occurrence to light up the site like streetlights would. Stars shone out as eminences of the sky, bright and resplendent. Henry smiled wide to have this view, a view that was not available in the city where its many lights hid the beauty above. They called it light density pollution. Henry called it progress shit, his standard term for anything that reduced his pleasures.

There were a few houses occupied already with 6 of the 12 completed properties lived in. The new habitants were very kind giving Henry gifts of cakes and bottles of expensive wine and aged whisky that he could never afford himself. Very generous. It was so different to be working on this type of development to one that was based in an urban area where all he normally got was a lot of aggravation and, of course, the occasional broken limb. All in all this exclusive development would have 30 houses, which was a pretty big build nowadays for an out of town site. They were large properties, each with five bedrooms, and were so expensive to buy that only the very wealthy dared to come and look. You should see the cars! Money almost dripped off them. And the women! My God. Such beauties. Yes, this site would do just fine. Just had to keep getting through the nights.

Henry quickened his pace, keen to get his rounds done and get back to his beloved newspaper reading. He had been looking through a superb article on air travel, something he hadn't been able to do for many years since the costs became so exorbitant at the side of climate change. New fuels were here though and the article reckoned it wouldn't be long before even Henry could be jetting off around the globe again. Now that really would be something! Henry had often wondered why a society that had made such incredible strides had taken so long to see the dangers of building it around so few choices for fuel. Money was what Henry put this down to, simple and pure greed. It was a paradox that a world that had funded new and exciting technologies and research, with the net effect being major breakthroughs across society, had taken so long to solve the fuel crisis. Still at last it appeared answers were working there way out to the common man! Henry would pass long hours at night reading of these changes and the ever-increasing transformation to the society within which he lived. He would marvel at science and wished that such breakthroughs had arrived earlier to save his sick mother who suffered terribly for years before cancer took her. The cancer wonder drug, the 'Angelica,' had arrived too late for her, but at least, thank God, it had arrived. Hopefully he would be luckier.

Yes, this was Henry, he thought, one of the lucky ones. To be living in these days, days of hope, of new beginnings and new insights. It was a new world, Henry considered, like the opportunity when the wider world was discovered, when the Americas and Australasia were found, when the moon was first triumphed! Yes indeed, it was a new world, a place that came with new dangers sure, but he felt protected by the firm hand of the coalition government. They didn't take any nonsense. New laws for new times, thought Henry, Britain once again protecting its own, leading the world in so many ways and making sure he would be safe.

And so here was Henry, 2 am in the morning on a brisk winters night. He was now around the back of the development towards the black woods, wind singing an eerie song through the whistling branches. Henry normally felt a chill around here where his walk from his cabin was the furthest away. He concentrated on the breathing technique that his good friend Dr McDermott from *The Times* had taught him, so that in turn he could keep his heart rate steady.

'Let in the breath and count to 5, let out the breath and count to five,' he reminded himself, his chant to keep the demons away. Henry had fastened this instruction over the door of his cabin, much to the amusement of the guys on site, to remind him of his mantra for these night walks. And so, as he strode out, he did just that. Breathing in, 1,2,3,4,5 and then breathing out and 1,2,3,4,5. It was a natural rhythm that flowed through his body, relaxing his brain and taking his mind away from the fears that wanted to take over.

Henry took the corner and turned to come back around the top of development towards the warmth and safety that awaited him in his trusted portakabin. As he did so he glanced towards a pile of earth that had been dug out as the last job of the day in preparation for the foundations of the next fine new house to be built. At this point, in slow motion, several things happened all at once. His feet continued to move forward, away from where he had been and back towards his welcoming TV and newspaper. His head had also turned towards his walk back but his heart rate had just doubled as his mind had caught an image, a picture that was stuck on pause and was not going away.

Henry found his feet begin to break out into a run, because, behind him he had seen, quite clearly, the bones of a hand stretching out from the dug up earth.

Chapter 2

# William

November 1943. Naples, Italy

'If I see that bloody smug smile on your face again I will personally have you march the square for the next five bloody days. Is that clear you ignorant little toad?!'

William did not enjoy the necessity that was to shout down young British soldiers, especially those who had arrived fresh from home, but they needed to learn the harsh realties of the battlefield right here on his parade ground. Most of the new soldiers in Naples were oblivious to the horrors of war that William had seen throughout the last 3 years of his tour in Africa. Rather, they had completed training within the comforts of home surroundings and the familiarity of British terrain and without the enemy looking to kill them at every opportunity. Sure, they had heard lots of stories about occupation and war, but every story, by the time it had reached a raw recruit, had been embellished to the extreme so that the version they had bore little association with the grim reality which was the terror of war. Their version was often heavily romanticised by the big screen, British morale necessity feeding their story with their inevitable return home as a hero, not as a memory.

Many of these young men then knew that war awaited, it was after all an unavoidable truth. Most too were ready for what they had prepared in their own mind of what actual battle was to be for them. Everyone knew of another family, if not there own, who had suffered loss in this war. These grim thoughts though could, in their mind, wait, for now they had arrived in Italy and its promise of sun and women. It was a real a challenge for William who right here and right now needed to refocus their minds on the realities of what lay ahead. It was an impossible task as the parade ground lay in the tender warmth of the Naples sun. The new recruits had after all landed in a country that seemed to rest between perfect azure blue skies and turquoise inviting seas, and this made Naples immediately so very different and exciting from the cold and grey of home. In many ways the still very warm autumnal city was a diversion, an enjoyable distraction from the fate that would await them. It was easier to conveniently overlook the not inconsiderate matter of potential for death or wounding from enemy fire and concentrate instead on the blessed kiss of the sun.

Of course William had been a new arrival himself to Naples only a month before, with the difference being he was now a hardened veteran from years of harsh and desperate warfare. Naples was indeed, despite the German occupation and the squalid conditions that were dominant, still an incredible city, notwithstanding the awful bombings and the massive decimation that was visible everywhere. Centuries of buildings that had coped with the threat and the real eruptions of Vesuvius were not about to bow down to a war and the effects of occupation.

The city, though, was also a very dangerous one. Recently, after a night out drinking had finished at the Bar Roma, William and several others had left the relative safety of Via Toledo in the hope of finding other establishments willing to stay open a little longer and serve allied soldiers keen to drink and be very merry. Sadly the backstreets offered a perfect backdrop for some local young men to fight and ensure these young British soldiers would know their place. The allied soldiers may have taken Naples, but drinking in their back street bars was a liberty they were not prepared to accept. As a result William had spent a week in hospital with an initial case of severe concussion and a lesson learnt too late.

A constant headache had left the hospital with him and it tended to grow worse whenever he was faced with a pressure situation such as the one that faced him now on the parade ground. At least he could handle it in the knowledge that his personal experience of being jumped by less than friendly local and extremely angry men, meant he had a story to make it all the more real to the new troops. Getting this story over was the issue.

Facing a bright spark on the parade ground, whilst having to endure the still present Naples heat and a banging headache, meant that William was about to lose it once again, and to do so in a fashion that he would not have thought possible of himself. Indeed his family at home would not believe it of their kindly spoken and joker of the party 'William.' In fact one of the side effects of these army years would be for William to have to spend the rest of his life seeking to forget these sides to the man he had become abroad with His Majesty's forces. War would leave its imprint forever on young William's heart and head. A simple truth of a man who had been to war.

As the private looked at his sergeant unfurling his torrent of sweeping verbal torment, William saw the usual succession of events appear in his eyes. Firstly the young man could be seen to be fairly cocky and sure of his place amongst his peers, pleased as anything that his note of cheek had caused a chuckle amongst the troops and made him the centre of attention. Then, as word after word began to fill his ears and generally drown out his own thoughts and the audience that were now no more than a memory, uncertainty began to take over. Eventually, as William's spittle began to run down the private's face and stony silence greeted the air around them, the squaddie was reduced to feeling isolated and regretting his once held position of strength. His face would eventually crack, showing William that the soldier now knew this was a sergeant not to be messed with and that he would be better served to keep quiet in the future.

As soon as William saw the eyes give way to defeat he would deliver a last volley of verbal abuse that normally threatened some dreadful detention, pause for dramatic affect, and then spin round on his highly polished boots and walk back to his position at the head of the troop. Here, whilst his back was still turned towards them, he would enjoy a small sense of achievement allowing an enormous smile to fill his face.

The sergeant's mess was one long joke about such incidents and as much as William would never like to be seen as too much of a hard man, such small trivia helped keep the boredom of war inactivity at bay.

William McTeer had been in Naples since the beginning of October 1943 being one of the first Allied troops to enter the city. It was a stop over that he had imagined would be easy and pleasant, after all was not Naples the city of majestic views, stunning weather and beautiful people. In fact history would note that Naples was to have the sad record of being the most bombed Italian city during the war. By the time William arrived, air raids had destroyed much within the city. Only recently in August the US Mediterranean Bomber Command had sent its largest raid of 400 planes. All in all Naples saw over 180 air raids terrorise its streets. Add to this the carnage inflicted on Naples by the Germans whose commander, Colonel Hans Scholl, had personally ordered that Naples be reduced to 'mud and ashes' before they left the city to the approaching Allied troops. Neapolitans sadly found themselves in the middle of a nightmare, as their former allies suddenly became their enemy, and an enemy that was to inflict immense brutalities against them. The Germans took it upon themselves to deliver a dreadful and brutal retribution on the city for 'changing sides.' War had decided that sides were there to be taken even though many Neapolitans had their choices made for them. It was unfair and it was shocking. In short, it was war at its brutal and bitter extreme.

And so the city that William had entered was a shock to him. The effects of the huge bombing campaign by the allies, coupled with incredible hardship posted upon the city by the Germans, was apocalyptic. Buildings mirrored the people being shattered to their core. Add to this the fact that the water supply had been ruined by the express order of Scholl to compound the devastating affect of food shortages, the people of Naples truly looked like they had been through hell on earth.

William's journey to Naples was after having served throughout the North Africa Campaign. He was part of the lauded Bernard Montgomery's British Eighth Army and he had seen far too much action that had hardened him to the terrors of war. And yet even he was shocked and disturbed by what he found in Naples. He had hoped the lack of sand he had virtually lived in for years, sand that had plagued his every waking hour in the deserts, would now be replaced with the beauty of Italy. Rather he found a city lost in plague and matching the bleakness of the Africa campaign.

At times the pure ferocity of the fighting throughout his African posting had been hard to bear. Far too many were now dead and wounded and a too often unthinkable question of whether victory was even possible plagued the soldier's thoughts. The fact that for long periods of time the British feared the German leader Rommel, and his audacious bravery that seemed to laugh at their own leaders, made for an uncomfortable nights sleep. Too often the allied forces had been outthought and outflanked and left with their confidence in tatters.

However the arrival of the new Field Commander Montgomery and his no nonsense approach had lifted the whole core of the British Eighth Army and their support divisions. A rumour circulated the troops that their new leader had said of Rommel 'after having an easy war, things have now got much more difficult.' This was to be an apocryphal truth that inspired and changed the campaign. A fighting force now stood freshly resolute and firm and the newly inspired British culminated the turnaround with the great surrender of the Germans and Italians in Tunis in May. It was believed by just about all that Mussolini was effectively defeated here, having devoted his destiny to the creation of a great Italian empire in Africa, a dream that now lay in tatters. With Italian soldiers committed around Europe fighting in battles that were becoming increasingly hard to win, Italy was bereft of soldiers to defend its coast and many in the Allied command saw a door opening into Europe through Italy. Winston Churchill called Italy the 'underbelly of Europe,' seeing it as the perfect place to step up through Europe and into the heart of German advances. William was very much right in the middle of all this action.

May saw Sicily taken and July saw Mussolini, the Fascist leader, summoned to the Fascist Grand Council, a council that had up to this point become a toothless one against the supreme Mussolini. With the Allied forces very much on their doorstep they now found their teeth and presented their once untouchable leader with a vote of no confidence. King Victor Emmanuel himself was immediately appointed as Commander in Chief and Mussolini found himself imprisoned. In general the Italian population rejoiced and their new Prime Minister, Marshall Badoglio, set about getting a separate peace agreement with the Allies away from the Germans. A secret surrender was signed on the 3rd of September but the Italians had counted against the typically obstinate Germans who immediately occupied Rome and forced a fierce counter attack, forcing Badoglio to flee and seeing Mussolini reinstated as Dictator! It was a yo-yo effect, which caught normal Italians in the middle of a catastrophe. Northern Italy became a German occupied country with much terrible blood letting between Mussolini's fascists militia and the anti fascist partisans.

It was into this cauldron of Italian against Italian that William was delivered, although Naples was now below the fighting lines and the highly impressive German Commander Kesselring who had retreated out of necessity to the north of the city and was refusing to yield even a metre of Italy without the allies paying dearly for it. It was the only way the Germans knew how to do battle and they were not about to stop just because of setbacks. They still believed in glory no matter the odds.

For William, Naples was to be a temporary stop, but a stop nonetheless! His bang on the head was also well timed, allowing him to have new recruit training duties for several weeks whilst many of his colleagues moved north into the vicious fight to take the Volturno line. The step out of the firing line was one that provoked dual emotions within William. First and foremost he wanted to stand shoulder to shoulder with his colleagues, but he also wanted to live. These were the sad truths of warfare. Fight and almost definitely face death, and face it far too often the closer you got to the front line.

Memories of such fateful days were far too numerous for William. In the second battle of El Alamein, Montgomery had launched an attack on the Germans that was to be a 'dogfight' that would use the British ability to fight with its infantry to superb effect. Yet these words do not explain, and can never explain, the simple truth of hand-to-hand combat that William experienced over two strength sapping weeks. The Germans were by this stage inferior and disadvantaged on many fronts, but their unflinching skill to fight with an intelligence and tenacity unmatched, meant that when they stood their ground the fighting would be inevitably fierce. In short the Germans greatest strength was simply that their reputation would strike fear into anyone who dared oppose them. It was a reputation that the Germans especially believed themselves, meaning they went into every battle with a distinct advantage of out and out confidence. So William, hardened by this time to the rigours of war, found new strength to be barbaric in war. On the battlefield there are no niceties. It is kill or be killed. It tended to be the new arrivals to the war that were not prepared for this simple truth. Their losses were always huge in comparison to experienced soldiers. A sad truth of the young being the lambs to the slaughter.

William though had not joined the war out of any desire to fight, to live out any child like desire of army. Rather this was the inevitable end of the process of his thinking that led him to believe he had to join up. He saw mankind as a whole, not as individual countries, and therefore killing one another was deeply objectionable to him and not just on religious grounds, religion being deeply rooted in his family, but also on clear personal moral grounds. He had argued this through with his older brothers and father with all of them failing to see anything but the need to stop Germany from their evil romp through Europe and, whilst William wanted to stop this too, he could not see past the nightmare of confrontation and ultimately the killing that had already started and would follow.

However there was another side to William that could not accept inequality and injustice and it was this side that won over the fight in his mind and convinced him of his need to fight come what may. So, William joined the war because he understood that his duty meant he had no choice but to risk his whole future with his fellow countrymen in any part of the world His Majesties Forces decided to send him. And send him they had. After initial training up in the cold of Stirling in Scotland he had arrived with crowds of other servicemen in Liverpool from where, amidst a sea of activity, his boat had left the relative safety of the docks for the dangers ahead. Thankfully his boat avoided the many German hazards, including the dreaded U-boats which seemed to have a ubiquitous quality to be everywhere, and he arrived safely in the heady mix that was Africa. Many were not so fortunate, their bodies forever lost to the ocean.

His time in Africa was hard. When the heat arrived it was as though it sucked the very air from his lungs. He had never known such an experience and was only heartened by the fact that every German, being North European too, would feel the same discomfort. William missed home so much that the aching for his return often seemed to physically cause his chest to ache. He missed the comfort of the local community, he missed his family and friends, and he even missed the more gentle weather that he now promised himself he would never curse again, no matter what the provocation it threw at him. His life had been so easy up to this point and now war had changed everything.

At least arriving in Italy was a physical move in the right direction. He was moving north! At this rate he would eventually arrive home and with any luck he would do so in one piece. He often reflected on the fact that the war had taken him to places he may well have never otherwise seen and for this he was grateful. Often at night, wherever he was, William would leave the mess and sit under the night breathing in the air of these foreign climes. This calmed him and connected him to the earth.

Naples in particular, in such a short space of time, had

made a huge impression on him. The city managed to still have beauty despite the many acts of violence carried out against it. Still it found itself touched by its friend, the Mediterranean sun, gently bathing standing property and ruined property alike as they all sat under the spell of a smoking Mount Vesuvius. This perpetually dangerous volcanic mountain gently tossed its ash at the feet of Neapolitans and yet they in turn continued to live in its path. William marvelled at the bravery of it all, living under a volcano that had erupted so many times that even the scientists had lost count. The last eruption had been in 1923 with the last serious eruption only 17 years earlier when over a 100 people had been killed. Vesuvius was only 6 miles east of Naples and it was clearly still pretty angry about something.

It was all a far cry from his home of Sutton in Ashfield where the area was filled with houses in terraced row giving way to terraced row in the gloomy Nottinghamshire coalfields. Yet the connection of smoke and ash made him feel closer to home than he had done for the last 5 years of being away. One day, he promised himself, he would come back to see Italy free from war within a Europe at peace with itself. Without hope, what did he have?

The people of Naples too were having an impact on him. During his recent enforced stay in hospital and the ensuing recovery time, William heard countless tales of bravery in the face of hardship and terror. He marvelled at the capacity of the Neapolitans to accept the Allied troops despite the fact that these same troops had colleagues who had bombed their city and killed their friends and family. Naples seemed to understand the precarious truth that casualty in war was an unfair yet inevitable truth. Maybe this had much to do with living their lives in an everyday real fear of an erupting volcano.

'You'll be home soon enough Lester!' offered William to his

friend. John Lester had been with William since Liverpool. They had fallen upon sharing a bunk and had both risen from humble privates through to ranked sergeants. John had also managed to remain behind in Naples with William having suffered from a dreadful stomach bug that at one point appeared to be killing him. It hadn't, but doctors had insisted light duties for two months. The two of them would travel north together in a few weeks time.

John was looking at a letter from his sweetheart at home in Workington, Cumbria. His was one of the few unmarried relationships to still be on with so many unable to allow for the time of being away.

'I didn't sign up to be away for 5 bloody years!'

'10 then?' offered William sarcastically.

'Very funny. Point 1 is that there is no chance we'd make 10 years of this and point 2 is that even you would almost certainly lose your sense of humour if this goes on much longer.'

'I know. Still, look at the time we have had. How many near death experiences would we have missed out on? Just think of the impressive stories you will be able to tell your Sarah when you get home. She is going to be overawed by the might, no the legend that is John Lester!'

John smiled. He loved to be with William. It soothed him. Together they had lost many comrades and friends and had come through so much. He found William to be a sensitive and caring man with a sense of humour that was black enough to help. He was also a lion in war.

'I know big man, I know. It's just 5 years! What else could we have done in 5 years? You could be the architect you were working towards. You could have a beautiful wife, a glorious house away in the countryside and at least two gorgeous children!'

'And a dog Johnny boy!'

'Indeed, a dog. What sort of dog?' asked John, laughing as he did so.

'A nice one!' replied William who had no real knowledge of dogs having never owned one and not being too keen on them really.

'Well, let's see now, maybe a Dachshund!'

'Your making that up!' replied William.

'I'm not! What about an Alaskan Husky?'

'Now you're just being silly!'

'OK. How about the same dog that our very own Winston has?'

'What type is it?'

'A poodle!'

'Oh I don't know. Just give me a dog!'

'Yes, but what type?'

'A brown one please.'

John and William were laughing hard now.

'OK we will make it a nice brown dog with two cute ears and four sweet chubby legs and a bark that sounds like angels singing!'

'Now you're talking John, but what sort of dog?'

'A German Shepherd of course,' laughed John on a roll, 'to remind you of this bastard war!'

'That's right, and I shall call it Monty after our glorious desert leader!'

'Lovely! Monty the German Shepherd it is. How's that for you William. That's your past as it could have been and your future as it shall be! Just the small matter of our destiny up north to come. If only this damn war would end. I swear, at this rate we could be retiring in Berlin.'

'If it's a free Berlin then fair enough.'

'Fair enough! You do make me laugh. If we have not won this 'war' in a year or so then we are wasting everyone's bloody time. It will have become un-winnable.'

'You mean the Somme effect?' asked William, seriousness eventually winning over some time in their conversation. It was a line of thought they had constantly come back to so many times before in the privacy of their own company. It was not the done thing to talk so openly about things that could be construed negative when there were others present. The two of them though were now in their own room, a rarity and a pleasure after spending time in cramped quarters throughout the last 3 years. Here in Naples they were in converted rooms by the docks and despite the squalor that was around them, it was far preferable to so much that they had experienced.

'Exactly! More and more death does not equal glory,' replied John.

The word death hung there for a moment and each chose not to dwell on it.

'Well, I think it will, soon. Let's face it we are closer to home than we have been for sometime.'

'True.'

'And the weather is even more bearable.'

'True.'

'I mean what month is it?' asked William.

'November.'

'And how, in any way, does the weather here mirror those cold and dark skies in England?'

'Good point,' replied John who was sat at his desk and had turned round to talk to William who had been dressing since returning from the rarity of a blessed shower.

'And the women,' sang William, his mind resting on one in particular who had captured his imagination.

'Ah, the women!'

'Are more like our beauties from home.'

'Apart from they look like goddesses and I am severely tempted to break my vow of chastity,' answered John.

'And the Pope's an Anglican!'

William smiled and looked at John. They laughed. They always laughed. It was a medicine to them and a way to get through the terrors that followed them.

'Let's go for that drink,' offered William, who had now finished making himself look beautiful. He was very eager to enjoy his first night off for weeks and get back to something that had been occupying his mind since the night he was last out in Naples.

'Sorry old chap but due to my recent stomach issues I am, as you well know, banned from the evil that is alcohol and so, as much as it pains me, I have to commit my evening to the many reports I have to write up for tomorrow. Look at this pile of work. You go. You know you want to and it's probably an evening you should do on your own.'

'Indeed, you are so right! OK, have a great night and I will see you later!'

For one final time, William pulled on his beret and checked over himself in the mirror. Whenever he saw himself in the mirror nowadays he tried to see the boy he had left behind in England. It all seemed so long ago. Then he looked very young and boyish, soft auburn stubble just appearing on his chin and temples. Now he saw a man, one who had just turned 23, with a strong jaw line that meant he got a bit of attention that frightened him more than excited him. His blue eyes shone out from his bright and eager face and he stole a wink at his image as he saluted to himself with a large grin written across his face.

John reminded him to stick to the main roads and bars and to take no chances. He did not want to have to come and get him from the hospital again.

'Is that clear Billy boy?' asked John, concern across his voice.

'Clear!' replied William, offering a comic salute and then leaving his friend to a night of boredom.

As William walked through Naples, the warm autumn night air lifting his spirits still higher, he reflected on the fact that he had been very fortunate throughout the war. He did this often, seeing it as necessary to honour the dead by recognising his own life that he still had despite the enemy's best efforts to take it away from him. William had been in so many near death situations since 1939 that he had lost count of the number of times he could have lost his life and had not. His dreams often reminded him of the screeching sound of a bullet as it flies so close to you that you actually hear its velocity. Far too many times he had been near to men who had died or been badly wounded by enemy fire and yet, save one battering around the head here in Naples, he had never been badly injured. It was truly miraculous.

He was on his way back to one of the places where he had been drinking the night of the attack when he had been badly beaten. Several weeks on though, and these streets were now much safer with allied forces and Military Police out in force. The Italians too, in the main, were warming to them and in particular the arrival of the Americans and the loot they had brought with them. Stockings were once again in circulation in the streets of Napoli giving the black market something truly valuable to trade!

William was going back to La Taverna La Libreria for one reason only. Accepted that the beer had been very good and he was in need of beer. Talking to John about the perpetual state of this war had convinced him of that! Also the bar had lots of books, hence its name, and some of them were even in English. William loved books. Reading was a passion and to find a tavern that combined food and drink and culture was almost as perfect as it got! He had never come across anything like it before in his life. Public houses at home were very traditional and he smiled at the thought of introducing a small library in the Market Tavern in Sutton in Ashfield. They would think him mad!

However the main reason was a moment in time that had thrown him completely and had left him in a state of flux ever since. Since that night his abiding memory was not the fear that filled him as he realised he and his comrades were helplessly outnumbered and were in serious trouble, but rather the glance that the young cameriera had passed his way when he was minding his own business leafing through an Italian copy of Shakespeare's complete works earlier in the evening. Given that William's grasp of Italian was 'loose' to the point of being hardly there at all, this was proving quite difficult but also, as the beer slipped down, quite amusing. His friends had left him to his books and arranged to meet him just down the road at Bar Roma. William was enjoying his third pint of Peroni beer. It tasted like a drink that had history in it and most certainly like no beer he had tasted at home. Lost in the drink he suddenly felt someone looking at him. It was very busy in La Libreria and there was no reason for anyone to notice him in the middle of a room full of Italians and servicemen, but someone clearly had.

William glanced up and saw two dark beautiful Italian eyes looking at him. The very sight of the young lady made his heart jump as much as any explosion had done. The young waitress from behind the bar was leaning forward on to her left elbow whilst using her left hand to play with her long dark hair. She was clearly off guard and had allowed her gaze to rest on a young man who had interested her very much indeed.

William's first reaction was to look around to see who she was looking at and, on turning around, he realised he was sat in front of the far wall and that there was, of course, no one behind him at all! He turned back only to find she had turned away and was carrying some drinks over to the other side of the restaurant.

Sitting back in his chair William glanced over to her, not wanting to be seen to be looking at the Italian young lady too intently, yet unable to do anything else. She was quite simply beautiful. Her hair fell easily down over her bare shoulders. Her dress was unable to hide a figure of slim beauty that fired William with interest and, though he tried to repress it, desire. William stole glance after glance and saw proud and smiling cheeks that stood out, eyes that were big, dark and bold, lips that reached out and called to be kissed and a neck that, with its golden colour, enticed the very core of him.

Caught in a mind that was now doing cartwheels William was no longer looking at Shakespeare, rather the book served as a cover that hid his over active mind that was in overdrive. He would need to leave soon or miss the men and the last few pints at Bar Roma. He could not chance being alone in the streets of Naples too late at night, and so the question was how to hear her voice before leaving. Maybe he could approach the bar, but if he did any one of the many staff could serve him and his chance would be lost. Maybe he could catch her eye and she could come and serve him? He decided that was the answer. Sadly, having tried his luck for several minutes, it was clear that she was not about to make the same mistake again and let him see her looking at him! In the end William decided he had no choice but to approach the bar and pay in the hope that she served him. This he did just as she sadly left the bar with some drinks for customers away from the bar.

'Il conto, per favour,' William asked the young, and effortlessly good looking barman, who in turned bowed his head in an over the top way that suggested some private joke was happening and William was the object of it. The two men exchanged smiles.

'Lovely evening!' offered William.

The young man smiled again and offered his tanned hand to William.

'Enzo Marinetti.'

William shook his hand warmly, realising as he did so that Enzo was probably his name so he politely offered his name back.

'I am William, William McTeer.'

Enzo offered William the bill.

'Hello William. You like La Libreria?' asked Enzo in a thick Italian accent, a broad smile causing William to feel even more comfortable. He felt his heart beating and sweat form on his brow as he waited for the girl to come back to the bar.

'I love it. It is so unique.'

'Unique?' asked Enzo, not recognising the word.

'Ah, yes, erm, a one-off.'

Enzo regarded the Englishman with a puzzled expression.

'It is not like at home,' offered William.

'Ah, yes, not like at home! What is?'

'Indeed,' replied William, thinking of the bar girl and wondering whether to ask the friendly barman about her. William looked over Enzo's shoulder towards the door that led away from the bar. She was not there. Enzo was very much enjoying William's discomfort. He had already seen his sister and the young man try to not be seen looking at each other for the past 20 minutes. William returned his eyes to Enzo who had maintained his abundant smile.

'You come back again?' Enzo's voice was full of mischief.

'I will. Grazie mille. Buona sera Enzo.'

'Buona sera William.'

Crestfallen William paid his bill and left the La Taverna La Libreria and stepped out into the cooler Naples evening.

'Mi scusi!'

A sweet voice in the night caught William off guard and he turned to see the girl who had so captivated his heart standing right there before him. She was holding his beret in her hands and smiling at him, a smile that lit up her face and lit up William's too. They walked towards one another and stood there in a frozen pose, her holding his beret, and he with his hands held tightly behind his back and his heart beating at what seemed like double time at least.

'Mi scusi signor,' she repeated after what seemed an age and held out his cap. William reached out instinctively and took his beret off her, their fingers touching for a sweet moment as she passed it into his grasp.

Had she meant to do that, thought William as he smiled pathetically at her, words escaping him for the first time in his life. The girl smiled at him once again, awkwardness filling the gap between them. Time began to run away from them and the girl, feeling the silence far too much, turned to leave.

'Arrivederci signor.'

With this the girl smiled once more and turned to step back towards the restaurant.

'Mi scusi signorina!' William almost shouted this out, words that would not come earlier, now falling out far too loudly. He was simply desperate to gain her attention and try at the same time to regain his thought flow. I must be sensible and make a suitable impression here he warned himself.

She turned back and stepped forwards towards him, her face upturned with a questioning look that appeared kind and interested. William recognised he had one last chance to make a better impression than the pathetic attempt he had mustered so far. Gathering himself he smiled as warmly as he could and then ventured some Italian.

'Grazia mille signorina. Parle Inglese?'

'A little Signor. Your hat, it was on the table.'

'Yes, I was distracted!' Distracted! What a ridiculous thing to say! William saw a chasm opening up before his very eyes.

'Dis-tract-ed?' Repeated the girl, thankfully not understanding the word.

'Erm, yes, erm, late, tardi!'

'Ah, tardi. Si.' A cheeky smile was released. She knew full well what William had meant even though she did not understand the word. He was clearly still distracted now.

You have such a beautiful voice, thought William, his heart doing somersaults! Her voice was so soft, so smooth, that as it entered William's ears it caused him to forget himself and by the time it reached his brain her words had lost all meaning other than the fact that he knew he wanted to hear more. Then there was the further problem of the lips that were letting out those words. Those lips were impossibly arousing. It was too much for poor William who found himself lost for a few moments again in his head. A further moment of awkward quiet passed. William then pushed out his hand for a formal handshake and said,

'My name is William!'

She took his hand and warmly shook it, smiling at him whilst she did so. She recognised William's awkwardness as being so very British. She had seen it in many others, but in William she felt peculiarly touched by it and moved to a deep joy that she had never experienced before.

'And my name is Francesca.'

Their hands lingered slightly too long for what was a first formal handshake but both did not seem to mind. William released her hand first, thinking it was the right thing to do as a gentleman, and asked,

'Do you work here?' knowing of course that she did and hearing the stupidity of the question as he had asked it. In his head William firmly kicked himself.

'Si signor. My mama and papa. Is their business.'

'Oh, super! Absolutely wonderful, splendid in fact! Very nice,' babbled William, unable to stop words coming out. 'I will be back really soon!'

'Buono signor. I shall tell mama and papa.' She smiled mischievously at this, very aware of William's discomfort and growing in her own confidence in front of this young

Englishman. In fact her parents would be mortified to see her talking so openly to William like this, although clearly an Englishman was far preferable to the Germans who had brought nothing but hate and disgrace into their fine city. The Quattro Giornate uprising had helped see them leave and regained some much needed pride and the Italians were now rising and wanting their country back for themselves. The Marinetti's were far from sure of whom to trust, but they did trust their own and had their hearts set on Francesca marrying one of Naples fine young sons in due course. For now though there was a war to get through and a Naples to rebuild.

For her part Francesca could only act upon what she felt and in William she saw a softness that was not something she saw in many on the local young men. Many of them were loud and brash, highly opinionated and very sure of themselves. When she had been at the bar lost in her thoughts she had looked at William struggling through an Italian narrative, and she had felt something she had never felt before. It had caught her out and it was not until William 'caught' her looking that she realised just how engrossed in him she had been. Standing here on the Via Portacarrese gave her the chance to explore this a little further.

'You met Enzo?' she asked, eager to keep the conversation going a little longer.

'Yes, Enzo, good chap.'

'Chap?'

Oh the way she repeated these words! William felt as though he was in heaven. If this moment could go on for all time, it would be too short a time.

'Er, man, good man.'

'Si. He is, what you say, wonderful.'

Wonderful! Was this her boyfriend? William quickly scanned her wedding finger and was relieved to see no ring there. Francesca saw his disquiet.

'He is my brother,' she declared, happy to see William's face immediately lift.

'Your brother! Of course he is,' William was almost beside himself with joy at this news.
'Wonderful man, yes, quite wonderful.'

Francesca was laughing at this display. She had never met such a man, so beautiful and yet so unsure of himself. It was instantly appealing and set her own heart racing. Suddenly aware that she had been out of the bar for too long already, she offered William her hand again and said,

'Buona sera William. It has been good to meet you.'

William then did something, which took them both by surprise. He lifted her hand to his lips and kissed the back of it, then gently released it and said,

'Buona sera Francesca. I will be back, soon. I,'

Time almost stood still as Francesca waited for the magic to end.

'I will look forward to coming back soon Francesca. As soon as I can! I will come and see you. I will bring you a book.'

Francesca smiled once more, her very smile again melting William's heart. In turn his stumbling language, his obvious inability to be forward and in any way presumptuous, was beyond touching to her.

'Grazie signor. I would like this, very much.'

The street was busy, people enjoying the night and the arrival of the allies. So much was happening around them, so much noise and life, and yet the two star crossed lovers heard and saw none of it. They were in their own encased bubble of time that was impregnable to all but themselves.

'Buona notte William.'

William looked at Francesca. An almighty smile filled his face and any thought of keeping his feelings together had caved in to a clear infatuation that was written across him.

'And buona notte to you Francesca.'

She turned half away, and then quickly turned back to him, walked straight up to him and kissed his cheek whilst resting her hand on his arm. She held his dreaming eyes for a moment, unspoken words of future meetings passing between them, and then she turned and dissolved into the Naples night leaving William feeling like he had never, in his whole short life, felt before. It was love.

Walking back, November having now arrived, William replayed his meeting with Francesca. In truth he had done little else since it had happened. They had indeed exchanged several notes to each other, the number increasing due to the hospital stay. The notes had become progressively more open about just how much they were both looking forward to seeing one another again. William had promised to bring Francesca a book that she could add to her library. Francesca told him she looked forward to receiving the book and that in return she would cook him some of her special risotto. William, who had no idea what 'risotto' was, told her he could not wait. The notes were formal yet playful, with both trying to use each other's language, and both clearly underlying the impression they had made on each other. The romantics believe in love at first sight and here was the belief incarnated. In the middle of turmoil, of hate and retribution, the instant pleasures of a new love had emerged.

The book idea had not just been a spur of the moment thing to say. William was prepared because he had with him one of his favourite books, which he would happily give to Francesca. Byron's poetic prowess was, to William, a thing of great beauty. Piece after piece reminded William of so much that was important to him. He had found Byron as a poet of choice at his school. There was something about this wild young man that captivated the young and impressionable William. Partly it was the simple fact that someone so magnificent had lived so close to his own home with Byron's home being only a few miles away at Newstead Abbey. William could therefore walk in the same places Byron had walked, breathe the same air and see the same sights. It made his poetry more real and accessible to the young McTeer. His fundamental Christian parents were not so keen and Byron was most definitely not a role model they wanted their children to follow. It was too late. William's love affair with the poet's work had begun and many of his books, and in particular the book he would give to his love Francesca, would stay imprinted on his brain for his life.

'Hours of Idleness' was first published in 1807 with a wonderful preface from Byron in which he writes to the Earl of Carlisle and suggests many might think his time could be better placed than simply filling the role of a poetic writer. Byron muses that his work will be found to have many faults and that it would struggle to find anything new to say given the incredible age of fertile minds that he lived in. These words of self doubt and self-depreciation by Byron had always stayed with William and connected to his own self-depravation of any talents he may have had.

By giving Francesca this collection he was saying two things. Firstly he wanted her to see something of himself through the words of the poet, words that William himself struggled to get over, but that through the vehicle of poetry his true senses and feelings could flow. Secondly he wanted Francesca to keep the book by way of a connection between them and, if by some magical chance they were to have a future together, then this book would draw them so.

He hoped that time would not have eroded her memory of him, but that rather she would burn for him as he burned for her. His one thought, the thought that he had held since leaving Francesca that night four weeks earlier, was his abiding hope and dream for her to want him. That somehow, when he walked back into her life and they met once more, that her eyes would open wide with happiness and betray the restless nights of thoughts, matching the nights that he had experienced, as she had considered would she ever see him again.

It was an unusually warm night, certainly much warmer than it would be back home in November! In fact nothing here in this war was anything like home. It was all very surreal, a journey that William had got on and had no idea how he would ever leave it. He was a passenger with no hope of being in control of the next stop. All he could do was stay on the ride to the best of his ability.

William was a fine chess player, happy in the game that started with a simple move and turned into a complex attrition of time and nerve. He saw the war as a big chess game with ultimately his only chance of survival being a mixture of luck and skill. The former was the most important and many times he had seen servicemen lose their lives, or at least part of their bodies, due to be being simply unlucky. It could have been so easily William taking the bullet instead was he not lucky enough to have been standing 3 feet to the left or right.

John called it 'destiny.' Others called it Gods will. William knew it only as time. Time moving and his life still amazingly moving in it. He felt no right to call on God as being more merciful to him than others. Why was that even possible? As for destiny he felt just as guilty! Why would destiny smile on him and dismiss another? It was easier to just accept each day as it came, what time had delivered, and in turn, hope. It was hope that allowed him to sleep at night, hope and a sense of duty that enabled him to get up in the morning. Indeed it was this small hope that he now clenched as his time, time he had been granted to make amends for his colleagues misfortune. Francesca was a dream and every bullet that had missed him meant he could be here now.

He crossed the Piazza Plebiscito, busy with allied servicemen and busy Italians. How must this solemn looking Piazza have looked before Europe decided to use it as a battlefield?

He rounded on to Via Toledo, heading up the street that was lined with a mixture of buildings of ancient quality and others that had been bombed into history. It had become a city that had turned in on itself and had done unspeakable things to itself and its soul. Many of Williams colleagues had been only too pleased to find beautiful Italian women throw themselves at their feet and be willing, for payment, to do anything to please. This left William cold. It was not in his nature. He was a romantic. William carried no feelings of blame for anyone, no sense of self-righteousness. Rather he just felt hopeless at the squalor of human degradation that war had inevitably brought to the streets of Naples.

You could still see on this grand street, named after a Spanish viceroy from glories past, the beauty and splendour that was Naples; but it was difficult. This war had not been kind and much work would be needed when this dreadful time had passed.

William walked past Bar Roma, and the crowds that filled it, and down the small alley that led to La Libreria, and there his eyes played tricks on him. Where Francesca's tavern had stood was now replaced with rubble. There was nothing. It was gone. It had become another hopeless casualty of this futile war as it took more lives and left the survivors bereft. A German bomb had left another shocking statistic that would all too soon be forgotten.

William's dream was crushed. His hopes of love in a war of brutality, lay shattered.

Chapter 3

# Francesca

March 1948. Florence, Italy

'My dear William,

This is my 12<sup>th</sup> letter to you and still no response. I cannot stop writing in the hope that one of my letters will find you alive and tell you what happened to me, tell you how I feel about you.

I am sending this letter to a new address I have through the British embassy here. My uncle got the address. I hope this will reach you William, dear, precious William. I must know of you and that you know of me.

Every day I wait for your letter and no response. Are you there William? Are you alive? I know you are. I sense you are.

Naples seems so far away now, and yet it is still only a matter of a few years that I lived in my Naples.

I tell you the story again in this letter that we were bombed yet I was saved. I don't know why? God knows I have asked why many times.

I was at the market collecting what little I could for the kitchens when I heard the explosion. Something in me died that moment. I knew. I ran back to mama and papa but it was no good. Only fire and death greeted me.

My brother, Enzo who you met on that night that seems like

36

*a dream now, was with me, and he held me back from running into the fire. There was nothing left and he pulled me back. Neighbours, dear friends all, were badly affected. The whole row was flattened like it had never been there. I went a little crazy for a while and was beside myself with fear and anger. After I came round I tried to get a message to you but it was returned saying you had gone. I cannot tell you how alone I felt and how I wept.*

*We stayed with friends for a little while which was hard on them, as you know how little food was there. They were saints to us. As soon as we could safely leave we went to my grand papa's house in the country. Together we grieved.*

*You will see I am now in Florence, staying with my aunt and her family. They are wealthy Florentines and wanted me to have opportunities. Aunt thinks I have natural ability to paint and so that is what I do every day. Uncle teaches me English! You will see if you ever get all my letters how my English has improved!*

*Enzo is not with me. He went to fight with the resistance and I do not know if he lives or die, though I have had stories that he died in the spring of 1944. I guess I will never know for sure but my heart tells me he is now at peace with my family and I will not see him till the new life.*

*William, I have written so often in the hope that you can know two things. Firstly that I am alive! We had just a moment of time but I know you would wish to know this. I thought of you coming to see me and just seeing the ruins of my house and the street and how hard that must have been. What must you have felt?*

*Secondly I am writing because I need you to know something. It is something I tell you, not to feel you must do anything in return for I hold you to nothing, but just so that you know. I very much hope that you are very happy back in Britain, that you have found in normal life something to rescue you from the horrors of war. I want you to know though William, dear William that I think of you every day. Since I first saw you, you melted my heart.*

37

*I hope you can forgive my intrusion William.*
*If you could write, even just to tell me you live, I can live.*
*Your,*
*Francesca*
*xx*


William
June 1948. Sutton in Ashfield, Nottinghamshire

*'Francesca – you live!!!!*

*I got your letter this morning and you cannot know how it has affected me. I have sung and I have danced!*

*You tell me I melted your heart! Francesca, you have my heart. From the moment I saw you, you had my heart.*

*Francesca – YOU LIVE!!!!*

*My sweet darling, my Italian beauty, my love.*

*I am an Englishman but knowing this news means I can overlook all my English reserves and cry out in writing how I really feel.*

*What am I to say other than I now count the moments until I can see you again? When can this be my love? I will work as hard as I can and save money until I can get out to you. Maybe in a few summers Francesca? Would your aunt and uncle approve?*

*I clearly made it through the war. John, my closest friend, made it too. We headed north pretty much after I had been to see you and thought you were dead. I asked about you but no one seemed to know or wouldn't say. It was all a dreadful mess. How you must have felt faced with that sight Francesca I will never know. It was good you had your brother Enzo. He was brave to join the resistance. You must miss him dreadfully. If only I could hold you now my dear Francesca and soothe you.*

*War just closed around me and I carried on looking out for John and he for me and we made it. Some of the things we saw, that we did, but no matter, these are all behind us now.*

*I was home late in 1945 and went back to my studies to be an* architect and that's what I'm doing now in Nottingham. I'm doing pretty well actually.

I have your book too my love, the one I was bringing with me that day. I shall bring it to Italy. You will have to wait a little while longer!

Thank you for writing.

I am sure of this fact – that my life is complete with your letter.

If that is enough for you then that is fine. I wish you a lifetime of happiness.

If you would like to see me then Francesca, my sweet love, know this;

I WILL BE WITH YOU AS SOON AS I CAN!

Write soon,

William

xx

Chapter 4

# William and Francesca

May 1952. Florence, Italy

As the train turned beautiful Italian countryside into the outskirts of stunning Florence, William nervously caught a glimpse of himself in the carriage window. At 31 he looked decidedly youthful and yet, with the meeting with Francesca only minutes away, nerves frayed at his mind, which was already doing cartwheels. She would be 25 now and coming up to her 26th birthday in July and, William reasoned, she would be even more beautiful. She had sent him photos that had simply melted him, photos that he took with him everywhere and now sat safely within his jacket pocket. What would she really make of this Englishman, a man so different in looks and character to what she was used to. He had replayed his thoughts in one of the many letters they had sent to one another over the years that had passed before this arrival was possible. Francesca had assured him of her love for her gentle Englishman, her undiminished feelings that had never left her, only grown.

William knew that now, with Florence and his beloved Francesca waiting for him, this would all be put to the test. Would they really be in love after such a short face-to-face meeting? Would time recognise a relationship that had grown based on longing to be with one another but without actual time together. Their letters, long and heartfelt, showed feelings into which each poured their heart in a way they had never done so before with anyone. This thought gave William hope and he relaxed a little. They may not have physically been with one another, but they had shared their hearts and this was the true measure of what they really felt.

William had hoped to be with Francesca much sooner but he had faced several obstacles. Firstly Francesca's aunt and uncle had been insistent that the two young lovers must be sure of what they felt before committing to William coming over to Italy. Whilst they knew only too well Francesca's devotion to William, they wanted time to make sure that love based on a chance meeting was really true. What they did not want was to in any way see Francesca's heart broken any more than it already was.

From their early letters William and Francesca were clear that they saw their lives together, and so they set about planning exactly that. Initially, at least, they agreed that William would join Francesca in Florence and together they would build a home. From here they would see were fate would take them. There had never been any talk around William coming over for a holiday. After all the costs were too high and the journey too long to allow them to have any length of time together. No, they were clear; William would leave England just as soon as he had built his career to the level he felt necessary and come and live in Florence.

Further William knew only too well that Giovanni Tolentino, Francesca's uncle, would be able to use his connections to get William jobs far easier if his architects portfolio had some real substance about it. This would take time. By 1952 William had built an impressive portfolio that would get him work across Italy giving both him and Giovanni the required confidence. To this end the two men wrote to one another with the young man regularly keeping the older man updated as to his work and his successes. In turn Giovanni encouraged William and assured him of helping him make progress when he would eventually arrive in Italy again. These letters had the added benefit of giving Giovanni confidence in the young William and his true devotion to Francesca. A hard working and talented young man he could trust and use.

So finally William was arriving in Florence having built a good income behind him. He had funds in the bank and felt he could now offer Francesca not only his love, which was undoubted, but also the stability of a proven career backed by capital.

The minutes had passed and the train pulled into the beautiful Firenze station looking so impressive and splendid compared to the grey stations William was used to at home.

He scanned the platform hoping to see Francesca but he was in a rear carriage so his view was not good. The train came to halt and busy, chattering Italians, spilled out to the warmth of the station, leaving William to pull his two heavy suitcases down from the overhead tray and struggle with them off the train. As he did so, sweat on his brow and fear of what might be still in his stomach, he felt the eyes of someone on him. As he turned she came running towards him, her long dark hair flowing behind her and an almighty smile across her face.

'My William, my William!' Francesca called as she ran and jumped into the arms of her man, arms that intended to never let her go again.

William, having dropped his cases to the catch the embrace of his lover, now spun her around, laughter and tears spilling out of the two of them as the years of separation quickly faded away with the reality of beautiful reconciliation. That embrace, that sweet embrace, would never be bettered in the whole of their lives.

Two weeks gone and the two of them had seen all doubts of how they would truly feel about one another gone. They had been inseparable and had talked non-stop about anything and everything. They had much to catch up on and they did so with absolute relish.

Today was a Saturday and was the last weekend before William would start on his new job working with the famous Capella's. Bernado Capella was one of Giovanni's oldest friends and, having seen William's impressive portfolio, had been happy to take on the young Englishman.

Francesca had chosen a favourite spot of hers for their picnic, high up in the jewel of the impressive Boboli Gardens on a slight incline of smooth grass with the shimmering view of Firenze before them. William had enjoyed a perpetual smile pretty much since the moment he had received the letter from Francesca back in 1948 and now, here in Florence at last, he had to almost pinch himself to convince him that this was for real. To have served in Italy in the war, and now to be back as a guest in peacetime was surreal. What was also surreal was that Francesca had come to Florence after losing her family in Naples to be with her aunt and family. She had moved from a liberated city to an occupied one, though the occupation of Florence did not leave the city in the same calamitous state as had befallen the unlucky Naples. Incredibly though William too had passed through Florence in August 1944, not knowing that the girl who he thought was now dead, lived just out of the city. Oddly in the week or so that he recuperated from highly active duty in the centre of Florence in billets within a convent, he found he could do nothing but think about Francesca. The short removal of the hum of war left a place for his brain to concentrate on what might have been. His time then in Florence had been a time of tears and loss.

It was a beautiful day and, as the sun reached high over the city, climbing ever higher in the heat of the sky, Florence was picked out in all its glory. The rooftops shone spectacularly as their bright terracotta tiles warmed up in the heat of the early afternoon and reflected a shimmering haze. Church steeples stood out as beacons and Francesca pointed to them, excitedly sharing their names and some of their history.

'There, though William, is the star of the show rising high above all.'

Francesca leads William's eyes across the Ponte Vecchio, spared during the war by a last minute telegram by the German high command, and onwards on to Brunelleschi's stupendous dome, which is visible from every vista around the city. The view is absolutely breathtaking with the multicoloured Duomo rising high behind the marble clad Baptistery as they sit together at peace within the Piazza del Duomo. The colours of the patterned exteriors are made even more noticeable because they stand out against the more duo tone effect of the rest of Florence. This was a building built to stand out and impress, and that is exactly what it does effortlessly.

'It is amazing,' William says, in a near state of hypnosis, bewitched by what he is seeing and the beautiful young lady by his side.

'This beautiful city Francesca is so very different to home. You really can't imagine the contrast. No wonder you paint. Your mind must always be alive surrounded by such subjects. I look at this view and feel almost as if I have no words because its beauty takes them all away.'

Francesca smiled at William, her William, and placed her hand around his cheek and cradled it so.

'In that case the city to you is like you are to me my love.'

He took her hand and kissed it, allowing the moment to linger as he took in the very core of her. He was happy, so happy.

It had taken William several years of hard work to restart and then build a career, and in turn build the funds that would get him back to Italy. Francesca's family had kindly offered money but William would have none of it. He wanted to arrive in Florence with a skill that could earn him money wherever he was, and so he set about becoming the architect he had started to become before the war intervened. Graves and Barnett had readily welcomed him back. They viewed William as a young man with great potential and were delighted that he had made it back in one piece. Many others had not.

Within 5 years he had completed his studies and had risen to be one of the senior architects within the team. His rapid rise through the ranks was due to some helpful timing of retirements, some casualties of war who never came back, but also his incredible aptitude to grasp a project and move it forward. His drive and determination stood him out amongst the generally slow and less than enthusiastic people around him. William was making up for lost time and his towering energy was testimony to this fact. His employers took note and made use of it.

His pay too was rising and as Britain rebuilt itself, William found himself in the right job at the right time. By 1952 he had gained something of a reputation, with his project experience being particularly strong. He had been involved in the design and reconstruction of several large jobs with a plethora of these adding to his burgeoning portfolio and building a really impressive CV. It was this of course that had allowed Francesca's uncle to get William into the Capella's highly respected and long-standing practice.

'Will you be happy here William?' asked Francesca, concern in her voice.

'I'm here with you!'

'Yes, I know, but will there be enough work to keep you happy?'

'Of course! It's amazing, inspiring. It's what I need. This work will set my career up for good.' As William spoke his face was at peace, happy, joyful. 'And with you and your family I shall be very fulfilled indeed.'

'Yes, my family already think the world of you, this is true. But William, your family, I fear they will miss you and you them.'

William's parents were both alive. He had two brothers and two sisters. All of them lived in and around Sutton in Ashfield and were involved in the coalmines in some form or other. His sisters, both younger than him, were excited about Francesca and Italy and both wrote regularly. His brothers, who were both older, were pretty distant about it all. The war had separated them with neither brother serving given their work in the pits. It was work that had aged them much beyond their years and they viewed their younger brother with jealousy, mistrust and silence. Any love there may have been in their childhood was all but lost now.

His father too was a distant man and William had never known a conversation that was not serious in nature. Rarely had they known any intimate times and this had not changed since he had gotten back from Italy. William's choice of a career away from the pits had taken away what little warmth there had ever been between them, a bridge impossible now to cross.

'You could have any job in the pit William,' his father would say, 'with your brain and my influence you can build a career here. New technologies are coming William, new ways of doing things, and it will take bright people like you to implement them.'

But John McTeer's words were lost on his son. William had lived in the shadow of the mines for too long. He saw the worry lines almost visibly grow across his mothers face once his two older brothers joined the procession of local young men who went down the pit to earn their living. The two brothers were not blessed with academic abilities showing no aptitude for schooling at all, and so their path into both becoming mineworkers seemed straightforward. And yet such a route meant facing extreme conditions and hard labour. Joan McTeer had been around mines for too long to not know the dangers that this would present to her older sons.

William's father had left Scotland with his young family in 1928 to move to the Midlands as a pit manager. His experience was perfect for the thriving Midlands pit community and he settled into the role with a relish. He loved the dynamics of mining and soon became a community leader, a man with much to impart but with little left over for his family at home.

Many nights, with the three elder men out of the house, saw William and his sisters spending time with their mother and the bonds here meant that these partings were the hardest when he left home.

'Do you know,' William began, gently stroking Francesca's arm as they relaxed on a soft cashmere blanket, 'when I was at war, I thought of nothing else but them and friends and home until something happened, something that changed my life forever.'

'Yes, war can change everything,' replied Francesca, her Italian accent lightly touching her words. Her English, previously heavily accented and broken, was now superb. Her aunt and uncle both spoke English well and Francesca had worked hard to ensure she had a great command of the language in time for William.

'Not war Francesca! You! Since I saw you I have lived these moments every day. Now I breathe again, now I'm here, here with you.'

Francesca felt she could not be any happier. Her high

cheeks seemed even higher as her smile filled her beautiful sun kissed cheeks.

'And where shall we live William, what of our future?'

'Well that depends on you.'

'Me?'

'Yes, you. Beatrice says you are going to be a very famous artist!'

Francesca frowned.

'My aunt says many things.'

'She loves you very much.'

'And I her.'

'She thinks you very talented.'

Francesca's face-hardened, a clear look of determination for William to see.

'I am me,' she declared.

'That you are my love, that you are.'

William ran his hand down the back of Francesca's long dark hair. They were sat under a tree that allowed the sun to reach them but took the sting out of its warmth. It touched her brown shoulders and arms and William, as he ever was and would be, was entranced by her.

'She says you can paint wonderfully,' William offered, eager to see her smile.

'I can do many things,' Francesca countered abruptly.

'Yes, true, and all of which I want to see, but Beatrice tells me you can really, really paint.'

'I am me. I will do what I do. It is not talent. It is me.'

'Right. I see where we are going. As long as I do not say it is good or bad or indifferent, but simply refer to the fact that you paint, that's OK?'

Francesca looked at William, holding his eyes with her own. She was not going to make this easy for him. He needed to understand that her art was a big part of her life and that it was as natural to her as breathing, but that she was not interested in whether people thought it was good, bad or indifferent, and she did not enjoy anyone having a view. To her, it was simply what she did. William needed to know this and support her in this.

'Only I will be my critic. Look William, yes I paint, but I see it as private, myself with my work. I don't want to think of it as talent. It is just me, my thoughts and my ideas, coming out on to my canvas. That way I keep all this pure. Just about me and my thoughts, my ideas. Italian art has a rich tradition in money and I hate that.'

'Yes, I see,' replied William, slowly getting used to the flashes of temper that shot out of Francesca like a safety valve, 'your art is just about you. Well what will happen with just you coming out on to your canvas?'

Francesca considered the question.

'I want to paint for the rest of my life. Not for money. For me because I have to.'

'And if money comes?' asked William softly.

'Then it comes.'

'And Beatrice says it already has.'

Francesca frowned. Her aunt had been too vocal as always. She would speak to her about this later.

'Some people are very kind!'

'And some people recognise what is worth buying.'

Francesca met this remark with silence and looked away. William quickly decided to change the subject, realising that he had put Francesca on the spot and that she was clearly uncomfortable with this.

'You know some people say I have a talent too!' he offered.

'And you do! Uncle says your work is unique and exemplary,' replied Francesca, a smile instantly returning to her face as she turned back to William.

'Your uncle is an intelligent man,' replied William with a cheeky grin.

'He says you have an eye to challenge what is normal and that you have a great future.'

'And you see how easy you say that of me and yet I

cannot say it of you?' William replied and immediately regretted raising the subject he had just sort to change.

Francesca waited, stooped in her thoughts for a while, but allowing a small smile to work the corners of her mouth, acknowledging as she did so the truth in what William had said.

'We will never be the judge of one another, that is what I am saying.'

'We will not! I agree, whatever we do I am here for you my love, whatever and whenever and without any sort of judgement at all!' William smiled widely, loving the way Francesca's cheeks rose when she smiled and creating small dimples under the cheeks. He reached over and took her hand, gently stroking it and holding Francesca's hot gaze.

'So my beautiful young man, where will we live to carry out our destiny?' she asked her young Englishman.

'Well dear Francesca I will live where you live. That will be enough for me.'

'I would like to think we will go back to Britain one day if that is what you want.'

William looked at Francesca, her big brown eyes full of Latin intensity and desire.

'Could you really leave Italy?' asked William, touching on a subject they had toyed with through their letters but not really dealt with. William had assumed he would be living in Italy for a very long time and not returning to Britain for many years, if at all.

'Yes. I think it would be good for me and my art.'

William was genuinely taken back.

'I am surprised.'

'Why?' asked Francesca, hearing the doubt in William's words, asking her whether she really wanted to leave Italy, whether she really could leave Italy.

'I will be ready soon. Italy will always be my home but it holds too much memory for me. I will need a new place and I like what I hear and read about Britain.'

'You do?' asked William with genuine surprise, seeing the view before him and wondering how anything at home could really touch this.

'I do! It holds such rich history, such a tapestry that I can be part of and you know, after all this war, there will be regeneration. Britain will be rich with culture.'

'It will!?'

'Yes my love, it will.'

William was thinking around the many times he had found Britain to be stuffy and anything but ready for an artistic revolution. In the Midlands particularly he had often felt oppressed by the lack of interest in books, poetry and paintings. Still, he had learnt much during the war from army colleagues of a Britain he did not know. The cities seemed to have much more going for them. He had heard too of places like St Ives in Cornwall where an artist's colony had been created and many in the town accepted art as a right and something to celebrate. When someone had told him about St Ives he had not believed them, but another friend he had made from the area had confirmed it. There was clearly much he did not know about his own country and maybe Francesca was right.

'Where would we go?' asked Francesca, 'to Nottingham?'

'Too plain. It will be a long time before any cultural revolution hits the Midlands! Besides, it is too near my family.'

'I would like to be near your family!'

William gave Francesca a shake of his head.

'I love them all; you know I do, but not living near them. I feel I have done too much to be back there and trust me, you would not like to be near my family. They will stunt our growth and look to suffocate us.'

Francesca frowned at William. She thought about telling him he should feel differently about his family but then she checked the thought. William had told her in his letters about feeling like an outsider to his father and brothers. What right did she have to tell him to feel any different to how he actually felt? They had just pledged they would not judge one another and she was not about to break that pledge now.

'London then?' asked Francesca.

'Very big and very grey. I think you would love it and then grow to hate it.'

'I would like to live near the sea. Lorenzo Gondoli, one of my tutors, spent years at a place called Edinburgh. He says it is cold, very cold, but spellbindingly beautiful. He says the light stretches across the city as the sea kisses and plays with the land. He says the seagulls sing to you and the sky opens up your head. Have you been?'

'It sounds like I will,' William laughed, a shot of excitement ripping through his brain as Francesca had lit up a distant memory. 'I am from Fife, Kirkcaldy to be exact! It is just north of Edinburgh, on the east coast.'

'You lived in Scotland!?' shouted Francesca, thrilled at a connection she had not known existed.

'Well yes I am, but only as a young boy. My father got a promotion in his job and so we moved down to England.'

'Do you remember much about Scotland?'

'I remember sunshine and the sea and, of course, seagulls. I remember being very happy. A carefree child. We had good times.'

'Then it's settled. Let's both go there and be carefree children again!'

They shook hands to make an agreement. Making plans together was so much fun. Their futures lay ahead like a map waiting to be drawn and it took up most of their happy conversations.

They ate a picnic prepared by Sophia, the Tolentino cook, much earlier that morning. The food was typically Italian and William loved it. The freshness of it all and the fact that its seeming desire was to not only test the taste buds, but to challenge them too. This was not like food at home where post war Britain looked very bland compared to the explosion of colour and texture that he was experiencing in Florence. Nearly everything about his every day now was a euphoric rise, a reason to move on to the next moment and this was best demonstrated by the food now laid out before him. Tuscan flatbread, torn and dipped into fresh extra virgin olive oil and mixed with garlic and rosemary, was a delicacy he had never experienced before and Francesca laughed at how such a simple food for her was a wonder for William. The hamper contained so much. Fresh tomatoes on the vine, succulent mozzarella, home baked bread, smoked salmon, ham, anchovies, basil, locally made burrata, rich aubergine and luscious peppers. And then the wine, all the time they drank so much wine! His body was alive with scents, tastes, sounds and sights that made him feel more alert and excited than he had ever felt before.

'What is this wine? asked William, as he let more of the sumptuous red slip so easily down his throat.

'Chianti.'

'Chianti? Sounds like it has come from somewhere oriental!'

'This I will have you know,' declared Francesca whilst picking up the bottle to show it off, 'is Colli Fiorentini, produced on the hills around Florence along the valley of the Arno. You are drinking an historic wine made right here. It is delicious is it not?'

'Everything here is delicious,' offered William, the alcohol affecting his manners as his wandering eyes fell from Francesca's face to her bare shoulders. Francesca, who was also feeling the effects of the wine from a bottle they had just about finished, coloured in her cheeks.

'Do you know how much I love you Francesca?'

'Yes. I think I do.'

As she smiled her cheeks rose and as they did it seemed

to emphasise her thin jaw line and her soft brown neck. The watching William was captivated and hot with the sensations he was feeling. He leaned forward and gently kissed Francesca, her soft lips, moist from the wine, setting his body on fire.

'God you're beautiful.'

'I am not!' replied Francesca, happy with the compliment yet unable to accept it.

'Try telling that to the men who watch you from everywhere.'

'They are Italian,' Francesca replied hotly.

'They are lucky.'

'Lucky?'

'They have been able to look at you all these years.'

Francesca begrudgingly accepted the compliment, feeling it best to stop William making her so self-conscious.

'You are beautiful and you embarrass me so stop this talking about me. Let's talk about you.'

'Alright. Me. Well, what is there to say?'

'That you are beautiful!'

William laughed very loudly indeed. He thought he had a certain quality, but certainly never saw himself as remotely beautiful. No one had ever said such a thing to him.

'I don't match your Italian boys.'

Francesca hit him on his arm with real force and became quite serious.

'You are my William. You are my beauty. You never need to compare yourself to anyone. Never.'

William rubbed his arm and looked at her, her lips pouting as she took in deep breaths.

'I don't. I won't. Did I say something wrong?'

'No William. I am Italian. There is a side to us that is fire and sometimes it burns. If you say something silly, I will hit you.'

'And if you say something silly?'

'An unlikely occurrence,' she said, allowing a small smile to escape, 'but should it ever happen, you will scold me in a soft and careful manner and I am highly likely to both resent the rebuke and ignore it.'

She stroked his arm where she had hit him, her face softening as she did so.

'You are so different to what I have always known. You must never doubt me.' As she spoke, her voice became very serious causing William to concentrate on her words and pull himself back from the effects of the wine.

'I never have and I never will. I doubt myself though.'

'Why?' Francesca asked, real surprise in her voice.

'Well, I am only me. I lack many things.'

'What do you lack?'

'You know, things.'

'Like what William?'

William took a deep breath, surveying the beautiful scenery before him and thought how to put into words why he felt quite often inadequate.

'I guess I feel like I have a lot in me, you know deep in me, but that it doesn't often seem to come out in the right way, you know, enough. Does that make sense?'

'Yes, it does. I feel that in myself all the time. Don't you see yourself in your buildings?'

'Well I try, but the clients invariably want what is so normal, what is traditional and plain. Trying to get acceptance for new ideas is very hard. Anyway what I deal with is bricks and mortar so no, I don't see much of me in my buildings.'

'So you don't express yourself, show outside what you are on the inside?'

'I am English!'

'Ah, English. You must come out into the sunshine.'

'Yes. That's me! I am a man who lives too often in the shade.'

'Then we must shine some sunshine on you!'

'I'm in the right country then.'

William looked up to the sky, letting his head roll back into the warmth of the dappled sunshine as it touched through the leaves of the tree and on to his face.

'You know, I do write,' William said.

'I know! Your letters were beautiful poems of love. You carry that notepad too with you everywhere! What do you write?'

'Oh, you know, this and that. Ideas for buildings. Thoughts of what I could do here and there. I find it really useful to be able to scribble down thoughts or else I forget them. Ideas are at their best when they are just formed don't you think? Otherwise your mind has too long to dwell on them and the idea becomes moulded into your own normality! I think that's why people see something different in my work.'

'That's good. I like that. I can use that! You know, I write too.'

'Yes?'

'Yes. I write a journal of my days. You are mentioned a lot.'

It was nearly two o'clock and the people of Florence were either sleeping or in some well found shade. The visitors to the city stood out as the ones still out in the sunshine. William was very thankful for the shade of the trees.

Francesca played with her long dark hair, gently twisting it into braids that fell apart instantly when she let go of them.

'I think the main reason I paint is because I use it to release what is in me. Maybe you should paint!'

'And you would laugh, a lot! I can only draw buildings.'

'You can draw out my heart William. When your letters arrived, such words, such passion. William, you can use words and you melt my heart. It is through your words that you, my love, paint.'

56

William smiled. He had to admit that he found words easier to come by than many. Maybe it was his fascination with the poets, a fascination that meant he could recite line upon line and such memories found their way into his own way of thinking.

'I love you Francesca.'

Francesca took William's hand, lifting it to her mouth, and kissed it.

'And I love you William McTeer, I love you!'

William looked at Francesca, breathing in everything about her.

'She walks in beauty, like the night of cloudless climes and starry skies; and all that's best of dark and bright meet in her aspect and her eyes.'

'Byron,' breathed Francesca, 'the poem you first sent me before sending me the book.'

'I thought it more apt than The Wild Gazelle! Although, come to think of it…'

Francesca hit William's arm again, but this time with less force and accompanied by laughter.

'You have real beauty William!'

William let the words enter into him. He was warmed by them.

'Really?'

Francesca looked at William, as though she were studying him to draw him.

'Your auburn hair is beauty. The way you grow it, longer than is tradition, is right. I love the way you push it behind your ears, as it falls down your neck and curls out.'

'Yes, yes, I know it needs cutting!' laughed William, blushing at Francesca's words.

Francesca ignored William's inevitable and typical self-deprivation.

'And your face William is one I have drawn a thousand times since that very first moment I saw you. I know it like I know my own. Your blue eyes shine, big blue eyes that I am lost in every time I see them. Your smile makes me smile, invites me to smile. There, that smile you do now.'

'You've thought about this haven't you!'

'And your slim, muscular body is like that of...'

'Of Michelangelo's David!'

They were both laughing now.

'Yes, that's right, only better.'

'Do you want to see some of my slim, muscular body?'

Francesca shot William a look of hunger and passion.

'Yes.'

William laughed.

'Then you'll have to catch me first!'

He stood up, picking up a half drunk bottle of wine with him, and ran up the bank, closely followed by Francesca who was laughing too much to run with any speed. They ran by the entrance to the formal garden at the top of the Boboli and passed several well-dressed tourists who exchanged withering glances at the impudence of the young lovers. Such downright decadence!

Down past the wall and several seemingly conspiratorial statues, and round the back of a magnificent fountain before falling down a hidden grassy bank and into a quiet corner of the gardens. There William took his love into his arms and looked into her eyes and told her he would love her forever. There Francesca stroked the beads of sweat from her lovers forehead and told him she was happier than she had ever been in her whole life. There, William and Francesca, made love for the first time.

# Chapter 5

# Robert

July 1st, 1963. Edinburgh, Scotland

It was a perfect day to be born. There was not a cloud in the Scottish sky as the world welcomed Robert Giovanni McTeer. He was a beautiful baby weighing 7 pounds and nine ounces with one freckle on his right cheek that touched a face that already suggested a smile.

Francesca looked at him with adoration and would, for the rest of her life, continue to look at him in the same way. He was treasured from the moment he was conceived and would feel the strong love of his mother with him throughout his life. This was her gift to him.

Chapter 6

# Angus

July 1977. Edinburgh, Scotland

If it hadn't been for Angus, Robert would be dead. No question.

They were enjoying a long school holiday before returning to Fettes, and had been playing into the evening on one of those mid summer nights where the day seems to have the possibility to stretch into infinity. And then in the twilight of the day, in one simple moment, Angus saved Robert's life.

The two boys lived in the glory that is Edinburgh and they loved their city. Of course, they did not see it as a city, rather a playground of opportunity. It had been a wonderful summer to enjoy having been superbly kicked into gear at the beginning of June when seemingly the whole of Edinburgh took to the streets for a party to celebrate Queen Elizabeth the second's silver jubilee. It seemed to the boys that Edinburgh had been in constant party mood ever since.

Edinburgh took on a whole new life in summer. The cold winds that blew off the Firth of Forth let up for a time, and the seagulls, encouraged by warmer currents, enticed you to believe that you were much further south in Britain than you actually were.

Robert knew the city so well, the back streets as well as the more obvious thoroughfares. As he had grown up, Francesca had taken Robert on long and seemingly unending walks around the city and its wonderful array of art galleries and bohemian bars and coffee shops. He had sat for hours on studio floors making up some game or other whilst his mother and her friends, old and often new because she had a habit of picking up friends wherever she went, would talk about whatever they talked about. Memories of feelings and smells he remembered lingered in his brain all his life, so that even in later life he could enter a gallery and be taken back to these times of being with his mother. He would return then to favourite memories of stealing a glance at her as she laughed at some joke or other, her long dark hair falling across her face, her eyes alive with excitement and passion. How he loved her, really loved her. He had the same dark hair and dark eyes that his mother had, and his skin too carried a darker shade giving him the look of a young Italian boy. Like his mother, he was beautiful to the eye.

Now at the grand age of 14 years old, he and his friends were considered old enough to roam free around Leith where they had lived since William and Francesca moved to Edinburgh in 1959. Though Robert had known no different, he felt Leith was a pretty superb place to live being so central to many great things for a teenager to roam around and do. And then, of course, there was the city centre. Although this was still officially out of bounds to them unless accompanied by someone over 16, this did not stop Robert and his friends making regular and ever more daring sortie's into the city centre to experience the treasures to be had. Normally though this was best avoided in summer with the tourist scrums that would change Princes Street and the Royal Mile into toe-to-toe carnage. Much more fun was always to be found along the river, their river, north to the Royal Botanical Gardens and onwards to the port and the never without a dull moment quayside. Yes, Edinburgh was indeed a fine city to grow up in. So much to entice and intoxicate a young mind.

Robert had only just turned 14 and believed himself to be as close to an adult as it was possible to be without actually being called one. It was as though he could almost sense the special elixir that would soon overtake his body and transport him into the magical world of adulthood, as though he could almost touch it!

His best friend, Angus Jefferson, had also turned 14 in May, and the two of them felt a whole new world of possibilities opening up to them. This summer in particular had seen their parents entrust them much more with where they were allowed to go and when they had to report in. Add to this where they went without telling their parents, and the possibilities were becoming endless.

The boys had been through all their schooling together, both of them living at the North side of the Waters of Leith, Robert on Ann Street and Angus around the corner on Dean Park Crescent. Their mothers, who were very good friends, had brought their boys up together and, despite the challenges that age can bring to young relationships, Robert and Angus had stayed best friends throughout. Robert was the much more exuberant child, a born leader, happy to be in the middle of a group of people either familiar or strange and orchestrate proceedings. He was never more alive than when conducting conversation and activity towards some great aim or effort, particularly and always preferably if such lofty endeavour was of his own making. Even from a very young age he had seen all that life offered him as a challenge and if there were not one in front of him, he would invent one so that it could be beaten.

In many ways Angus was opposite to this. He was a compliant friend who offered no opposition to any of

Robert's plans, only support, love and gratitude. When Robert would become so engrossed in something to the extent that others either walked away or let him down, his old friend Angus would be there for him, an ever willing springboard and support for all he sort to achieve. Angus idolised Robert, adored how he was and the ease with which he could have ideas and inspire people. They were only young lads but already the battlegrounds and the formations of their lives were becoming clear to them. What was strength and what was weakness was spelt out clearly in the playgrounds and parks of Edinburgh and to Angus, Robert was an inspiration that lifted his spirits and helped him believe that he could have a piece of his confidence, a piece that would help him move forward to be a braver young man.

It would be unfair to say Angus was an easy conquest friend for Robert, an obedient servant with little inside other than to follow. Rather Angus had his own special abilities and qualities too. He was incredibly intelligent and ahead of many of his fellow pupils, which given he was at Fettes being arguably the best school in Scotland, was some going. Young Jefferson was a bright educational light at the school and much was expected of him in terms of his future education and career. The same was not true of Robert who often caused his parents to be exasperated by his lack of interest in pushing himself in terms of his education.

Both Angus and Robert were in the minority at Fettes insomuch as they were day students and not boarders. Also most of their friends out of school who lived near them did not go to private school and so the net effect saw the two boys often lean on each other by way of support and belonging.

They both looked an idealised and pretty picture coming home in their school finery that included the highly distinctive chocolate and magenta blazer, something that filled their parents with pride. In fact it is said the colours were chosen to represent the mud and blood of the rugby field, the harsh reality of which Angus and Robert felt very often on the cold wind swept sport fields that awaited them. Rugby at Fettes was not just a sport, a way of advancing physical fitness, but rather something to be ingrained on the boy's minds. Rugby was a code for life with harsh lessons that if learnt properly could aid the young men throughout their whole lives. The fact that several Fettes old boys had won the almost impossible to get Victoria Cross through valour of the highest order, added weight, if it were needed at all, to this view.

Angus had a firm grasp of what he was looking to achieve in life. He wanted to follow his father into Oxford and law and no one doubted he would do just that. It was a clarity of aim that impressed all his masters and friends, including Robert who aspired in turn to learn this skill from his trusted friend. Robert saw in Angus qualities he did not have. The patience, counselling and longevity of Angus kept Robert going, kept him focussed, and as a result the friendship grew and grew meaning they learnt from one another.

Recently Robert had discovered that he could climb out of one of the top floor back windows, which overlooked their glorious city garden, and pull himself, quite easily, on to the flat piece of traditional lead covered roof on to which it opened. The garden went back 100 yards with an old magnificent stone wall as its boundary. It had been an overgrown garden, almost a jungle his father had said, when they had arrived. It was a challenge that Francesca had taken on with happy vigour. The garden was now divided into sections. The patio area with its large dining table and benches including a covered pergola so that the frequent Edinburgh rains could not stop happy outdoor festivities. The play area which, when Robert was younger, had included an enormous sand pit, had now become a sunken pond with active pond life and a totally over the top Ravenna Italian fountain that kept getting blocked. Once William had fallen over in the pond and emerged covered in algae, coughing up dirty water and swearing he would never enter the pool again. Francesca and Robert had only just stopped laughing when William took off his Wellingtons and discovered in one of them an unfortunate goldfish! They had all nearly choked with laughter at that. Sadly the fish had simply choked.

From here under an arch, you entered the formal area, which had deep borders with immense colours and sizeable and stunning shrubbery. Francesca would spend many hours in the garden, not just with her beloved plants, but also because to the bottom corner she had her private garden studio with floor to ceiling sliding patio doors that she would often have wide open no matter what the weather. A specially fitted flat roof jutted out to stop the rains lashing into the room allowing her to keep her doors open whenever she liked, the smells and sounds of the garden floating into her. Yes this Italian girl had come from the warmth of the Mediterranean and acclimatised herself to the often-harsh winters of the east coast of Scotland.

The studio had oil fired heaters that Francesca would only use when she remembered how cold she was or when her adoring son joined her. He had his own drawing table near his mothers so that he could come and go whenever he liked. Other than William too, no one else was allowed in the studio. It was Francesca's secret haven, her quiet space, and the place where she could be herself.

William told his son one cold February night, as they sat in the warmth of their kitchen looking out to the light at the end of the garden where Francesca had been encamped all day working, that his mother was a free spirit.

'What's a free spirit?' the young 6-year-old boy had asked his father.

'Someone who looks like your mother,' William had replied.

The next day, a Saturday, on one of their long walks around the city, Robert, who was gripping his mothers hand as they climbed up the steep Scotsman Steps to Market Street, asked Francesca,

'Mummy?'

'Yes precious?' she had replied, happy as ever to be on the move with today them being on their way to meet an old artist friend in Grassmarket.

'Daddy says you are a free spirit.'

'Does he indeed!' laughed Francesca, slowing down to allow little Robert to keep up with her. 'And what made him say that?'

'Because you paint in the dark and the cold with your door open.'

Francesca smiled, letting the warmth of the knowledge of her husband and sons love wash over her.

'Well, if your Papa says I am, I must be.'

Robert considered this answer and wondered why William had not called him a free spirit too.

'Mummy?'

'Mmm?'

'Can I be a free spirit too?'

Francesca stopped and knelt down to face her young son face to face.

'You can be whatever you want to be sweetheart.'

And with that she kissed him on his forehead and they continued their climb.


The Ann Street garden continued to the other far corner and the back of the garden. Here was the vegetable plot, the huge white octagon greenhouse, and, possibly, Francesca's proudest part, the compost area where anything and everything was deposited to rot and use again in its eventual decomposed new life. Francesca had brought her gardening ideas and abilities to her new home from the fresh gardens of Italy.

'Everything is here for us,' she had told William as they looked out to a garden that was a hopeless mess, a garden that was so badly lost that it had put so many people off buying the house. 'This garden will feed us, in our minds and in our bodies!'

'So you like it?' asked William, seeing the potential of adding real value to the equally run down house, but struggling to see how they would find the time or energy to get into the jungle.

'I love it! It is us. It has been waiting for us!'

'It's not too much work then?' he had asked, concerned that they would take too much on and that this would in turn take them away from their vocations.

'The work will make us better people! This house and its garden will help us in our work William, not hinder us,' Francesca had replied with pride, knowing what William was thinking.

'We had better buy it then!' smiled William with a cheeky glint in his eye.

The Estate Agent watched them, as he had watched 10 more couples look around this old Georgian house on Ann Street, which was one of the most outstanding Georgian terraces in the whole of Edinburgh. The properties here were strong and sculptural, yet also softer and more relaxed than much of New Town. It was as though the architect, Sir Henry Raeburn, had specifically designed the Street in sole honour of his wife, Ann, to replicate her character in a row of actual buildings. The street was fortunate in position too, being surrounded by a beautiful green landscape that gave it a glory all of its own. Further, and just below them, ran the beautiful Waters of Leith having travelled 24 miles from the source at the Colzium Springs at Millstone Rig and down, through the Harperring Reservoir, past the ruins of the Cairns Castle, and dropping into Edinburgh itself. Here the river arrived at Dean Village on the site of the old watermills in a deep gorge dramatically spanned by the highly impressive Dean Bridge. All this beauty and impressive scenery was outside the front door of this house and yet this property had not sold. It was, in estate agent speak, a property needing the touch of a developer, a visionary. The house could almost be said to have not been touched, apart from simple additions, since it had been designed in 1817. William though, as a brilliant young architect, saw what the shell was and what it could be. Francesca saw this and more.

'We'll have it!' declared William to the startled Estate Agent.

'You will?' he replied with a surprised tone that he immediately regretted.

'We will!'

The Estate Agent had been unable to suppress an actual laugh of relief, which was further duly noted by William and encouraged him to ask for an even larger discount which would later be begrudgingly given.

Over the years they had done much work to the house with William overseeing most of the changes and updates, including restoring the many Georgian features of the house as well as adding as much glass to the back of the property as the planners would allow him to do. William planned the work and old builder friends came in and carried it out with the ever-watchful William busily following them around and ensuring all was done as he had planned. He was, in builder speak, an awkward client.

Since coming to Edinburgh he had set up his own business adventurously called 'William McTeer Ltd!' His reputation had grown in Florence and his CV, with its large portfolio of work, had become very impressive and well known. He worked from the office he had set up at home, which was a large room on the ground floor at the front of the house. William could see no need to add what he saw as unnecessary expense with a swanky city centre Edinburgh office. The business now employed 3 more people and despite the need for more space, William resisted. He would rather stay small and be cramped, than lose his home luxuries, which he loved, and add costs, which he hated.

The garden though was all Francesca's work and by all this really did mean all. She must have got through 20 large refuse skips over the years as she gradually dug out the garden and, as William had done inside, found much that was original and beautiful including a sunken secret garden area with original stone work. The restoration of this alone took her almost a year. Around the garden she gave structure and added many playful touches including statues both formal and modern situated throughout. Many pieces you would not know were there unless you knew where to look. Robert knew where they all were after many years of losing balls of all shapes and sizes throughout the garden and needing to retrieve them. Between him and Angus they had named every statue, the majority of which with names of various Heart of Midlothian players.

On this particular July night, with Robert's parents, William and Francesca, wrongly assuming their young charge and his wild haired friend were in Robert's bedroom, Robert and Angus had carefully lifted their exhausted bodies out onto their high vantage point where they could feel like kings of the world.

'I don't even like girls,' moaned Angus having again been harassed by the guys in the Park as to why he was once more spotted following Mary McGowan home. This despite the fact that she lived a mile away from his own house and thereby ensuring a massive, and hard to justify, detour.

'You like boys then Angus?' asked Robert with a big grin across his dirt smeared face. They had been playing football for what seemed like a 4-hour game that had included 2 fights and an eventual glorious victory for their team. It was a victory secured once Robert had dealt with the opponent's best player with a casual yet effective trip. Robert refused to allow the game to be over until it was clear his team had won with a resounding score line, which meant the game had gone on so long that a third of the players had already given up and left before the game was officially over.

Angus had tried to ignore the boy's jibes but he was, unlike Robert, quite sensitive.

'Mary's just a friend, well more my mother's friend's daughter as you well know,' he had reasoned, speaking as much to Robert as he was to himself.

'Yes, of course. And she's got them tiny wee tits developing,' Robert had replied, purposely adding more amusing embarrassment on to his friends shoulders.

'Has she?' offered Angus as casually as he could and pretending instead to be taken with a distant view out to the sea.

'Yes stupid, you know she has! She's lovely and she thinks you are too. You can tell by the way she is when you're around,' offered Robert with an air of adult knowledge in his voice.

'Can you?' asked Angus, too quickly.

'Yes,' smiled Robert with the easy conquest of his friends true feelings, 'when you finally walk away from her she follows you with her eyes.'

'She does?' asked Angus, a keen a happy tilt adding itself to his voice.

'She does. Just one piece of advice Angus.'

'Yes?'

'When you are talking to her, talk to her eyes and not to her breasts.'

Angus had not prepared for this conversation. He was ready to stand his ground on not even liking girls, but the simple mention of Mary's breasts had caught him out and set him feeling that strange sensation he kept getting whenever he saw the girl. He had, like all his friends, a vague idea about girls and that one day they would grow up into the mysterious world that his older sister Annie was now inhabiting. She was 19 years old now and seemingly in another world and being, to Angus and his straightforward mind, very weird. Strange hair, bizarre make up, moods so variable that you never knew what was coming and, to top it all, a seeming disregard to inhibition that meant she walked around the house naked causing his friends to call round far to often. She played her music very loudly too to the exclusion of anybody else's likes or feelings in the house. It was music that was normally played by people who looked just like her on their elaborate album covers. Further Annie had also taken to smoking with exuberant excess. She smoked when she got up over breakfast, when she sat for hours in front of her mirror doing her make up, when she came down for dinner and when she went to bed. It was horrible and Angus had already vowed to never ever smoke. His dad was finding it all too much and seemed to cope by being out of the house more often than ever. Angus tried to do the same.

Mary though had opened up his mind to the possibility of girls. Her stolen glances caused a strange nausea to well up within him. Any sense of being cool that he had, which was little enough, would immediately dissolve, and he would find himself following her without talking to her. She didn't seem to mind.

Robert offered further observations.

'Well when I say she thinks you are lovely, I think it is more in a cuddly doll sort of way. She'd like to stroke your hair and dress you up in wee fancy clothes Angus!'

Robert laughed, satisfied with his joke and making up

71

for the fact that he wished he could feel what Angus was feeling. Angus looked a little mortified and, as he often looked, a little confused.

Robert stretched up and walked to the edge of the flat roof.

'Careful Robbie,' called Angus.

It all happened so quickly really. Robert had done this many times before but maybe not walked quite this far out. Maybe he was showing off for his friend, or perhaps tiredness simply caused him to be careless. Maybe the light of the day had made him giddy, but whatever the reason, he was overstretching the mark. The end of the roof was extremely worn from years of Edinburgh weather and, under the heat of a hot sunny day, meant there was no grip whatsoever for his feet. He was wearing worn dark blue adidas samba trainers with little to no tread left. As Robert heard his friend call out to him, and he turned back to reply that he was totally in control, his left foot slipped and he began to fall with his feet first, off the roof. It was four floors down and would take him straight onto a slab filled terrace that would offer no soft landing.

As he fell, his knee caught the edge of the roof, immediately stripping off the top layer of skin and pushing him outwards. His chest, then chin, caught the old gutter that stood resolutely at the side of the roof, and both knocks encouraged him to react with blinding speed by flinging out his arms to ensure his hands caught the edge of it. This they did, arresting his fall and seeming to pull his arms out of their sockets at the same time.

In that brief moment as he held on, his legs dangerously swinging like a hideous pendulum below him, all he could think about was his summer fading away and the pain that awaited him when he would unquestionably fall. As he did so his fingers began to slip on the hot lead guttering and he awaited his doom.

And then, almost as fast as it had happened, it was all

ending as Angus, a bigger and stronger lad than his friend, was pulling him back onto the roof, scraping his own arms as he did so and causing more cuts to find their way onto Robert's arms and legs. This would take some serious explaining to his parents.

Exhausted the two friends fell back onto the safety of the back wall and, as the fading evening sun calmed their nerves, they began to laugh and revel in the beauty of redemption.

Chapter 7

# Robert

May 1982. Sheffield, England

Having spent far too much time occupied with the delights of beer, music, football and girls, and far too little time spent on his studies, Robert now found himself sat outside the office of Ronald Jones, a rather domineering type of man whose sole intention in life seemed to be that of intimidation. This was not a character trait that Robert was particularly fond of or looking forward to meeting on a one to one basis, particular given that Mr Jones, who was head of his course and the Sheffield University Business & Economics Department, appeared to be using it almost exclusively on him of late. Yes Robert could accept that his first year of higher education had been less than successful. Grades had been somewhat patchy and in some cases not awarded at all. He had managed to keep matters from his parents and had taken the hopeful view that there was always next year. He suspected Mr Jones was about to tell him this was not necessarily the case.

The fact was that Robert was at University primarily because it was expected of him, and not because he wanted to be there. His father William had long since underlined to him that university was a privilege to aim for and excel in, and yet education had left him cold. To be told by his father from a very young age that this right was one of the things his father had fought for, nearly lost his life for even, left Robert with little choice but to comply, but he found himself unable to do so with any level of real enthusiasm.

Robert had enjoyed an upbringing that included an education that no doubt many others would have made much more of. Going to one of the best schools in Scotland should have meant he could have hand picked any of the top universities in the world. As it was his grades were mixed and it was only by impressing at interview with Ronald Jones himself present, that he had managed to get on to the Sheffield University Economics course. For William this was an immense disappointment as this was neither the university, nor the course, he had aspired for his son. William had always had a firm belief that Robert could achieve much more and that Robert's seeming inability to break through his own lethargy was nothing short of a serious failing of a son to his parents. He fell short of telling Robert this, which was very difficult for him to do, but the unspoken words were felt by both. Francesca had spent much time soothing the family waters, hoping her hard work was allowing the older man and the younger son time to move on. She knew it would take time and hoped that Robert would come out of Sheffield with something that both men could be happy with. 'Hope is the dagger with which to pierce the heart of despair,' she told herself and then promptly added the words in her daily journal for inspiration.

Robert was under no illusion that William expected good grades now with the expectation being a first or at worst a 2:1. Sadly neither grade was a likely outcome that Robert was confident of. From University the pathway, Robert knew, would be in his fathers mind into William's growing business. However Robert had never enjoyed the prospect of joining the architects world and try as he did to encourage himself to be more focussed he was, ultimately, just plain bored; bored by the prospect of a path seemingly made for him and bored by his university studies that seemed so extremely dull and devoid of what he actually wanted in his own day-to-day life. It was not as if many of his teachers over the years had not poured on him accolades to try and inspire him, always with the addition of a phrase 'if only he would apply himself more wholeheartedly.' As a young scholar he had been able to drift along with his natural intelligence and drive, meaning he stood out and excelled. As he had gotten older his luck was running out. His grades suffered because he simply did not know the subjects and general high intelligence was no longer enough. His time of leading the pack was behind him and Robert felt the sting of this but did not know how to deal with it.

The young man longed for the discovery of something out there that would fully involve him and energise him with a commitment that he could attach himself to with a vigour that really would make his father, and himself, proud. Robert found this energy when he was with people, out at night in the great metropolis that was Sheffield, a city he had fallen in love with, with its people and with the hum of the place. Over less than an academic year Robert had gotten to know key people within the out of office hours community. He knew where the pop stars and DJ's hung out and he knew the majority of them and, more importantly, they knew him. He was right in the centre of organising student parties and events. He had become the focal point for much that was seen to be cool in 1982 within the student union. Normally such positions fell to second or third year students, but to Robert leadership in an area where he wanted to be involved came naturally and people easily fell under him and his command.

Then there were the other rewards. Girls, drugs and

the thing that made it all go round, money. Yes Robert was making serious cash and lots of it. Be that from arranging gigs and taking backhanders or setting up dealers and taking cash. He didn't care where it came from. All he knew was that the side industry he was in was making him rich. His had already changed the rust bucket Fiesta his mum and dad had sent him off to University with as their gift for his education with a 3-year-old red TR7. He was the envy of his year. He liked that.

Robert considered himself a very lucky man indeed to not only be in Sheffield in the middle of the exploding pop culture that was the early 80's with awesome bands such as ABC, Heaven 17, The Jam, Roxy Music, Soft Cell and so many others filling the cities venues, but to also be in the actual city that gave birth to the Human League's 'Dare' album in his first Autumn in Sheffield. 'Don't you want me baby' was the song of the year and every nightclub played it in every form it could. Robert had read somewhere that Bowie himself had announced at a gig in 1979 that the Human Leagues synthesiser pop revolution was the future of rock and roll, and this had helped him choose Sheffield as the city he wanted to come to, sensing there was something here for him. Now he was actually here in the middle of the musical revolution of the decade and he loved it. The whole scene seemed tailor made for Robert's character and so in the environment of modern day culture he excelled, even modelling his hairstyle on the now famous Phil Oakey lopsided haircut. Sadly these out of course achievements were probably not about to satisfy the indomitable Ronald Jones and would certainly not impress William.

As Robert sat waiting on a hard plastic chair made, he felt sure, to make people feel uncomfortable, he sat thinking through the seriousness of what no doubt awaited him whilst mixing these thoughts with various events he had coming up. On one side of his brain he considered a plethora of excuses that he was preparing for his father after what would probably be a 'leave the building and don't come back' edict from the meeting that waited. On the other side of his brain Robert worked through the line up for the forthcoming weekend of events that included several parties and much good fun to be had, not to mention the good weekend cash to be made. And this was his problem. He had a magnificent over active mind that wanted to be in several places at once. Such thinking had not been conducive to match his structured education in economics!

'Come!'

The call bellowed from behind the office door causing Robert to sit up straight and look quickly to his left and right. Was it he that had been summoned? He was aware that he was feeling remarkably hot and a cold shiver from behind his neck started a mild panic to fill his young body. He looked across to Mr Jones' PA, a pretty girl who Robert was sure he half recognised, who was busy typing.

'Excuse me?' Robert asked, in an over the top polite voice, 'is he calling for me?'

'Yes,' replied the girl, looking up and catching Robert's eye.

Robert looked to the door that was waiting for him and then back to the girl.

'I hope you don't mind me asking but don't I know you?'

The girl nodded, a small and slightly embarrassed smile on her face.

'Erm, yes, we have chatted at the Student Union a couple of times. Last weekend at the late night party?'

'Yes, that's right!' declared Robert, not remembering the girl exactly, but now placing her at one of the weekly Union party events that he organised. Maybe they had only chatted, but his head was remembering some heavy kissing too. His embarrassed thoughts were thankfully interrupted.

'Now Mr McTeer,' came a further loud and gruff voice, 'unlike you I have not got all day and the clock is quite clearly fucking ticking!'

Let off received, Robert climbed to his feet and immediately became aware that he ached in a manner that suggested he had chronic flu. The truth was that prior to being told to appear at the office after the morning lecture he had been feeling as bright as the preverbal button. A successful night in Sheffield had seen him at last go home with Sandra Moorhead and, having lusted after her for the whole of the year, the night had been a long and memorable one. However the affects of far too much alcohol coming face to face with a stressful meeting was now kneading its way into his temples.

He gently opened the office door and was greeted by an office that was so dark his eyes took time to adjust.

'Shut the door and sit down,' said Ronald Jones far too loudly and without looking up as he sat busily filling in some forms on his desk. Ronald Jones was an unremarkable man to look at and yet you remembered him. Middle aged, relatively in shape without being athletic, unkempt greying hair that somehow seemed to suit him, and a face that was alive and confident. His choice of clothing was invariably a linen suit, a white shirt and a colourful tie always falling away from his collar despite his top button always being fastened. He would wear brown brogues and red socks that matched his red braces. These were his trademark and how people would always describe him. The overall effect was one that meant he had a presence, a presence that after spending any length of time with him turned into an aura, the unmistakeable feeling that you were in the environment of someone who left an impression on you for years to come.

Pipe smoke filled the room and partly disguised the piles of books that filled shelf after shelf around this large room occupied by the Head of Economics for the

University. He continued to write and Robert tried to calm himself. He remembered his mother telling him that if ever in a state of panic the most important thing was to breathe deeply and slowly. This was good advice as Robert immediately realised he had been doing neither since entering the room. A deep breath was duly taken only to result in the intake of copious amounts of pipe smoke causing Robert to cough uncontrollably. Without looking up, Ronald Jones lifted his right arm and pointed towards the corner of the room where a sink and selection of glasses stood. Robert made his way over to the sink and gently filled up a glass, taking his time to ensure that he got himself under control so that he could handle the oncoming expected onslaught. His hands were clammy and he could feel the beer from the night before begin to perspire out of him. He knew he must look very rough indeed.

'Tick tock, tick tock Mr McTeer. Come on, come on!'

Robert turned round, spilling water on to the floor and his black Adidas Beckenbauer trainers, and made his way back to the chair. As he sat down, Ronald finally looked up.

'Robert,' he started, looking him straight in the eyes and making Robert in turn look down, 'it's good to see you looking so incredibly crap! Well done. You must be very proud of yourself!'

'Well, I've been up late, you know, working.'

'Working? Hah! Of course you haven't you pathetic little boy! You've been burning the bloody candle at both fucking ends have you not?'

'I do like candles,' let out Robert before immediately regretting the smart reply.

'Don't be impertinent Robert. You're in enough trouble already.'

Ronald let a moment of silence fall between them and, as he did so, he kept his gaze firmly on Robert who almost visibly shrank in his chair in response and dropped his head.

'Now then,' Ronald went on, 'here we are, just you and I. No one to see me kill you.'

Robert looked up, offered a little smile, and was relieved to see the Head of Economics return it.

'You are a gifted boy, no, a gifted young man. Do you know the full potential that lies beneath your grasp?'

'The full potential? Is this about my last paper? I can really explain...'

'Quiet Robert. Your papers are not why you are here. Christ Almighty Robert. Do you think I, the highly renowned Ronald Jones, the Head of the University Business and Economics Department, Chair of the Sheffield Business Club, Board Member of the National Association of Macro Economic Studies, Chief Fucking Man all round, would waste my time having you here to talk about your work to date! You have been coasting my dear boy, coasting, and do you know why?'

'Well, why? It's a good question and I'm glad you asked, you see....'

'Ah my dear boy! You amuse me greatly! You are bloody well bored out of your much under used brain. Am I right? Of course I am right. I am always right Robert. This is my gift.'

'Yes, undoubted, but...'

'When I am done Robert you may talk but until that time, and I shall tell you when that time arrives, you can keep your mouth well and truly fucking shut. Is that clear?'

This last tirade was delivered at a rather loud volume with a clear threatening tone, and Robert considered whether to just walk out and be done with it. However he saw in his minds eye his Dad waving him off just after Easter and the look, which William had given him, imploring his son to make them proud. In the memory of those eyes Robert was reminded that he really did owe his parents more than to be thrown out so early. Even he could see the sense in getting a decent degree, though what he would do with it was another thing entirely. He looked up and simply said,

'Yes Mr Jones, quite clear. I am here to learn from you.'

Ronald Jones smiled at that and sat back in his old office captain's decrepit leather chair, the arms worn away and the tan well and truly faded. He began.

'Good, and yes, you are here to learn from me. Let me take you back in time young man. When I interviewed you some time ago now I was struck by one thing alone, the way you could hold a room. In your interview it was your personality alone that carried you and therefore everyone listened to you. In your pathetic self-deluded mind you probably thought we were impressed by the smart flouncy school you went to and your trumped up curriculum. Some of them of course probably were, but not me. Rich retarded bastards the lot of you. No, I watched and listened. I saw a room waiting on your next word, impressed, no besotted by you despite the fact that you had nothing particularly brilliant to say. You have, and I think you know this, to be a true gift.'

This was an unexpected turn and Robert's confused brain began to do somersaults. He had been rather upset to hear his parents described in such a false way and whilst part of his head began to raise valuable objections, his mouth wisely managed to keep counsel. Ronald, in full flow, continued.

'At the moment you have demonstrated this gift by pissing it down the South Yorkshire drains but, and I have this on good authority, you have matched this pissing with an exuberance of character that has half of the well and good in the Sheffield social scene knowing exactly who you are. You are making money are you not Mr Mcteer, and good money at that!'

Robert was now spell bound. How the hell did Ronald Jones know anything of the sort? Was he being followed!

'Close your mouth Robert. It is not a pleasant sight. It is

82

my business to know what I need to know. As I said, you have a gift to match my gift and I have plans for you Robert that I believe you will fulfil.'

'Plans?'

'You agreed to keep quiet Robert but I shall let that one word pass.' A thin smile spread across the older man's face as he turned to his left and pulled a file into the middle of his desk, allowing the few silent seconds to drag longer than they needed to.

'Have you ever thought of becoming a property tycoon Mr McTeer?'

'Erm, well, maybe?'

'And what have you thought?'

Robert considered the question. Maybe this was a way that the wise old economics professor was testing him to see what he had learnt so far from his studies. Maybe, just maybe, all was not lost after all.

'Well, that property is something we all need and will always need, and given the simple laws of supply and demand, a key phrase used by Adam Smith himself in his book The Wealth of Nations, issued I believe in 1776, property would appear to be a safe bet. Given therefore that we live on an island that has an upward limit on what we can build, and given our population continues to rise, property would be as good a business as any Mr Jones.'

'Indeed young Robert, indeed.' Ronald held a broad grin now. The very mention of Adam Smith, the accepted father of economics, had gained Robert several brownie points.

'Do you know where the property market is set to go in the world?'

Robert opened his mouth to speak, only to see Ronald Jones put his finger to his mouth in a silencing gesture.

'I shall tell you where Robert. Up, up and up like there is no fucking tomorrow. Sure there will be hitches along the way but the man who is ahead of the game will never look back, do you hear me, never look back! The world is changing. Thatcher's fine capitalist revolution is with us. We have left the dark days of depression and small-minded left wing thinking, and we are swiftly moving to a free market that will allow free enterprise never before dreamed of and that, dear boy, will make us very wealthy indeed. Soon salaries will rise to extraordinary amounts and the middle classes will become the new rich whilst the old wealth will run out like steam from an old broken kettle. And then, and mark my words Mr McTeer, the super rich will be born out of being in the right place at the right time.'

Robert was now gazing intently at Ronald Jones as he talked so coherently and with such conviction about the beauties of capitalism, and the way that good old-fashioned bricks and mortar would be the very cornerstone of the growth of the western civilisation and, indeed, the world. He was a man on a mission and for some reason that Robert could not work out; he was delivering this vision in detail to him!

'And that is why, young Robert McTeer, I hoped you would turn out to be the type of young man I thought you might be.'

'Might be?' asked Robert, letting the many questions buzzing around in his head try and make some sense of what was happening here.

'Yes, indeed. Let me tell you a story. How old is your father?'

'Dad! Erm, not sure really. Just past 60.'

'And is he remarkably wealthy?'

'Well, no, not really. He's certainly not the man you described earlier in your tirade on Fettes parents,' Robert said quickly, forcing the words out bravely so that they would be spoken before he had time to reconsider. 'He does OK though. You know, he has a nice house and good job.'

Ronald looked at Robert, admiring the words he had shared in support of his father despite the fear he knew the young man felt in his presence. He softened his voice and asked,

'A nice house you say. Does he own other houses?'

Robert laughed at that. The very thought that his father could own more than one house was preposterous for many reasons. Firstly and predominantly William would not see the point financially. Why waste money on something that they could not fully use. William very much believed that anything they bought needed to be used until it could not be used anymore. The Ford Cortina 1600E had been at the top of its class when, in 1968, the McTeer's had bought it. Now, 14 years on, William would remind Robert that the 'E' stood for 'Executive' in 1968 and it still stood for 'Executive' now! The fact that 14 years on it had dated somewhat, and that fourteen Edinburgh winters had rather dented the bright exterior and once shining gleaming bumpers to become tinged by rust, did not dampen William's enthusiasm. Seeing that old lump of a car come to Fettes on many an occasion was, to Robert, more than embarrassing. The parent's car park was like a who's who of the luxury car market, plus, of course, William's Ford Cortina!

William McTeer Limited was the same. It now boasted 6 employees, all of whom worked out of the McTeer family home. The business now took up much of the ground floor with an extension now added to the house to simply keep the back of the house for the family. William still had no intention of spending money on an office when he could save money and stay on Ann Street.

Robert didn't actually mind this as most of the McTeer team were in their mid 20's and they were all pretty cool, so Robert got to exchange music and cigarettes with them. Besides he spent so little time at home now that what did it matter if his parents wanted to not have a private life!

Francesca positively revelled in so many people being around all the time. She got to use the brave ones as models and found the whole set up as wonderfully bohemian. By good rights the neighbours should have complained given the ins and outs from the McTeer household every day but they didn't. Instead they joined in the silliness and turned most late Friday afternoons into an end of week and start of weekend party.

William also objected to the ownership of things he saw as excessive from a political viewpoint. He was not too left on his beliefs as he saw private house ownership and private education as a God given right. However he viewed the overly wealthy with absolute suspicion and despite the fact that he lived in arguably one of the nicest parts of Edinburgh, a fact that he constantly reminded Robert was due to the benevolence of Francesca's family, William would never accept that he could have a second house that others could be living in. To him second properties were a way of driving up house prices and depriving the locals out of their own properties. He once told Robert that buying a house was a trick of a capitalist society to tie you into their ethics for good.

'My Dad would not be happy about having a second home or a second anything sir.'

'Not happy? Is he mad? Does he not see all around him the wealthy getting wealthier?' asked Ronald, genuine surprise and deep disdain in his voice.

'He does. It makes him sick,' replied Robert, with a mixture of respect for his fathers strength of belief but also despair as he could not understand the man.

'Envy is it boy?'

'No,' replied Robert in a level voice, 'pure belligerence.'

'Ah, belligerence!' Ronald smiled at that. 'His loss I say.'

'I do too sir. I have told him as much on many occasions. He has more than enough money.'

'And he does what with it?'

It was a good question. Robert reasoned his parents were pretty wealthy. Certainly much money had come their way from Italian family bequests. His parents though were known benefactors of many matters including diversities from art galleries to shelter projects to care homes to homeless children in deepest South America. If there was a cause, Robert could count on his mother to both find it and persuade William to join her and support it. No wonder his Dad had not moved the business on. He probably didn't have enough money left after giving it all away.

'My parents do lots of charitable work sir.'

Ronald lifted his eyebrows, pulling them together in an amazed expression.

'Well, well, well. Quite astounding. And he wonders why you don't wish to follow his lead!'

Robert laughed at this. Having had years of listening to his parents go on and on about this need and that travesty, it was great to listen to a fine selfish man after his own heart. He had long since reasoned that he would make money, and lots of money, for himself first and not be tied to such small aspirations as his parents. Only after great wealth had found Robert, he often reasoned, would he give some away.

'Where do you want to be when you reach your father's age?' asked Ronald with a real interest in his tone.

'Happy. Rich. Free.'

'And how will you do this?'

'Investment sir,' replied Robert readily.

'Investment?'

'Yes. I have enough about me to be very successful. I just need to find what fits.'

'Indeed. That is why you are here.'

'It is?' asked Robert, hoping with all his inner self that Ronald would clarify exactly why he was there as soon as possible.

'Yes. It is. Do you want to be in your 50's and only own one house Robert?'

'No sir. I would like properties around the world.'

'Why?'

Robert was beginning to enjoy this. At home Robert felt that talking about wealth was akin to talking kindly and enthusiastically about the joys of whipping people senseless. The mere mention of wealth would cause his father to become extremely edgy and his mother to get ready for her feed the world speech. As a result the dreams of wealth had grown very large in his own head and not made much more of a journey.

'Because I like the thought of it.'

Ronald rested back in his chair. This was all going very well indeed. Ronald held up his hand as though calling for a moment of peace before the delivery of a great speech. Presently he cleared his throat, took a sip of water and then began.

'Robert, let me tell you something. Despite my dashing youthful looks I am in my mid 40's and do you know what I have been doing with my life? Well, I had spent my life-teaching students the plain beauties of economics when one day I realised I had not been teaching myself. I stumbled upon a little scheme that involved buying land and old property. It was a bit of a scam to be honest with you, but no one was really losing. It was just that I was gaining the most. A few years on and I have now built myself an enviable portfolio. I say enviable but to an outside man they may say I have built a mixed bag. Some fine property here and there, but elsewhere they may view what they see as acres upon acres of worthless land and rubble, and yet, one day young Robert, and one day very soon, it will be worth many, many millions of pounds. This is simply the start and the future has no full stop, no full stop I tell you! History is remembered more often than not because of the bravery of those who took decisions that would change the world. I have taken such decisions, my buying habits bravely predicting what will come next. Out of my dreams, my actions, will flow out history.'

Ronald opened the file in front of him and placed in front of Robert picture after picture of building after building, field after field, map after map. Each new piece of paper was placed down with a quick explanation as to why it was on the Ronald Jones portfolio, the potential for profit.

As intrigued as Robert was, he was now beginning to get worried. This was either the most elaborate one to one economics teaching session he was ever going to get, or he was part of a jigsaw that would hopefully soon make sense. The rigours of the night before were now really beginning to close in, and his poor troubled head was crying out with pain. Concentration was key and he must understand what on earth was happening. He took a sip of water.

'OK – I hear you, but what are you telling me all this for?'

'Ah yes, Mr McTeer, good question. Patience. We are nearly there. The future, my future, is based on one simple truth; namely that property will win the day. Agreed?'

'Yes, based on what you are saying, and with my limited knowledge, I agree?'

'Well, I am many things Mr McTeer, a brilliant economist and a forward thinker being some of my best attributes; but an evangelist, a bright leader of people, an inspiration to others? These things I am not. I am too bombastic, too angry most of the time, to full of my own self-importance to lead a team, an organisation. In short, I put peoples backs up.'

A pause filled the air. Ronald sat back and enjoyed the end of his favourite black walnut pipe, allowing time for his words to sink in to his young audience of one. Robert could almost see his own thoughts going round in the thick and rich pipe smoke circles that hovered around the room.

Ronald Jones fixed a hard stare on Robert and simply said,

'You are an evangelist and the time has come for me to place such a man into my business.'

Silence.

Ronald Jones leaned forward in his chair and made up another pipe. Slowly he lit up and gently inhaled and then, as he did many times on many days, he smoothly let the smoke drift into the office air, watching it rise and form its own dazzling shapes as it did so.

Robert simply looked at his Department Head and waited. If he was swimming, he was right out of his depth.

'I have waited for the right man to cross my path for four years Mr McTeer, and I am here to tell you that you are that man. I am offering you the job.'

'The job?'

'Yes, the job. Well done.'

'Well done?' asked Robert, dazzled by what he was hearing.

'Yes, well done. You are now the Managing Director of Jones Ltd. Within a few years you will be a multimillionaire. You can thank me later. You can keep your sideline ventures in place. They will keep you dirty and I do need you to stay dirty. You might even build a few good contacts for us. Now leave me alone to get on with matters.'

Robert thought he should perhaps stand but found himself almost glued to his seat. He had been sweating heavily but suspected it was not this that was holding him down. Unable to move he decided to do nothing.

Ronald had turned his attention to some document but now stopped writing and simply looked up over his glasses.

'And you are waiting for?'

'Right. Nothing really other than everything. Will you be writing to me with any of this?'

'Don't be stupid. Of course not.'

'Right.'

'When would you like an answer?'

Ronald gave him a very hard stare. There was no need to give an answer when both men knew this was going to happen.

'Right. I see. The old fashioned assumed close. Yes, well, I'm in then. Good. And when do I start?'

'You've already started Robert. You started the moment you met me.'

Robert stood and walked towards the door, a sense of elation beginning to build inside him.

'Oh and Robert,'

'Yes sir?'

'Get your bloody hair cut.'

'Right. Will do.'

Chapter 8

# Alison

July 1982. Sheffield, England

Alison Collins was a lost soul, a wandering spirit that was struggling to find any semblance of what she could call her own calling in a world that more often than not bored her to distraction.

She had been working as Senior House Manager at The Crucible Theatre in Sheffield for two years now. She had worked here part time throughout her English degree at the University and when she had finished that, passed with a first of course and top in her year, she easily fell into theatre life. She was young to get the job, but she had impressed so many people within the theatre with her drive and determination that they were hungry to get her on board as soon as they could. The job to her was easy, a mere matter of course, and allowed her more importantly to mix with artists who lifted her spirits. They were fellow travelling souls, forever looking to fill their voids with the characters of parts they could live for a few hours each day. Some people found actors the strangest people. Alison found them the most normal of people because they were, in the main, true to their predicament, namely that life was a one off, a show, and a set of happenings. It was not mapped out on a piece of paper that was an obvious dot-to-dot map of how all would be well. Her family back home in Nottingham believed this to be true and it made her ill to even think about it. Life was not black and white. It was an accident waiting to happen, a journey that had no fixed definitives other than the fact that whatever you had planned for yourself, you would most definitely get something else too. Alison viewed life as first and foremost cloudy with, if you were lucky, a glimpse of colour along the way. To be involved with actors was to see people reaching out to touch these colours, to try and turn the normal into something worth having.

The job at the theatre gave her the platform with which to use her best talent, which was that of simply listening and turning what she heard to something to her advantage. She had an uncanny knack of listening intently and being able to replay what she heard in a way that made people think. This generally made people calmer and more open to exploring issues that they had previously been unable to see past. She found that she often had complete strangers open up to her and share great secrets and then walk away from her lighter in their face. She knew that this was a gift and one, that had she not felt so totally devoid of faith, would have been perfect for the church for her to use along side the rest of her devout family.

It was probably the levelling out of life, the ying and the yang principles that seemed to Alison to rule so much of the universe, that meant this ability to give ease was equally measured by her own severe lack of inner quiet. She was forever feeling there must be more, and more often than not she felt left with a sense of being short changed. The Crucible Theatre had been good to her but now she had to admit that there was a big hole deep inside her just getting wider. She needed a new challenge, something that would match her ambition with her outlook on life.

For now though her job, and the friends and contacts her job brought, kept her in the game of life and stopped the onslaught of insanity. For now what she had would just have to do.

Each night at performance time, Alison would be highly visible for her team. She was a tall lady at 5 feet and 10 inches and this, connected to her striking looks, high designer heels and her long blonde hair, hair that had been long as a child and she had kept long, meant she attracted attention. It helped her with her job, helped her stand out in a crisis, helped her be alluring when she needed to be, and dominant when it was called for.

It was one of her many tasks to ensure all was well with the theatre and the theatre goers who on capacity would number over a thousand people. And so, one warm July evening, when she saw an interesting looking middle aged man vigorously expressing concerns about the nights play to one of the bar staff who was looking brow beaten and a little terrified, she stepped in to discuss it with him in person. She listened impeccably to Ronald Jones listing several reasons why this particular Shakespeare tragedy had been just that, a tragedy. After a while he stopped complaining about the play and started asking about her. This was her talent, her power. She loved reeling a person in and turning the situation, any situation, into something far more interesting. They got on well, exchanging interesting views and conversation. He returned the next night and sort her out again to talk. She expected him to ask her out and he, she suspected, knew he would be turned down. What she was not expecting though was the chase. Ronald Jones clearly knew what he wanted and after several sets of flowers and calls, she decided that she would give him the benefit of dinner. After all he was clearly a man of great interest and character and she was in need of being entertained.

Sheffield was a fantastic city but Alison had tired too of

her circle of friends. University education was a great way to experience life, but it left a pretty bitter taste afterwards when the reality of the next 50 plus years hit home. She needed excitement; something to burn her from inside, and to date only the pretty one-dimensional fixes of sex and drugs had kept her from going insane. She was tired, tired of going through the motions that the circles in which she moved kept following. Work, drink, drugs, sex, sleep. Tomorrow work, drink, drugs, sex, sleep. The day after had the variation of missing the sex. The day after the drugs. It was becoming a drag and Alison had fire she wished and needed to burn. And so this welcome arrival of this older man, a clearly highly educated man with more than a hint of secrets was worth investigation. What she uncovered though surprised her. Ronald Jones was very, very wealthy. After several dinners he began to open up, as all men did to her, and shared his life. He operated a dual life, highly acclaimed university professor to the vast majority of people who knew him, but highly asset rich with a clear knack of deal making on the side. It was this 'on the side' that he started to talk about more and more as their meeting together had become regular. He was trying to impress her and clever enough to know it was working.

'You see, I never really intended to get so filthy rich. It really is a hobby, simply economics in practice. I had become tired of just doing what I had always done and I saw an opportunity in a piece of land. It just looked right; do you know what I mean? The right piece of land in the right place. I knew it was only a matter of time before it would become highly marketable and I was right. A big PLC wanted it and would pay for it. I held out and then the price became too irresistible. I took this money and thought I could pay off the mortgage, you know get straight, but the elixir of buying and selling was too much. I was hooked and I was off and running.'

'When was this Ronald?' asked Alison, unprepared for the fact that she was feeling sexually turned on by this man of increasing interest sat before her.

'1973. I had been teaching here for 10 years and had put some money aside. Susie had left me and I thought, what the hell!'

'How long were you married?' she asked, too hastily and with too much interest.

'Married! No chance. Living in sin and had been for 7 years. I think they call it the 7 year itch.'

'Isn't that only if you are married?'

'Apparently not!' Ronald replied, smiling with the inner knowledge that his charms appeared to be working.

'And she left you?' asked Alison, mischief in her voice.

'Yes she did. Crazy fool,' smiled Ronald, seemingly not worried or slighted by his ex leaving him or Alison asking about it.

'And did you miss her?'

Ronald looked at Alison. He could not really understand how this beautiful stranger had come into his life and caused him to be so incredibly open about himself. Maybe it was just a timing thing? Maybe she was actually interested in him? Either way he felt he could trust her, that for the first time for a long time he had someone he could talk to. From the moment he had met her one thing was abundantly clear to him and that was her use to him professionally. He saw in Alison rare qualities of absolute single mindedness and abject loneliness. Such qualities were perfect to add to his future and that of Jones Limited. Another perfect pillar for his plans of corporate growth had come into his life.

'Yes, I missed her. For a long time actually. The emotion surprised me. I think the buying and selling helped me move on. I think it still helps me move on.'

'Makes you feel more alive?'

'Yes, makes me feel more alive. Life can be pretty boring can't it?'

Alison looked aside, tears suddenly stinging her eyes.

'Yes, Ronald, it can.'

Ronald had seen the tears. He was not surprised. It was not hard to sense the desire for more in someone when you felt it so hard yourself. He knew there was much to be gained from looking after this lady.

'Don't you ever think there must be more?' he asked her.

'I do, often,' Alison replied, looking intently across the table and hopeful more was on the agenda.

'And that's why you are here isn't it?'

'Well, let's be honest,' a smile filled Alison's face as she looked straight at Ronald, 'that's why we are both here isn't it! I cannot remember not longing for more, not approaching a corner and thinking around it there might not be a better option.'

'That's because you are a warrior Alison,' declared Ronald, preparing to have a bit of fun with this beautiful and fascinating girl sat before him.

'A warrior?'

'Yes, a warrior. Helena Frisk did some work in the 50's on different types of personality. I covered it off in my degree and it stayed with me. We are all types of people. There is a homemaker, priest, tradesman, handmaiden, farmer, teacher, politician, and, wait for it, a warrior.'

They both giggled. They were enjoying themselves as barriers between them continued to fall away.

'It all sounds very Middle Ages to me Ron.'

'Exactly! It is, very middle ages, but that's the point. Life was once much more basic than today's busy world with huge choice. If you set aside the fact that gender and birth were a key part in what you became, and you have to so that it fits our time, you can then place yourself in the path you would have naturally become. No modern take on what you made yourself into because of the greater opportunities we have, but rather just eight raw, basic things that you actually are.'

'It's just too obvious, too slimmed down for my liking.'

'Exactly! It is meant to be. In Frisk's work you are forced to choose, choose the key components that make you. If you just see the headlines you may choose too hastily. You for instance might pick yourself to be a handmaiden.'

Alison cast Ronald a hard stare who returned it with a broad smile. Ronald went on,

'But you need to drill down. She gave each heading five key components and then finalised it all by saying, just as you would if you lived in those dark days, you had to choose.'

'And what did you choose?'

'Well, my dear pupil, at first assumed I would be a teacher, after all that is what I do. However drilling down she used headings that left me cold.'

'And so?'

'And so, wait for it, I am a warrior just like you.'

'Just like me? I see. You think you've got me all figured out already! And how do they look, these mighty warrior types?'

'They are single minded, free spirited, selfish beyond all others, enjoy danger and can only be truly happy with like minded souls.'

'You really know all this stuff! Ronald Jones, Professor of Economics, Head of Department, owner of a superb portfolio of investments painstakingly built over many years, and follower of mumbo jumbo!'

'Mark my words Alison, you are a warrior.'

She smiled. She liked playing these games with this intriguing man. It was time to probe further.

'So, why, having found money and lots of it, have you really stayed at your little old University? Aren't you bored? You surely don't need the money!'

Ronald nodded, pleased, it seemed, to have the question.

'Honestly? It's my life. That's the simple answer and the truthful one. My students, they are what I enjoy the most. I like to lead, inspire, open up their small brains and pour in ideas.'

'You like power Ron. You are not a teacher, rather an infiltrator of young idealistic minds!'

Ronald laughed. She had summed him up perfectly.

'That I am! Gives you a warm glow doesn't it! My teaching does one more thing though. Since starting Jones Ltd I have been aware of my need for my future.'

'Your future?' she asked, wondering what was coming out next.

'Alison, I am pretty good at what I do, but I deal with my real estate on a one to one basis. I neither have the time, the personality or the needed information to do what I do to the scale that it could now be done.'

'You wish to scale it up don't you!'

'I do. I have the money for it and I look after some pretty impressive young minds.'

Alison saw Ronald in a new light. Not only was he incredibly intelligent, brave and wealthy, but he was cunning too. Such a combination!

'You are using the education system to find your team?'

'I am.'

Ronald looked so pleased with himself. Alison sat back and studied him for a while. What was he plotting?

'And have you found anyone yet?' Alison enquired, wondering just how far Ronald Jones had got to date.

'I have,' he replied happily, 'I have just appointed him as my Managing Director.'

'Not a student?'

'Yes a student! He will be a genius.'

'As your MD though!' Alison was almost lost for words. The cheek of the man. The most incredible risk to appoint someone so young for your future.

'Yes, my MD. Ingenious yet mad isn't it. I have found a

most extraordinary boy. He is bored out of his brain doing my degree and he is longing to express himself in the market place.'

'Does he know this yet?'

Ronald smiled. His plan was all set to go, coming together before his very eyes.

'Yes. He does. I told him just before the summer break.'

'You mean you asked him?'

'No. I told him. As simple as that.'

'And how did he take the news?' Alison was at this point wondering if Ronald was slightly mad, not that this possibility was in any way putting her off him.

'Naturally he was delighted.'

'I suppose he's a warrior too?'

'Oh yes, very much so. In fact I would go so far as to say this boy is a warrior king.'

Alison was clearly taken aback. From the moment she had met Ronald she had been impressed by the fact that there seemed to be so much more to find out. This was clearly the case. He was not a 'safe' choice. Rather he was living life on the edge making decisions against clearly thought through criteria that to many would seem like very real madness, but to him was perfect sense. She liked that a lot.

'And he's OK with all of it?'

'OK young lady, OK! He's the luckiest man in the world. Of course he's OK. I'd go so far as to say he is probably beside himself with joy.'

Alison took a sip of their third bottle of ridiculously expensive Bordeaux wine from the Mouton Rothschild chateau.

'Wow! Well Mr Jones I have to say you've got me. I don't know if you are a genius or about to see it all go down the pan, but I suspect you know exactly what you are doing. You know what you want and you get it don't you.'

Another smile filled Ronald Jones face. Alison was a perfect find. What a run he was on! It was time to deliver his killer line, his pièce de résistance.

'And that's why young lady I am asking you to join the firm'

Alison's heart immediately began to beat faster. Had she not known that this was where it had all been leading to?

'You are?' she asked, her voice breaking slightly as she did so and betraying the excitement that she felt could actually explode out of her heart.

'I am. I need eyes and ears in Jones Ltd, to be kept updated from the inner sanctum.'

'You want a spy?' she replied, unsure what he was saying and wanting to be clear of her value to him.

'No, not a spy! Of course not. I totally believe in Robert. He will do very well indeed. However business can be a treacherous affair and a man in my position cannot be too careful. I need a highly intelligent person who knows exactly what they want too in the middle of my company. I need a person to ensure it stays the right side of the law and the right side of looking after me. I want you to be Robert's right hand Alison and in turn my right hand. Can you do that for me?'

Alison looked across at Ronald. She had been stroking his hand as he had been talking, aware that she was feeling extremely turned on and was desperate for sex with him. Whatever journey she was on it was far more exciting than the one she had been on to date. Even up to the start of this evening she had thought that she had been playing Ronald Jones. Maybe she had to an extent. Now though it was clear that he had been playing her. Whatever was happening there were no doubt that these were new rules and far better than the ones she had been playing.

'I can do that and much more Ron.'

'Well in that case welcome to your new position of Operations Director in Jones Ltd. You start on Monday.'

'What about my notice period?'

'You start on Monday.'

Alison nodded.

'I start on Monday.'

The plan was becoming a reality. Jones Ltd had another new employee.

'And now dear girl, if you would be so kind, how about we retire to my apartment for a good fuck?'

Alison actually felt herself blushing, which surprised her. This man had a hold over her.

'I was hoping you would get round to that.'

'Oh yes, as with everything,' said Ronald, rising from his chair, 'all good things come to those who act!'

Chapter 9

# Robert

Summer 1982. Edinburgh, Scotland

It would have been very difficult for Robert to tell his parents about his sudden change in career path, as they would have struggled, particularly his father, to believe him. Why should they? After all it was all so fantastically bizarre, the most incredible of turnings on his hereto normal journey of life. And so he chose the easy option and didn't tell them at all. The great news was that after the glowing first year report that Ronald Jones had kindly provided this all made for a most unexpected, enjoyable and somewhat smug summer break. These reports would follow for the next few years, each as glowing as the last, as Robert would make his way to the first class honours degree despite never attending a lecture again.

William in particular was delighted with his sons incredible progress, progress that he had written off as virtually impossible only months earlier. There were so many questions he wanted to ask his son about how the change in performance had happened and why, but for now these were probably best left unspoken. Rather better to just enjoy the accolades his son was now getting and get excited about the boys future again! William even began to entertain thoughts that maybe his son would, after all, be able to step up into his business, thoughts that for some time now he had gravely placed aside assuming they would never happen. Robert, it seemed to William, had never been able to concentrate on any one thing for too long and as a result getting him through an expensive education had been at times a very tortuous process. The times William and Francesca had been called into Fettes and asked to take hold of their sons education were too many to remember, or indeed to want to remember, and they had hoped that a University education and time away from home would be just what Robert needed. It now seemed that indeed it was as Robert had now, wonders upon wonders, begun to flourish. It transpired further that Robert had even been working hard in an office job to earn extra money and that had purchased a nearly new shiny sports car, a bit flash for William's liking but this was not a time to call Robert for that. No, this new Robert was a fabulous revelation to his father. It made William's step lighter and he found himself feeling better about almost everything.

Francesca too saw a lightness and confidence in her son that had been worryingly missing when they had last seem him in the Easter break when he seemed downcast and was unnaturally quiet. The new buzz around him absolutely delighted her. All was, at last, back on track. Both the men in her life spent the summer with a fresh brightness about them and it was wonderful. They were even happy with one another, a fact you could see as they had just returned from Tynecastle Stadium still talking about the referees ineptitude and not Robert's!

'A joke!' declared Robert.

'A disgrace more like,' added William.

'Makes you wonder what qualifications you need to have to be a referee doesn't it!'

'Clearly not an eye test!' said William, hanging his coat up in the beautifully tiled hallway and causing Robert to laugh and repeat the words 'eye test' over and over as they walked into the kitchen.

'Good game darling?' asked Francesca, putting out fresh spaghetti Bolognese onto the waiting warmed bowls.

'Yea, a good game,' responded Robert, kissing his mother on her cheek and going over to sit down at the kitchen table, 'in fact a fine game! The boys were magnificent if you overlook their general inability to play football.'

William laughed hard at this causing Francesca to grin widely as she sat down. So often over the years the relationship between father and son had not been a close one. They had continued to try and paper over the cracks but both men knew the gulf between them. Their characters were so different, too different. And yet, this summer, they had been able to move forward and no one was happier about this than the lady in both their lives, Francesca.

Robert too had enjoyed his holiday, basking in an easier time of things at home thanks to his new mentor, the great Ronald Jones. It was all beyond exciting and Robert continued to pinch himself wondering how this had all landed in his lap. The one final hurdle was preparing the way to tell his father about his new career path and he thought about gently preparing his father for his not joining him in the business, but one tentative approach early on in his holiday on the subject saw William become a little emotional and Robert quickly backtracked. There would be time for this in due course and the blow would be much softened by the outstanding success that Robert foresaw and a clear need therefore proven for Robert to be involved in matters away from architecture. After all when his father discovered he was the Managing Director of an outstanding real estate company surely he would have to be happy. Maybe even William and his team would be able to do project work for Jones Limited. Robert could get them major project work from which his father's business could make so much money and grow. Yes, that should soften the blow.

Robert had never found speaking with his father easy. It was difficult to understand but a mixture of their very different characters and them being from different times with different values meant they rarely saw eye to eye. The fact too was that Robert had given in on his father very early on, something that surprised his mother and upset William. There was much done on William's part to bring the boy round; trips with his son to as many Hearts games as they could manage, football on the park, walks and talks. Somehow though, whatever they did together, it could not solve the distance between them. Robert was unmoved by William. He simply didn't get his father. He found him too open, too easily pleased, too involved with minutia and too inspired by what to him was simply uninspiring to the young man. Robert had always felt a call to be great, to be involved in something big and to satisfy his incredible belief in capital and the value of being, if at all possible, filthy rich. Such beliefs were the absolute opposite of his father and time was never going to bridge this. There was a measure of respect for his father who had served bravely in the war and was recognised in his field of architecture, but these things were matters Robert could not turn into anything of real significance that would ever make his father more than a peripheral figure to him.

Francesca was different. Robert looked at his mother and felt a peace that kept him calm. He found her beautiful. Not just in how she looked, although he recognised this from a young age, but in how she used her character to be there for him. He never felt, as he did with his father, that the relationship was hard work. There was an ease between him and Francesca, a turn of friendship that asked very few questions. As Robert got older he knew that Francesca would have been uncomfortable and no doubt angry with many of his choices, but she stayed loyal to him and never asked of him in the same way that William did, never offered him pleading eyes but always simply loving eyes. That was his abiding need and that was what his mother gave him, her gift to him, her precious son.

His mother also produced something that others from far and wide admired, greatly admired. Francesca Marinetti, having kept her maiden name as an artist, was known throughout the world for her paintings. Her aunt, Beatrice, had taken a latent and raw talent and helped it grow. She had done so to give her young charge an independent career, but also to help Francesca move on with her life after the devastating losses that had befallen her at such a young and tender age. Francesca's work was built up over several years with several tutors that Beatrice and Giovanni had employed. Then in 1947 they showed Francesca's work, without her knowledge, to a senior tutor at the Academy. He was an old acquaintance and friend, giving them his time to review what he thought would be a polite refusal. In fact the tutor, the highly respected Phillipe Battison, was taken aback by what he saw. In Francesca's work he saw a student who was not trying too hard. Her work was clearly natural to her, an ease of hand that drew you into the work. He was totally and immediately smitten and Francesca's entry into the Academy followed the next term. By the time William had reached her in 1952 she was already beginning to specialise on the human form.

During the 50's Francesca Marinetti found her work become collectable. She did not choose the path or work for the success. It simply found her just as her work had found Mr Battison. By the time they arrived in Edinburgh she was painting exclusively nudes. She used few colours but strong and vibrant shapes. Light and shade were what first caused her to draw, and these basic understandings were what she now used every day, extenuating the effects of the light conditions she was working under.

Robert was not to become an artist but he did have talent with an eye for drawing. Some of his earliest memories were happy times with his mother painting in her studio and being like her, being her young apprentice. They would spend hours throwing on colours on to a blank canvas, creating magical masterpieces that they would then unveil to William by way of some grand show later in the evening. Three of these pieces remained in pride of place in the McTeer kitchen, framed and looked at proudly everyday.

As he had gotten older the burden of his mothers name and her renowned ability meant he preferred to stay away from being an artist himself. He knew he would never reach her status; find the depth of humanity that you saw in her work. He would, though, be profoundly affected by her work for the rest of his life and never be able to walk past a piece of art without sizing it up and comparing it in his minds eye to his mother work.

Francesca understood her relationship with her son and the fact that she was closer to Robert than William could ever be. It had happened quite naturally and she went with the flow of it all. She understood very early on that swimming against that tide would have sunk her. And so Francesca demanded nothing from Robert and simply accepted him for what he was. Losing her parents in the war meant she found herself unable and unwilling to shape Robert in any way other than for him to see her for what she was. He would then make his own choices. She would watch William try so hard with Robert, try to help his son see what was right and what was wrong, but she knew these were quite simply their ideals and not her sons. She would leave Robert alone to form his own pillars from which he would build, for better or worse. It was his life to make.

And so Francesca kept herself detached from the shifting dynamics between the two men in her house. To become involved would have affected her mind and her work and she would not for her own sanity and inspiration allow this to happen. Many years before she had simply decided that they would work through their relationship in time or would not. Such was life. Her temperament would inspire William to try and emulate her quality of standing away from life and just letting it happen. He failed most every time, but at least in his failure, his wife's love made him feel less uncomfortable and, as time and failures went against him still more, he learnt to be more accepting and less self critical. He would never have Francesca's temperament but then again he had never known the sense of loss and desolation that she had know in 1943.

For William and Robert, Francesca was a light, a beacon. She gave them both hope but for very different reasons. William drew strength from her to be easier with his life whilst Robert drew inspiration from her to make life notice him.

Robert found that he grew up quickly over the summer holiday of 1982. This was primarily due to the additions to his reading material as Robert, yes the previously young work-shy fop, became a veritable sponge for information. There was much to be learnt and Ronald had sent his young apprentice home with a small suitcase of books and papers that he would need to familiarise himself with. Added to this, a steady stream of packages arrived each week from Sheffield for him to read. Robert took to the task with admirable vigour and found his fascination in land and property and wider issues boom. It was as though someone had taken the lid off a wonderful secret and now Robert was sprinting to catch up on what he did not know.

William and Francesca started the summer having to stop and stare at the sight of their son lost in a pile of books but then, as the weeks moved on, the sight became the norm. William, always an early riser, would even find his son sometimes up before him in the study, hard at work. Never had such diligence been witnessed before! It seemed there were not enough hours in the day for Robert to be able to read all he wanted to read.

When their son was out, which were now the exception and not the rule, his parents would go through his books and see what he was reading. Advanced economic books and essays, Law Society journals and Government and Finance studies were what they expected to find, and sure enough they did find in abundance. What surprised them though were the copies of books by such classic masters as Marcel Proust, Fyodor Dostoevsky, Gustave Flaubert and Henri-Marie Beyle. In turn these were complimented by poetry from Blake to Byron, Keats to Wilde and Brooke to Heaney. The inclusion of Byron brought William full circle as he found a copy of the exact same book that he had posted to Francesca all those years earlier. The finding of the great poet in Robert's reading material gave William a warmth of security and a connection to his son, albeit an unspoken one between them, that he had not felt for some time.

Previously Robert had simply never felt the need to know what these books could tell him. Now the switch had been flicked and his need for knowledge gripped his very core. He was determined to return to Sheffield as a man of real substance and not the boy that he now saw he had been. He had reflected many times on the meeting with Ronald Jones and though an element of suspicion and wonder would cross his mind, he actually believed what he had been told. Robert had never been short of confidence and so he knew that he had much to offer this older man, and offer him he would! He intended to return to Sheffield and blow him away with the incredible progress he had already made.

His parents in turn were astounded with the man they

now found before them as he turned almost before their very eyes from a self absorbed boy to a man of depth and quantity. At the dinner table they were regaled with questions of politics, economics, and culture. Their son had suddenly found a hunger to find out about the world he lived in. William even found himself reading up on subjects in his day, eager to have conversation with his son in the evening to strengthen the bonds between them.

'I see in the paper today that Sheffield is set for more decline Robert, the cutlery industry shrinks still more and our eastern friends steal our steel industry from under our very noses. What's left to build the country Robert?'

'It's a good question Dad and one our politicians should have an answer too.'

'And do they Robbie?' asked William, eager to test his young son's grasp on politics.

'Of course not!' replied Robert, eating his dinner as always with incredible speed. 'You taught me quite clearly that politicians are often the last to know what really needs doing. Nothing's changed there but don't you worry!'

William smiled at the small compliment. Maybe his son was learning about real life after all.

'Why should we not worry?'

'Well, decline means opportunity Dad. You should know that. Remember what the war did to Britain? 50's depression and the 60's opportunity that followed. I mean, come on, you rode that rollercoaster and started your agency on the back of it. Don't you worry about Britain. It's going to be fine, just fine.'

William exchanged a look with Francesca. She had a big smile on her face.

'And you Robert, will you be fine?' William asked, leading the conversation towards Robert's future.

'Me Dad? I'm going to be more than fine. I'm going to be very fine indeed.'

William looked at his son. He had long since known

they were not alike, that Robert's life would be very different to his own. He just didn't understand his son's confidence, his unreserved optimism for his future despite his failure over many years to seize the benefits of the education that was placed before him.

'Why? Why will you be very fine indeed.'

'Because my dear father, I have landed on my feet.'

'Landed on your feet?'

'All in good time Dad, all in good time.' Robert rose from the table, picking up his now empty dinner plate which had been demolished with the speed of a young man on fast speed forward almost all of the time.

'Thanks for dinner. Great spaghetti Mum, as always! Must be that Italian thing you've got going. Anyhow, must go. I'm meeting my dear Angus. Don't wait up.'

'How lovely,' replied Francesca, 'give him our love and tell him to come round so I can feed him up.'

'He won't need asking mum, you know he'll be round here the first moment he can. I'm surprised he doesn't sleep here rather than at his home as it is.'

Francesca laughed. She was well aware of the way dear Angus loved the three of them. It was very sweet.

He went out the door, patting his father on his back and kissing his mother whilst whistling some pop tune or other as he left.

Francesca reached over the old dining table and took her husbands hand, lifting it to her lips and gently kissing the soft skin in between the thumb and first finger. She knew he needed it.

'You know you've got to let him go William, he's not you.'

'Well, he's not you either,' replied William too quickly and instantly regretting the heat in his voice. Why his son wound him up so was a complexity that he so wanted to be rid of in his life.

Francesca smiled.

'No, he's not. There's no law that says he should be either of us William. You know that. At least he seems happy and that's all that counts.'

'Is it? Is that all we wanted my dear?'

Francesca held William's hand in the middle of her own, gently squeezing it with a soft rhythm. She loved her husband so much. From the very first moment she had seen him in the bar in Naples she had loved him. They said love at first sight was nothing but romantic nonsense. Well, she was full of romantic nonsense and so was William.

'Yes, my sweet love, that's all we ever wanted.'

Over summer Robert made sure he still found time to catch up with his best friend Angus who was home too from Oxford University for the holidays. Angus had progressed as planned in his father's footsteps and was now studying Law as one of the truly chosen few within Magdalen College as an undergraduate. From here he would join one of the country's top legal firms and build his future. It was an easy path for him and, to Angus, one that seemed as always very ordinary when compared to what Robert was doing.

'So he just offered you the job?'

They were sat at The Castle Bar on the back looking over the very fine views across the rooftops and down to the historic Grassmarket. Robert had shared the whole story of the meeting with Ronald down to every last detail just in case Angus picked up on something obvious that he had missed. Now Robert just sat with a big grin on his face.

'Yes, he did!'

'And you said?' asked an incredulous Angus.

'I don't really remember. I was so relieved and happy.'

'What? The most incredible thing happened to you and you don't remember?'

'Well, the truth is my dear boy that I, yes even I, was

113

shell-shocked. I mean, my God! I was just amazed.'

'I bet but,' and as Angus spoke he put on his serious face to add gravitas to the question, 'are you sure about all this?'

'Of course not!' laughed Robert, 'he might be mad for all I know or just want to get into my pants along with everyone else in Sheffield.'

'Exactly! This man is possibly a nutcase!' replied a relieved Angus, pleased that his friend had not lost all sense of reality. The story he had just heard reminded him of those people who become part of some strange religious sect and seemingly overnight lost all sense of everything they had ever known.

'Yes but then again, what is the alternative?'

'That he may be the real deal and this could set you up for life?' offered Angus begrudgingly.

'Indeed,' said Robert, a huge grin on his face.

'And if he is the real deal?' asked Angus, wondering where Robert thought he could take this.

'I will milk it for all it is worth. This is my chance to hit the big time my dear friend. Big money for a big future. It is, quite simply, perfect!'

Angus smiled. In Robert he had always seen the strength and daring that he lacked, but in turn he always left his meetings with Robert feeling stronger and more ready to address the shortfalls in his own character.

'Well I hope it is everything you wish for and more.'

'And if it is,' Robert reached across the table and placed his hand on top of Angus's resting arm, 'I will be needing you.'

'You will?' Angus said, looking up through his long hair that fell in front of his eyes.

'Of course I will. I always need you, you know that.'

Robert spoke a genuine truth that they both recognised. Their friendship was very deep. They knew they were better with one another and the miles that now separated them for most of the year had not changed that. Robert went on,

'I tell you I have read more over the last few weeks than I have probably read in my entire life and the one thing I am sure of is having excellent legal counsel that I can trust on my side is imperative.'

'You mean in your pocket!'

The two of them laughed. They both knew that is exactly what Robert meant.

'Angus, if a little dreaming is dangerous, the cure for it is not to dream less but to dream more!'

'Hang on Robbie, are you quoting Proust at me?'

Now they really started to laugh as Angus saw a small miracle develop in his best friend. The uneducated had become educated and the world had better watch out.

# Chapter 10

# Robert

October 1982. Sheffield, England

Summer ended and the return to Sheffield arrived. An immediate succession of meetings took place, including the introduction of Alison to Robert, and plans were quickly put in motion together with rules of engagement and reporting lines. The new office, all set up by Ronald and Alison over the summer, was handily placed across from Robert's favourite Italian restaurant, Mama's & Leonni's, on Norfolk Street in the Sheffield city centre.

Sheffield was not Edinburgh but Robert liked it just the same. In many ways Sheffield was the opposite of Edinburgh. Edinburgh was fit for a monarch, the royal mile leading elegantly up to the imposing castle, the views from which swept across the city and its great properties and immense beauty. Sheffield was a working mans city, built on hard labour and dark times. And yet this grit gave the city its soul. There was no doubting that Sheffield was very tired from years of decline, a decline that mirrored the slow and lingering death of its great industries. Its many suburbs were full of large and menacing looking buildings that saw the vast majority in sad neglect. In this respect the Waters of Leith and its empty mills and factories were echoed here.

This grim persona was not what Robert experienced though from the people of Sheffield who he found to be warm and generous with a soft South Yorkshire accent that caressed you in conversation. He supposed it was this accent, matching the softer Scottish tones of the Edinburgh people that had always made him feel at home here.

Robert had a pretty good idea of the areas throughout Sheffield already as he had spent his first year following his love of football. He may not have been the leading light in the University Economics year, but he was central to the football team playing the pivotal role of centre midfield general. He also played for the seconds for the university team itself. When he had time he went to watch both Sheffield Wednesday and Sheffield United play. It was his saving grace in his first year that the Sheffield City Council was being run by a left wing Labour contingent that insisted on having the lowest bus fairs in the UK. As a result he could travel from one side of Sheffield to the other for the princely sum of only 11p. At last he had a policy he could for once agree with from a left wing council. It left plenty of his far too generous allowance from his parents for other activities that he had made full use of in ways it was best they had no knowledge of.

Now back in Sheffield the two men talked through their strategies for Jones Limited. Buying land and property in this declining Sheffield market may have seemed to some like professional suicide, but Ronald Jones was adamant.

'Now my dear boy is the time to buy!' he declared to Robert using this repeated dictum that he greeted him with every time he saw him. They were sat in the corner of the upstairs floor in Mama's on a table for four that overlooked Norfolk Street below and had a view across to their office. This was almost the company table. Whenever any of them came over the staff would get them straight upstairs to their spot.

It was late in the afternoon and they had been 'in meeting' for a few hours. Robert had been given the boundary's under which he was to work. He was to find land and derelict properties that could be bought for a song. Strict codes of pricing were to be used for size and location. If the seller would not sell at the price required, Robert was simply instructed to walk away. Similarly everything had its price so there were strict growth percentages they worked to. If someone wanted to buy and the asset had grown by the required value, then they would sell. A simple technique and no room to manoeuvre. It would be their protection.

Therefore Robert would not need Ronald Jones's sign off as he could not go wrong, but he was to report weekly on progress and progress was needed. Over the years it was clear that Ronald had been very busy indeed. He had bought and sold and built some not inconsiderable wealth, but he had done so at the side of a very busy career and this had most definitely held progress back. Now, with Robert on board, he could trade up. In turn he would gear up his assets and look to grow much more across the UK, in turn reducing his risk base and increase his diversification.

'There are two things Robert that in life could stop us.'

'Two things Mr Jones?'

Robert had continued to call the senior man by his formal name and this suited Ronald just fine. Respect was important. You could build an empire on respect.

'Indeed. Death and spirit. If we have the stomach for this, and the constant ability to lift our game to where the requirement is, then we will be immeasurably successful.'

These conversations were as much about building rapport between the two men as they were about building business direction and increasing Robert's experience as quickly as was possible.

'Well, we have the spirit!' declared Robert happily.

'We do that young Robert. We are cheeky, opinionated and ready to move mountains. I suspect until the grim reaper arrives we will make money like there is no tomorrow.'

'And what of circumstance?' asked Robert, keen to know what could falter their plans. 'What if things conspire against us? The market for example. What control do we have over national, even international events? World war, economic meltdown, inner city riots, political expediency that leaves us without our assets. Mr Jones, what of circumstance?'

Ronald lent back in his chair and gazed out on to the street below. The sun was gently shining its warming autumnal rays across the old buildings that had stood tall and proud in this part of Sheffield for many years.

'You know Robert, just down from us is the Lyceum Theatre.'

'Yes, across from the Crucible.'

'Correct. It has lay derelict for years and in so doing it shames this city. And yet across from it sits the Crucible, an ugly building if ever I saw one, designed by a certain Tanya Moiseiwitsch. She is famous for her set and costume designs and in my opinion should have stuck to that rather than visit her design on us and yet, and yet my dear, dear boy, whilst the elegant Lyceum falls apart, the ugly Crucible theatre prospers.'

Robert listened intently. He had learnt over his summer to take in information and become a sponge for it. Listening to Ronald Jones was an almost religious experience. It was as though he was sat at the feet of a great apostle, a famed guru, and he intended to take it all in. Ronald, very aware of his pupils rapt and adoring attention, went on.

'Any why? I shall tell you why. It is a simple truth. The Crucible theatre prospers because inside it has a soul, and that is its greatest prize and the reason for its success. Do you go to the theatre often Robert?'

'No sir, I'm afraid to say I do not. I guess you are going to tell me that I should.'

'Yes you should. You need to go. The theatre has much to teach us in a way the cinema can never teach us. On a stage you get to see a real person act out their part and in so doing mix it up with their personality. It is riveting stuff regardless of how good or bad the production is. There is no second take as on the films where they can go and go again until they get it how they want it. No, on the stage Robert the actor has one chance, one moment to deliver. It is spell binding and an inspiration as to how we can live life. I will get you signed on as a member and you must see every serious production there is to see. It is a vital part of your education. Understand?'

'Yes sir. I do. I look forward to it.'

Ronald smiled at Robert. He had indeed been a taken aback by the progress his young protégé had made over just a few short months. What unending possibilities were there then with the months and years that lay ahead for them?

'You see Robert, Ms Moiseiwitsch does nothing for the people of Sheffield with her external design but she does everything for the watching crowds on the stage created inside. To listen to Macbeth declare that 'life is not a walking shadow but a poor player that struts and frets his hour upon the stage and then is heard no more' on that platform, is to be entranced into a world all of your own. Do you understand what I am saying Robert?'

Robert pondered his words and then said,

'That it is not the building that makes the money, but rather the essence of what the building means to the buyers that makes the money. The paying public have chosen to honour the Crucible and therefore it prospers.'

'And they honour it because?'

'Because it makes them feel better, or more alive, or both!'

'Exactly! You are coming on so well Robert, you really are,' said Ronald, clapping his hands together with joy. 'Our job is to find what will affect people to give us their money above and ahead of all others. Robert, you will learn to ensure that whatever the circumstance, that you are one step ahead of it. Our job is to make our futures secure and our drive will do just that. However history and the many books I have had you reading teaches us a very clear truth, that we are the truth by which our lives will be measured. We are the truth Robert, we are the truth.'

As Ronald had spoken this last sentence he had done so looking away from Robert. Their relationship had grown so much and whilst it was clearly one of teacher and pupil, it was developing into one of mutual respect and shared vision. As he turned to face Robert, Ronald's eyes were moist with tears.

'Robert, I am not, as you know, a man given over to my emotions. I am a man focussed on what I want and what I must do to get it. You are testimony to this and will be so for many years to come. And yet at this moment I am sad because of the people, my father in particular, who are no longer with me to share my vision and their loss to me underlines the truth in what we have spoken.'

Ronald had fixed Robert's eyes as he said this, and whilst Robert was surprised to see an emotional side he had not seen before, he was taken with the steely intent by which Ronald Jones had spoken.

'I won't let you down sir.'

Ronald smiled.

'I know,' he said, 'I won't allow it.'

Ronald let the words sit between them as he lit up a fresh pipe and Robert in turn lit a cigarette. For awhile they sat in silence, their smoke meeting in the air between them, lingering and creating a heavy cloud.

'Tell me young man, what do you understand of the essence of the play of Macbeth?'

'Well,' started Robert, gathering his thoughts as he did so, and then relaying in textbook fashion a short synopsis of the play. 'It is sir a story based in my own dear Scotland of prophesy and murder. It is Shakespeare's shortest tragedy based on the most heinous of crimes, that of regicide. Macbeth acts hastily and on the premise of words from others that he should have the Kingship. He makes mistake after mistake and is backed by his wife who is a quivering mess. In short the tragedy is as much about what happens as how it happens.'

'Indeed. Do you know that often the last performed play in theatres across the land is Macbeth? It has become the embodiment of its own curses. It is a play that has taken on its own power, its own spell of intrigue and power, so much so that actors will often not mention the word Macbeth whilst in a theatre for fear of being cursed themselves.'

'Wow, I didn't know any of that,' said Robert, impressed by the power of words.

'You see Shakespeare wrote it for reasons we will never know but we can guess at. What is clear is that he wanted to make an impression with a dark and powerful work, possibly the darkest he would ever write. It is said he used actual witches spells in the text and this is the reason for the effects it still has today. I believe in making your own destiny and that's why I believe in Macbeth the play, not Macbeth the person. He was a fool. A doomed and headstrong victim hoodwinked by the powers of others who used his woeful lack of judgement to lead him down the path of terror and tragedy. Robert, over the years ahead you will have many voices that feed into you. They will promise you great riches and they will make you question what you and I have. You will need to face this.'

'Surely you don't expect me to ever question...'

Ronald held up his hand.

'Yes I do. In time you will question all. I want you to

remember this conversation and remember Macbeth. He murdered his king and his walls came tumbling down. I won't let that happen to us and neither must you.'

'Of course not,' replied Robert with real conviction in his voice. He had no intention of ever letting Ronald Jones down. He looked to Ronald, smiled, and said,

"But life itself; my wife, and all the world,
Are not with me esteemed above thy life.
I would lose all, ay, sacrifice them all
Here to this devil, to deliver you."

Ronald smiled, truly touched by the quote.

'In quoting Bassanio you do yourself great credit young man, great credit indeed.'

They sat in silence. Each lost in their own thoughts and comforted by their conversation. There was much to be done but for now it could wait awhile.

Chapter 11

# Building the Business

June 1985. Sheffield, England

The buying and selling began and Robert was extremely grateful for the clarity of his mission as it made his position in front of clients easy. He got used to being very hard nosed in his conversations, making his position on purchase or sale clear and then simply walking away. He was amazed with just how often people would call him later to accept terms they had only hours earlier said they would definitely not, under any circumstances, entertain. Such was the power of his position that he became hardened and imperious to the people he dealt with. He had no time for small talk and no need for it either. He learnt to only have in his day what he needed. He calculated that on any day this gave him an extra two hours to place more in it and Alison, in turn, saw to it that he had plenty to do.

Almost at once Jones Ltd saw its balance sheet grow considerably, though it had very little need of an empire of staff, and their needs were simply managed by Alison Collins, the Operations Director who Ronald had personally appointed. Robert had immediately noted that she was fiercely attractive but did not question the appointment as he got to know her. Alison clearly had a strong outlook on what life should give her and in turn give Jones Ltd. She would not be messed around and this strength of character was a perfect backdrop to the message Robert was delivering out in the market place.

Between the two of them Robert and Alison managed the small yet effective team that they acquired, several of whom were ex students who had worked at some time under the watching eye of Ronald Jones and had been recruited accordingly. Each one was highly focussed and brought a specific skill into the tight unit. It was a team geared up for finding opportunities, making sure they knew where the next big thing would happen, and ensuring that they bought it at the right price. Research and contacts were key and their off balance sheet cash dealings were testimony to this. Jones Ltd stuck rigidly to its principals of selling at a set profit. There was no need to be greedy providing they got the decisions right in the first place. An early lesson Ronald had instilled into Robert was that greed would cause you to hold on too tight and you would lose focus.

'Greed is always the downfall of a great man or a great empire Robert, always, no question. Look at Ancient Greece or Rome; look at the Spanish Empire or the British Empire, look at Macbeth. It was always the same. Empires that floundered and fell apart because it was never enough. They forgot to look after what they had and to do so wisely. Thomas Fuller said 'If your desires be endless, your cares and fears will be so too!' Robert, let us not be greedy.'

And this was Ronald Jones watchword. It had made the man and for now Robert was happy to follow the example to the letter.

'Good day Robert?' asked Alison after a long day that had seen a five hundred acre site with unbelievable potential purchased and bought at far below its estimate value with a potential upstream value of twenty times plus the price paid. Further a government purchase on a land strip had completed and had made Jones Ltd a small fortune. Alison stood at the doorway to Robert's office, pen sitting suggestively in her mouth.

'Just a bit! I am ecstatic. I'm off to Dexter's to celebrate. You busy tonight?'

'Yep.'

'Hot date?'

'Always.'

'With Ron?'

Robert had guessed at the pair's secret within months, although it was clear that it was a secret and needed to remain so. Throughout the early days of the business arrangement, Robert had learned a lot about the hard-nosed side of running a business, about protecting the asset above all else. He knew that Ronald Jones was a hard man from the moment that he had met him, and that to build the business, this precious business, Ronald was right to take every step possible to protect himself. The fact that he had brought in Alison as an ally was just plain common sense. As it was Robert could clearly see why he had chosen Alison who he found extremely bright, very intelligent and a very highly focussed businesswoman. He needed Alison as much as Ron did and he was pleased to have her with him.

What Robert had not bargained for was that Alison was a player too. She spent the first year weighing him up and finally decided that he was her longer term future and so she told him all about Ronald. From that point on their connection became the stronger one, whilst Alison continued to use her relationship with Ronald for her own pleasure and her own gain. Jones Ltd was being built on deceit after deceit and yet it was flourishing at an incredible rate.

'You know it,' replied Alison, offering Robert a mischievous wink.

'Try to not tire him out too much. I have him in on the meetings tomorrow at Dore.'

'It's him you need to be speaking to. He has a remarkable libido for one so advanced in years.'

Robert covered his ears in mock exaggeration and made a loud humming noise whilst walking past Alison and towards the exit door.

'You take care. I need Ms Property Tycoon back in tomorrow at 7am sharp.'

'Yes sir!'

Robert almost skipped out of the office. Making money could not be easier. He had in 3 short years become a highly successful businessman that mixed it with whoever he met. He had, as Ronald had put it, 'that extraordinary quality that marked him out as a genius, namely that he had no fear.'

No fear. Was it that simple? He once caught his Dad at a football game between his beloved Hearts and Rangers grasping for breath and holding for dear life the seat in front of him.

'Are you alright Dad?' asked the startled 15-year-old boy.

'Don't worry son, just a slight bit of panic. Fear not, it's not my heart! It will settle down.'

And it had. Five minutes later William had been laughing along at a song the Hearts fans had put together about the legend that was Drew Busby and Robert was amazed. He saw then panic as a weakness and decided that his father's weakness would never be his own. The fact that William had served throughout the second world war, seen terrors that haunted him still most every day of his life and had gone days without sleep just to stay alive, escaped the teenage Robert. Weakness was weakness and he was having none of it.

Robert had always felt indestructible. Maybe the fact

that he had faced death on the roof all those years earlier with Angus had given him this confidence. Also his mothers unlimited belief in him from as long as he could remember had always made him feel he could walk on water. He knew, clearly knew, that he had no intention of allowing himself to succumb to anyone or anything. He intended always to live life as it was meant to be lived, namely for his enjoyment and absolutely for his personal excitement. And so whilst he had curtailed his extra activities, sometimes so tired after a full day that even he came home to simply sleep, he still found himself out in the middle of the city most nights for at least a connection or two. As people saw Robert grow in stature, more and more of them wanted a piece of him and he found many an interesting proposition coming his way. Some of these involved business deals he could put through Jones Ltd. Some he could not so he financed them himself. 3 years on from starting in the business Robert had his own portfolio. It included cash and property and he was also the proud investor in a drugs ring run by a prominent DJ who ensured Robert personally had what he wanted and when he wanted it. Alfie Adams was his friend from his student days and he had Robert's trust. When Robert became wealthy he had his money too.

'Hi Robbie, usual?' asked Sam, bartender, founder and majority shareholder of Dexter's.

'Indeed. You OK on this mighty fine day Samuel?' breezed Robert, clearly on a high.

'I'm good thank you. It was a superb weekend again wasn't it. As you know we were pretty packed Friday and Saturday bringing those pound notes in.'

'Yea, Saturday was some night wasn't it!' replied Robert who had been thinking back to his two girl conquest in one of the back rooms ever since.

'And I see you've had a good day?'

'Ah you noticed my chippy demeanour! A great day, thank you, a great day!'

Robert looked around the bar. He had been coming here for the last 2 years having met Sam Dexter by chance in a club one night. They had got on famously and immediately struck up a friendship that had led to Sam inviting Robert to join Dexter's. It was his own private members club, a club that welcomed new members by the personal invitation of the owner only. In one respect it was quite odd being a member at a club where everyone was a friend or connection of the owner, with the members having no obvious link other than that. However Sam Dexter knew so many people from such an eclectic and more often than not impressive background that the connection was ideal. It had already provided some huge deals for Jones Ltd with many more pending. Robert was sure to keep his new friend on his side and earlier in the year had invested some money in the club and taken a minority stake. He had overpaid for the stake on purpose.

'There you go Robbie, a pint of the black stuff for you to enjoy.'

'Thank you very much my good man! Alan in yet?' asked Robert, having scanned the bar and not seeing his friend.

'No. He called earlier though and said to tell you he will be in just after 8.'

'Great. Gives me time to read the papers.'

Robert made his way over to his favourite corner. There were several very comfortable chairs and lots of newspapers and magazines. Dexter's had become something of an oasis for him, a place to relax and be with the people he wanted to be with. Sam was really something of a genius having created Dexter's out of a nothing type of bar that had once been here.

It was reached by a discreet set of steps that went down to the club from the main road across from the side entrance to the Town Hall on Surrey Street. The steps were totally innocuous, set, as they were, in between an entrance to a barber's shop that must have been there for 50 years and a Bank that had no doubt been there for longer. This inauspicious start to the club continued as you arrived at the bottom of the steps to be faced by a black and well-worn heavy looking door that would not have been out of place in an old prison. Three slow knocks followed by two quick ones were the code for John, the doorman, to open the doors viewing hole to ensure you were indeed a member and then, at last, entry to another world!

Through the entrance foyer and its impressive Edwardian tiled floor and past the locker room and the very slinky dark marble toilets, and then on to the main body of the club decked out with expensive oak floors that held the bar which filled the wall to the left where it led into the wonderfully slick restaurant at the top corner. Dotted around the sides of the main room were very comfortable armchairs mixed with designer pieces of furniture with pieces of Mies van der Rohe, Eero Saarinen and Charles Eames to relax in. Further around the far wall were several private booths to allow more intimate communication to take place with handily placed curtains for a more private audience, such as the one Robert had enjoyed at the weekend, to take place. The walls were adorned with large pieces of art, all of them original, and some of them worth a great deal. Robert was not sure whether the club was the right place for a Smith or a Frampton piece to sit, but sit they did, looking out at the bar and taking in the view.

This was a club put together with a great deal of thought and love for the benefit of members who were prepared to pay for the privilege and enjoy and respect the anonymity and beauty that the club gave to the member. It suited Robert totally.

'Robert McTeer as I live and breathe!'

Robert looked up. A man in his late 20's with dark hair,

a slight tan and cheeky smile stood before him. It was his main contact in the Sheffield constabulary and very good friend, Alan Seymour.

Robert happily jumped up and the two men embraced.

'Good to see you man!' said Robert with great enthusiasm. For some reason Alan had always brought out a smile and sense of joy within him.

'You too dear boy. Good day?'

'Always. Just a few more million made. You?'

'You know it. Some good stuff to tell you about. Another?' Alan nodded to the empty Guinness glass.

'Need you ask!'

Alan Seymour was a Detective Inspector within the Sheffield Police Department. He was relatively young for such a post and had risen to the dizzy heights on the back of a superb education, a connected father and an array of successful and high profile arrests. Robert had met him through Alfie Adams. The friendship had grown and now the three of them were together in business, a business that allowed Alan to turn illegal drugs into cash for the three of them and a cut for Alan's close-knit team. It was a thoroughly easy and successful way for Alan to wash his dirty finds into the money flow with no one to ask awkward questions and no need to waste time on low life scum on Her Majesty's over worked legal system and far too crowded prisons.

Alan returned, placing Robert's dark pint with its deep cream head down in front of him and lifting his own in the air.

'Will you join me in a toast my friend?' he asked.

Robert smiled, stood and lifted his glass.

'And what are we toasting?'

'To Freddie Brownlow!'

'Freddie Brownlow?' asked Robert as they pushed their glasses together and sat down.

'Indeed. Freddie very kindly donated some useful pharmaceuticals to our collection earlier today.'

'Oh, did he indeed! How good of him!' replied Robert, chuckling as he did so. 'Does he know of his donation?'

'Is the Pope an Anglican?'

Robert laughed. He always laughed with Alan.

'And where's Freddie now?' Robert asked, knowing the probable answer already.

'Northern General.'

'Ah, that old chestnut. Still, if you mess with drugs! Is he poorly?'

'Very much so!'

The two men toasted themselves again.

'I saw Alfie last night. Things are going well. He's being asked to get involved in the Nottingham scene again. Shall we?' asked Robert, who always bowed in these matters to Alan's greater knowledge of the criminal fraternity boundary rules.

'Not yet. There's some pretty big and quite frankly weird stuff kicking off there. It makes the mining riots look like Sunday school summer trips.'

'Really?' asked Robert, finding it hard to believe that much could match the turmoil, the hate and vitriol that the mining strikes had caused in the area.

'Yes. You wouldn't believe some of the stuff we are seeing. There's some especially hard bastards coming in from abroad so I say let's stay where we are strong and can control the collateral damage.'

'You're the man!' said Robert, raising his glass again to his friend.

'No you're the man!' returned Alan. 'On a far more pleasant note, how was the magnificent and highly sexy Jennifer?'

'She was, well,' Robert flushed a little. Jennifer Greatorex was one of the clubs late night dancers and he had finally taken her home. 'She was, as you might expect, very experienced!'

'Oh, I see! Too hot for you Robert?'

'Get lost! She was very kind and I was very lucky!'

That made Alan smile widely.

'And are you seeing her again?'

'Of course. Tomorrow I hope if I can get the meetings over in Dore done in time.'

'Well I leaned on Jenkins earlier so he will fall into line for you. He needs me more than he needs O'Mally.'

'Well I have a little parcel of photos arriving for O'Mally in the morning at his office which he will be seeing prior to seeing me.'

'A parcel! How nice of you! You really are most thoughtful Robert. Have you sent him chocolates?'

'Underwear. Female underwear to be more exact. Also enclosed a few copies of some extraordinary photographs that include a few shots of his big hairy arse, clearly in thrusting motion. He will not want Mrs O'Mally to see those or, indeed, the press.'

'Ah, the old bribery route?'

'Indeed. Rarely disappoints. I think he needs his wife and her fathers money more than he needs that land.'

'I think you're right. OK, drink up, we have a hot date.'

'We do?'

'We do. We are off to see a hot tip for a future huge band at our favourite music venue.'

'Ah The Leadmill! What a delight. All those sweaty young nubile students just waiting to meet us.'

'That's right. We can play that older yet still young and with it card.'

'I am young and still with it.'

'Well, I look like I am!'

'You do, although that hairline.'

Alan punched his friend's arm as they said their goodbyes and left Dexter's. They stepped out into the Sheffield June evening, quite warm with the city centre quiet given it was a Monday. Turning left, they trailed down Surrey Street laughing and joking about one thing and another.

'It's a beautiful car.'

'I know but how much!'

'Alan, trust me, I'm getting more and more loaded everyday.'

'Buy me one then!'

'You get me the Mills Land cheap and I will.'

'You're on.'

Across Arundel Gate, a busy road being a main artery route that passed The Crucible, and down Howard Street and the stretch of large and ugly Polytechnic buildings.

'I just said to her, Sally, if you insist on wearing that uniform I will have to insist on carrying out a daily strip search.'

'But she's a policewoman in uniform! She has no choice.'

'Exactly. Robbie, you are the man.'

'No you're the man.'

'Exactly.'

Down to the busy junction that to their left housed the Student Union, named after the heroic Nelson Mandela himself in 1982, and the busy and dirty bus station that seemed to stretch for miles.

'Have you seen a View to a Kill yet?'

'Seen it, I'm in it!'

'Yea, right. Like they'd have you in the secret service!'

'Robbie, seriously, I was an extra.'

'Really?'

'Of course not!'

A right along Shoreham Street and then dropping down to the cigarette littered steps to the end of The Leadmill Road and their arrival at the venue. The Leadmill sat in a converted flourmill that had been, as much around it still was, derelict. The building had some history having housed The Esquire Club that in the 60's had seen, amongst others, The Who, The Small Faces and Jimi Hendrix all perform. Somehow this pedigree left a spirit that the founders of

The Leadmill sort to re-create, partly out of a desire to have an arts club in the City, but also out of pure desperation to give the City some much needed heart and soul.

The bouncers welcomed both men who they knew very well indeed, and showed them through.

The Wedding Present were on stage, music blasting out across a smoke filled auditorium.

'They're loud!' shouted Robert into Alan's ear.

'Good though eh!' replied Alan as one of the pretty young female bar staff arrived with two bottles of beer for them. Robert gave her a gentle slap on her bottom and winked at her as she walked away. He didn't see her mutter an expletive under her breathe in return. She would not therefore be a conquest for Robert at any point later despite the fact he fully intended to seek her out and try it on!

'Quite a lot like The Fall I'd say,' Robert said.

'Yea, or The Buzzcocks.'

'Now you're talking. If they reach half that height.'

They stood and listened to David Gedge and his band lay out their tracks, an album not yet out so this was a rare privilege. After twenty minutes Alan nudged Robert and they made their way through the crowd and through to the stairs to climb to one of their secret spots, the roof.

As they arrived both men lit up and looked up to the Sheffield night sky, the noise of the night traffic rising from far below them. Alan produced a bottle of whisky and, taking a drink direct from the bottle, passed it over to Robert to do the same.

'Where will we be Robert in 10 years time?'

Robert took a large gulp of Jack Daniels and let it bite into his throat as he considered the question.

'We will be here Alan. You and I.'

'And will we have changed?'

'Oh yes. We will be older and we will be wiser, and we will have more wealth than you can imagine.'

'Oh, trust me, I can imagine a lot of wealth.'

Robert laughed.

'Yes you can you greedy bastard. Listen man, we are going to make serious money and no fucking idiot will be able to stand in our way. We are a team, a perfect bloody team and we will do what we need to do to get what we want, when we want.'

'You are an evil bastard,' smiled Alan with glee in his voice.

'Takes one to know one,' replied Robert with a nod.

'To winning all out battles then, no matter what!' declared Alan raising the bottle in the air and then taking another large gulp before passing the bottle to Robert who did the same.

They paused, allowing the moments to pass.

'I was lucky finding you Robert. You're going to be something.'

'I am something you sentimental fuck, and so are you.'

The two men embraced, finished their cigarettes with a last intake of smoke, and then made their way down to meet their quarry for the night.

# Chapter 12

# A Visit Home

April 1989, Edinburgh, Scotland

In less than 7 short years Robert had transformed Jones Ltd. The company, the brainchild of Ronald Jones, had become a business making profits of tens of millions of pounds and in turn made Ronald and Robert very wealthy men.

Robert in many ways had become an almost archetypal child of the Thatcher revolution. From a student going nowhere in the early 1980's, he had sprung forward to grasp the ideals of free markets and entrepreneurialism. For him the 80's were a golden age, a time to sink down the roots that would ensure his great wealth that would bloom for the rest of his life.

Jones Ltd had surfed on the wave of open for business Britain and, as restrictions had fallen away, Robert and his team had made every use of the governments eagerness to allow free trade to prosper with the humble British Pound doing all the talking. After many years of economic difficulties, the 80's brought some much-needed calm with interest rates and inflation both falling. Jones Ltd flourished magnificently on the back of this. They were on the radar now and people who mattered were either aware of them or becoming aware of them. Several approaches for 'talks' around what they were doing and partnerships were batted away. There was nothing to talk about. Jones Ltd was its own business and would not be sold, the power base ever diluted.

Therefore at the age of only 25 and nine months, Robert was already a millionaire three times over and living the life of a young man without responsibility and with every possibility seeming achievable. He kept two apartments, one in his beloved Sheffield city centre, and one down in highbrow Chelsea for his many London trips. He had two sports cars, the Porsche 911 Carrera, this being the high flying executive car of choice, and a classic 1958 Bugatti Road Car. It was a life he had dreamed of and a life that his father could not understand. Indeed William viewed the 1980's as a decade of indecent excess that, he said, would have repercussions for decades to come.

'Dad,' reasoned Robert on a trip back home one weekend having taken Emily, his wife, to share some exciting news and see the family home for the first time, 'we have to move on from the war you know. That was then and this is now. It's called progress.'

Father and son were outside on the terrace, enjoying an unusually warm April afternoon and sat to the side of one another at the weather beaten outdoor table. William studied his son for a few moments, his fine tailored clothes, the soft tan showing off his latest trip abroad, and his designer shoes that probably cost more than the value of William's entire attire. It would have been easy to enter into an immediate argument, particularly with Robert's purposeful goading in mentioning the war, but instead just one overriding emotion sprung to the fore of William's mind.

'I love you Robert.'

'Ah Dad, stick to the argument!' Robert almost got up to walk into the house. His father would always revert to raw emotion. It was claustrophobic and unrealistic and Robert would have none of it.

'But I do. We don't say it enough, in fact you don't say it all.'

'Of course I love you,' Robert replied, quickly pushing out the words and making them sound as he had said them, that he didn't really know if he meant it or not.

A small moment passed before them, William pleased with his small victory, Robert unsure as to why he had given in so easily.

'Why?'

'What do you mean, why?' replied Robert, frustration heightening in his voice as he sort to keep himself calm. Why did his dad have an effect on him that no one else in the whole wide world had?

William just looked at his son, a warm and loving face meeting his son's attempt to draw battle lines. Robert softened a little as a result, seeing an ageing man before him who just wanted to be loved. For his mother's sake he took a deep breath and told himself he would try a little harder, after all they had the whole of the evening to get through yet.

'Well, you're my Dad.'

'And?'

'And what?'

William smiled and took a few breaths. Francesca had spent years telling him to be more relaxed with Robert and accept him for what he was. Now it was William's turn to take a breath and remind himself that they had guests and the evening ahead to enjoy, not mope through.

'We are different son. Very different. I know that and I want you to know that I am comfortable with this. The difference between us, that's OK.'

'Have you been on a course Dad?' asked Robert with an awkward smile. William laughed.

'I know I probably should have! Years ago would have helped wouldn't it!'

Both let that comment sink in. Out in the garden spring was well and truly coming to life. Buds were showing everywhere and the Forsythias and Cherries offered a multitude of colour. Birds sat ready for their evensong, excitement building as the time drew nearer. A beautiful white butterfly took flight across the lawn causing William to point and laugh.

'That's a Large White lad, did you see it?'

'The butterfly?'

'Yes, a Large White. Very early in the season though. Too early in fact. Beautiful specimen Robert, little tips of dark colour on its forewings with the female having black spots on the wings too. Incredible. And early. So early!'

Robert could see the enthusiasm his father was having simply because he had seen a butterfly! He almost wanted to cry for the old man. Were they really related!

William sat back in his chair, letting the warmth of the sun caress him; pleased he had been able to bring something beautiful from nature to his son's door.

'You know Robert, the point is, the one I am trying to make and no doubt badly, is that I know we will never win each other around to a way of thinking that is like a foreign language we have never heard before!'

'At last! Common sense prevails! My father joins the real world!'

William smiled. His son was a one off and he knew that. Robert had a singular mind all of his own and there was no way that he, humble William, would ever affect it. Still, it was something he would not give in on, he would continue whilst ever he could to drop little bits of life as William saw it into his son. Something of deep beauty might just stick he reasoned.

Robert continued.

'You know Dad, my view is, and I am not having a go here, just agreeing with you as to how we view things so differently, so don't be so defensive?'

Robert asked this whilst leaning forward in his chair and opening up his hands in a let's talk motion. William inwardly rolled his eyes but outwardly just managed to nod and offer a weak smile.

'Well I am decided that your politics are short sighted, small minded, badly positioned and never able to work. History proves it. The only place where your politics will ever work are in fiction. That's why you love poetry.'

William laughed now, part of desperation and part out of humour. Poetry indeed.

'You fought for an idealistic vision Dad, a vision that was already clearly crumbling as Russia and America divided the spoils. Your dream never stood a chance.'

William nodded to this. There were some truths in what he was listening to.

'And then, in post war Britain, we lost our way. We believed we could still change our world, when in fact the world was changing without us. We fell back in the race Dad, Japan, France, Germany; you name it, all moving on without us. Our ways of doing things, our stiff upper lip and doing the right thing! Well, in short, it's all bollocks. We had become the poor man of the economic world, sat hungry in the corner whilst the developing world laughed us. And that, quite simply is why we needed Thatcher.'

William raised his hand, asking his son to let him interject.

'And there we will forever disagree. A lot of what you say is true, but is it so bad that people dream; aspire to make a brighter future, where the needs of the many are provided for? You see, to me, Thatcher is everything that is bad.'

Robert laughed sarcastically. His father knew so little of life it was almost frightening. William went on,

'I know that the economy looks better, that much of what we see day to day seems to be getting better, but have you taken time to look behind the cracks Robbie?'

'What cracks?'

'There you go, what cracks indeed. How do you think she's saved so much money?'

'Good management?' offered Robert with a smirk.

'By not placing it into the needy of our society!'

'The money wasters you mean that bled this country dry in the 70's, the very reason we needed the 80's Thatcher revolution.'

William took a deep breath again. He was going to keep controlled this time. He had promised Francesca. She had been particularly clear as to his expected behaviour! William lifted his glass of wine and rocked it to and fro allowing the colours to catch the light through the reflections from sky and garden. The wine, intoxicated by the air, lifted its aroma and the effect calmed him.

'Some of them, yes, but many no! The social service budget has been cut. Education budget – cut! Housing budget – cut. In fact worse, housing is being sold off! Add to this the privatisation that has placed our crown jewels into the hands of the private sector.'

'Where it will be more effectively managed Dad, just what was needed.'

'And one day be sold overseas! Just what is not needed because one day we will need to buy it back.'

'Ah come on Dad. How likely is that?'

'Mark my words Robbie. We are setting ourselves up for a brain drain as our people go overseas where our assets will follow. You've already commented on the increasing economic prowess of our overseas competition. Their wealth will be our downfall.'

'You've been reading too much George Orwell Dad.'

Now it was William's turn to smile. His son using great thinkers such as Orwell even in a conversation was something he was still getting used to.

'Nothing wrong with Orwell son.'

'He was a Trotskyist.'

'He was a democratic socialist!'

'There you go! The same thing.'

'Orwell was right about many things Robbie and you should take time to read more of his writing. You know that in 1984 one of the slogans he used was 'ignorance is strength.' I think that is true for you. You are ignorant of many of the dreadful social problems in this country of ours and this is your strength. The terror that is visited on millions is not visited on you. You don't understand it and, in fact, you choose to believe much of it is self inflicted and often imaginary and therefore nothing that need concern you and do you know what?'

'What Dad?' asked Robert impatiently, desperate to get inside to the safety of his female admirers, hearing his father's words and not listening fully to them.

'This is your strength. You can be totally focussed on building your empire without worrying about the problems that do not concern you.'

'Dad, why do always feel you need to dampen my enthusiasm, take away my fun?'

'I don't son. I just want you to be realistic.'

'About you dampening my fun?'

'About life.'

'Well, I guess that's why you're there!' suggested a now irritated Robert who fell back into his chair, pushing his hands through his thick dark hair and on to the back of his neck which was now aching.

'I guess so,' replied William, tiredness taking over his brain and leaving him feeling somewhat exhausted.

Francesca appeared at the French doors, a picture of happiness and delight. She was dressed simply in a pure white dress to her knees and black leggings down to her ankles. Older and yet still so slender and elegant, she offered her two men a beautiful open smile.

'Oh, how lovely to see my two men chatting so nicely. That's very precious indeed.' Her voice betrayed a tone of saying well done to them both. William and Robert in turn exchanged a knowing smile. If only she knew that she had, in fact, arrived just in time to ensure one of them did not have to make the decision to walk away. Rather they could now all pretend they were in Francesca's happy little world and that result would do just nicely for both men.

'Tea is ready!' she declared with a triumph akin to man's landing on the moon, disappearing immediately as she did so.

Robert arose immediately with William following heavily behind. The two of them left the patio and filed through to the dining room where Emily and Francesca joined them laden with a home cooked Francesca special lasagne. It was complimented by a hearty salad covered in a special extra virgin olive oil mixed with herbs and garlic that was imported from friends in Florence.

'This smells absolutely gorgeous Francesca,' exclaimed Emily, her South Hampstead High School and Cambridge University accent causing William to automatically run it through parrot fashion in his own mind, his own east midlands roots having never left him and causing his own accent to regularly be mimicked. He would look forward to doing a suitable impression of Emily to Francesca later. William very much liked the young girl though. Emily, a strikingly beautiful woman, had a softness to her that appealed to the older man. It was softness that was plainly missing from the people that Robert generally surrounded himself with, such as that incredibly intense Alison Collins. What a strange woman she was!

'Thank you Emily. It smells almost as good as you look!' replied Francesca causing the young girl to colour slightly at the compliment. Both Francesca and William liked their daughter in law a lot. It had been a whirlwind romance between Robert and Emily with them being introduced to her 2 months before the marriage in 1987. Robert said he had seen her and knew she was the one, which Francesca found very romantic and William kept his counsel. It all seemed rather sudden and William was convinced his son had married purposely into old money and elite society. Even Francesca would not dismiss the idea but told her husband to give them time and, two years on, they seemed happy enough.

'Where are you living the most?' asked William, eager to understand how having two houses could make any sense whatsoever.

'Well,' replied Emily, 'I spend most of my time in Chelsea near Mum and Dad and my friends, and Robert joins me a few nights each week. He does so like Chelsea don't you darling!'

William threw his knee far too keenly into Francesca's under the table in a there you go point. He had been labouring the issue to Francesca over many months that two houses could only mean trouble!

'That must be very nice for you having time away from young Robbie!' replied William with a not too heavily disguised sarcastic tone and a small smile that his son noted.

'I'm just so busy,' went on Robert, effortlessly ignoring his father, 'with work being such a great success. Do you know Dad, I just can't seem to stop making so much money!'

'Isn't that marvellous!' declared Francesca trying to keep everyone happy, whilst William responded by taking a large gulp of wine to wash away the indignity of having to listen to such talk. Robert continued,

'So much good fortune and I have to tell you both that it hasn't stopped at the business. We couldn't be happier could we Em?'

Emily returned a broad and knowing smile, and immediately Francesca knew what was coming next as she threw her own knee into her husbands.

'Are you pregnant?' Francesca declared, a big and excited smile filling her face.

'Yes!' replied Emily, a huge shriek taking over as Francesca almost ran around the table to hug her.

Congratulations continued as William fetched a bottle of champagne from the fridge and they toasted the expectant McTeer.

'When's the little one due?' asked Francesca as they settled down again around the table.

'October,' replied Robert, 'mid-ish.'

'Then here's to October!' shouted William as he sank another glass of champagne and the effect of the bubbles began to explode through his brain, 'I'm going to be a grandfather!!!!!'

Robert rocked back in his chair, the alcohol settling his own body down. It was good to see everyone so happy and amazing that the news of a simple child could make everyone so dewy eyed. He was happy, of course, but he knew a child could be many things from a perfect companion to a pain in the arse. Still, the news was a clear success and he was pleased. This was something he could deliver to his parents and make them very happy indeed. If only his marriage could have half the amount of happiness. Sadly he only saw one outcome for them and that was not going to be a happy Emily.

Later in the evening Robert finds himself alone again, this time in the lounge, with his father. Emily has found the allure of bed too much to resist. She rarely stays up past ten o'clock anyway and even less so since she became pregnant. They are watching Match of the Day, something that they have often done over the years. Meanwhile Francesca is lost in her studio away in the garden. When Robert was a little boy he used to think the distance between the house and the studio to be very far indeed. Even now, sat in the warmth of the lounge, Robert feels his mother is too far away, that somehow either the studio should be in the house or the TV should be in her studio.

He smiles to himself as he considers the absurdity of the thought he has had, that somewhere the little boy within him has just shouted out.

The football finishes and William looks across to his son.

'Well, that's me done for son. Sleep calls! Can I get you another drink before I go to bed?'

'No thanks Dad, I'll make myself one and perhaps take one out for Mum.'

'Great. She'd like that. See you in the morning.'

William stands and stretches, his ageing and sleepy limbs crying out for rest. He walks over to Robert and kisses his head.

'Night then son. Good to have you here and fabulous news again on the impending McTeer. I really am delighted and as for your mother, well she is beside herself.'

'Thanks. That's good. Night Dad,' says Robert, turning off the TV.

William slips away to dream of grandchildren.

Robert sits for a moment and considers the day and the big announcement of the little life that is growing in his wife right now. He has not really thought about it too much. He has been busy, really busy, and somewhat disinterested in Emily and whatever might be happening with her for sometime. Somehow this lethargy of thought has left him thinking little of the fatherhood that now awaits him and here, in his parent's house, he begins to allow thoughts of his child to take hold of him. Does he want a boy or a girl he muses? Emily had said she supposed he wanted a boy. Did he? He didn't know or hadn't really cared. Now, as the clock on the mantelpiece takes centre stage with its rhythmical tick tock, Robert imagines himself and a baby, his baby, in his arms. It wasn't such a bad thought after all.

He wanders into the kitchen and makes a fresh pot of coffee. He gets the old wooden tray from the side of the bread bin, and places on to it two large white china mugs, the sugar bowl, two tea- spoons, a bottle of milk and a plate for some ginger biscuits which he duly gets out of the biscuit tin. The kettle boils, its steam rising high into the kitchen ceiling as it completes its cycle.

Robert gets the coffee out of the fridge and opens the packet to be greeted by the fresh aroma that reminds him of childhood and the many trips he had with Francesca to what seemed like every coffee house in the city. God he loved her. Here, on Ann Street, more than anywhere else, he loves her. He picks a white rose from the beautiful bouquet in the hall and places it across the tray. He looks at his prepared tray and smiles to himself as he hears his mothers delight in his minds eye as he arrives at the studio. One final change was needed as Robert replaces the milk bottle with a small white and blue striped porcelain jug into which he places some milk. There, that was better.

He steps out into the cool night air and walks quickly over the now cold and carefully lit garden. Francesca had wanted no lights at all but several trips experienced by both her and William had caused her to accept a certain amount of garden lighting would be no bad thing. She had sourced some old black antique lights that were being replaced in the city by a newer version. A friend had set them up and they suited the garden just fine.

He arrives at the studio door, knocks softly, and goes in.

'Hey Mum.'

'Robert! How lovely!'

It is midnight and Francesca is in her element. She sits in front of a big canvas into which she clearly engrossed. She turns and comes over to her son, taking the tray off him and placing it on a small coffee table. She kisses him on each cheek and then shows him to one of the two old battered chairs that sit by the newly arrived coffee.

They sit down.

'Thank you Robbie. Beautifully done. You are coming on!'

'I'm not disturbing you am I?'

'Never baby. You are one of the two secret people who can come in here whenever you like. Now what do you think?'

The two of them look over to the white washed canvas, standing eight foot square and holding a figure in outline. There were no clear lines, rather a succession of strokes that formed the nude.

'I like it Mum. It's new for you isn't it?'

'Yes it is! Well done,' she replies, pleased with her son's knowledge of her work, 'I've been working on the idea that we are very complex people and that what one sees in a person is only a small part of what one is. The effect I am using of multi layering the outline is trying to replay this.'

'Yea? Well that's brilliant. It looks great, you know, very effective and different. Unique in fact. I haven't seen anything like it.'

'Oh!' Francesca says as she sees something on her picture. 'Do you mind pouring the coffee whilst I just touch up the last bit I was just on. It will annoy me otherwise. I won't be more than a few minutes'

'No, that's fine Mum. It will be nice to watch for a while.'

Robert had watched his mother paint for hours as a boy. Often his mother would have set up an easel for Robert to work on and the young boy would do just that, normally copying his mother's work as best he could and sometimes branching out into his own ideas. Eventually the young Robert would tire and curl up on one of the chairs in the studio and just watch, captivated by his mother's work and his mother.

As he pours the coffee, its warming and rich scent filling the air, he looks around the room. It was as messy as ever with canvas laid against canvas. He becomes aware of the many people represented by the work here and their eyes seeming to rest on him, almost asking him to search deeper into his own soul, which was something he took great care to never do.

'Mum,' asks Robert as Francesca takes her seat beside him. 'Why do you paint all these people?'

Francesca smiles.

'They ask me to either directly or indirectly.'

'You mean you ask them!'

Francesca laughed. Of course she did.

'And that's it?'

'I think I give them something to reflect on.'

'And what do you get out of the bargain?'

'I get to reflect too.'

Robert sips his coffee. It tastes good.

'You could have painted too Robbie. You still could.'

'No Mum, I really couldn't. Not like you anyway. I don't have your heart. I have a different life.'

Francesca knows what he means, sees his struggle of control over humanity. She knows they are different people and she is not about to try and change him. Even so she feels a little sadness begin to pull at her mind. It came from time to time and she was an expert at batting it away. She begins to do so again but Robert is not finished.

'Do you worry about me Mum? You know, like Dad?'

Now Francesca takes some coffee and weighs up her response.

'I try not to think about it. I have always left you to be you. You will make your own choices.'

Robert heard the concern in his mother's voice and feels the tiredness begin to kick in. He had been working at full tilt now for too long. His personal life was a mess with much fun but not with his wife who he avoided as much as he could. Now a baby was to join the mix. His parents were near saints and try as he might he would never ever be anything like them. Here, in his mother's studio, he felt as close to his conscience as he ever would and he could not cope with what he was feeling. It was easier to not feel at all.

'Mum. I love you, you know that don't you.'

'Yes Robbie, of course I do.'

'Well that's enough isn't it? Enough for both of us?'

'Yes,' replies Francesca, placing her cup back on the tray and leaning over to pat her son's hand. Robert looks up to meet her gaze.

'I'm just tired Mum. It's late. Hilariously I can't match my mother's stamina for late nights! See you in the morning.'

He rises, kisses her cheek and steps out of the studio, leaving her to fear that her son was further away than she had thought. Francesca considers this for a few moments, allowing the realisation that her son, her Robbie, was struggling. Could she, his mother, help? Was he asking for her to do more, say more? She looks back to her canvas and her mind begins to get caught up in that too. For several minutes she feels herself pulled between the two.

Ten minutes later Francesca was lost once again in her painting. This was something she could do.

Chapter 13

# The Birthday Party

Summer 1989. Ashover, Derbyshire, England

It was the last day of June and Robert had arranged a meeting with Ronald Jones to discuss his position and the ownership of the company. The arrangement of an excellent pay package was something that Robert had simply outgrown. He had become, in such a short space of time, Jones Ltd. The money and assets had all in the beginning been Ronald's but now the vast majority of the very core of the portfolio, had all been constructed and was now managed by Robert and his team. It was time for this to be recognised. It was time for change.

Ronald was ready for the meeting that had been brewing for some time and had drawn up, via his solicitor of many years, a highly generous offer of a 25% stake in the ownership of Jones Ltd for free, with an option to purchase a further 20% of the share capital for a mere one million pounds. He had run the whole thing by Alison who seemed suitably impressed, though strangely non-committal on how Robert would view the offer. To Ronald it seemed immensely equitable and fair. He was giving away ownership for free and offering a further stake for a steal. He viewed the matter as a common sense of action that he needed to take. Put simply, Robert had far exceeded his most optimistic of expectations and he now deserved his reward.

'You see Robert this offer is made because I want you to know your true value to me. I want you to know your future with me is assured. I want you to know I appreciate you.'

Ronald spoke in a friendly tone. He recognised the balance of power had shifted and was keen to allow Robert to truly take over and feel like he was in control. Over the last two years it had become noticeable that Robert was no longer subservient in anyway whatsoever. Meetings were far fewer between the two men and they were far less enjoyable than they had been. Matters of business were all discussed professionally but quickly, the younger man keen to get away and get on with his day. Ronald was busy anyway with his many commitments and Alison had given him no reason to be unduly concerned about Robert, so the older man let matters continue hoping all was well.

'Mr Jones, I do know that,' Robert offered, in a still, calm voice.

'You do! Excellent. That's so good.' Ronald settled back in his chair, relief flowing trough his body.

'I do know my future is assured Mr Jones. I also know that you have needed me as much as I need you. After all it's been your cash with my brain.'

Ronald noted the word 'been' with concern.

'It is my cash Robert, and indeed my support of you to make more for me, for us!'

'Yes. Indeed. You see that's why we are sat here today. Something has to change.'

Ronald was surprised by the words even though they were delivered in a non-threatening steady tone. Why had Alison not made it clear to him that Robert was unsettled, that he was not being given what he clearly thought he deserved? Where was this conversation going? Everything seemed to go into slow motion around them, Ronald's senses going into overdrive to concentrate on what was coming next.

'What do you mean Robert?' Ronald asked, trying desperately to keep calm.

'Mr Jones, let me respectfully first of all say that without you I would be in a place far different to where I am today.'

'A bed-sit on the Ecclesall Road perhaps?'

Robert smiled. It was probably true. Before he had met Ronald Jones, Robert had been heading into unchartered territory. Would he have made a success of himself? Robert's self belief gave him an emphatic yes, but he also knew that he would almost definitely had not been anywhere near as successful as he had been, and certainly with the speed that he had grown his wealth, had the older man not found him and catapulted him into the big time.

'Maybe not even that glamorous,' Robert replied, 'we can only guess at what would have been. However I also know why you chose me. You saw skill and boredom and you knew, if your calculation was right, my ambition would be lit and your future would be set.'

'I did Robert, to be sure I did,' acknowledged Ronald, his brain remaining on high alert for the conversation that was clearly coming.

'And so you see I now need to be sure of my future.'

'And 25% for free doesn't do this?'

Robert paused. The offer was a generous one and one that he could hear his father and Angus telling him to be grateful and accept.

'No, it doesn't.'

The words were delivered in a level voice with no emotion whatsoever.

Silence filled the gap between them.

They were meeting out of the city in a pub on the Lodge Moor Road on the outskirts of the City of Sheffield. At Lodge Moor you were at the gateway to the Peak

District and that made the land here potentially very valuable. The hospital, which had been founded in 1888, had not been developed with the future in mind. It stretched for miles and miles and was a site manager's absolute worse nightmare as well as being a cash pit for repairs and running costs. Robert knew, through his many contacts, that its days were numbered. He had ensured that Jones Ltd was best placed to benefit from its inevitable closure.

He had just shown Ronald around the site, filling him on the many plans he had. It was all very exciting and had pounds signs written all over it. The last obstacle had been a major landowner to the south of the hospital who let the land be used by the hospital for a minimal fee for the good of the patients. The land was pivotal as it covered the main road arteries that any future development would need if it were to be a success.

He was called George Braithwaite and he was an eminent man, highly respected and the Chair of the hospital committee. He was highly connected and had been totally against the sale of land, his and the hospitals, because he knew once it was gone it would be lost forever. George was a man of money, of capital, but he also believed in social justice and care for all. Selling land that had been used for a hundred and one years and more for the help of sick individuals made no sense to him at all, no matter what the immediate value of the sale money would provide. It was a short sighted nonsense, the type of planning that the Government was showing itself to be open to far too often, shoddy work that in his opinion was doomed to failure and he was having none of it. Negotiations had therefore been tense for several months and Ronald had come to the meetings today expecting matters to remain in the balance at best and yet, amazingly, the opposite had occurred. A pale George Braithwaite had attended the meetings in a most cordial and polite fashion, and had agreed a sale within ten minutes. The legal documents were all prepared by Angus' team who were in attendance in great numbers and the deal on George's land was completed without any further aggravation. Robert left them all to conclude matters, taking Ronald on the tour of their new purchases.

'How did that happen?' asked Ronald as they left the conference room.

'A simple matter of knowing which buttons to press Mr Jones,' declared Robert and walking away at pace.

'What buttons?'

Robert stopped, allowing a heavily breathing Ronald to catch him up.

'Do you want to know?' asked Robert.

Ronald considered the question and the implication within the question.

'No, I guess not. Well done.'

'Thank you.'

Business concluded and the two men had retired to the nearest pub and sat themselves in the corner away from the few locals who were in to conduct their own appointments with their trusted pints of bitter. The pub itself was in need of a major revamp. Stains littered the old chairs and carpet, the smell of too many cleaning products rising above that of the smoke that wafted around them.

Ronald looked at his young protégé and considered what he had become and, as he did so, he found a rage begin to build inside himself. He had already endured the fact that he knew his girlfriend was sleeping with young Robert to get as much information on him as possible. Indeed he had encouraged the liaison, accepting the need for such action. However what made this worse was that he was sure Alison actually enjoyed it. Still the information passed back was invaluable. It meant that he had taken steps to ensure the business cash was followed meticulously and all deals clearly listed and passed by him. Of course he knew Robert had his own side shows of growing businesses but there was no question that this had in any way impinged upon Jones Limited which was an unqualified success.

And yet here they were, Robert regarding his offer with disdain. Why, Ronald asked himself again, had Alison not warned him this would be the outcome? Surely she knew what Robert was after? Ronald, though, also knew how highly regarded Robert was, and that Alison would be protecting her own position. She was clearly waiting to see how this would play out. Clever bitch. The thought of her naked in Robert's arms filled him with fresh rage. The simple fact was that the generous offer had been one he fully expected to be readily accepted, should have been accepted. He had expected more than thanks, he had expected gratitude. Anger now took over in a swell of emotion that came all at once, sweeping aside the caution he knew he should probably still be exercising, and he exploded,

'Robert, I fucking made you boy. I took you from obscurity and I made you. Don't just sit there and be flippant with me boy. I will not be played by you, you hear me, I will not be played by you, you fucking dickhead! Jones Ltd is mine, all mine. I found you and I will find another you. There, how do you like that? You'll be left with your tiny dick in your hands, trying to make a living out of the poxy drug addicted peasants you supply without Jones Ltd to give you the cash flow. You will forever regret the day you sort to outfox the King of Scotland! Bastard,' he spat, words leaving him as his breath ran out and his eyes blackened over with the fog of hate.

Bored heads turned and Robert offered them a smile. He heard the rant, indeed, expected it. It took him back to distant memories of sitting outside Ronald's office all those years earlier, full of fear and expecting the worse. The fear though now had long since gone and had been replaced by a confidence that most people felt as intimidation. Robert now only felt pity for the man before him, pity that he spoke in the way he did, pity that he thought he could ever ride rough shod over Robert again, and pity as to what would now play out and where it would leave the unfortunate Mr Jones. Of course Ronald was right, he had indeed given Robert the opportunity, but hundreds of millions of pounds of profit that had gone into Ronald's pockets was more than thanks. Now Robert saw that it was time for the founder to move aside. Still speaking slowly, quietly and calmly, Robert laid it on the line,

'The thing is Ron, and I really think it is probably time that I called you that, don't you? The thing is Ron that you have made me and so sat before you today is a pretty near as dammit version of you, and this is why you should be afraid because I am not just you. I am the new incarnation and as any new version, I come with all the necessary changes. I am a much younger version of you so my energy levels are not restricted, but I am also far more calculating and far more ruthless. Nothing stands in my way. Nothing. You know that. Every fucker that ever meets me gets to know that eventually, one way or another that I will prevail. I am 100% bastard material and you, Ron, will bow down to the new King of Scotland. But be assured, I am no Macbeth! I am the devil.'

'You little cunt!'

Ronald felt his chest tighten and the room seemed to close in. Robert saw the older man's discomfort and knew the game was now his.

'Now calm down Ron, we don't want you overdoing things now do we. I am simply telling you the facts. I will be fair with you. You deserve it. I will look after you and honour what you have done for me.'

Ronald took a sip of his drink and allowed his body to settle a little. He would not be brow beaten by Robert. He would try and keep it together. He needed time to fight this, to get his head around what was happening.

'What do you want?' Ronald asked, anger written through his voice and across his face.

'No shareholding. It's yours to keep. Why should it be mine?'

Ronald looked at Robert. He saw a slight smile cross his face, which had the affect of annoying him still further.

'I don't want your company now Ron. I want your inheritance.'

The words held their own in the air between them. Robert simply waited. There was no conversation to be had, no bargaining to be made. He had become used to the fact that what he wanted, he got. Ronald, on the other hand, was astounded. This was never how he had thought it would turn out.

'That's impossible Robert. You can't have my inheritance! How can you ask for it?'

'I'm actually not asking. I'm instructing.'

Ronald shot to his feet and jumped across the table, knocking over the glasses of beer and sending them crashing to the floor. He gripped Robert by the collar, pushing him back against the cigarette stained wall.

'You fucking can't instruct me!' he shouted, spit hitting Robert's cheeks, the very breath of the old man filling his lungs as the senses heightened.

Robert, enlivened by the attack, held a passive smile. There was nothing more to say, although he hoped the barman would get over quickly as Ronald's grip was starting to hurt and he was beginning to struggle to breathe, not to mention the damage that was probably being done to his highly expensive tailored shirt and suit. The barman duly arrived.

'Break it up lads! Fucking hell! It's normally the young hooligans causing uproar, not the suits,' he roared, pulling the older man away and forcing him to relax and slowly release his grip on Robert.

Ronald rocked back and stayed standing at the opposite

side of the table to Robert who in turn gently dusted his shirt back into shape and sat himself back down. As he did do he produced two £20 notes and handed them to the barman.

'Just give us five minutes please.'

The barman, a middle aged man who looked 10 years older than he was, shot the two of them a look of distaste and returned to the bar shaking his head.

Ronald held his position, breathing far too heavily, sweat dripping from his brow.

'Aren't you going to sit down Ron?' asked Robert, his voice so calm that it was as though this was the most normal set of circumstances in the world.

'Fuck you Robert. Fuck you! My answer is simple. My answer is no.'

Robert smiled. It was a smug grin that only added to Ronald's anger.

'That's your prerogative. Let's not be hasty though. It's my big party tomorrow night and we can chat then when your temper has calmed down. It can't be good for you, a man of your age, getting so over excited. Goodness knows how you cope with Alison who incidentally is just the best fuck in the world, don't you think? That arse, my God, such beauty. I prefer taking her from behind. Can't beat it don't you think?'

There was so much Ronald wished to say, so many ways in which he wanted to hurt Robert right now, but he knew his temper had let him down and he now felt as bad as he had ever felt in his life. So calming down was the best advice he could have had and in that respect alone he considered Robert was right. Murder, which was the only thing on his mind, would destroy them both and lose all that he, that they, had built. Maybe a night's break for them both would see a more reasonable apprentice.

'To tomorrow then Robert. It gives us both time to think.'

Robert lifted his empty beer glass.

'Yes, to tomorrow.'

A big party had been Alison's idea. They had made love in the office after a spectacularly successful day in which several deals had all come together. They were on the floor by the sofa against the corner of Robert's office, the late evening sun visible through the window that opened out onto the Sheffield skyline.

Robert lay with his head on Alison's naked lap as she stroked his hair.

'Have a big party Robbie! Let everyone see what you've become. I'll get the usual crowd there and some nice to haves.'

'And have them we will!'

Robert laughed. Even his party could be a great big networking event! Was there no end to what the two of them could achieve?

'You are fantastic, you know that don't you?' Robert said, massaging Alison's right hand that he held in his own.

'Of course I do! If you're a good boy I'll come to the party without knickers on too. That should get you through the event.'

'A party it is then!'


Robert and Alison had an arrangement. From early on it was clear to Alison that Robert would be running Jones Ltd one day and so she had told him of her duplicity allowing the two of them to be careful and to satisfy Ronald and his understandable curiosity. They knew Ronald was a highly intelligent man and would not be blind to Robert siphoning off any business, and so they decided to build the business and feed Ronald what they wanted him to know and think. In time they would ask for the business, but not before they knew it was truly theirs.

They did not love each other in any traditional way in

so much that they had no hold over one another that asked for any level of commitment. They knew they would never be husband and wife, never parent children and never live together. And yet on a level, on their level, they cared for each other deeply. They accepted their need of one another. They understood that they were highly driven individuals and that many people would feel uncomfortable with them. This strength of character was a natural wall that with each other was not a problem. Time that they spent together was relaxed and their relationship had grown.

Each though had their own private life. Robert had met and married Emily Grayson two years earlier. It had been a whirlwind romance based on absolute love for Emily but never that for Robert. He liked Emily, finding her funny and beautiful, but he did not have time or the appetite for love. Emily's father was well positioned in society and the City, and the marriage helped Robert in all sorts of social circles, changing forever the people with whom he would do business and the new stratosphere he would be able to work in. Alison had done her homework and Robert did the rest. Emily was now heavily pregnant with their first child due in the autumn. Robert was happy, though the marriage was becoming an increasing burden with Emily asking for more and more of his time, time that he simply did not have or wish to give. Trouble was therefore brewing and would need to be faced in time and dealt with in time.

Alison remained unattached to one partner but attached to many. She continued to live her life out of her order of needs, yet having found Jones Ltd, or rather having been found by Ronald, the rest of her life seemed to fall back into place. Now the casual relationships, the easy lays, the ability to be how she wanted and yet walk away to her own life; all of these things made her feel much more fulfilled. She would never change. Having found Ronald and then Robert, she would never need to.

It was a perfect summers evening for a party. The Peak District country house hotel that Alison had chosen for Robert's party was quintessentially British. Built in the 12th century on the outskirts of what was then only a tiny hamlet called Ashover, and extensively rebuilt and added to in the 17th century, Milhaven House was classic in every detail. Its hidden gem, and the reason that privileged garden enthusiasts knew about the house, was its heavenly landscaping. Spacious courts with their decorative gateways and garden houses, with finial caped walls and tightly trimmed hedges, impressed the eye and drew you into a space of wonder. Colour was absolutely the order of the day in the borders with magnificent planting based on an historic tradition. Variegated aralias, flowering grasses and lush and pure white dahlias sang in a chorus of beauty. The trained eye could see argyranthemums, penstemons, crocosmias, purple heuchera and continus standing out in the height of a stunning English summer day.

The quizzical wanderer would find many treasures in the gardens of Milhaven which covered 8 complete acres of laid out gardens including delicious lawns, sumptuous ponds and delightfully full borders with many exotic finds. Particular interest was given to lavender, roses, valerian, camomile and elecampane varieties as all were grown in abundance in Ashover's rich and important past, where each were dried out and used in particular for medical research.

Milhaven House was an important landmark and gave a clue as to the grand history that Ashover had once enjoyed. The village had been superbly situated in the middle of lead mines, limekilns, coalmines, stone quarries, flourmills and many other industries. As a result trades had grown up within it including shoemakers, nail makers, basket makers and rope works. The latter had enjoyed a fabulous reputation with their ropes once stretching from Moor Road down to the church gate and said to be the longest ropes ever made in the country. Ashover had therefore grown rich and had built fine houses from its prosperity, property that today remained as a clear legacy of those times. It was, then, a beautiful village with wonderful houses, chocolate box village pubs, incredible scenery and a village school that every parent from the surrounding area and beyond wanted their child to go to. Term time school rush hour was a traffic nightmare as the expensive four-wheel brigade descended on the small lanes in and out of the village causing locals to moan and send unanswered letters of complaint to the local council.

Throughout all this period Milhaven had stood proud over the success of Ashover down in the valley below it. The views from the house were extensive in all directions, and on a clear day you could see the counties of Yorkshire, Lincolnshire, Nottinghamshire, Leicestershire, Staffordshire and Derbyshire. The views included the beauty spots of Slack, Bradley Tor, Cocking Tor, Ravensnest, High Ordish and Ashover Hay. It was a delight, a haven of euphoric peace and pleasure away from the busyness of the cities below.

It was in the corner of one of the laid out lawns, late in this divine mid summer afternoon that Robert found his parents. They were ageing now, he thought, with even his mother looking too small in frame. Robert noticed though as he got closer to them how good they still looked. He was proud of them for that and hoped their genes would follow him.

William was sat on an old wooden seat, the early evening sun resting on his face as he let his neck gently fall back and his smile greet the warmth and kindness of its rays. On his ears rested his headphones, which released music from his Sony Walkman, a piece of technology that his father had found too irresistible to resist. To be able to listen to his favourite pieces whilst being out and about was a match of perfection to William.

As Robert got closer to them he saw that his mother was crouched by a pond taking photographs that she would no doubt attach to her studio wall and work from. Francesca adored a good garden and knew all about the gardens at Milhaven being such a keen gardener herself, and so she had come prepared with her camera to catch some inspiration to take home. She used her old Rolleiflix TLR film camera, refusing to follow so many modern developments in photography, but rather happy to use her old friend and develop the prints herself in her darkroom at home.

Francesca heard Robert's footsteps and turned.

'Robbie, my Robbie, happy birthday darling!'

She rushed towards him, held him by the shoulders and kissed both his cheeks. Robert eased into his mother's embrace, thrilled to see her and to feel her adoration for him.

'I see you are still striving ahead with modern technology mum!'

Francesca looked at the camera in her hand and smiled.

'What was good enough for Lee Miller is good enough for me, my sweet bambino. You know that! I don't need to spend hundreds of pounds just to make me feel better, unlike some of us!'

Robert smiled. He had heard it all before. At least with his mother it just felt like banter as opposed to a lecture from his father.

Francesca stood in front of Robert and sized him up.

'You are looking tired and carrying no weight.'

'Isn't my svelte like figure a good thing Mother?'

'No Robbie! Unnecessary thinness is never a good thing. I have seen this for myself, as you well know, and I do not want to see it in you. You should always carry a little weight because you never know when you'll need it.'

'As in times of famine?'

Francesca smiled. She had long since chosen the path

165

of least resistance with her son. As a child she had given him everything and now he had to make his choices and make them he had. From a turning point in Sheffield, Robert had mentally and physically left them. In truth Robert was an ambitious child, with a drive and determination that he had not inherited from them. His mentality was always that he was right, never wrong, and that he had to be top dog in pretty much everything he ever took part in. It was a trait she recognised from her Papa, and one she now saw clearly evidenced in her son. This probably helped her accept Robert's character more readily than her husband who was never going to understand his son.

The two of them now turned to William who was looking up at the two of them with a big grin on his face.

'What are you listening to Dad?'

William continued to smile at them. He couldn't hear Robert's voice as the London Symphony Orchestra were in full flow playing Elgar's encapsulating Nimrod at an extraordinary volume.

Francesca stepped over to her beloved husband and gently pulled the headphones away from William's ears said,

'Your son wants to know what you are listening to darling.'

William stepped up out of his chair and walked over to Robert, placed a hand on his son's cheek, and smiled.

'Happy birthday Robert!'

'Thanks Dad,' replied Robert, feeling a sudden burst of unexpected genuine warmth for his father.

'It's good to see you son. I was listening to your favourite composer.'

'Bono?'

'Very good. How did you know?'

'It was the way you were moving your head. The exact rhythm to 'Where the Streets have no Name."

'From the seminal Joshua Tree album?'

Robert looked at his father, astounded by his knowledge. Francesca laughed.

'It's Joe from next door. Him and your Dad are doing a musical swap to educate each other.'

'That's Joe the spotty 12 year old?'

'It is!' replied William with a tremendous sense of satisfaction, 'except that he's now 15 with even more spots and looking to make a career in a band called Polaroyd. Quite the guitarist actually and the band are fabulous.'

'You've seen them?' asked Robert, amazement in his voice.

'Seen them,' replied Francesca, 'he's their manager!'

Robert looked from his mother to his father and back again to see if this was a joke. It wasn't. A wave of jealousy passed through him and he decided to not dwell on what he had just heard. It was, after all, his birthday.

'Well, bravo to Joe!' said Robert, forcing out the compliment and hoping they could move on to more pleasant matters.

'Quite right! Well this is all very nice isn't it boys!' declared Francesca, delighted to be surrounded by her two favourite men of her life.

'Yes it is,' replied Robert, letting his eyes drift across the gardens and taking in the view, which was, even to a mind such as his, quite impressive. Why oh why did his father have to upset him so?

'I wondered where you both were,' he said, forcing his voice to be light as he did so.

'Well we got here last night,' said Francesca, sensing her son's unhappiness and regretting sharing the news of Joe and William's friendship.

'Last night! Thought you'd get here early for a bit of monkey business?' Robert goaded, smiling at his little joke.

William and Francesca both laughed.

'Now then Robbie, no need to be coarse,' smiled Francesca, delighted to see her son now laughing with them.

'Your mother wanted to explore the area and,'

'And I've fallen in love with it. This is just divine. Do you know how far you can see from here?'

'America?'

'Don't be so facetious!' Francesca chided.

'OK. Erm, Sheffield?'

'Further, much further!'

'Really?' now Robert was interested sensing there was more to this area than he had realised. Maybe he should be buying up some land as an investment. If there was planning to be obtained you could sell property here for a pretty profit indeed.

'Boys,' declared Francesca addressing the two men before her, 'when I die I want you to bring my ashes to these peaks.'

'Francesca!' called William, a small chill running through his body.

'No, no, I am fine and I will outlive you both and live forever and so on but I'm simply saying that when I die, which I will, then please, leave me here. I can look after my grandchildren and help their minds and their dreams soar through this air!'

Francesca was so happy. She felt free and very much alive, her senses open to all the light that had flooded into her day.

'OK Mum, you've got it. Ashes on Ashover Hill. Sounds almost poetic!'

'Well, whilst we are on the subject, I don't want cremating,' offered William.

'Dad!'

'Well I'm just joining in the happy chitchat. Burial for me and if your mothers going to be here then get me here too, but buried mind. Maybe we could get on to hymns if we've got time? I've always been a big fan of 'Always Look on the Bright Side of Life,' not technically a hymn in the traditional sense, I grant you, but to a Monty Python aficionado, such a song is meat and drink!'

'So what have you been doing today?' asked Robert, totally ignoring his father who was clearly drunk or had a personality collapse, or both, and addressing his mother with a change in the conversation.

'Well, we've been out walking and,'

'And Francesca has taken lots and lots of photos.'

'I've got some lovely shots!'

'Of course you have Mum. You always do. And what did you do Dad whilst Mum took her shots?'

'I considered the meaning of life!'

'And?'

'Not much else really.'

'No! What did you find out?' Robert asked, half teasing and half curious.

'That I am nothing and yet everything all at the same time. That I understand myself more than anyone, and yet I do not understand myself at all. That your mother stills spins my world and that without her I would fall off the edge. That if I could be anything else for just one day, it would be a rabbit. Shall I go on?'

Francesca lovingly touched William's arm. Robert rolled his eyes in mock resignation of the fact that he would never understand his father. He considered him a fool.

'Well that's good Dad. I'm pleased for you. Write it down and maybe there's a book in it! However, right now, are the two of you going to honour us with your presence? The parties kicking off and Em's parents are here and really looking forward to seeing you two, well mum at least. Try and avoid the rabbit eureka moment dad will you? You do know how important Em's dad is don't you.'

William bristled at this and was about to reply when his wife jumped in.

'We are coming in now darling,' replied Francesca, ignoring Robert's last comment and hoping William had too, 'We want to dance tonight don't we William?'

'We do indeed,' managed William, who had been

genuinely looking forward to a night of revelry, 'we were hoping you might have a live band on playing some boogie time jazz?'

'I have!' replied Robert triumphantly, regretting the dig at his father and pleased to be giving him good news, 'really I have. The band have come up from London and will be playing their first set in around an hour.'

'You know how to lay on a classy party son, I'll give you that.'

It was the last four words that picked the fight that no one wanted but always seemed to be there, waiting to happen.

'You'll give me what Dad?'

Francesca placed her hand on Robert's arm.

'It's nothing son, let's go in and have a great night.'

William stood still. He looked at his son and just saw a stranger. He saw a young man who was highly and stratospherically successful at his career, but somehow it meant nothing to him, his father.

'I'm sorry son, I meant nothing by it. It's great to see you.'

'Never enough Dad is it?' said Robert, shaking his head, turning away and beginning to walk towards the house.

'What? What's never enough?' asked William, pushing a softness through his voice to try and ease the space between them. Robert turned around and stepped back towards his parents.

'What I achieve.'

'I don't care for what you achieve, I care for you.'

Francesca looked on with the inevitable feeling of tiredness that rose within her. She had been in the middle of this for many years now. She felt exactly what William felt, but she managed to deal with it and just accept what she was given. William had tried, so much he had tried, to come to the same place. Clearly he needed to try some more.

'Yea right Dad. Just forget it. Come on, let's go and enjoy the party.'

'Not like this Robert.' Francesca caught her son's arm as he had turned to go back to the house. 'Your Dad and I are so very proud of you and we just want to know you are happy, that you and Emily are happy.'

Robert waited a moment. He looked at them both. He loved his mum, that much was sure, and maybe even his dad, but he didn't need them. One day no doubt there would be time and a need to see them, but for many years now the fact was he was very different to them and whilst he loved his mother very much, his father was just way too different to even try.

'OK. Fine. Sorry for overreacting.'

'As always.'

It was William, the words spoken before his brain had managed to send the hounds out to stop them escaping.

Robert turned to Francesca, kissed her on the cheek, and turned to walk at pace back to the House.

William looked to Francesca and smiled awkwardly.

'I am a fool my love. The words…'

William stopped. Tears filled his eyes.

'Just came. I know. I sometimes think your words come like the images that fill my head. We can't stop them.'

'I'll go and apologise.'

'You will, but later darling.'

'OK. Good. Let's freshen up and give him time to simmer down first shall we?'

They hugged. They always hugged. It was their safety net and their warm blanket. Their beauty was in some ways Robert's undoing.

William and Francesca joined the party two hours later. It was gone 8pm and everything was in full swing. The main room and adjoining bar were full of faces, many of which they had never seen before and had no idea who they were. Emily joined them and placed names to people and William, who recognised the names, was now able to place them to the people he now recognised from the vacuous world of politics and business. There were many celebrities present too, most of them of the younger variety and none of whom he had a clue that they were or what they were famous for. Francesca made it her duty to try to never watch television and absolutely never read the mass media, so the list of guests that included exclusive society from Westminster to Pinewood, meant even less to her than William. Coming from Italy had helped her totally cut herself off from the media of a foreign country, even though that country had since become her adopted country. She did though do a much better impression of pretending to be impressed than William, who seemed to drop his head and shoulders visibly as he realised he was in the middle of a dreaded society party.

'And how are you my dear?' asked Francesca smiling at her daughter in law's proud bump on display for all the guests.

'I'm fine thank you Francesca. I've never felt better actually.'

'That's the pregnancy high my darling!' said Francesca, stroking Emily's arm without realising she was doing it.

'Yes, it is,' replied Emily, feeling Francesca's touch that made her feel loved and cared for.

'And names, do you have any yet?' asked Francesca, keen to put a name to the expectant baby.

Emily smiled, a little nervously. She was not a confident girl for one so blessed with upbringing and beauty.

'I guess I can tell you.'

'Of course you can my girl!' voiced William with a big grin on his face as the warmth of his beer gradually began to take away the sadness of his earlier meeting with his son.

'Well, if it's a girl, and we don't know because I didn't want to know, then we will call her Jasmine.'

'That's a beautiful name,' beamed Francesca.

'And if it's a boy, we will call him Taylor.'

'As in the man who makes your husbands expensive suits?' enquired William.

'No dear,' corrected Francesca, ' it's spelt t-a-y lor and it's a modern name and beautiful at that.'

'Modern name, I see. In that case here's to them both.'

And the three of them raised their glasses and toasted the expectant child.

'Where is your delightful husband Emily?' asked William who was keen to make amends for his earlier faux pas.

'Well, he said he had some business to attend to back in the room. I'm sure he won't be long.'

'Right. Well I will leave you two beautiful ladies if I may be so excused, and go and see if he minds me apologising for upsetting him earlier.'

Both ladies smiled at him, Francesca out of love and pleased he was going to put things right, and Emily because she never really understood William and would now be left alone with Francesca who she loved very much and found extremely easy to talk to. She had some questions she wanted to ask about Robert. He had become more and more short tempered of late and maybe Francesca would know how to handle him.

William makes his way up the stairs to the suites on the south side of the house. The Pendragon Suite had apparently been used by all sorts of famous people including various nobility, facts he had picked up from the hotel information sheets he had read as he waited for Francesca to be ready earlier. Why she had to take so long to perfect perfection had always mystified him and despite giving her this line on many occasions, she continued to take as long as she wanted to get ready. It had taken many years, but he was now used to it and was able to use the time to satisfy his own leisure pursuits of reading and music.

He rounds the top of the banister, a huge wooden affair that must have taken many craftsmen a very long time to master, and then follows the helpful sign down the corridor that leads exclusively to the suite door that opens out into the south wing and the apparently wonderful Pendragon Suite. As he does so he hears raised and angry voices and something in him tells him to slow down and stop and listen and not to knock on the door.

'I will fucking not sign that fraudulent will. You will not have your way by force and lies and deceit and as far as I am concerned you and the bitch and your little brigade can all rot in hell.'

It is a loud, angry voice. One that William can just about place.

There was a quieter voice replying to this and William makes out the tone to be that of his son's, Robert. The affect the voice has on the angry shouting man is not good.

'I don't care. I'd rather die than sign this you bastard!'

A pause as whatever was happening in the room took a breath and William feels a rush of the old panic that occasionally plagues him, begin to claw at him again now. What was happening and was Robert alright? Then William hears his son speak slowly, clearly and easily.

'Then if you'd rather die we'd better grant you that wish don't you think?'

William finds himself replaying the words whilst panic and bile rise to his throat when a soft bang is heard from the room followed by a crash to the floor. Robert's voice is heard saying 'you know what to do, deal with it,' and William's mind is screaming that a shot, muffled heavily by something or other, has been fired. Now William finds his world is falling away as he has heard his son's voice speak of and be involved with what he knows without doubt to have been a murder. Any effects of the alcohol that William has drunk has now been lost as the stark truth of what faces him now hits him full on.

Some movement then follows with hushed voices that now William cannot hear. They are lost to him now and he finds himself suddenly very confused and disorientated. He assumes he is about to faint and to steady himself he finds his hand moving automatically to the door. He is also full of the parental need to be there for his son despite what he knows he has just heard. Then, as his hand touches the door handle, he hears Robert's voice, definite and calm.

'Simple suicide ay Alan! What a shame. No, a pity indeed! Bastard.'

Another voice, one William does not recognise, shouts 'The King is dead, long live the King!'

Laughter follows and William stands in a daze.

Then a set of footsteps can be heard coming from deep within the suite and towards the door that William is standing at. William reacts out of pure instinct by racing back to the end of the corridor. He has just managed to turn to appear to be again walking towards the door, when Robert steps out.

'Dad, what are you doing here?' asked Robert in absolute surprise and with more than a little anger.

'Robert, are you OK?' replies William, asking the wrong question immediately.

'What do you mean am I OK?' snaps Robert.

As Robert speaks, he does so very loudly ensuring, William knows, that those still in the room would know he was not alone. Robert closes the door far too quickly and begins to walk towards his father, the initial mixture of anger and surprise in his face being carefully removed.

In those few moments William resolves to try and keep his mind out of Robert's affairs. He had come here to make an apology. Whatever Robert was involved in was clearly desperate and dark and William's involvement would only confuse matters. Maybe he could talk it through with

Francesca later and they could decide together how best to handle this. Now was not the time. William makes a conscious decision to soften his tone, to try and appear quite drunk, and to make it perfectly clear he had come up to Robert's room for one reason only.

'You know, after our earlier upset. That silliness of mine and once again putting my big foot in it. I love you son,' slurs William, falling on to the wall in a minor miracle of acting drunk.

Robert looks back to the now closed door behind him, and then looks back to his clearly drunk father. No sound was heard from the rooms behind him. Whatever had happened in the Pendragon Suite was now being dealt with in a silent manner.

Robert steps forward. He looks calm and feels calm but seeing his father before him was like a message from God himself. Why did there have to be this conscience always following him around. He stills his inner self and walks up to William, placing his arm around his shoulder and gently leading him away from the suite door.

'I'm fine Dad. We're fine. Come on; let me help you. Take my arm.'

William leans into his son, holds on to his offered arm and bizarrely notices the sweet smell of his aftershave.

'It's just how we are Dad, just how we are,' repeats Robert, his mind racing through a thousand thoughts as he continues to take his father away from the suite.

William hears many answers to this spring through his brain but he manages, remarkably, to suppress them all.

'Yes, it is,' he says simply.

William considers his next line carefully. He wants to give his son the chance to offer him an explanation of what had just happened, for Robert to say something that William could believe in and take heart from.

'Did you hear that shouting? It seemed to be coming from up here somewhere; I couldn't make out where exactly. Probably the effects of three too many beers!'

'I did Dad, that's why I was coming out, to see where it was coming from,' says Robert, calmly and without any hint of concern in his voice. 'Still, it all seems quiet now. Probably just some rowdy guests! Nothing for you to worry about. Now come on, let's go and enjoy my party!'

William's heart sinks. All his fears for his son are rising to explosion point in his head. Clearly Robert is involved in something dreadful and yet he seems totally at peace. That thought only adds further sorrow on the older man's shoulders as he realises Robert was clearly used to dealing with situations like this. What on earth was he like? Who was Robert McTeer? What had they created?

As the two men walk down the stairs and people greet the young starlet Robert as though he is some hero of theirs, William decides to break the habit of a lifetime. What had just happened would need to be kept from Francesca. It would break her heart and William would not allow that to happen again. Not now, not ever.

Chapter 14

# Desolation

September 1992. Edinburgh, Scotland

'I'm coming, I'm coming. For fuck's sake!'

It seemed to Robert that whoever was knocking on the door had been doing so for far too long and certainly far too loudly. What was wrong with leaving a note! He was dressed only in a towel having left the shower and an extremely attractive girl, who's name he did not even know, much sooner than he had hoped to do so. He would be giving whoever was at the suite door a piece of vitriolic spite that they would remember for a very long time.

Prior to this rude interruption Robert had been having a good time being back in Edinburgh. The exclusive Balmoral Hotel was certainly as good a place as any to look out at the skyline of one his favourite cities in the world. Robert had travelled extensively, seen most of what the world had to offer, and yet it was his home city of Edinburgh that continued to beguile him in a way most cities could not touch. The history, the light, the views; the astounding way that the golden stone of the stunning buildings came alive to your eyes.

It was actually business he was here for, an attractive development opportunity on the outskirts of Leith that had caught the eye, but he would pull in seeing some of the old crowd and, of course, see his parents. He had seen very little of them over the last few years, finding it increasingly hard to make the effort after the big Ashover birthday party and the highly unfortunate incident with William's inopportune arrival at his suite. That had been a death knell for them really and whilst Robert was sure his Dad knew nothing, it just underlined a feeling of distaste he had for him.

Robert had also reflected on his parents in general and given he had virtually nothing in common with them he just stopped making the effort. After all they were just two old love birds hung up on each other and their little lives, and whilst this was all well and good, he found as he got older there was no good reason to see them. In fact they, and in particular William, had a negative effect on him, reminding him that his chosen life was so very different to theirs and in affect making him question some of his choices. These were questions he did not need, that could not come between him and his important business decisions. No, Robert would do his duty and see his parents when he really had to, but such get togethers were now very limited and normally limited to family events, more often than not around Jasmine. He knew his parents would be upset that he had effectively cut himself away, that they would never understand, but that was their problem, not his.

Robert was being remarkably successful despite a very difficult economy, and was firmly established as a big fish in a wonderful pond of opportunity. Now that Jones Ltd was all safely in his hands, he and Alison had set about a radical period of uber growth marked by an extensive increase within the team matched by high risk gearing of all asset classes. The old profit and loss percentage point's model approach went straight out the window to be replaced by the high tech computer models of a new generation and a team of highly trained analysts to operate them. Diversification too was the new Jones Ltd watchword with in particular Robert's team launching into the world of finance and the beauty of hedge fund management, or as Robert called it, printing money management. By the time the summer of 1990 had arrived Jones Ltd was almost unrecognisable to the company that had been in place a year earlier.

Times too were very different. The days of entrepreneurialism without end were sadly and somewhat inevitably going. Margaret Thatcher was disappearing too; sliding backwards in popularity as she took decisions that alienated her party and lost touch with what the country wanted. Britain had changed and it appeared she would not. In ridding Jones Ltd of Ronald Jones, its founding father, Robert was ensuring a new dawn that would burn brighter and brighter. To stand still was to risk burning out in out of date ways, ideas that may have served Ronald but that were ultimately never going to build massive growth and wealth, which were Robert's dream. Thatcher's dream may have been over, but Robert's dreams were in full steam ahead mode. His name would live on as a byword for breathtaking success. He would make sure of that. His was a legacy destined to be born.

Robert and Alison had recognised the warning signs of an economy running out of steam in the late 1980's. Ronald was not impressed by their plans for change, insisting what had worked before would continue to work. Surely, he argued, this was their safety net, the simple means by which they had made their success assured. Maybe it had been. What was clear though was that an economy ravaged by higher inflation and double digit base rates would be in difficulty. The press coined the phrase 'negative equity' in the early 90' as property prices fell for many people far below what they have paid for them in the first place. Residential ownership became a doomed occupation for many, clearing them out of their savings and causing them to have to hand back the keys to their homes and start again. Life long ambitions were torn apart as economic reality hit Britain's hard.

However to ride such a market you needed to be asset and cash rich and Jones Ltd was heavily blessed in both cases. In such a market there were infinite bargains to be had, incredible deals to be done that were simply not there in the late 80's. Now was the perfect time to build the stock for a recovery that would surely come. As others, including the once impregnable Ronald Jones, had become frightened, Robert and Alison had plotted for Jones Ltd to strike forward with focus and bravery.

One of Robert's favourite books was a 1st edition of Samuel B Griffiths translation of Sun Tzu's 6th century BC 'The Art of War,' bought for him by Angus for his 23rd birthday. Angus had been desperate to out wit his ever increasing impressively read friend with a classic book that Robert had not read and that he had hoped would blow him away. It had. Robert took to the book like a duck to water and read and reread it before buying copies for all the team. What impressed him most wasn't just the fact that in a mere 13 chapters Sun Tzu seemed to sum up how to run his business, but also the unbelievable list of people who had gotten there before Robert in reading the work. Even Napoleon was said to have been under Sun Tzu's spell. Apparently scores of Vietcong leaders could actually recite passage after passage and used the book as their bible to fight the Vietnam War and stand against the might of the American armies.

Many quotes had stood out, but one particularly surprised Robert and came back to him time after time. Sun Tzu suggested in Chapter 6, which covered off Robert's favourite topic of weak points and strong,

'Whoever is first in the field, and awaits the coming of the enemy, will be fresh for the fight. Whoever is second in the field and has to hasten to battle will arrive exhausted. Therefore the clever combatant imposes his will on the enemy, but does not allow the enemies will to be imposed on him.'

The quote hit Robert like a lightning bolt and stayed with him. He considered that Ronald was playing too safe; taking fewer and fewer risks, and as a result was letting others get their first to new opportunities. Even worse others were coming along and buying Jones Ltd stock at the agreed profit level targets and then going on to make a killing themselves. No, it was time for Robert and Jones Ltd to be first in the field, to find those opportunities ahead of all others, and then watch others come over the hill and pick them off at will. Power was Robert's drug of choice and he fully intended to control the game and make his fortune huge.

He reached the suite door, arguably the best in the hotel, and angrily swung it open. Two police officers in uniform were not what he was expecting.

'Mr McTeer?'

'Who's asking?' asked Robert, several lines of thought running through his mind all at once, his anger at seeing police uniforms having left him to be replaced by confusion.

The older officer of the two, job weariness written across his face, repeated the question in a voice that suggested some serious matter would follow.

'Mr McTeer?'

'Yes, of course, it is my room after all,' replied Robert, sarcasm throughout his voice.

'Can we come in?' asked the officer, walking past Robert as he did so. The younger officer stayed routed to his spot, a strange look of emptiness meeting Robert's steely gaze.

'Well if you must,' announced Robert, turning and following the older officer into the entrance hall of his suite.

'Please,' Robert offered, softening his voice and pointing through to the lounge area, its windows opening out on to extensive views across to the castle and up Princes Street. As Robert followed them in to the room, he picked up loose clothing, some of it his and some of it his guests, and pointed to the sofas for the two policemen to take a seat.

'Do you mind if I just throw some clothes on?'

'Not at all sir.'

Robert quickly retired to the bedroom asking himself if any loose stones could have caused this visit. He and Alan were always so careful. They considered themselves untouchable but maybe someone had made a mistake. Alan covered everything for him. There was no trace. Confidence rose in Robert and he gathered himself. It must be some other matter.

He threw on some jeans and a T-shirt and then, on his way back to the policemen, went into the bathroom and asked his visitor to leave, passing her the clothes from the lounge and bedroom and a considerable bundle of £20 notes in the process.

As he walked back into the lounge, taking a seat by the window, the girl quietly left.

'No need for the young lady to leave on our part sir,' said the older policeman, missing nothing and yet with no suggestion in his voice that he was offering any thoughts as to whom the lady may have been.

'Oh, Janie, yes, she was leaving anyway. Shopping, obviously! No worries, she'll be back later.'

'Of course. Mr McTeer,'

'Robert, please.'

'Right, Robert. Well I am PC McBride and this is PC Neale. I am afraid we have some very bad news.'

At this point PC Neale dropped his head causing Robert to become immediately alarmed. PC McBride continued.

'There has been an accident sir, a very serious accident.'

These words, words that you read in a book or see on a film or watch in some TV series, these words were now being delivered to Robert. It was as though someone had literally opened a door and let out pure fear, rather like opening a door to the outside on a cold winters day and the cold air coming in so quickly that it chilled the bones within seconds.

'It's your parents sir and I'm afraid it's very bad news.'

Robert sat perfectly still, staring through the men sat in front of him as the colour left his face and a sickness rose in his gut.

The words continued to come, entering his head and being stored as though recorded, words that he would replay over and over again.

'Your mother is dead sir. Killed on impact. I really am so very sorry sir. Your father is at the Royal Infirmary and is stable.'

Francesca, Francesca, Francesca. Dear, beautiful Francesca. No, no, no screamed his head.

'It was on the A1. A surprisingly dangerous road really. The lorry driver had lost control of his vehicle. He is stable too and will be under police custody as our enquiries continue.'

Robert sat, stuck to the spot as his perfect world was turned upside down and emptied out like trash. His mother dead and his father critically ill because of some drunken fucker who would be dealt with in the fullness of time. How had this happened? How?

'Would you like us to take you to the hospital sir?'

Robert let his eyes meet those of PC McBride.

'What?' he asked, his broken voice limping out.

'The hospital sir, would you like us to take you. We can do that now sir. We would like to.'

'Right, yes, yes, that would be appreciated. Thank you.'

Coat collected and within minutes he was sat in the back of the waiting police car. Rain was falling on the streets of Edinburgh. Sorrow for all time. Francesca was dead.

'Dear, dear Robbie. How are you?' asked Alison, taking Robert's tear stained face in her hands. She had driven up from business in Newcastle as soon as the police had called the office and the message had been relayed to her. She had arrived at the hospital only three hours after Robert himself had arrived. Dear Alison. Always at Robert's side.

Robert sat at the end of the ward where William now lay in a side room. He was asleep, full of morphine. His heart beat strong and he was yet to awake and discover the loss of his precious Francesca. There was no way of knowing just what this would do to him. Francesca was his life.

'I am empty. I just feel numb really, although very angry with the lorry driver. Very fucking angry.'

'Is he alive?' asked Alison, softness in her voice.

'Yes. But he won't be for long,' replied Robert, too loudly.

'OK,' hushed Alison in a soft voice, 'all in good time, all in good time.'

A few moments rested between them, Robert feeling calmer for Alison being with him.

'And William?'

'Broken legs and ribs and an arm and heavily concussed, but overall the doctors say he is remarkably lucky apart from the fact that he has lost the person to whom he has clung all his life and that she will never, ever be able to come back to him.'

At this Robert did something Alison had never seen before. He cried, really sobbed. She held him close into her bosom and rocked him back and forward in a slow, gentle rhythm.

'She was a beautiful lady Robert,' Alison whispered as

she stroked his hair and his tears fell down like soft summers rain, 'a beautiful lady.'

2.00am came and went, the wide-awake son sat with the still sleeping father. A chair by the window offered a view of nothing but a dark and wet night. The misery was complete.

William's bruised and battered right hand lay by his side and Robert looked at it. A hand that had held a gun in the Second World War and had fired off bullets to save the man who fired them. A hand that had claimed that of a fair maiden in Italy and brought her back to live in Edinburgh. A hand that had steadily put together drawings that had launched many buildings and even some design classics. A hand that had held that of a young boy as they walked by the Waters of Leith on a hot summers day and the father had told the son how much he loved him. A hand now stripped bare of the love of his life.

Robert then did something he had not done for many years. He picked up William's hand, held it to his face, and kissed it and once again the tears flowed from the young man's eyes.

The next morning and identification of his mother completed and his father still to come round, Robert left the hospital and, turning on to the Old Dalkeith Road, he walked aimlessly in cold driving rain as the never ending traffic sped past him, their inexhaustible tail wind rushing against his face. As he reached the edge of the Liberton Golf Club with its rolling parkland soaked after days of rain, Robert paused and stepped on to the outskirts of the course. As he left sight of the road and his world became solitary for the first time since he had heard the news of Francesca's death, he suddenly felt an almighty crashing pain of anguish descend upon him. As he did so he fell down on to his knees, and screamed out loud shrieks of hurt whilst tears mixed with rain lashed down over his face. This was pain that would leave an everlasting impression and, as it washed over him, it brought a sort of calm and a defining clarity.

He had already become hardened in the world within which he lived. Francesca had been his soft bridge back to his heart. Now he would become like stone. Him against the world.

Chapter 15

# Holiday

1st July 1993. Bourg, France

'Happy Birthday Robbie!' Angus beamed with a wide and excited grin. His face was coloured red from too much sun and wine and his heart was happy from relaxing all day by the pool with the four children. He had not laughed so much for far too long and the youngsters, who were all now exhausted, were getting happily settled down by their mothers for a good nights sleep, whilst he and Robert set up the BBQ for the four of them to enjoy late into the night.

'Thank you Angus. It is always a pleasure to enjoy my birthday with you by my side! Without you it would not even feel like my birthday. I would like to propose a toast.'

Angus nodded his appreciation at the suggestion. Both were gleaming with the affects of several glasses of Bordeaux wine, which was far too easy on the palate and as a result far too easy to drink.

'To my best friend Angus who, throughout my 30 years of life on this earth, has stood by me like a bear, a pillar and a rock!'

The two men pushed their glasses together.

'And I would like to add to that toast if I may Robbie.'

'You may,' replied Robert with a mock bow.

'To my best friend, on this, his special day. May your days be long, your health an ever present and your career, and therefore my career,' added Angus with a nod and a grin, 'be a continuing great success.'

'Cheers!' declared both men, pairing their glasses in celebration of their good fortune and fine hopes.

The two families, a party of eight, had arrived into Bordeaux airport three days earlier and were now just about settled into the beautiful French Chateau which sat on the outskirts of a pretty and undeveloped village called Bourg overlooking the Gironde river and beyond. The holiday had been arranged for nearly 9 months and by the time it came they were all ready for some down time from life at home. Emily had booked the holiday in the October, the week after they had cremated Francesca and taken her ashes down to Ashover Hill just as she had requested. William had been in a dreadful state, physically and mentally, but at least he had been able to leave the hospital to attend the funeral. It had been a grim affair, though there was much to celebrate in the life of Francesca Marinetti. Her 66 years had packed in some amazing things and her legacy was vast. They had all drawn some hope from that, even her boys, William and Robert.

William over time had reflected greatly on things and he took much solace in Francesca's life. He was surrounded by many good friends built over the long and beautiful years they had enjoyed together, and he was coming to terms with things at home in Edinburgh without her physically by his side. He was talking seriously about having a life change which would include selling the business and home and moving to North Cornwall, a place that he had always loved. Emily and the children had been up to see him on a few occasions, as had Angus and Maddie, but Robert had not returned to Edinburgh since the accident. Father and son had hardly spoken at the funeral and it was painful for those close to them both to watch the relationship, at least what was left of it, finally breakdown before their very eyes. The glue that had been Francesca was gone and now the two had simply fallen apart.

Robert had dealt with the loss of his mother by being away from home more than ever, finding more and more business trips to fill his time and occupy his mind. The business was going through a period of intense growth and busy acquisition and it was very easy to get lost in the work. He had pulled away from his home life finding Emily far too demanding and the obvious need to build his marriage too difficult to face. In truth he was no longer interested. Instead he relied greatly on Alison who gave him all he needed without any emotional attachment. It was easy that way and suited them both just fine.

Emily had confided in Maddie that matters between her and Robert were now very difficult, a fact that was clear even in public life to most observers. He was rarely at home and when he was he paid Jasmine very little attention and Emily even less. They had moved into an impressive and large detached property in pretty Totley, south west of the industrial City of Sheffield and on the outskirts of the Peak District, just before Jasmine was born with Robert insisting the child should have fresh country air. And so they had bought a huge old house that had recently gone through some major refurbishment with the owner sadly running out of money, and losing his marriage in the process, just prior to completion. As a result they picked up a relative bargain with its 4 reception rooms, 8 bedrooms, games room, indoor pool, tennis court and 10 acres onto open fields and the beginning of the peaks. It was beautiful. Sadly their marriage was not and this beautiful house was not about to mend it. Robert had married, in truth, for the reasons of business and class necessity, and now the strain of a lack of any deep and meaningful relationship was becoming too intense a problem for them both.

Emily had hoped that the birth of their second child Taylor, who was born on the 17th October of 1992 just after the accident, would help the marriage. It had not. Therefore the two-week break in Bordeaux was a make or break point for the marriage. Angus and Maddie had happily agreed to take as much as the strain as they could to allow Robert and Emily time to discuss and somehow try and rebuild what little they had left. With little Edith now 3 and Charles 5, Maddie and Angus knew only too well how time seemed to simply disappear with little children, leaving little energy left over. Certainly it was not a good time to try and build on the embers of a dying relationship.

Robert was busy looking after the BBQ and Angus stood by his side gazing across the view that stretched in two directions. One across the ancient Gironde River as it fed into the magnificent Dordogne River, and the other view across stunning vines that filled the vista with an excitement of the good Bourg wine to come.

'It's good to be here Robbie, the eight of us that is. Our happy little band. I mean, I know the kids all get to see each other but not like this, you know, all of us, together. It's been too long really.'

'Aye. Of course it has, but life seems to need quite a lot from you and I at the moment doesn't it.'

'That it does,' accepted Angus willingly.

'And that's the truth Angus and only you and I can really understand that truth. I know our good ladies try and be supportive, but they cannot understand how our business needs us, heart and soul Angus, heart and soul! Whatever it takes. 24 fucking 7 eh? We leave no stones unturned. We are that impressive.'

Jones Ltd and Burns & Co were both growing very quickly indeed. There never seemed enough hours to complete the workload and whilst Angus tried to balance his work life with time at home, Robert seemed to revel in doing as much as he could without any regard to the consequences on his family.

Angus was a partner within Burns & Co, an old and respected practice based in Nottingham and to whom he had gone after his superb first obtained at Oxford. The exemplary degree result was never in doubt, as was the fact that this together with his father's reputation who had been a well respected and senior judge, meant he would have a pick of jobs. He chose Burns & Co because in the first instance they had offered him a ridiculous salary with a contract that would see him become an equal partner within 2 years subject to performance criteria. He had seen Robert soar on the back of incredible income and Angus saw Burns & Co as in some small way a chance of moving in the same direction. Secondly Burns & Co were ideally located as they were based in Nottingham and that was near to where the love of his life lived. He had met Maddie on his course at Oxford. She was an exceptional talent and they were undergraduate adversaries vying for top spot throughout their academia. By the time the first summer holiday had come and gone they had realised just how much they had missed each other and their relationship began. Therefore a move to Nottingham was the perfect solution as Maddie was clear that this was where she intended to work and live to be near her friends and family. Nottingham too was close to Robert and therefore the future of his success.

They were married 4 years later and moved into Southwell, a beautiful small town on the outskirts of Nottinghamshire that was full of history and stunning buildings. They had rented a house that sat off the main pedestrian thoroughfare. From its back bedroom window you could see the magnificent Minster spires that towered over the area. Last year, after Maddie's income had finally begun to flow, they had taken their joint salaries and bought the largest house they could afford, this time backing on to the wonderful park and even closer views of the ancient cathedral and its brooding towers.

Burns & Co had 5 more partners, all of whom were over the age of 50 and looked to Angus to bring in fresh ideas and direction. With the Jones Ltd account a forgone conclusion and a gift from Robert to get his old friend started, Angus had brought all this and more, and as a result his salary had grown with exceptional dividends, as the partners feared he would leave them and take the big account he had brought elsewhere. In fact he had no intention to do so. He knew the other partners would all retire in due course and that would leave him all he had built and all they had built too!

Whereas Angus had chosen to become a solicitor, Maddie had always wanted to be a barrister. Her father was a barrister and she had loved going to court often and watching him in action, finding the way he held a jury in the palm of his hand to be both powerful and liberating. She had never been a girl who excelled in sport or would win a beauty pageant, but put her in a debating class and she would always win the argument. She was a mirror to her father's ability and the career path to become a barrister was almost a calling.

'Maybe you should hand more over to Alison?' offered Angus, carefully trying to bring the conversation around to Robert and Emily.

'Angus, my dear friend, Alison handles far too much already. My life is how I want it, you know that.'

'Well what about James, or Sarah. They are both bright young things. They probably don't have your commitments and you could add more on to them. I tell you the work they pass through my office is...'

'Unbelievable. Yes, I know.' Robert turned the steak and added more oil causing the flames to shoot up in anger. The spite of the fire intoxicated him. 'You know I enjoy it. I get a buzz out of it. I live for the buzz of my day, not to be at home tending my garden, so to speak.'

Angus had heard this many times before and he knew it to be true. It was, in part, true for him too but not in the all encompassing way that it was for Robert. Angus wanted to tell Robert that he needed to protect his home, protect the relationships he had built that were so precious but, as was normally the case when he spoke with his best friend, he felt unable to intervene, to offer advice that might upset him. What was worse was that he knew the moment Maddie arrived she would give him that look that said 'have you had a word with him?' Angus would raise his eyebrows in a 'what can you do' look, and Maddie would look away, feeling the hurt for Emily and anger at her husbands inability to, as she saw it, ever really stand up to the nonsense that was Robert. Here was no love lost between Robert and Maddie, just the simmering need to be pleasant because of Angus.

Angus took a large mouthful of wine and breathed in the warm French night air. A change of subject was the best policy!

'Is William really going to go and live down there in Cornwall?' Angus asked with deep wonder in his voice.

'He is indeed,' replied Robert matter of factly and without any trace of melancholy in his voice.

'Why?'

'He says he wants peace.'

'Fair enough, of course. But still, Cornwall!'

'It is still in Britain Angus! You do make me smile. It's not the back of beyond.'

'I know but, well, it's Cornwall! It's miles away. What the hell ever happens in Cornwall?'

'It is beautiful, from what I can remember.' Robert had gone to Cornwall a few times as a child with his parents, the long tortuous journey down from Edinburgh being rewarded by wide golden beaches and a sea that, unlike at home, you could go in without getting frostbite!

'What about friends? I mean in Edinburgh he knows just about everyone.'

'It is Dad we're talking about Angus! He will make friends easy enough, he always does. Besides the Edinburgh clan will no doubt be down to see him often enough.'

'And what about you? When will you get to see him?'

A moment of silence. This was a difficult question.

'Well that's the rub, I don't think he wants to see me.'

There had clearly been a breakdown in the relationship between Robert and William for many years. Still, with Francesca gone, Angus had naively thought that matters might improve. Clearly they had not. Maddie was appalled by Robert generally and the fact that he had not been up to Edinburgh to see his father since the funeral made her even angrier. Robert was the subject Maddie and Angus fell out about most. It wasn't even that Angus often differed in Maddie's views of Robert, but rather that he felt he had to protect his friend.

'He does Robbie, of course he does. He just needs time.'

Robert turned to Angus, placed his arm around his shoulder.

'Angus, why do you always feel you need to fix things. Some things are not there to be fixed. Dad and I have never been close. You know that better than anyone. I probably used to annoy him when I was a baby for all I know! We have never seen eye to eye and it's not going to start now. Now Mum's gone I have no reason to beat myself up about it. Dad knows how I feel. He's always wanted a different son and I've always wanted a different dad. He got me and I got him. No crying game required. It's just life and we have to get on.'

'Robbie, that's not true,' replied Angus feeling a little hurt for William, who he was sure felt very differently to Robert.

'It is true Angus, and even if it's not, my life is too busy to worry about it. Dad's moving on so I say Amen to that. Gives him less time to have a go at how I do things. I'm 30

195

for fucks sake, 30! I mean, come on, it's time to stop trying to make something work that is never going to work don't you think!'

Angus did not really know what to say. His own father, who he loved very much, had died two years previously and the effect on him was deep and debilitating for a long while. In truth it still affected him. The memory of his father and the warmth that he felt would touch him at different moments and leave him feeling the loss as well as comfort. To think Robert could turn down the gift of a father seemed inconceivable, even more the fact that William was in mourning and would soon, and incredibly, be living far from all his friends in Cornwall. Besides all this Angus loved William dearly. He thought the man was a saint and as close to perfect as he had ever known. They had always got on so well, talking about many issues and laughing so very often. Francesca and William had been a massive part of his life and he loved them both very much. How could Robert not do the same?

'I can hear you thinking Angus. Cheer up old man. It's my life. Dad will be fine because he's doing what I am doing – getting on with things. Dad is a man who can turn water into wine. He will revel in a new life, a new page! He does not want me on that page and, quite frankly, I don't care because I have not, for as long as I can remember, wanted him on mine. Now, it's my birthday, so stop trying to fix my life, or if you must let's talk about things we can fix. Come on, let's talk about happy subjects.'

Angus looked at his friend, weighed him up with his eyes. They were so different and yet so reliant on each other. William would have to live his life without his son and it appeared Emily would soon be living her life without her husband. There was nothing he could do about it. At least he could tell Maddie he had honestly tried. Angus knew there was one thing he could do and that was to be Robert's friend, his best friend.

Angus gave Robert a huge grin.

'OK. You win. If that's what you think is right then I'm sure you know best. I'm still going to go and see William as soon as he has moved in.'

'Good. He'll like that. You know he loves you very much indeed. You're the son he never had!'

'Robert!'

'We both know it's true Angus. You're the blue-eyed boy and our middleman, our go-between! Give him my regards.'

'I shall give him your love Robbie.'

'Good for you Angus. Give him that as well.'

Much later, after the food had been eaten and the wine had been drunk, Angus and Maddie had made their way back to their room with Maddie keen to talk about what her husband and Robert had discussed, time having not allowed this update to take place up to this point! Angus, in turn, had simply fallen asleep on the bed whilst Maddie had been in the bathroom. The mix of the sun and the wine had clearly been too much for him. As Maddie kissed him on his forehead and pulled a thin single sheet over him, she heard raised angry voices begin to sing out in the garden. They had enjoyed a relatively pleasant evening, all of them trying harder with it being Robert's birthday. Eventually Maddie had pulled Angus up from his chair and left Emily and Robert to have a hopeful romantic end to their evening. Clearly this was not happening.

'You will never change Robbie, you don't know how to.'

'Oh come on Em, you know how things have been for me!'

'There you go!' screamed Emily, 'I don't know. We don't talk. You don't see me!'

'We see each other all the time,' said Robert, defensively and without any conviction.

'When? When do we see each other?'

'Now?'

'Yes, now, because I arranged a holiday hundreds of miles away from home as the only chance I would have of seeing you away from that blasted, precious work.'

'You mean the work that means we are beyond wealthy and has set us up for life?'

'What life Robbie? What fucking life? Hello! Have you seen us, taken a look at us?'

'Oh come on Em, you love it! Your big house, big car, this club and that club.'

'Trappings Robert to fill a broken heart!' Her voice broke as she said that and there were a few moments of silence.

'Come on Em, it's my birthday, let's not fall out.'

'Let's not fall out! If you would love me Robbie, as you promised you did.'

'Oh come on Em, leave it.'

'Why did you marry me? Why?' Emily was working herself up.

'Oh please, not now. Stop being so hysterical and keep your voice down. Do you want to wake up Bourg on your account?'

'I hate you Robert! You take what is good and you suffocate it.'

'What!'

'You, you, you! No room for anyone else, not even your father!'

'Emily! For Christ's sake!'

'Don't come near me you bastard!'

'Em! Ow!'

A pause in the night allowing the insects to make themselves heard.

'Sorry Robbie. Are you OK?'

'Fine,' replies Robert gruffly, 'why hit me?'

'Sorry sweetheart, sorry, I really am.'

'Do I really deserve that?'

'Well no actually, you don't. I know you have been through so much.'

'I have. My wife hitting me is not helping.'

'I know. I won't do it again.'

'You said that last time Em.'

Crying oozed out of the girl. Sorrow and sadness and loss falling through her tears on to the warm French lawn, where it disappears and is gone forever.

Maddie pushed the french doors quietly shut, locking out the anger, vitriol and confusion floating in the late night air. She did not like Robert. Never had. He had a confidence alright, a confidence that could move mountains, but where was his humanity? When Angus had first introduced her to him on a trip to Sheffield, he had been so full of himself that she had almost wondered whether Angus was the right choice for her if this man was his best friend. Over time she had come to realise that oddly Robert's confidence was what Angus fed on, it was this that gave him what was lacking in his own character. She realised then that she would have to put up with Robert.

Still, she felt for Emily. A lovely attractive girl who had seen her hopes for a life of love dashed in pools of greed and loneliness. If she had ever had Robert, ever really had his love, then it was clearly long gone now. Emily was clearly struggling to keep things together and all now seemed lost. Maddie gave the marriage 2 years tops and suspected Emily would be asking her to help with the divorce.

The next morning arrived with the heat of the previous day. Robert made his way to the breakfast table having been awoken by the noise from the pool where Edith and Jasmine, dear friends and inseparable when they were together, were playing. He walked into the kitchen to find

Maddie feeding Taylor in a high chair that looked far from secure.

'Good morning Robert and how are you today?' said Maddie, trying with much effort to put sincerity and friendliness into her voice.

'Oh, erm, fine thank you,' he replied, opening the fridge to take out some juice.

'Sleep well?'

'Not bad. You?'

'OK, although a drunken Angus is never a good sleeping partner. His snoring could wake a dying man.'

That made Robert laugh.

'Nasty bruise over your eye Robert,' observed Maddie and immediately regretted saying it knowing the reason for its appearance.

'Oh, yes, knocked my head on the door. You know, strange room at night, too much drink. Silly really.'

'Well, nothing that this fresh country air won't help clear up in no time.'

'Right, quite! Where is everyone?'

'Well, the girls you have heard of course!'

'Indeed. I suspect the whole of Bourg has heard them too. We'll be receiving a neighbourhood visit no doubt soon. I shall say they are all yours.'

Maddie flashed Robert a tart smile that told him they may as well be for all the time he spent with them. There was no love between the two of them, each putting up with the other because of their shared love of Angus.

'And the rest?'

'Well Angus said wouldn't it be lovely to have fresh croissants for breakfast and so he's taken Emily with him to use her command of the language and Charles to have a 'French village' experience.'

'Ah, good old Angus. Ever the adventurer. Is that fresh coffee?'

'No. I'm making some more though.'

'Oh. Great. Do you want some help?'

'No, it's all under control.'

'Right. Well I'll go and see the girls.'

'Sure. They'd love that. I'll bring you some coffee out when it's ready.'

Robert escaped into the brightness of the morning. It was only 9 but already the heat was rising. Jasmine saw him and screamed with delight at his appearance. She jumped out of the pool and ran to Robert to throw herself around him. Edith too followed her slightly older friend and wrapped her dripping body around her favourite uncle causing his trousers to now be quite wet.

'You little monkeys,' called Robert with fun in his voice and picking the girls up, one under each arm. He ran to the pool and jumped in with them, their screams of delight welcoming Angus, Emily and Charles as they arrived back at the villa gates.

'Morning Robbie!' called Angus as behind him Emily slipped quietly to the kitchen and the safety of Maddie. Charles made to follow the clothed Robert into the pool but Angus caught him by the arm.

'Trunks on first old man!'

'But Dad! Uncle Robert hasn't.'

'True, but your uncle Robert is very silly and you are not.'

Charles looked to Robert who shrugged his shoulders and climbed out of the pool dripping wet.

'Trunks I think are for the best,' he said to the young boy.

Charles looked at the older man who had emerged from the pool, his clothes clinging to him as the water poured from him, and nodded his head in agreement before disappearing to get changed.

'Great night last night!' declared Angus who had heard none of the argument and got up too late to be briefed by Maddie.

'Yes it was my friend,' replied Robert, happiness in his voice as he tried to just remember the good parts of the evening.

'And do I have a treat for you!' said Angus, joy almost palpably oozing out of him.

'Really?' replied Robert, keen to let his friend have the joy of sharing the nature of his trip into the village.

'Yes indeed. We've only gone and got fresh croissants!'

'No!'

'Yes! From the village. A little bakery. All French it was with a little old woman and everything! It was very sweet. I even used some pigeon French!'

Robert laughed. How he loved the fact that his friend, his oldest and best friend, could make the most normal of things seem extraordinary. He placed his wet arm around his shoulder.

'Shall we go and eat them then?'

'Yes,' replied Angus with excitement in his voice as they turned to walk to the house.

'And what happened to your eye? Looks like someone hit you!'

'They did,' replied Robert with no hint of irony in his voice, 'they did.'

# Chapter 16

# William

May 1994. Port Isaac, Cornwall, England

'It's good to see you Angus, really good to see you. Come on in and take a seat.'

'Thank you William. It is of course splendid to see you, though finding you was quite a job. I had no idea you had decided to live so far away from civilisation! I'm surprised you've actually got electricity down here. You do have electricity down here don't you?'

William laughed. He had always really liked Angus. Sadly his voice had become quite Queens English over the years with it now only bearing a faint hint of the Edinburgh lilt, but he still maintained something in his face that reminded William of the exceptionally sweet boy he once knew. Further William saw in him a man that had kept his good heart, and in that he hoped Angus could in some way be a protector for his son. Now that Francesca was gone, and his own relationship with his son was as distant as it had ever been, he knew Robert needed Angus more than ever.

'Port Isaac is hardly the back of beyond Angus!' declared William.

'It is to me William. At best I am rubbish at finding

anything. Getting to the right court on time is hard enough for me, so coming here is like asking me to go to the moon! I found the coast road to Port Isaac, eventually, but then there was the no mean task of navigating the smallest lanes in the history of the world, irate farmers in their Defenders, irate locals in their Defenders, and cattle, who incidentally do not have Defenders, blocking the road en masse and absolutely oblivious to the shrill of my horn. The kids loved it all, obviously, and Maddie told me to enjoy the moment. I am sure she was enjoying my discomfort as much as I was dreading it. You have to laugh at that don't you! Anyhow I finally dropped them all off at Port Gaverne, enjoying that moment immensely of course, and here I am.'

William laughed throughout this monologue. Many city folk amazed him. It was as though life outside a city was backward, somehow cut off from the real world. To William, he had found a release in Port Isaac, a quiet that had touched him and helped him find some peace to counter his immeasurable loss.

'Well I suggest you don't do too much sightseeing whilst you are down here otherwise you will get very lost! How long are you down for?'

'The week.'

'Brilliant! And you are staying at?'

'The Port Gaverne Inn. Seems OK actually. Probably full of modern day pirates of course but the décor is pretty good. Admitted it's not The Balmoral, but it will do nicely William.'

'Oh Angus, you do make me smile. Not The Balmoral indeed. It's an ancient and pretty coastal inn and it is nestled next to a virtually unspoilt bay. You're very lucky Angus to have got in.'

'Aye. I am. You're right. I'm just a spoilt little city man in every way and simply used to my ways. You can take a man out of the city but you can't take the city out of the man.'

'If I was a younger man I'd try.'

'And it would be a pleasure William to let you. Anyway, we are all here now and, despite the cattle attack, we will no doubt have a lovely week. Tell me, the cows don't go down to the beach do they? I really don't know what I would do if faced with one of those beasts.'

Anyone else and William would have thought they were taking the rip. Not dear Angus.

'No they don't, fear not. You are safe down there.'

'Ah marvellous. Well it is fair to say that the kids love it and Maddie will be in her element.'

'Excellent. I shall very much look forward to seeing you all at some point. Good of you to come round straightaway then.'

'Couldn't wait William. I was desperate to see the house that had dragged you away from Edinburgh life.'

'Just the right time Angus, I don't think I could have stayed in Edinburgh. And this place, well, it's the right place too.'

'How did you know about it?'

'The house?'

'Well, yes, but Port Isaac too. How would you find out about a place like this?'

'Well, we called here many years ago, the three of us. Robert would have been about 5 or so and we were holidaying down at Polzeath, which is just down the road. We found this place on a drive one day and we came back, the year after I think it was, for a fortnight. Oddly enough we stayed over the way there in another cottage and so when I saw this on the Internet it seemed like it was perfect for me. Keeps me fit up and down the lanes.'

'Lanes William! They are like mountains! I couldn't do it.'

'Oh you could.'

'No, really, I couldn't. Still, it's clearly right for you. And you're settled in alright?'

'Fine, really fine. Come on, let me show you around.'

William had bought an old cottage towards the top of one of Port Isaac's many little pathways that led up from its spectacular atmospheric harbour. From the back garden, small yet well stocked with all manner of exotic plants, he could look down to the brooding harbour with its flower lined pretty lanes falling down each side. The cottage was detached and traditional in the sense that it was a simple lay out with the front door leading into a good-sized living room that covered the front of the house. Its two large and elegant bay windows sat proudly on either side of the beautiful wooden door. Behind this, and to the centre of the house, was the inner hall that went off to the kitchen on one side at the back of the house, and to the simple yet elegant dining room on the other. A beautiful spiral staircase led up from the hall at the back of the house. It looked out through a tall and impressive window that took in all the view of the harbour and allowed precious coastal light to stream in.

Angus could feel the peace of the house touching him as he was being shown around, and it moved him greatly. There was a sense of calm, of thought, an essence of which touched him and had the effect of setting him at ease.

At the top of the stairs to the immediate right was a bare wooden floor bathroom with a stunning old eggshell blue painted roll top bath. Two bedrooms sat on the front of the house, each with smaller bay windows that matched those downstairs in the living room. Finally you came back to the back of the house and the third bedroom, which in this case was being used by William as his study.

'It's beautiful William!' declared Angus, happiness oozing out of him as he did so.

'Thank you Angus. Your kindness is much appreciated. I know it's not Ann Street, but it has its own charm doesn't it!'

'That it does William, that is does! Was it like this when you bought it?'

'It was good, you know, in good condition. All I had to do was clean it out, remove some scary wallpaper, and paint it.'

'You got someone in I assume? A Cornish pirate with time on his hands!'

'No Angus, I did not! I did it myself you cheeky bugger! I enjoyed it.'

'Wow! Good stuff. If I tried to paint I would probably get more on myself than the walls and have a nasty injury to boot. Probably fall off a ladder and break the old collarbone too.'

William had used stone colours to give a backdrop to each room and then filled the walls with their pictures including many of Francesca's. So many more of Francesca's had been left behind, donated to the National Galleries of Scotland. William considered it was the least he could do given how much support and joy they had given his Francesca over the many years behind them. He had not discussed it with Robert who he assumed would not understand giving away what were now very valuable paintings.

'Are you writing your memoirs William?' asked, Angus, pointing with his eyes to the old mahogany writing desk in the study that looked through the sash window.

'As a mater of fact Angus I am!' replied William with glee. 'Francesca always said I should record my journey's through the war and so that is what I am doing.'

Seeing Francesca's pictures had already moved Angus and now the very mention of her name by her husband hit like a heavy weight punch but he noticed that William seemed unperturbed. William sensed Angus's thoughts and placed his hand on the younger mans shoulder.

'It's OK Angus. I miss her dreadfully. She was my life. From the moment I first saw her in Naples I knew. She knew! But things have to change. It is the way of things. I have my memories and her paintings and we had many beautiful years, and for that I am very thankful. She is with me. She helps me. I feel her, every day.'

On the wall facing the window of the study Angus saw a self-portrait of Francesca. It was quite a simple piece, only small and using soft colours that highlighted the character of the artist. Her hair was long, as she wore it when she was not working, and she looked out of the picture, as she would have looked in to the picture, with a questioning look that underlined her inner doubt.

Angus saw the piece and took a deep breath.

'William, where was this? I've never seen it.'

William grinned.

'Hardly anyone has. I kept it in my study at home'

'How old is she there?'

'Oh, about 41. I insisted she did it. She didn't want to of course.'

'No surprise there. She was so beautiful. Every time I saw her she took my breath away.'

'And mine Angus, and mine.'

Angus started to cry. He had told himself on the walk over to William's that he would go and comfort the old boy. He had lectured himself to give William a strong arm to lean on. Now his tears turned to sobs and his good intentions were left as that.

As he cried, and William held him tight like a little boy, Angus felt relief and peace fill his body. After a few moments Angus stopped crying, his body relaxed in William's hold, and gently the older man stepped away.

'Is that better?' asked William, a softness and care in his voice that was typically William.

'Yes. Yes it is. I'm so sorry, I really am. I came over here to comfort you!'

'Don't be ridiculous. You never say sorry for feeling raw emotion Angus, never.'

'Yes, but…'

'Never,' added William with force in his voice. So many

saw human emotion as weakness, Robert of course being one of these, and this was something that had always annoyed William.

'OK. Thank you.'

'Come on downstairs. We shall have tea in the garden. It's a beautiful day after all and we must always make use of beautiful days.'

Twenty minutes later and after a full tour of the garden that included every plant named, the two men sat at the garden table. Four weather beaten chairs surrounded an even more weather beaten table. On it sat a wooden tray with an ancient white teapot with an old and chipped blue and white milk jug and two china mugs that declared their support for the National Trust. A biscuit tin full of ginger biscuits accompanied the tea.

'It was always Fracesca's bag, you know the gardening. Somehow working in this garden has given me a further connection back to her.'

'She was an incredibly wonderful lady William.'

It was funny because Angus had thought about what he would talk about to William on this trip for many months ever since he had rung him to tell him of their plans. He had thought through many different topics but was clear on one topic that would be best to probably avoid. Twenty minutes later and Angus was continuing to still talk about the topic he had thought it best to talk around.

'And her work in the 1960's was probably the making of her do you think?' ventured Angus.

'Yes, I do. She experimented much more. She let the cat out of the bag.'

'What do you mean?'

'Well, for a long time Francesca fought against being the artist she was and being the artist she could be. She had such immense talent but with it came letting out emotion and that, my dear boy, was something she fought against.'

'Yes well, with us British understandable but for an Italian!'

'Well it was the war Angus. She lost her close family. She lost so many dear friends. She had raw memories that could break most of us and she was afraid of them. We would talk about it so often and she would agonise over her choices and her dreams, but I knew time would help her. And then one day we were in Paris and called in at The Louvre as we always did, and there was Degas there, lots of Degas, and there were some quotes from him. In one he said, and I'll never forget it, 'The heart is an instrument, which goes rusty if it isn't used. Is it possible to be a heartless artist?' I think then she got it. She knew she had to just let out what wanted to come out and then her pictures took on a new life. She was good already, but she became great.'

'Wow. That's beautiful. Have you told anyone else that story?'

'No, actually, I haven't!'

'You should.'

'Yes, I should. I will add it in my ever growing memoirs!'

The two men let their thoughts drift as the sun touched their faces and the sounds of the day caressed them.

'This is beautiful,' gasped Angus, suddenly overcome by the sense of everything surrounding him. 'William, when can I move in?'

'Do you want to have a quieter life?' asked William, slight mischief in his voice.

'Do I want a quieter life! Well I do, I guess, but I don't. I mean my life is crazy but it's great.'

'And do you have time for what matters most?'

That hit a spot. It was as though Maddie had called ahead to prep William.

'No. The truth is I do not,' replied Angus honestly. 'I know that I'm guilty too of not allowing my heart to live.

My heart is best kept locked up where it does not think too much. I've got too many other things that need my concentration and I cannot be deflected!'

'Now none of that young man. You must be true to yourself.'

Angus smiled. True to himself indeed! He was struggling to hold his family commitments up with work being so busy. William had finished his working life now, but Angus was building his. There was never any time, just the promise that one day there would be time. Surely that was enough wasn't it?

'I hope to find time to be me as soon as I have that window to do so!'

'Well, don't wait too long or you will follow our Robert. How is he?'

Talk had inevitably fallen to Robert. Angus was pleased that William had brought it up as he wanted to reassure the old man, but not be seen as being pushy on such a sensitive subject. William saw the concern in Angus's face.

'Don't worry yourself about Robert and I Angus.'

'I wasn't!'

'You were.'

William looked across to the harbour. Port Isaac was so far away from it all. Here he had so much time to think. He had found that matters that concerned him took on a new perspective. It was as though a fog fell away and he was able to see things more for what they were to him, not what he thought they should be.

'Yes, you're right. I do worry about you both falling apart. I don't like it. I tell you both the same things you know,' said Angus.

'Well that's nice of you, but, and it's an important but Angus, I am moving on and so is Robert. Can you imagine Robbie in a place like this?'

Angus laughed.

'He'd go mad!' he said.

'He would. Look, I am actually not thinking about it all too much anymore. I feel released here and it feels right.'

'Really?'

'Yes. Really. All my life I have been very busy, you know? From my early life where we worked very hard for little reward my die was cast. I know you all think you are part of a new life that leaves little time to live, but trust me, when I was a lad starting out, they worked me 6 days a week and gave me four weeks off a year including bank holidays. And for the privilege of having no time left over I was able to earn a relative pittance!'

'You sound like a Monty Python sketch!'

They laughed.

'I know, but it's true! You see after the war I did something that changed my life. I took the plunge and went to live in Italy for quite a few years. Thankfully Francesca spoke brilliant English but I learnt the Italian language too, took my trade over to Florence and worked hard with it. Then I came to Edinburgh and Francesca and I worked all hours to build our future. We had each other of course, but it was hard work. Those early years, you know all about them I am sure, when you don't know if your business will stand out enough to be noticed and continue to be noticed.'

'You stood out William. I mean what other business working on major projects throughout Scotland was known for working from home!'

'Yes, we caused a few eyebrows to be raised then. People thought I was a little potty but they couldn't deny the strength of the work and clients just came. My point is that right up to Francesca's death we were both working and working and now I'm ready to stop working and I wish every day I had enjoyed more time with Francesca. I will never get that time back now. That's why it was easy to sell the practice, easy to leave Edinburgh and come here. It was the right time. Does that make sense?'

'Of course. Maybe when I'm your age, what are you? 56 eh!!'

'Well done! If only! Don't wait Angus or you'll find it has passed you by and you don't want that do you?'

Angus smiled. He had come here to help William deal with his issues. He should have known William would be looking to help him.

'I'll be fine William.'

William looked at Angus with a stare that suggested he was not so sure.

'I will!'

'Well you better. That wife of yours is a very special person. Special people deserve special love. How old are the kids now?'

'Well, Charles is 6, going on 16 of course. And little Edith is 3, nearly 4. A real cutie.'

'Wonderful. I can't wait to see them.'

'Well let's do that William. Maddie wants us all to go to the harbour tomorrow. Why don't we call for you around 11 ish? A spot of coffee here for Maddie to see the place, she is desperate to see the place William, and then a splendid day out. OK for you?'

'Well, if it's no trouble?'

'No trouble! Maddie would hit you for saying that! She can't wait to see you and I can't wait to show off the kids to you.'

'Good. Wonderful in fact! I shall look forward to seeing you special people.'

'You're very kind.'

Angus paused, weighing up the next sentence that he wanted to say to William.

'You know, Robert too is a very special person. I just can't get my head around why you two can't get around to seeing each other. I don't want to labour this William. You two are at peace with this, it seems. It's just me. I can't understand it! I love you both, you know, and, well, it just feels wrong.'

William poured fresh tea and considered his next words.

'You know Angus, when the two of you were young, you stood out.'

'Me?'

'Yes, you. To me that is. The fact is you didn't know you stood out, probably still don't if I'm guessing correctly. That to me is special. Now I know Robert is special. Look at all he's achieved. I'm not oblivious to all that my son has done you know. I can't even pick up a paper without seeing him or something related to him being in it! It's just that I've never been able to appreciate it. It never felt right and now I've had time away from it all to really see how I feel, well I understand it more.'

'Well to me it just seems mad, the two of you apart. He should be here for you.'

'And I should be there for him, but we aren't. I agonised over the breakdown of our relationship for years Angus.'

'Breakdown?' asked Angus, interested by the word breakdown that suggested an actual set of issues that had clearly caused much upset and this eventual separation.

'Well yes, breakdown. We gradually fell apart. I think it was only for Francesca's sake that we both stuck at it for so long. She was far closer to him Angus, accepted his choices and I never could. He will be a very different man without her here.'

Angus knew this. Robert was noticeably more brusque, even with him. He had less time for people. Things were even more black and white to him than they were before and that, for people who knew him, was pretty hard going. Angus's staff were always on their guard when Jones Ltd called. They knew, more then ever, that things needed to be absolutely 100%. There was no room for error or there was hell to pay, and if Robert ever got involved it would invariably lead to someone's job going.

'But he's done very well for himself, very well. He's building an empire William.'

William nodded his head, his face though grave.

'I know Angus, as I said I know he's achieved so much. And you are with him, and that makes me very happy because he needs you more than ever. Things are, well, they are never simple.'

Angus said in his head that Robert needed William more than ever, but he checked the words and stopped them from coming out.

'It's just that we are so very, very different, Robbie and I. I love him you know.'

'Of course.'

'But I will probably never see him again.'

Angus nearly choked on the fourth ginger biscuit he was eating. William waited for Angus to clear his throat and regain his composure.

'Sounds odd doesn't it, a father not wanting to see his son.'

'Erm, well, in truth, yes.'

At this William looked across the view to the dark cliffs that sat either side of the harbour. Their shade matched his mood now.

'Angus, there are things you do not know, things that are best left alone. My son has made choices and his life will be led by those choices. He is as different to me as day is to night. Whilst Francesca lived we all needed to see each other, but now, well let's just say that now we do not. Robert is evil. One day he must and will pay.'

A gentle summer breeze swept Angus's unruly hair away from his eyes. A pair of seagulls flew closely overhead, their voices raised at the excitement of the harbour below. From the house Radio 4 and it's chatter of voices made their way out into the garden. Below them a neighbour cut his early summer grass with a petrol mower, the noise echoing around the small gardens and the stone properties and walls. Angus heard none of it.

William placed his hand on Angus's knee.

'Now then, come on laddie. No need to be too concerned. Well, there probably is actually, but there is nothing you or I can do about Robbie. He has set his path long ago and his course will not be for the changing.'

'But, but….'

'I know. I've spoken out of turn, said too much. Don't you worry. Just be there for him but not at the expense of your beautiful family who are waiting for you now so come on, off you go and let's see each other tomorrow. I will very much look forward to it.'

'Of course William, that's why we are here in the back of beyond, to see you!'

Angus rose from the chair, his head feeling giddy as though he had been drinking rather too much over too short a space of time.

'Now remember, I am here for anything you need. Just call. Any time. Probably best to forget what I just said about Robert though.'

'I really don't know what you are referring to William,' said Angus, William's words running around his head.

'I know you don't. Forget about it, that's for the best. Forget I said a word. Enjoy your break, my god I think you're ready for it!

The two men embraced by the old cottage gate and Angus left in a real state of confusion. He walked up an alley and then along the top road of Port Isaac, past the small shops at the top of the hill along New Road and the garage that looked as though it was stuck in the 1950's, and then down the hill to the inn. He felt a whole range of emotions but at the heart of it he felt anger at both William and Robert for not facing whatever demons they had with each other and for not making them right. He would tell Robert what his father had said and tell him to go and make it right! To think the relationship had broken down so far that William called his son evil! It was all so bizarre and out of character.

Angus thought of his own father. If only his own father had lived he knew full well he would never have allowed such a gap to break them apart. As he had that thought, he scolded himself for it. What right did he have to judge what he did not know? He was a solicitor for goodness sake. He should know that more often than not, truth was fiction and reality a lie.

He was also very confused. What on earth was William referring to when he said Robert had made 'choices,' that he was 'evil and would pay!' It sounded absolutely hideous and so unlike William. Whatever had happened had obviously led to William saying he may well never see his son again! He would discuss it with Maddie over supper. She would know what to do. She always knew what to do.

By lunch the next day Angus and Maddie sat with William on the harbour beach eating a beautiful picnic bought at one of the bakeries by the harbour. It was delicious with far too much for them to eat but they were giving it a fair go. The weather was pleasant for a May day with the sun putting on a brave effort to convince the adults to remove their jumpers and brave the still cool breeze. The tide was out and the beach became a makeshift car park for those who had braved the tight drive down the winding Port Isaac lanes to the bottom of the hill.

Edith and Charles ran around the beach picking up stones and playing with the delights that the tide had left on its retreat out to the sea.

'God it's good to be here,' said Maddie, heartfelt relief flowing out of her. 'Back home just seems to be so manic, you know, jobs, family, demands and so on.'

'Well you're welcome to come down and see me anytime you please Maddie. You know that. You don't have to wait for your daft husband to take time off. You know where I am now.'

'Oh William, you really are the sweetest thing,' replied

Maddie, taking William's hand in hers and gently patting it.

'If you're going to hold my hand Maddie, you can stay, no need to go back at all!'

'Put Edith down!' shouted Angus, noticing Charles was holding his young daughter upside down in the air whilst she screamed with possible delight or terror. It was hard to tell.

'It certainly is pretty special,' Angus offered, looking across at the Port Isaac harbour, looking remarkably untouched given the new money that seemed to be flooding in around the county. 'What would the developers do with a place like this?' he asked no one in particular, but regretted the obvious and unfortunate link to Robert. He had told Maddie all about William and his outburst about his son. Maddie was worryingly not at all comforting, saying that maybe William had seen Robert for what he truly was. This was not helpful and had caused Angus to have a fairly pitiful sleep.

'Thankfully Angus this would not be for your modern day developer such as my dear son. They want a harbour where they can moor their large and expensive boats and, as you can see, this is splendidly no good for that. Also they want lots of access and, happily, look at these nightmarishly thin roads down to the harbour. You and your Range Rover brigade Angus wouldn't stand a chance. No, I don't think Port Isaac is set to lose its soul anytime soon.'

Maddie had the biggest grin on her face. It was so true. Money thought it could buy up the world but maybe the world had other ideas. She always loved to see a good fight back of any variety.

'Edith, don't eat the sand!' cried Angus, William laughing as the young girl elegantly stood and spat out as much as she could whilst her older brother just watched and clapped his hands.

'More tea?' asked Maddie, undoing the largest flask

that William had ever seen.

'Yes please. It's wonderful tea. You know, it is so good to see you all looking so happy. I worry for you all.'

Angus caught Maddie's eye and raised his eyebrows.

'Well you mustn't worry about us William,' said Maddie, 'we're fine, sort of.'

'Sort of?' asked Angus, a note of concern in his voice.

'Yes, sort of. It's no use putting a brave face on just for William,' replied Maddie, looking across at Angus with a frown.

'I wasn't. I thought we were fine.'

'We are Angus. It's just that you are too busy most of the time.'

'Yes, well actually William has already lectured me on that very point.'

Maddie smiled, leaning over to William and kissing him on the cheek.

'You really are a wise man William, seeing through to the heart of the matter.'

Angus looked hard at his wife. He was sure she was making a point about Robert and this was hardly the time or the place. William nodded in the children's direction.

'It appears they want to explore,' he said. Charles had arrived at the side of a small boat that sat patiently on the beach, and he was trying desperately to climb in. Edith was stood loyally at his side, bucket in one hand and spade in the other and clearly unsure whether to try and follow or just wait.

'I shall leave you two young lovebirds to decide what you would like me to cook you for tea. I suggest we pick up some fresh mackerel from the harbour if you like. It really is delicious. Leave the little ones to me.' And with that William walked at pace across the beach to the children, their faces brightening as he arrived and lifted Edith high into the air, spinning her round and tickling her under her arms.

'More, more, more Uncle William, more!' she called.

'Me next Uncle William,' cried Charles, his attention shifting from the boat and stretching his arms out to the older man.

'He's great isn't he,' asked Maddie, her admiring eyes watching the scene before them.

'Yes he is,' replied Angus, 'yes he is.'

'And you're great too Angus.'

Maddie looked at her husband, smiling at him as his face lit up with the compliment.

'I'm really not am I? I am too busy. I clearly spend too much time with my work and I miss out on times like these and quite honestly my sweetheart I cannot see a way out of it. I mean the business needs me Maddie. The work we have is so huge and I have to make sure it is all perfect, absolutely flawless.'

Angus purposely missed out the reason they both knew everything had to be so perfect, namely Robert.

Maddie listened patiently. It would have been easy to jump in but she needed to try and find something constructive to say.

'Look Angus, just try a little harder will you? Try and find ways of your team being more there for you and, and please don't take offence, please try and stand up a little more for yourself with Robert.'

His name seemed to follow them everywhere and had even made its way on to this beautiful day and this almost hypnotic harbour beach.

'Maddie,' Angus took her hand, 'I love you, more than anything else in this world. I love you.'

He leaned forward and kissed her, their lips touching and both feeling the warmth of intimacy.

'Let's have a lovely holiday shall we and no more talk of you know who.'

'OK,' smiled Maddie.

# Chapter 17

# Back to business

June 2000. Sheffield, England

'Hi Robert, can you talk?'

It was Alan Seymour on the phone and he sounded dreadful.

'Of course I can talk, why do you think I answered!' laughed Robert trying to lighten his friend's load.

'I mean, can you talk freely, privately?' replied Alan, his voice sounding very strained and upset.

'Yea I can. I'm on my own in my office. There's no one else here, just me. Calm down man, you are scaring me. Are you alright?'

There was a silent pause, the sort of pause that indicated things were very much not alright.

'We have a problem.'

'We?'

'Yes, very much we.'

'Well, when do we not have a problem!' offered Robert, trying to lessen with simple words whatever nightmare it was that they so obviously faced. He knew Alan was never a man to panic and as a result Robert's heart was already racing.

'We don't have problems like this,' replied Alan in a flat tone.

A silent pause. This was not good.

'Are you sat down?' asked Alan.

'No I am not fucking sat down, I'm now stood up and agitated. What's the problem?'

'Alfie's dead.'

Robert quickly sat down, his legs feeling very vulnerable to giving way. Alfie Adams had been one of his best friends since he first came to Sheffield and together with Alan they ran a tremendously profitable line in addictive drugs.

'Robert. Robert! Are you there'

'Yes, I'm here.'

'Are you OK?'

'No! Are you?'

'No. Of course not.'

'Where are you?'

'At The Club.'

'The Club' was the name of the bar and nightclub that the three of them jointly owned. Robert had bought it for a song in 1991 as the economy faced melt down and no one wanted to invest. Jones Ltd had been investing in everything it could get its hands on and the building that they used for The Club was a left over building that became surplus to a deal. A late night drinking session led Robert to offer the building for free for their idea of having their own club, subject to Alfie running the business and Alan protecting it. They all shook on it there and then. It had been a tremendous success with the grand opening in the spring of 1993 happily coinciding with the face of UK music beginning to change along with the gradual re-awakening of the British economy. Things were changing anyway with the free spirit rave movement that had created events that appeared and then disappeared overnight, slowly become more difficult to arrange. All types of old school and new dance music adapted and began to move inside. The timing of The Club caught this perfectly.

Within 2 years Britpop had arrived and The Club became one of the coolest places to hang out in Sheffield. The sideline of predominantly ecstasy sales was enormous.

'What do you mean at The Club?'

'He's here and he's very much dead.'

'How?'

'Look Robbie, let's not talk any more on the phone. Just get down here as quick as you can.'

'Sure. Are you alone?'

'No, but it's my boys that are with me. No one else, so don't worry.'

'And is it contained?'

'Yes, all shut up here and will remain so. We have control.'

'If we had control he wouldn't be fucking dead.'

Silence.

'OK. I'll be there in ten minutes.'

Robert quickly squared his day with Alison who would be more than capable of fulfilling all his engagements. From the office, which now took up several buildings on Norfolk Street, Robert broke out into a run. Down a very busy Fargate, past the Cathedral that acted as an oasis of calm in the middle of the city, and then on to the aptly named Paradise Street which ran down from the back of the cathedral and was home to The Club.

Two detectives, both Alan's men, were guarding the door and expecting him. Robert nodded to them. Words were not exchanged. In through the main door and there was Alan, waiting on a seat at the bar, two straight whiskies in front of him and ready to be downed in one which they both duly did. Alan filled them back up.

'I want to see him!' said Robert, panic and sadness in his voice.

'You don', trust me you don't.'

'I do!' insisted Robert.

'It will never leave you if you do,' replied Alan, holding up his hands as he did so.

'Even so.'

Time waited as Alan played with the sight of Alfie in his own mind.

'OK. I guess you need to.'

Alan motioned with his head towards the back of the room where one of the raised dance floors was positioned. Robert walked towards the stage and as he did so he saw by the right of the stage the feet of a body. Moving to the right, the body took a name and the view of his friend became clearer. He stopped. Alan joined him and placed his hand on Robert's shoulder.

'Robbie, that's close enough son.'

Robert took a few deep breaths and took in the sight of his dead friend. Where his eyes had been now each socket wore a gold coin from which blood had oozed out and lay below him.

'What the fuck? spluttered Robert.

'Yea. It's bad. This was planned and this is no normal set of killers.'

'And his eyes?'

'He was shot through in each eye.'

Robert's stomach lurched. He stepped back, away from the body, and took several deep breaths. Now Robert was very worried.

'Is that not some kind of signature killing? Robert asked as he regained some sort of composure.

'Yes, I'm afraid it is. Come on, let's go and sit back down.'

The two of them returned to the bar and away from their dead friend's body.

Two more whiskies were poured and emptied.

'Who found him?' asked Robert.

'Me. Pippa called. Said he'd not returned home. I came here as the first obvious place to check and, well.'

Alan swallowed hard and Robert placed his arm around his shoulder.

'It must have been awful Alan.'

Alan simply nodded.

'Then I got the lads down and closed it down.'

Pippa was Alfie's partner of several years. She was well liked by both Robert and Alan and had phoned Alan earlier that morning when she awoke to find him not at home.

'And no one else was here?' asked a frightened Robert.

'No. I don't believe so. If I had to guess the killers brought him back here so that we would find him here. They knew what they were doing.'

'So who fucking did this?' asked Robert, so many questions flooding his pounding brain.

'Russian mafia? Armenian Gangs? Certainly European,' offered Alan with clearly no clear answers yet.

'Why?'

'Well it's not what we are doing in Sheffield, that's for certain. We are small time compared to them and we keep a tight ship. We don't bother them. This isn't their patch.'

Robert looked over Alan's shoulder and towards the stage.

'I think we have,' replied Robert quietly as a new fear brushed down his spine.

'What do you mean?'

'Alfie said he wanted to try Nottingham.'

'And?' asked Alan quickly.

'Well, I said no. After all, you have always been clear on that being a bad idea.'

'And?' Alan's voice was raised now and agitated.

'It was last month when you were in Spain.'

'And it couldn't wait?'

'He said just a club or two and that he had contacts. He said he would prove it could work and then impress you accordingly.'

'By getting himself killed? For fucks sake Robbie!'

Robert looked at Alan and just shook his head.

'Sorry.'

'Sorry?'

Robert just sat still, his misery complete before him. Alan struggled to keep his temper under control. His friends had seriously messed up, but at least Robert was not lying dead on the floor as well as Alfie. He leaned back in his chair, measuring his words for the way ahead.

'Look, this is a nightmare for which you will be very sorry indeed for a while to come yet.'

Robert looked at his friend, anger rising.

'Robbie, you fucking idiot, we are dealing with mad men here.'

'What do you mean by we? You and I were not involved!'

'Guilty by association my friend. As sure as they came after Alfie they will come after you because your name is on the bar too.' Alan's name was not showing on any paperwork given his position in the community.

'Fuck.'

'Yes, fuck.'

Silence sat over them as they let the gravitas of the situation settle. Alan found his anger dissipate as sorrow for Alfie mixed with fear for his good friend Robert, a man who also was responsible for keeping him extremely wealthy.

'Look Robbie, you need to disappear for a few weeks.'

'Disappear!'

'Yes.'

'I can't just get up and go!'

'Well yes you can. Either in the sense that you physically go somewhere for a while or in the sense that they will send you somewhere forever.'

'Shit.'

Alan lit a cigarette and handed it to Robert before lighting one for himself.

'I'll deal with it. I just need time to find them and deal with them.'

'You can do this?' asked Robert, his eyes nervous and suddenly looking very tired.

'Yes. I always do don't I? It will just take time. These guys are serious players. I have my scouts out already and I am on it, but having the next target out the way would be helpful.'

Robert thought through what faced him. He could run most things by phone. Alison would do the rest. Over the years Jones Ltd had grown into an international company. The brave steps that they had taken after taking control of the company had paid dividends. Their asset bank was now worldwide and growing still. The model too had changed with Jones Ltd now running massive commercial property funds for investors in a market that showed little sign of abatement. Robert was beyond wealthy. He was now one of the nouveau super rich with all the trappings to show for it. And yet here, in his back street dealings, in his very own playground, he had become unstuck and people were out to kill him. What if they came for him before he could get away?

'Have you phoned Pippa?'

'No.'

'No?'

'Oh Hi Pippa. Alan here. Delighted to report that Alfie's here with his eyes missing and blood all over the place. On the positive side it appears the killers left you some gold coins!' replied Alan mimicking the conversation they knew he could not have.

'OK!' said Robert, holding his hands up. Alan took a deep breath and softened his tone.

'I'll phone her in a bit and tell her I've found nothing and not to worry.'

'Not to worry! Fuck, she'll probably already be beside herself. And then when she finds out about this, well, I mean, fuck.' Robert was sat holding his head in his hands, his fingers pressing in on his temples as he tried to push some sense into all of this.

'I know Robert, I know. One things for certain though;

I need to get him out of here and away from any connection to this place.'

Robert just stared at Alan.

'Any other ideas?'

Hopeless resignation filled Robert and his face showed this.

'No. You're obviously right. It's just, you know.'

'I know. He is, was, just the man, the main man and our very good friend. It seems wrong but he would have had to do the same if it had been you or I.'

Robert nodded and patted Alan on his arm.

'Where will you take him?'

'To the Don. Buys us a bit of time and nature will do its bit. I'll make sure someone finds him in a few days and let plod take care of it. In due course it will hit my desk and I'll do the necessary.'

'And Pippa?'

'As soon as he is found, I promise. I'll take care of her.'

'OK,' Robbie stood up, 'I'd better get back and get Alison to sort out things.'

'Where will you go?'

'Do you want to know?'

'No, best not.'

'And you are sure you can deal with it?'

'Yes! It might take bribery as well as inevitable death for the morons who did this, but yes, I can deal with it. If necessary I will get our European security guys in on it. It's just for now, you are a sitting target in this city. Get out for a few weeks, have a well earned break.'

'A break! It's not like I'm going to fucking Butlins is it?'

'Look, all I'm saying is you need to disappear so you may as well take some down time. When you get back let's get some decent security around you too. Even you are not invincible Robert. You have serious enemies in the crime world and the business world. Let me look after you properly now, yea?'

Alan had been warning Robert about security for some time. Robert nodded. There was nothing more to say. The two of them stood and hugged. As Robert walked towards the door, Alan called after him,

'And one more thing.'

'Yes?'

'Take the kids.'

'Take the kids?'

'Well, better safe than sorry. You could probably do with some time together anyway.'

20 minutes later and Robert was driving back to Totley to get some things together. Jasmine and Taylor were at school and he would phone the schools and tell the heads about a surprise trip that had just become available through a business connection. It was too good an opportunity to miss for the kids, he would tell them, would be great for their education. The fact that Robert was on both boards of Governors and a major source of external gifts into the respective schools would see the normal frowns cast on pupils taking term time holidays waived anyway.

He had not mentioned too much to Alison. They knew each other too well for him to need to. Alison was his unquestioning right hand. She knew if Robert needed to get away for a few weeks at the drop of a hat there would be trouble enough that he needed to deal with. That was all she needed to know.

'Suzie please,' asked Robert, waiting on the phone to be connected to his fiancé of two years.

Susanna Valentine was 10 years Robert's junior. He had met her at The Club and unlike all the other women he met and more often than not had a one night exchange, he could not get Susanna out of his mind. Apart form the age difference they were very alike in character, the strength of Susanna's nature taking Robert aback. Her birthday was 2 days later than his and it was her 23<sup>rd</sup> she was celebrating when they had met.

Susanna was a dynamic woman on her way up the banking corporate ladder at a speed that left her competition floundering. She did whatever it took to make her days a success and now, just shy of her 27<sup>th</sup> birthday, she was the banks youngest Area Director handling the whole of South Yorkshire. She was a beautiful lady, tall and strikingly attractive with Italian looks inherited from her mother's side. The connection back to Francesca was obvious.

Susanna was also a strong character, a lady who was not to be Robert's easy shoe in. She asked Robert in detail about Emily and the breakdown of the marriage. She told Robert he was a bully and that Emily did not stand a chance. No wonder she had experienced such a dreadful breakdown, Susanna had told Robert on an early date. Robert had thought to take offence at the way his new girlfriend spoke to him, and yet he actually found the challenge of the banter a welcome refreshment to the normality of people being sycophantic around him, not that he minded the latter of course. He bathed in it daily and it kept him dirty.

And so the relationship had developed. It was a lively relationship, one that would often see the two of them argue and explode in a rage at one another, but also one that saw them make up with great gestures often accompanied by lustful and extremely passionate sex.

'Hi gorgeous!' said Susanna, 'ready for tonight?'

'Ah yes, that's actually why I'm ringing. I'm afraid…'

'Robert! Tonight's my area dinner and you need to be there. You've known about it for months. I told Alison this could not be moved under any circumstances!'

'Yes baby I know, but something's come up.'

Silence was offered back down the phone.

'Suzie, I know this will not make any sense at all, but a job has just collapsed and I have to get over to Spain to see the main investor. It can't wait. It's me or we lose millions, literally millions.'

The theme of silence continued.

'And so I have to go now,' continued Robert.

'Yes, I understand,' replied Susanna at last, upset in her voice, 'but why not tomorrow, or the day after?'

'Because he leaves the country for his own holiday the day after tomorrow and I therefore have no choice. You know I would not want to miss your dinner.'

Susanna laughed.

'Of course you would!'

'Well, yes, you know it's not my first choice of a night out with a bunch of overly interesting bankers.'

'I'm an overly interesting banker!'

'Yes but clearly, you are in every way an exception. Honestly I wanted to come.'

'Only because I promised you a night of unrivalled passion to follow!'

'Yes, well that helped, of course. Look, I've got no choice, I have to get there and get this done. I'm taking the kids.'

'Out of school?'

'Yes, out of school. I thought it would be good to have some time with them. Maybe a couple of weeks.'

'You did?' asked Susanna, amazed and pleased by this development. Robert had rarely shown any signs of being a doting father other than in the area of provision, an area he was very good at in making money and serious amounts of money.

'Well don't sound too surprised!' replied Robert, putting mock hurt in his voice.

'Well, I am! To be honest I'm delighted. It will do you all the world of good. They need it.'

'Really?'

'Of course they do Robert. They don't see you. They are beautiful kids. Their mum is in London, a shadow of her former self, and you are never at home. Of course they need you!'

Robert let the words pass. She was right of course.

'Well look, if you can get some time, you should come out.'

'Maybe darling, if I can,' she replied, pleased that he had asked her. 'It's a busy time for me, you know that. Besides, it would be good for the three of you to have time just on your own.'

'Well, your call. I'll ring you.'

'OK. You owe me one.'

'And I can't wait to give it you.'

By 4 o'clock Robert found himself doing something he had not done for far too long. He parked in the car park at Birkdale and waited with a host of other parents for little Taylor to run out of school. The little man would be expecting to find Sofiya, the au pair, to be waiting for him so it would be quite a surprise to find his father there. It was a routine Taylor McTeer was used to with the two of them then going on to Ashdell to pick up Jasmine who, being 3 years older, was doing longer days.

Sofiya had been a godsend to the McTeer's. Emily had found her through an agency and she had joined them from the Ukraine from just before the birth of Jasmine. The stay was supposed to be 5 years maximum but nearly 11 years on she was still with them. Sofiya had grown used to Robert and simply accepted him allowing her to get on with her life. To allow Robert any more space in your head was to allow him the ability to dominate you and this happened with most people. Instead she and Robert had no relationship and this allowed them both to just get on with things without the need for dialogue.

In many ways he reminded her of some of the men back home who were always involved in some activity or other that seemed to place them above the law. One of these was her older brother and the things she knew he did sickened her. In turn Andrij despised his sister for how she made him feel. The escape, because that's what it felt like, to the UK was for the best for them both.

Sofiya felt very protective of her charges, dear Jasmine and Taylor, having been at their side throughout the nervous breakdown that gradually destroyed their mother's personality and the accompanying failure of the marriage. What came first was unclear, but Sofiya knew any woman would need to be unbelievably strong to stand up to Robert together with the ability to overlook so many things. Emily was never going to be that woman.

Robert knew that in Sofiya he had a bridge for the children to feel able to stay with him and feel protected. He looked after her accordingly, paying her far more than what was usual for such a role, and giving her an annex to the side of the house for her own to do what she wanted with. He neither liked her nor disliked her. He simply accepted her as she did him. It worked for them. They both knew what they got out of the arrangement and the benefits and excuses it gave them.

This summer afternoon though was seeing Robert pick the children up. Robert saw Taylor first, a shock of messy blonde hair all over the place making him stand out from the pristine Birkdale crowd. A feeling of parental pride swept up in Robert, mixed with the need to protect his son now from the dangers that were out to get them. Robert watched Taylor scan the group of parents for Sofiya, and then saw his face explode with a huge smile as he saw his father. He bounded up to him and jumped into his arms, both of them laughing as he did so. The Birkdale parents brigade would have something to talk about now.

An hour later and Jasmine's reaction was a cooled down version of the same, leaning into Robert to allow her head to be kissed, and walking back to his car with a proud smile across her face.

'Now then kids,' declared Robert as they made their way back to Totley through the early evening traffic, 'we are going on a holiday.'

'Holiday!?' they both cried almost in unison.

'Yes, a holiday. It's about time isn't it?'

'But what about school Dad?' asked Jasmine, an eager student and very well drilled by her teachers in the need to be on top of her studies.

'I've cleared it with the school Jas so don't worry. Aren't you worried about missing school Taylor?' asked Robert with a smile as he already knew the answer. He looked in his mirror to see his son grinning back. Taylor would not miss school.

'So, we are catching a plane tonight,' announced Robert trying to sound as up beat as possible.

'Tonight! Wow!' said Jasmine, now tuning into the adventure.

'Yep. We fly to Barcelona in Spain for a few days,'

'We know where Barcelona is Daddy, we're not stupid,' interrupted Jasmine.

'Indeed. It's good to know the education I pay for is paying dividends. We can get our bearings and then drive down to Seville. Do you know where that is darling?'

Jasmine pulled a face for her father, which was duly noted and made them both laugh.

Robert had figured that if anyone actually tracked the fact they had flown to Barcelona, they would then struggle to place them at Seville being a 1000 kilometre drive south.

'Can we watch the football at the Nou Camp?' asked Taylor, being football mad and, like his father, an Arsenal fan.

'We can visit! It's not the football season is it but we can visit the grounds at Barcelona and Seville. Is that OK Jas?'

'Yes, great!' replied Jasmine who, having been brought up in a house where both men and Sofiya adored the game, found that she was fascinated by it too. If only her school would let her play it but sadly it was not on the timetable for Ashdell girls.

Taylor sat in the back of the top of the range and suitably one off black Range Rover Vogue, going through the Barcelona players he knew from his play station game. Exotic names of Rivaldo, Figo, Kluivert, Puyol, Xavi and Cocu filled his mind.

'Can we meet Figo Dad?' he asked.

'He's playing at the Euro's son! We'll have to watch him on the TV.'

'Oh. OK. Cool.'

'Daddy?' asked Jasmine, burning questions filling her mind as she tried to make sense of it all.

'Yes darling?'

'Is Sofiya coming with us?'

'No, she will look after the house for us whilst we are away.'

'Right. What about Susanna?'

'Would you like her to?' asked Robert. The relationship had been gradually building between them and they all seemed to get on quite well.

'If you would.'

'But would you?'

Jasmine thought about it. She quite liked Susanna. She smelt nice and made her laugh.

'Yes.'

'Well, if she can get over for a few days, she might join us.'

'And,' Jasmine was looking out of the window, the gentle space and feel of Totley coming into view, 'will mummy be coming?'

Emily had lived in London with her parents ever since she went over the edge 5 years earlier. Robert had found her in the bathroom with her wrists bleeding heavily and an empty bottle of sleeping pills by her side. The medics who got to her so quickly saved her life. From that point on Emily's parents had taken her back to be with them and looked after her as she tried to regain her mind. As she had, the inevitable and messy divorce had followed. Occasional visits for the children would happen either in London or Sheffield, but for Emily it was emotionally damaging. She was still very much dependant on a cocktail of drugs and professional support several times a week to help her cope, and seeing her children was usually too much for her causing great upset for all. Taylor didn't seem to mind too much. He had no real memory of Emily and to him Sofiya was as good as his mother. They were very close. Jasmine though had never been able to pull away. She got upset when she saw Emily and still talked about her often.

'No Jas, your mum will be with her parents as always. Maybe one day you can go on holiday with her too. She'd like that.'

That pleased Jasmine.

'Yes Daddy. I'd like that too.'

# Chapter 18

# Taylor

Winter 2010. Spain

As Taylor left his home, the only home he had known all his short life, he had resolved it would be better for all concerned if he never came back, or at least not for many years to come. For too long now he had been fed up with his life in Sheffield and yet he had coped, rolled with the good and the bad.

There were many reasons for Taylor's unhappiness. His school had brought much upset with its philosophies increasingly alien to how he viewed life. Robert called his son a wandering hippie to try and insult him and fire him up. In fact Taylor took the jibe as a compliment, seeing himself as a free spirit desperate to get away from the school and father who constantly tried to pin him down. What exam results would he get, which university would he attend, which course, what grades, what career path would it lead to and what were his plans and his aspirations? Taylor had answers to all of these questions, but they were answers that would not be satisfactory to the school or to the ever hard to please Robert.

Taylor loved his father insomuch that he had deep feelings for Robert simply because he was his Dad. Other than that though there was very little for the young man to cling on to. He rarely saw Robert and when he did see him they exchanged few words. Even these were normally connected to his father telling him about the way he should be living his life and he in return pretending to listen. He had long since realised it was pointless trying to offer a view that was different to his fathers. All this did was extend the conversation to hours of deliberation that was boredom personified. No, better to just take the lecture and allow the patriarch to think he was getting somewhere. And so the relationship had floundered.

Anger would have filled many young minds. Not Taylor. He simply accepted the relationship as an inevitability given the fact that his father was clearly more committed to most anything above spending time with his children. These were the facts, he reasoned, and they were not about to change so why get upset about it? Robert was Robert and nothing he could do or say would ever alter that.

So, after much thinking and planning, Taylor had come to a conclusion that he saw as inevitable. He would never change his father, but he could change his own situation and that is what he would do now.

Things had been coming to a head some time now with the ever-increasing burden of being the son of the famous Robert McTeer. The local papers covered stories of him all the time, the nationals too. Now Taylor was even having to watch his father on TV. It was all far too much and the expectation that came with this and the obvious life path that Taylor must now walk was just too big a weight to carry. Time had been a valuable lesson and the result of this was what Taylor now knew to be true, namely that the moment had come for him to be as far away from the McTeer influence as was possible.

At least when his sister, Jasmine, had been at home things had been more bearable, more fun sometimes too.

How he missed her. She rarely came home nowadays staying in London with her life down there. Why would she do any different? At least when she had been home he had an ally. Now, with Robert and Susanna, who he didn't mind especially though she was too much like his father, always arguing then making up like children, he just wanted and needed out.

Having turned 18, Robert had bought his son a brand new top of the range Porsche Boxster in shining 'look at me' black. It was a present that was typical of the highly esteemed businessman, all ostentation for as many people as possible to see, and bearing no relation to the lack of any real connection between father and son. Taylor knew that such a gift was the envy of many but he also knew the baggage and calculations from his father that it came with. Robert was expecting much from Taylor in his last year at Birkdale and Taylor knew the university course that would follow would all be looking to lead to the one thing Robert had always talked about, namely the addition of Taylor to the ranks at Jones Ltd. It was his Dad's stated intention that his one and only son would carry on the dynasty he had begun. Taylor knew this would never happen.

His friends told him not to worry about it, that university would give him space to be away from it all and make his own plans. They did not know his father! Robert could affect the life of a specific field worker on an Indian tea plantation if he chose too. His Dad's meddling was done with such subtlety and through so many meshes of people, that Taylor often reasoned it would take a whole field force of a secret service agents to catch him out!

Taylor's thinking was simple. To complete the path that Robert had mapped out for him with perfect exam results, that he was well on the course to achieving, and going to the right university would only exacerbate the situation. Now was the time to make sure he would not be ladled with the intense pressure he had felt for too long now. He would break the cycle and simply walk out of his life, leave the education ladder that he was on and the inevitable path that it would have led to. Taylor knew Robert would be appalled but calculated he had bigger issues to deal with than a drop out son. Time would heal and if it did not it was a chance he was ready to take.

Taylor was not to be alone on his escape. A year and a half earlier, in the summer of 2009 at a friend's party, Taylor had met a girl he fell in love with at first sight. He was not looking for a girlfriend, even less one that would change his life. He was outside on the covered veranda with several friends drinking far too much beer and passing round a bottle of vodka. The resulting inebriation was inevitable. For Taylor the discovery of alcohol had seemed to come all at once having gone from having no interest in it to suddenly enjoying to excess. His body was taking time to get used to this new drug that was hitting his young blood stream.

He had turned to the lounge in the house, the French doors wide open, and saw a group of people dancing to the music that was blasting out of the stereo. Friends and friends of friends were people that he recognised instantly but there, in the middle of the dancing, was someone he did not know. Her short blond hair, cut in a very straight and chopped style, allowed her face to stand out and Taylor couldn't help but stare. Her high and made up cheeks and laughing eyes drew him instantly to the sight of her. She was a petite and slim girl wearing a tight white cap sleeved T shirt with a picture of Jimi Hendrix painted across the front, and a short dark skirt leaving a gap to red knee length tights that led down to white pumps. She was using these to dance with great energy, and dance like Taylor had never seen anyone dance before.

He had walked over to her in a trance, the alcohol

adding to the dreamscape he was now in, and stood to the side of her. She continued to dance, seeing him there like a lost puppy, but lost in the joy of moving to the latest Tiesto Latin dance mix that filled the air.

After a while she stopped, turned to him, put her hands on his shoulders and shouted into his left ear,

'Are you going to dance or just stand there like a weirdo?'

To which Taylor responded by energetically dancing until she decided to stop which was 45 minutes later. Taylor considered himself fairly fit playing football twice a week and going to the gym at least twice more, but he was sweating so much by the time they left the dance floor that he felt himself positively lethargic compared to his new dance partner. She seemed untouched for having danced for what must have been well over an hour at high energy. She was like a nymph, a mythological spirit. There was an untouchable quality about her.

Taylor picked up two beers out of the ice bucket and the two of them fell into the cool welcome of the garden.

'Who on earth are you, if that's where you are from of course?' Taylor asked as they lay down on two garden steamer chairs and, lying back, lay looking up at the starlit evening.

'Charlie Gable,' she said, sitting up on one elbow, a big smile welcoming Taylor's gaze and offering her hand to be shook.

Taylor pulled himself up and responded by warmly shaking her hand. It was small and warm and smooth and he did not want to let go.

'I'm Taylor McTeer and I am very, very pleased to meet you.'

'And me you cute boy,' Charlie responded and dropped back onto the recliner.

Taylor heard her say cute boy and was not sure if it was

compliment or she was having fun at his expense. Still, he was here in the garden with her, so he counselled himself to stick with it.

'How come I've never met you before?' asked Taylor, still resting on one elbow and looking down at Charlie, her soft complexion moving him deeply. Charlie knew he was looking at her and she let him do just that as she fixed her eyes on the sky above.

'Wasn't the right time I guess.'

The answer stalled Taylor for a moment. What did it mean? She really was from another planet! After a few moments of silence that underlined Taylor trying to come up with a clever line that was not forthcoming, Charlie got up on one elbow again and looked at Taylor.

'You're quite a good looking guy aren't you!'

'Well, I, you know.'

'I do know. Your long wavy dusty blond hair,'

'Shit,' thought Taylor who had spent ages washing it then straightening it before coming out. Sweat always made his hair curl.

'Is just so wonderful. I could spend hours running my fingers through it.'

'You could?'

'Yes Taylor, I could and I almost certainly will assuming you interest me and don't turn out to be some sad rich boy caught up in nothing but yourself.'

'Oh, I'm not that!'

'Really?' Charlie replied, a cheeky glint in her eyes. 'Tell me about yourself then.'

And so Taylor had done just that recounting all that was good and bad and leaving out nothing. Normally he would hide certain things, particularly the wealth of his father, but speaking to Charlie he had felt there was no need to hide anything at all. And then she had told him about herself, that she had never known her Dad and that her Mum had died when she was 10. There was no other family to look after her and so she had gone through several foster homes before ending up next door to the party household 4 years ago. She wasn't bitter, rather philosophical, accepting her fate but determined to twist it for her future. She deserved that didn't she? Taylor knew, as her story had unfolded before him, that he had found someone who would understand him.

As they spoke their path began, their future road started here. The party had ended and everyone had either bedded down for the night or left, but not Charlie and Taylor who stayed put in their garden furniture and deep conversation. They spoke until sunrise and then, as Charlie stood at her front gate watching Taylor walk down the road to catch a bus home, the warmth of new love just seemed to have come and taken over.

From that day to this they had never failed to spend several hours together and here in the winter of 2010, Taylor was making his way to her to run away together. They were now both 18 and could therefore in their own minds do what they wanted. Charlie, or Charlotte to her foster parents, had been ready to run away all her life. Meeting Taylor was a dream. Here was a fellow traveller with whom there was excitement to be had and dreams to be made true.

So, as he pulled up outside Charlie's house four hours later in the old VW Beetle van he had just bought off a house bound hippie who wanted his van to go to a good cause, Taylor felt a lightness of spirit he had not felt for a long time. The Porsche had finally proven useful giving him much needed funds to add to the McTeer / Gable travelling fund.

Charlie skipped down the drive of her house off Abbeydale Road. Her foster parents were both out at work and Charlie had taken the liberty of lightening them of various household appliances including the kettle, toaster, and coffee percolator. She left a lovely note, thanking them for the last 4 years, after all they had been nice people, a little distant, but nice. Further she left £50 saying she hoped this would cover the items taken, and that the decision to leave had been taken rather quickly, hence their being no time to go to the shops! She knew it was cheeky but it was done now and it made Taylor laugh a lot.

The two of them had talked so much about what would make them happy, which dream would most suit them, and they had kept coming back to sunshine, café culture and music. Taylor had a thing about Seville, a place he had visited for several weeks as a child, and when googling the area Charlie had fallen in love with it too. Seville offered a place of culture and history, as well as being wonderfully close to the ocean and a place for them to follow one of their favourite pastimes which was surfing. And so it was decided that they would one day set up a café of their own in Seville. They would immerse themselves in the local culture, and live as new people without anybody's expectations and pre conceived ideas of who they should be upon their shoulders other than their own.

The plan had been for the move abroad to happen after 'A' levels had been completed and their dues repaid to parents and schools. However after one long drinking session following a crazy party, the two of them had decided waiting was just going to cramp them by painting them further into a corner that they had no intention of going in to. And so the summer escape trip that was to see them travel across France, through Barcelona and down into Southern Spain, settling in Seville for simple jobs that would give them much needed experience and contacts and handily help fund their café running dream, became a winter plan instead.

Charlie had looked into what was required and thankfully the need for visas had been lifted for UK nationals so the passports were enough! They both conveniently lost their passports so that brand new ones with up to date photographs could be obtained, which given they both looked like children on the old ones was just as well. They wanted to enter their adventure looking like adults! Cash was set aside. Secret packing of clothes was begun. Laptops with i-tunes were updated and foreign plug adapters purchased. Favourite books and photographs were added and they got themselves ready. They told no one what they were doing. It was too dangerous to do otherwise. The main problem was Robert. He would have gone mad and the outcome of that was unthinkable. Far better to do this themselves and build a new life with new friends. In time they would be able to invite their past lives into their new one. All in good time. All in their time.

The excitement was almost too much to bear and several times they both found themselves wanting to tell their best friends about their plans, but they stood firm knowing that one loose word would make the journey probably impossible. Robert would have seen to that.

And so as the end of November closed in, the two of them started their journey alone, away from a bright yet very cold Sheffield.

'And that's better,' reasoned Taylor as he crunched the van into second gear as it pulled out on to Abbeydale Road and into the city, 'because we will have more time to get to know the area and make contacts.'

'Brilliant!' declared an ecstatically happy Charlie.

'And we can save lots of euros from our jobs and tell everyone about our plans.'

'Apart from those we don't want to know,' added Charlie.

'Indeed.'

'And we can basically party longer.'

'And harder.'

'Oh much harder,' laughed a Taylor feeling remarkably chilled and free.

And so the happy journey began. The two of them heading south on to the M1 to an uncertain future, but at least a future they felt they had some control over. Their cash fund was just over a highly respectable £150,000 made up of £25,000 left over from the sale of the top of the range brand new Boxster, a £15,000 loss over 1 month that would have made Robert beyond angry! A further £50,000 from savings in Taylor's bank account made up of inheritance monies from his grandparents, and just over £70,000 from Charlie's banking, most of which was from a Trust Fund that she came into from her deceased mother estate on reaching 18.

They figured that this would get them started providing they could add to the fund with work in Seville. They would live frugally and carefully and defy anyone who would have thought they did not have it in them. Thankfully the recession of the last few years had lowered costs of most things around Europe and the two were hopeful this would add to their opportunities when they were eventually ready and able to invest.

The phone calls home that evening from a call box as they had reached France were far from easy. Robert had told Taylor he would be disinherited, Taylor needing to hold the phone quite a distance from his ear as his fathers words exploded down the line. Charlie's kind foster parents turned into bitter ones in only one day, asking for a further cheque for £100 for goods taken to stop them contacting the police! Charlie sent them £101 and enclosed a nice card with a picture of a coffee shop on the front.

Still, with the difficult calls made and the plan well and truly out of the bag, they felt even better about what lay before them. Within 2 days they were on the south west coast of France just north of Biarritz and enjoying some winter surfing. Surfing suited them, the chill out circle that seemed to follow people who liked nothing more than to lie in the ocean and be carried back and forwards by its waves.

A stop off in Barcelona followed that saw the intended 2 days turn to two months. Neither had been to the city before and the attractions of the old city and its culture were too much to walk away from. They got bar jobs and in this time began to grow into adults just off the Placa Reial. The very supportive owner, Christa, let them park their remarkably reliable campervan out at her place on the outskirts of the city. Taylor and Charlie stayed in a small room at the top of the bar from which their window looked down into the pageant that was The Placa Reial with its immense architecture and stunning interiors. They would glimpse down through their open shutters to lives below that were full of opulence and style. Down beneath them was the pedestrian zone that never stopped humming as life continued 24/7 around the Three Graces in their fountain and the magnificent Gaudi lamps, all towered over by the neoclassical facades of glorious buildings and the stunning mature palm trees. On a still night it was like looking down on to a classical film set.

The pay was very little, though they got free use of the flat which helped enormously, but the Christmas tips were great and despite a few purchases that included a painting of the Placa that Charlie insisted she buy off a street artist, they would eventually leave Barcelona several thousand euros up.

On the early hours of a Catalan Christmas morning, Charlie returned to her room exhausted after an incredibly busy and full on day. She opened her door and was greeted by what seemed like hundreds of tea lights lighting their room. Single red roses led her through to the tall balcony window where a white table cloth sat elegantly over their small window table, a bottle of wine already opened and two glasses ready to fill. Her heart was lifted and, as she turned, there was Taylor, big grin on his face, his hair tied back and looking very wonderful with a white shirt tucked into his favourite blue faded Diesel jeans. He stepped up to her and kissed her before gently stepping back and handing her a small wrapped box.

'I thought we said no presents?' asked Charlie dreamily.

'We did. This isn't a present though; it's much more than that Charlie. It's a statement of how I feel about you, what I feel for you.'

She ran her finger under the wrapping paper, keeping her eyes on her man. As the paper fell open she looked down to the small box it had uncovered and she opened it. There sat a white gold ring with a beautiful oval blue topaz gemstone that had a wonderful and dreamy intense colour. A tear fell on to Charlie's cheek as she looked to Taylor and thought about the many things she wanted to say and share, to tell him how she loved him and how he had changed her life. It was quite simply the nicest thing anyone had ever done for her. Words though were lost as for now she found herself perfectly overcome with happiness.

'The stone is a blessing for sleep and rest Charlie,' ventured Taylor, unsure whether her quietness and tears were a good sign, 'and that's what I wish for you because,'

Charlie looked into Taylor's eyes, tears now streaming down her cheeks.

'Because?'

'Well, because, quite simply, I love you Charlie Gable.'

And that was that. Sobs of joy followed as she fell into Taylor's arms. After several minutes of uninterrupted sobbing Taylor gently asked,

'Are you OK baby?'

'I'm happier than I have ever been in my life Taylor. Please don't ever let go.'

Taylor smiled at his love, pulling her towards him and

kissing her on her soft forehead. He then wrapped his arms around her and held her tight, kissing her head constantly as he did so. He had no intention of ever letting her go. She had become his life and he loved her dearly.

As the cold weather descended over the Catalan capital, Taylor and Charlie said their good byes to the many friends they had made in such a short space of time, and headed south for their destination of Seville. Christa had got a friend lined up to give them bar work, which would again add to the 'dream' pot. As they set off from Barcelona, a long drive ahead of them, they talked through their plans.

'How old were you when you went to Seville?' asked Charlie who had only left England once, and that was to Paris on an arts trip a year earlier.

'I must have been around 8 or 9,' replied a very happy Taylor, a happiness that had not left him since Charlie had jumped in the camper van back in November in a cold and wintry Sheffield. He felt free for the first time in his life.

'And tell me again about that holiday babe, everything you can remember.'

It was a story Charlie had heard many times before, but normally just snippets of it. She wanted to hear on this journey the full version.

'Well, we hardly saw Dad as a rule, as you know, but that summer, for some reason, he took time off and we had three weeks over here in Spain. We flew into Barcelona, I don't really remember that bit, and then the rest of the time down in Seville, just Jas, me and him.'

'Why the holiday, the time set aside?'

It was a question that had perplexed him and Jasmine for many years. Why, in the middle of their childhood, had Robert turned dutiful father, only to return to normal service when they had gotten back home.

'We don't know! It was weird, but good weird. I think he just had a moment, a guilty moment no doubt, where he thought he would try being a parent, and so for those 3 weeks we all had glimpses of what it could have been like. We stayed in this pretty amazing hotel called Alfonso the 12th ish or something like that. It's far too posh for you and me,'

Charlie hit him suitably hard on his upper arm.

'We will go in and visit anyway. What's the worse that can happen!' laughed Taylor, rubbing the throbbing arm that was also holding the steering wheel.

'You'll find out you are still posh enough to fit in!'

Taylor smiled. He had been working hard on slowly breaking up any airs and graces that still clung to him. The south Sheffield accent that he had helped a little, albeit he had to remember to make it sound broader than it was.

'Anyway, this hotel had everything and Dad must have paid a fortune. Jas and I would spend hours just exploring the place whilst Dad did his business stuff.'

'I thought you said he took a break.'

'Well as much as Dad could take a break. This is Dad we are talking about! He was on his phone a lot, I remember that. Anyway, Seville was just amazing. We were there in June and it was hot.'

'June! He took you out of school?'

'Yes. Amazing isn't it.'

'More than amazing Taylor. He was up to something.'

'Probably, but to be honest we were just happy to have him, to have each other and play happy families.'

Charlie stroked Taylor's neck. She had never liked Robert who she found condescending, short tempered, rude and, worst of all, a Tory. Still, he was Taylor's father and he was the only father he would have. She reasoned it was not her place to ruin this memory so she backed of.

'We would wander the streets aimlessly, jumping in and out of the shade that we could find. Every street corner had open-air cafes and there was always some festival or other on. Even as a child it was so alive to me, you know?'

'Yea I know. I can't wait. And what did you do, you know, you were there 3 weeks!'

'Well it's a long time ago now and mostly I just remember laughing, a lot. You can imagine with my Dad that remembering a time when we laughed a lot would stand out!'

'It's OK. We'll get therapy for you when we can afford it,' replied Charlie laughing. It was so good that they both had issues with their upbringing. It helped them understand each other.

'Jas and me would play in the pool for hours. We'd run around the hotel and its gardens, full of real orange trees! In fact that's Seville! Full of real orange trees! The hotel, the 13th! It's the 13th!'

'What is?'

'The hotel, Alfonso the 13th, I remember now.'

Charlie laughed. It was so cute seeing Taylor get so excited about remembering such a small detail. The memories of Seville were clearly very special to him.

'Well-done sweetheart. You have a memory that works!'

'I thank you!'

'And your Dad? Did he spend any time with you really?'

'Well that's the thing. He did, he actually did. We took a car out lots of days. Went to the coast. Took boat trips. Had lots and lots of meals. Even Uncle Angus came out for a few days.'

'Angus came out? I thought you said it was just the three of you?'

Charlie was well versed in Taylor's family and extended connections. She had even met Angus a few times and found it difficult to believe the timid, kind and jolly faced man she met, was the Managing Partner of some high powered law firm, let alone Robert's alleged best and oldest friend. They seemed so very different.

'Well, you know, Angus just doesn't seem to count. He

251

is always there. He came out on some business, as always of course! Story of my life with Dad. Always even with pleasure there has to be some business. Mind you Angus is fabulous and I remember laughing with him so much on that holiday. I'm far closer to him than Dad as you know. I mean, he's always been there for me, ringing me often to check I'm OK. Being like my, well,'

'Like a Dad sweetheart, like a proper Dad! Yea, I like Angus too. He's sweet.'

'He is. I've known him forever and he has always shown an interest in me for me. Unlike monkey nuts!'

'Well, at least you had a Dad to be upset with.'

Taylor did not reply other than to lean over with his left hand and squeeze her right thigh. Charlie never knew her Dad and when her Mum died at just 32, she left her 10-year old daughter with a brother who would not have her. Instead she spent her formative teenage years living within different foster homes. Thankfully these were all in Sheffield and the last one had given her some stability. Taylor fully appreciated the fact that he had parents and he had consoled Charlie on this many times.

'Your Mum, she would be so proud of you baby.'

'She is proud of me,' replied Charlie with a solid assurance.

'Yea, she is!'

Taylor and Charlie had spoken often about spirits, of life and of death. Charlie felt her mother with her, by her side. She told Taylor that she knew the moment she saw him that they would be together because her Mum gave her peace that it was right. Such thoughts were like a foreign language to Taylor, although he did have a sense of destiny. From a young age he had often stopped and thought about what was round him. He was very aware of space and light and a heightened sensation of time moving around him. He had never talked about these things until he met Charlie of course. Now they loved to talk about chance and fate, and the inexorable truths that followed them all the time. It was their language, their truth and their safe place.

'So your Dad played Dad for 3 weeks and you got your love for Seville. Why he did it will have to be one of the those great unsolved mysteries!'

'Jas thinks he was on the run from something.'

'Jas said this!' replied Charlie, surprised. She had met Jasmine many times now and really liked her. She was so much the opposite of Robert it was untrue. She was softly spoken, very kind in her nature, open in her outlook, and not at all career focussed. The thought of Jasmine thinking her father was involved in less than savoury matters was quite interesting and probably almost certainly the truth of the matter.

'Yep! Knowing Dad he was more likely to be on the charge after something. 'Anyway, whatever it was, it gave all three of us something positive to remember and as you say, at least I've got that.'

They spoke about Seville, and in particular summer in Seville, the whole of the journey south, and yet it was a late January day in winter that they entered the city. Still with temperatures over an average of 10 degrees centigrade, and with most days blessing them with sunshine, the two thought they had probably found heaven. They had loved the boldness of Barcelona, it's size, liveliness, the architecture of Gaudi and Montaner, the madness of a city that considered itself to have everything it needed, and was probably right! Here in Seville they found a different pace, a place built on art and culture that despite its size, and Seville is heavily populated, managed to make you feel you were in a smaller place.

The contact of Christa's was a man called Raimon Rodriguez who ran many bars, restaurants and hotels all over Seville. Christa had spoken highly of the two young English adventurers and Raimon was only too happy to have them. He employed many travellers feeling they gave his places a cosmopolitan feel. Further he found them accommodation in San Bernardo in an apartment just off the Calle De Enramadilla. It was very similar to the apartment they had been given in Barcelona being at the top of the block and being very small. However for the two of them it was perfect. From the windows it looked west over the green areas of Parque Maria Luisa and from there over to the river and on to the West Bank.

Little contact was made with home other than the occasional telephone call to friends and family. They only ever used landlines for fear of Robert somehow or other having them traced. They were both very protective of the dream that they were building and too afraid that to share where they were and what they were doing would affect this. However Taylor did confide in Jasmine who he trusted entirely and loved absolutely. She would not betray his confidence and the two kept in touch at least once a week. Jasmine was 3 years older than Taylor and had always been very close to their mother Emily. Emily had experienced a dreadful breakdown and Robert, as the marriage had broken down, had been given custody of both children. By the time Jasmine was 14, Emily had been able to work through a lot of her difficulties and Robert did not stand in the way of Jasmine going to see her down in London where she lived in an apartment near her parents. Their bond had grown and as soon as Jasmine had passed her A levels, she had gone to London to study where she lived near Emily. Here the two of them were able to begin to rebuild on their lost years.

Taylor had joined his sister on a few trips to London but somehow the bond between mother and son remained broken. Emily saw too much in young Taylor's face that reminded her of Robert and there was an air of suspicion that what was in the father would be in the son. This was a line of thought that was not helped when Robert let slip to Emily by phone one night that he had earmarked Taylor to step into his shoes in Jones Ltd. Taylor took the rebuttal from his mother in his stride. He could never really remember ever knowing her and clearly it was not going to happen now. Jasmine told him to be patient. Taylor told Jasmine not to worry on his account. It was what it was.

Jasmine had gone straight to The London School of Fashion where she met, for her, many fabulous people who inspired her greatly and gave her confidence and happiness away from home in Sheffield. Now having finished her course she was working for Alistair McKay in Chelsea and enjoying herself. She had stayed living in the same apartment, which she shared with a friend, just a few streets away from Emily in South Kensington. She saw her father infrequently. Normally this would be on her birthday and just before Christmas when he would arrive absolutely full of himself and like a whirlwind, and would take her out for dinner to The Ritz. Robert did not know how to do ordinary. He would ask her about Taylor and she would just smile and tell him that when Taylor wanted to talk to him he would do so in his own time.

'Just give him space Dad. He deserves that doesn't he?'

'No. Yes. I guess,' would reply Robert, a glazed look across his eyes that betrayed the hurt he was feeling.

Over the next year Taylor and Charlie set about working hard and adding to their bank balances, whilst looking every hour they could spare for where they wanted to set up a café. They both loved the idea of being by the water, but with prices so high on the East Bank, they started to look across the river. Here they found and fell in love with Triana, a traditionally working class area famous for its bull fights and flamenco artists. Ancient cobbled streets, beautiful architecture and with a strong gypsy contingent dominating the area, Taylor and Charlie began to dream of finding a place here. In time they set their hearts on being on the riverside along the Calle Betis, blessed with glorious views of Seville's many towers and belfries. There could be little better to do than to sit there, by the river, with a drink and watch the hours and the Sevillian's just pass by.

The two young entrepreneurs and dreamers placed their details with several estate agents saying they were prepared to rent or buy, with their preference being to buy a café with potential on the waterfront overlooking the Rio Guadalquivir. Prices were too high but they hoped for a miracle that something might just come through.

2 years passed and Charlie and Taylor built on their command of the Spanish language, added to their many friends and connections and most importantly added to their pot of money. They would take their short holidays in Western Andalucia away from the tourists that would flock to Cadiz. Here the Atlantic would power into the shores giving perfect waves for surfers to find their rhythm. They would travel, as ever, in their trusted camper van and sleep out under the stars. Here they would meet many fascinating people and make so many new friends. Beach parties would stretch late into the night as music and chatter entwined.

Amazingly during this period property prices had continued their fall. The world had been undergoing a long recession and Seville was not immune to it. However with business costs and running costs being so high, particularly the costs of food and energy, and as their experiences working with Raimon had shown, they began to accept they would have to lower their expectations. They had seen many properties over this period, many too expensive for them, but each with something that just didn't feel right. Charlie was definite that they must not accept anything but that which appealed to their heart and head 100%.

'We will know when we have found our café Taylor. We won't need to ask – we will just know!' she had told Taylor during a despondent night after yet another unsuccessful viewing.

And then in late March 2013 an agent came back to them with a proposition. An old lady was selling a café towards the middle of Calle Del Betis. It was in the location they wanted and had a view to match. The café was, along with many properties in this area, in need of some renovation, but with the Calle Pely y Correa area around the back of the property, the area was full of nostalgia and potential. They had no hope of being able to truly afford it but they could not pass up the chance to view.

They visited the café, called Casa Ana after the oldest church in Seville which was just a short walk away and was called the Iglesia de Santa Ana. It was Triana's most popular place of worship and at the centre of the community. Casa Ana seemed to have all of this life too and without meaning too, they immediately fell in love with it. It was very traditional and relatively small compared to many cafes on the riverside, but it was a treasure. The front was double bayed with a large doorway in the middle. There was a private area outside the front with old wooden tables and chairs and a covered pergola for those wanting to enjoy the view. It was of the same relatively small width as the front of the café. Inside its walls were decorated with numerous pictures of flamenco artists, bullfighters and sailors. There was a palpable sense of many years of Seville living in the place, its walls reflecting the people who had frequented the little Casa Ana and Triana. As you walked through the long thin café it finally opened out into a wider area with, in the corner, a lifted area, almost stage like, upon which there was nothing.

'What is this used for?' asked Taylor of the middle aged and very expensively dressed and reserved Spanish agent who had come to show them around. He seemed a peculiarly rich estate agent to be showing them around an old café and Taylor was not warming to him.

'It is for performance. You know, flamenco!' He announced this as though presenting an actual performance.

Charlie's grin, that was already aching because of how much she was enjoying herself, got even wider. Since they had been in Seville she had gained something of a reputation as a dancer. The flamenco, very Spanish yet uniquely Andalusian, had entranced them both and here was a place that seemed rooted in the tradition.

Finally, at the back of the cafe were two small doors with tiny windows of different colours from top to bottom.

'May I?' asked Taylor, checking it was OK to open them.

'Indeed, it all comes with the place.'

Taylor gently opened the doors to reveal a delightful courtyard area, covered in flowerpots on the floor and fastened on to the walls, and each overflowing with beautiful flowers. The patio walls were immaculately whitewashed, contrasting with the colourful display of geraniums and carnations in age-old terracotta pots, many of them cracked. Incredible scents of early blooming jasmines filled the air.

Taylor caught Charlie's eye. She was beside herself with joy. Taylor's heart leapt in response. They were finally onto something. This was a gem of a building, stuck in time in a place of history and beauty. Maybe the magic had at last happened.

Back inside, the kitchens sat behind the bar towards the rear of the building and they found them to be small yet tidy and more than adequate. There was also an access area out to the courtyard at the back, which in a hot sticky Seville working kitchen was a real bonus.

Just before the entrance to the kitchen door was a door marked private which led through to the personal quarters on the first floor. The three of them, the excited young couple and the aloof estate agent, walked up the tight stairs and through the entrance lobby at the top. From here you were led through to the living area that sat at the side of a small kitchen that wonderfully overlooked the courtyard. Then on and through to a small internal hall area. From here two small bedrooms rested with an even smaller bathroom sat in the middle of them. The whole of the living quarters were in dark ornate wood, most of it with highly detailed carvings. On the walls were scores of pictures of scenes from around Seville. Charlie was in heaven. As she walked through the apartment she let her left hand just drift across it and gently touch things, letting the sense of time and calm touch her.

Throughout the viewing an old lady had sat in the corner of the café by the door, half looking out of the window and half following the young English couple as they had made their way around. She had a look of a long life written across her sun-weathered face and she showed no expression other than the one that sat on her face all day long.

As Taylor and Charlie walked back out towards the main entrance Taylor turned to the old lady and asked in Spanish,

'Excuse me but may I ask, is this yours?'

The lady smiled slightly and nodded.

'It is beautiful,' Taylor responded.

'Have you lived here long?' asked Charlie.

Again the lady nodded.

'Wow,' said Charlie to the old lady who had now lifted her face to the young lady, 'it is the most beautiful place I have ever been to in my life.'

'So you like it?' asked the agent.

Charlie looked at Taylor. He had specifically told her that no matter how much she liked it that she should keep these feelings as hidden as possible. The property was already well over budget at €575,000 which would mean at best a mortgage, that they did not want, would be required. They would never have come to such an expensive place but the agent had insisted saying he knew it was too much for them, but that they should come.

Taylor had hesitated but Charlie had insisted. So they had come.

'Like it? I love it!' answered Charlie, far too quickly and far too enthusiastically!

Taylor smiled. Their cool card now out of the question he had to bring in some realism.

'Now look Senor Villa…'

'Didac, please senor.'

'Right, Didac. OK, here's the deal. We know this property is not even officially on the market and that price negotiation is probably out of the question.'

Senor Villa just smiled.

'Well my point is,' Taylor caught sight of Charlie's face, so happy and so pure. He wanted to kiss her there and then. 'Yes, erm, that our point is, this property is very much us, but very much too much for us without a mortgage, which we will probably not get for the size we need and even if we wanted to, which, of course, we do not, imagine such a huge debt in these days of difficult credit.'

'So you don't want it? asked Senor Villa, in a voice that suggested he knew he had them.

'Well we would need to discuss that but,'

'We want it!' offered Charlie, being of no use whatsoever to the bargaining position Taylor was trying to engineer. Coupled to this Taylor was also counselling himself that they had always said they would not start the business with a large mortgage. It was too much of a risk.

'Of course we want it, but we cannot afford it!' Taylor declared.

Taylor smiled apologetically at Charlie.

'I see your problem Senor. The question is what would be the right price for this property?'

'I guess the one you have it on for?' replied Taylor quizzically.

'Ordinarily yes, but this is no ordinary sale.'

Charlie and Taylor exchanged glances. They were in the middle of something here and were both at a severe disadvantage as neither had a clue as to what it was.

'Not an ordinary sale?' ventured Taylor.

'No, not an ordinary sale,' the old lady had spoken. Her voice was rich and warm.

'Why do you like Café Ana so much?' she asked in a deep and low voice.

'Well,' replied Charlie, 'we've been looking for the right place for the last 3 years. We wanted a place we could call our own; a place that was already special and that we could add something to for years to come. This place seems to be old Seville encapsulated all together. You can feel it can't you?'

The old lady smiled and again nodded. She then looked to the agent, nodded, smiled at Taylor and Charlie, and then stood and walked heavily and slowly past them to the back of the Café, through the small door marked private, and up into the private residence.

All three watched her go and, as she disappeared, Senor Villa spoke.

'If you want it, its yours. It will cost you, and only you, €250,000. This deal is absolutely confidential and must never be shared with anyone. Do you understand?'

Again Charlie and Taylor exchanged confused looks.

'That's less than half price!' exclaimed Taylor.

'It is, much less.'

'But, I, we,' Taylor was struggling to construct a sentence and his thoughts were even more confused.

'Why Senor? Why us?' Charlie cut to the chase.

'Because Senora Manara has lost her husband. The two of them ran Café Ana for 30 years. This was their life. She has no need for money. She just wants this place to go to the right people. She has watched me show 30 people around this place and not once smiled. Today she smiled. Today she sold Café Ana.'

And that was that. Due process took over and by the summer new ownership had taken over at Café Ana. The majority of the staff had worked there for many years and Taylor and Charlie had no qualms in keeping them on. The café seemed to have a life of its own with many locals having their time slot to come in and be served. The team in the kitchen, led by the sister and brother team of Penelope and Toni, served up a gastronomic feast of delights of chorizo sausages and Serrano hams, several types and sizes of deliciously succulent olives, wonderful fresh salads, shellfish of seemingly every variety, eggs plain or more likely stuffed with some delicacy, soups, vegetables, fish, meats and deserts to tempt all. Nearly all was sourced locally from a fascinating set of traders, many of whom called by in person to enjoy Café Ana for themselves.

Taylor and Charlie had so often talked about their café and the many things they would do to the place, the changes they would make. At Café Ana they made none other than some much needed decoration and repair and adding their vibrancy and personalities. What could they possibly add to something that was so perfect already?

Café Ana by day was a place to relax and breathe. People would stop by and chat for hours. Others would simply come and sit and watch the world pass by the café front. Others would call in for a quick chill fix, a time to enjoy a part of their day in their favourite secret café, the Café Ana. Others to read the papers, others to sleep, others still to gossip to their hearts content.

At night it became a place lit by the sound of live music and more often than not, dancing too. Musicians and dancers were never booked to appear. They just came, their guitars and dancing shoes with them. The sound of laughter and music and chatter would emanate long and late out into the warm Seville night air.

Taylor and Charlie got to know their regulars and would

sit and chat with them, sing with them and dance with them. It was more than they could have ever wished for.

By Christmas that year the business was already holding its own with monies left over from all the outgoings to provide Taylor and Charlie with a living too. It was a miracle.

On Christmas Eve, at around 3am when the usual suspects had finally left for the evening, Taylor locked up, as he always did, and collected the final takings from the till to take up to the apartment and lock in the safe. It had been an excellent year, a year that they could not possibly have imagined. They had made friends, so many friends, and welcomed friends from home too. Jasmine had come out for three weeks that summer and just helped in the bar. Lots of people did the same and two of their friends had actually left 'home' behind and had stayed on. The Seville dream had been too much for them to walk away from having worked its magic on them too.

Taylor smiled to himself as he caught sight of a picture of a flamenco dancer on the far wall. Before coming to Seville did he even know that this dance even existed? Now it had pretty much taken over their lives! Night after night it was open house in Café Ana. Locals would bring their guitars and as the evening turned into night the playing would begin. Hand clapping would beat in time with the ballerina's feet as she danced in high-heeled shoes. Often the ballerina would follow the beat with solos on castanets, the sound resonating out and making the whole café move to its pulse. Usually it was the locals who did the honours, many of gypsy origins whose family line went back for generations. Sometimes it would be an English girl called Charlie who would rise in her heels and feel the rhythm take over her body as she entranced the room.

Taylor had gotten to the door that led through and up to their apartment, turning the lights off as he did so, and was just about to open the door when he became aware that there, sat by the far wall behind the raised performance area, was a figure. Smoke rose above the person's head and the smell of a rich cigar floated over to Taylor.

Taylor took a deep breath. It had been a long night and he was tired. He didn't need a drunk to spoil his evening.

'I'm sorry Señor but you should not be here! We have closed. It is Christmas night and you should be home by now with your family. Come on, out you go.'

Taylor spoke quickly, his heart racing slightly as this last reveller had caught him out. The figure did not move and did not speak as Taylor walked back to the light switch to turn on a few lights so he could see clearly what he was dealing with. He turned back to the figure and then his heart really began to race.

'I am here with my family already. Hello Taylor. I've missed you son.'

Taylor stood, stuck to the spot with fear rising through his body and a cold sweat appearing on his brow.

'It's OK,' said Robert, a soft voice carrying no menace, 'I'm not here to get in your way.'

'You're not?' asked Taylor, rooted to the spot and feeling immediately like a young boy again and not the man he had become.

'Bring some fresh coffee over son and let's talk.'

'Coffee? You want coffee!' asked Taylor incredulously.

'Yes Taylor, I would like to take some coffee with my son.'

Taylor again took a deep breath. He thought of his precious Charlie above them and asleep in bed and panic began to rise and rise inside him. He looked back to Robert. He had no choice but to follow his father's request.

'OK. You promise no funny business?'

'Funny business! Come on Taylor, it's just your old man here to see his son. No more.'

'With you Dad there's always more.'

Robert smiled and nodded.

'Well, not today. I promise.'

'OK. I'll get the coffee.'

Taylor made the drinks in a trance. So many questions shot trough his mind, each one with him trying to answer it so that his dream with Charlie could not be affected. He looked over to his Dad who simply looked back and waved. This was very odd indeed. The Robert sat before him was like the Robert of the last time they were in Seville together. Of course he knew Robert would have long since known he was here. Knowing his Dad, Taylor was in fact sure he would have known where his son had been nearly from the start. Not from the very start though and that had always given Taylor a sense of satisfaction, that he had in some small way outwitted the formidable Robert McTeer. Somehow as the months had turned into years, Robert, and this was the miracle, had decided to leave them alone. Whenever he had found out where they were, and he would have found out, he chose to not come out and confront his son. God knows he must have wanted to, but he didn't. And now, after over 4 years, 4 long years where so much had played out in each man's life, here his father was.

Coffee made and the patio doors pushed open to allow Robert's smoke to escape, Taylor arrived at Robert's table, placing the coffee down between them and sitting himself down.

'Charlotte well?'

'Charlie is fine. Thank you for asking.'

'Is she?'

'Awake?'

Robert nodded.

'No. She will be fast asleep, blissfully unaware of the little drama unfolding underneath her.'

Robert leaned forward and patted his son's hand.

'Drama! I like that. Very funny.'

Robert sat back in his chair and looked around,

seemingly taking in every detail. 'This place is magnificent Taylor.'

'Yes, it is.'

'And you've done it.'

'We have,' said Taylor proudly, ensuring his Charlie was not left out.

'Indeed, the two of you have. Well done. It's wonderful!'

Taylor had been anticipating many things that were about to follow as he had made the fresh and strong coffee. A gentle chat full of niceties was not one of them. He poured out a coffee for each of them.

'I guess I should say I asked you not to come Dad.'

'You did, on many occasions, but I didn't come did I?'

'Not then, no, and I thought you would,' answered Taylor, truthfully.

'I thought I would,' responded Robert in kind.

'But you didn't and, now that you are here, I have to ask how. How did you stop yourself?'

'Honestly?'

'Yes, honestly.'

'Angus stopped me.'

'Ah, Angus. Of course good old Uncle Angus.'

'Indeed. When you first came out I wanted to....'

'You wanted to what Dad?'

Robert smiled and rocked back in his chair.

'Oh you know, be very angry with you.'

That hung between them. Robert held real fear over many people, Taylor included.

'So what do you want now Dad?'

'Truth.'

Taylor considered the answer. It was a confusing one.

'Do you need a kidney or something? Am I your last chance?'

Robert laughed out loudly, choking a little on the coffee he had been sipping.

Taylor had dismissed how relaxed his father looked on

the assumption it was a show, but now he was not so sure. His Dad was being nice. Maybe he had lost everything in the great worldwide recession! Maybe he was expecting another child! Maybe it was just Seville having this effect on him. It had, after all, done this before.

'Look Taylor. When you left me,'

'Left you! I'm not married to you Dad. Oh, and by the way, how is Susanna?'

'I have no idea. I left her a few weeks ago. We are not together any more.'

'Oh. Sorry.'

'No, nothing to be sorry about. We were never a perfect match, although I loved her.'

'Susanna was good for you Dad. She loved you.'

'Until she found someone else son.'

'Oh, sorry. Mind you it's not that you'd never played away is it?'

The two men considered each other, speaking honestly to one another was a revelation.

'Look son, finding perfection for me was never going to be an option.'

'You had mum.'

Taylor saw a movement in his father's eyes. That had hurt a little. Robert took a moment.

'I did. But I lost her because when she needed me the most I was not there. I was never going to be there, you know that. It's not in my character. We both know she was better off without me. I never really loved her Taylor, much as it sounds so crap to say it aloud. That's the truth.'

Robert waited. He knew these words were offensive and upsetting. He went on.

'So losing her hurt but not as much as if I ever lost someone I really, really loved. This is where truth comes in and the need to sit in front of you and be truthful with you. Despite everything, I want you to know that I don't want to lose you.'

Taylor waited. He gathered his thoughts. This sudden love fest was leaving him no more than lukewarm. It was weird and he was totally unprepared for it. It simply did not add up with the father he knew.

'Why now Dad?'

Robert lit up another cigar, the cool breeze from the night air in the courtyard catching the smoke and sending it up into the Triana winter sky.

'Because I thought I had given you enough time to let the anger burn out. I know why you came here Taylor.'

'You do?' asked Taylor, wondering where his father was going with this.

'Yes, we both do. Because of us; you, me and Jas.'

Taylor let a small smile pass across his face.

'Well, I liked the place Dad, sure I did.'

'And the fact that the three of us had such a great time here.'

'Yes, and that.'

'Well, I've thought about that, a lot as it happens. When I figured that out, that this place meant something between you and me, well, let's just say that put everything that has happened make more sense. It meant a lot to me. I know I've been a bad father in many ways,'

Taylor let out a stifled snort in agreement.

'And I am not here to play at putting things right. I appreciate it's far too late for that. I just made sure I had made a gap in my diary to come out here and tell you what I've told you. Just that. Nothing more. I realised as time took away my anger that you did love me, in some small way, and that just maybe part of you being here was about happy memories between us.'

Taylor lifted his eyebrows at that, though he knew there was some truth in it. Robert went on.

'Why else would you come to the one place where we have a shared memory of intense happiness? And I thought to myself that I owed you the honesty of coming out here to tell you something I have never really been clear with you on. It's simply this son, that I love you. Just that.'

Taylor looked at Robert, still looking surprisingly good for a man who had just turned 50. He decided to let the comment that he was a gap in his fathers diary go. Robert appeared to be in the mood for peace and Taylor had not seen his Dad like this for a long time so maybe it was best to just go along with it all. It would be unlikely he would have to see him again for another 4 years or more likely much more, so humouring the man seemed like a plan.

'You look well Dad.'

'And you do. Older. More like me.'

'Yea, right!' shot back Taylor, aware that he had seen his father in the shaving mirror far too often looking back at him. Genes could be a real bastard sometimes.

'Really! I saw it as soon as I crept in the bar like a spy!'

'Yea. Sneaky. When did you arrive?'

'Oh, around 1. You were busy, both so very busy, but happy, so happy.'

Taylor smiled. The observation was quite sweet.

'And you're really telling me you came all this way to tell me what you just said.'

'That I love you?'

'Yes.'

'Yes! It is.'

'Then fine, great even. I mean, I am pleased really. We can all move on. Truth is I loved that holiday here with you. We both did.'

'Thank you Taylor. That means a lot.'

'Really?'

'Yes, really. I haven't done much to enamour myself to you. It's just good that I did something.'

Taylor sat across from his father with a big grin now filling his face.

'What are you smiling at?' asked Robert, an automatic smile on his face in reply.

'Well, it's funny really.'

'What is?' asked Robert.

'Well the whole Seville memory thing.'

'Why?'

'Well Jasmine always said you probably brought us here just because you had to. You know, because you were having to run away or hide from something.'

'Did she indeed!' replied Robert, wincing inside at his own parental incompetence. It had long since stopped amazing him how lies could so easily hide the truth. However occasionally, and this was one of those times, he was caught short by himself, embarrassed by his past mistake.

'But I guess Dad even you wanted a family once.'

Robert leaned forward on his chair and passed a hand over to rest on his sons tanned hands that were resting one on top of the other on the table.

'Don't ever think that badly of me Taylor, please, not ever. I longed for you both. God you should have seen me when Em told me she was pregnant. Both times I cried like a baby. When Jas was born, Mum and Dad were there and together we all cried! The McTeers in unison, sobbing aloud.'

'And then there was me.'

'Yes,' and as he spoke tears came into his eyes. Taylor could not remember ever seeing this before or, indeed, ever speaking so deeply with his father before.

'Your birth was a blessing to us all. Mum was gone and then you came. I always thought you were her lasting gift.'

For a moment there was nothing to be said. Robert had shown emotion to his son for the first time since he was too young to remember. Taylor could hardly formulate a sentence. His mind was working overtime as he tried to balance up all the bad thoughts and memories of his Dad to what was currently happening. He was straining to try to not enjoy what was happening, seeking to keep balance in the knowledge of what he knew his father to be.

'Listen Taylor, I'm just over it all now. Over you leaving and the hurt that left. Over the fact that I made this happen by being a bastard. I'm over it. I'll never be what you needed Taylor, it was just not in me to be so. I just wanted you to know that I....'

'Yes?'

'You know?'

'No Dad, I don't. That's the point isn't it.'

Robert looked straight into Taylor's eyes, the older man's eyes that had seen so much hardness, now softening as he saw into what could have been in the eyes of his son.

'That I'm sorry. Don't expect it to change anything, I'm too old for that crap, but know that much will you?'

Taylor looked at his Dad, feeling his heart beating fast and hard against his chest cavity. As Robert had spoken his voice had broken and tears had fallen from his eyes.

'OK Dad. OK.'

Now it was Taylor's turn to rest his hand on his fathers.

'Right. Good. Tell me about what you've been doing then. All of it.'

And the two of them talked. They spoke at length about Café Ana. They spoke about home. They spoke about Jones Ltd and the unbelievable success around the company cleaning up after yet another recession.

'Recession son is a tool of the very rich to rub the noses of the world in the shit and trust me, I've been rubbing!'

They relived the Seville trip of what seemed like another lifetime ago, and laughed through the memories. Through it all Robert constantly told Taylor how his son could be doing things better, only for Taylor to smile and Robert correct himself. Robert talked about growth, buying more café's and turning them into a brand. This had made Taylor cry with laughter.

'Charlie would kill me!'

'She would?'

'She would. This is all we want for now and probably forever. It's enough. Why more?'

'Because it's in your blood!'

'No Dad, it's in your blood.'

Robert heard this and nodded. He had truly come to realise that Taylor was not like him. He saw his parents in his son and daughter. The irony was clear.

'I don't think you've ever reached that place of enough have you Dad?'

'No. I haven't. I never will. Sorry.'

'Bloody hell! That's 2 apologies in one night! No more please!'

They laughed again, the laughter being like a healing balm to their souls. Coffee had led to whisky and both were getting quite drunk.

'Charlie's important to you isn't she?'

'Yes she is. I love her very much indeed. More than anything or anybody.'

'Good, that's good son. She sounds perfect for you and I'm pleased you found her.'

Taylor thought about saying it was a shame Robert had not said such things in Sheffield but he let that go too.

'She says fate found us both,' offered Taylor, opening up his inner thoughts as he did so.

'Well I'm sure she's right. Do you know who would have loved this place Taylor?'

'Who?'

'Your Nonna.'

Francesca. The very mention of her released a sense of beauty into the room

'She would?'

'She would. She was an amazing lady you know.'

'I do Dad. She was one of the few subjects you would spend actual time telling me about! A free and beautiful spirit you would say.'

'Indeed, as are you. You're very like her.'

'Really?'

'Yes, really. She would have been very proud of you.'

Taylor almost felt a warmth touch his cheeks.

'You miss her?' asked Taylor already knowing the answer but wanting to hear his father say it.

'Miss her? Of course I miss her. Every day I think about her. She was too good for me though son.'

Taylor thought to ask more but he held back. The last few hours had been the nicest time he could remember he had ever had with his father and he was not about to ask anything that might spoil that.

'She left a lifetime of journals that one day I would like you to have.'

'Really?'

'Yes, a lifetime of hand written notes. It's pretty frank stuff so she doesn't hold back on me, but try and overlook that Taylor if you can. I will leave them to you in my will.'

'Oh, how pleasant. Something to look forward to!'

When Charlie found them extremely drunk 2 hours later, they giggled together like schoolboys. A quick explanation was given to Charlie whose initial look of fear at having the mighty Robert arrive was soon dispensed by the pure joy she saw in Taylor's face. Together they showed Robert to the spare bedroom and went to bed.

At nine o'clock on Christmas Day morning, with Taylor and Charlie fast asleep, Robert woke up to the sound of his mobile phone alarm and got himself ready. He left a note telling Taylor he didn't want them to leave it so long before they saw each other again. He fastened a cheque for €25,000 to the note with the PS at the bottom of the page asking Taylor and Charlie to use the money for a holiday of a lifetime. He then slipped out of Café Ana. As he walked down the Calle Betis towards the Puente de San Telmo on a crisp Seville morning with a gentle Andalucian sun brightening the day, Robert felt truly happy. He had done something good and made something right. If things had gone badly he had reasoned he would have had to tell Taylor about how he had enlisted the help of Didac Villa to find the young couples dream and how when he had, had paid the extra €325,000 to make the purchase of Café Ana possible. As it was things had gone far better than he could have expected and that secret was one that no one would ever need to know about now. Perfect.

Chapter 19

# Jasmine

April 2019. London, England

'If art is fashion, then fashion is life.' This was the great dictate that Esther Morton had drilled into her young charges at college from the first day and the first moment that they had arrived.

'Write it down, write it down! Make it the inextinguishable truth, the guiding maxim by which you live your days!'

The highly respected and highly charged Ms Morton was the Senior Lecturer at the London School of Fashion and a clear voice on why fashion dictated much of society without society even knowing it. It was her way of ensuring her students knew they were dealing with something that without which life would become very dull.

'In fashion,' she would say, 'we have the power to change lives. We can take a person on a journey from withdrawn and sad to confident and happy. We can do the converse too if we so choose. We can dress a movement. We can even dress a nation. We can, in short dear hearts, do what the hell we want. We are the true leaders of our world.'

Jasmine had never been a very confident woman. As a

young girl she had felt very much the difficulties within her parents relationship and the break up had been almost as hard for her as it had been for them. The after shocks were huge with Jasmine having to pick up the pieces with her mother, Emily, in London, as well as wanting to protect her little brother Taylor who no one, apart from her and Sofiya, their au pair, seemed to love with any kind of real care and attention.

As she had reached 18 the choices of life had crowded in upon her. The last year at school had been so difficult in trying to decide who needed her most and where she should go next and London was the winner. Her brother, and leaving him, was her main concern and yet, thankfully, Taylor had proved a very strong young man, a boy who knew his own mind and who seemed to have much more inner strength than Jasmine knew she would ever have. And so, with her mothers continuing breakdowns and the increasing vocal pressing that she needed her daughter to be closer, Jasmine made her way to London to study a passion she did have in life, fashion.

Over the years that had followed Jasmine settling into her London life, Emily had gotten much better, partly due to the fact that her doctors got her medicines right, and partly due to time. It allowed her to get real separation from Robert and to understand that she was still young enough to live a life. As Emily had reached out and found new friends and reacquainted with old ones, Jasmine had been able to be less concerned with her mother's wellbeing and have more time for herself. During this time she had discovered that whilst she loved aspects of fashion, she did not love the life around it. Unlike the highly assured Esther Morton, Jasmine found fashion to become, to her, increasingly transient and not connected to who she was and, as she did so, she fell out of love with it. It was Alice, her girlfriend, who suggested she try something totally new. She was 9 years into a career with Alistair McKay and she was heavily connected to some serious players in the fashion capital of England. Her Dad was proud of her, which was a first for their relationship, and was even talking of his daughter having her own brands. It was probably this that caused her to take the most reflection and consider her future. Jasmine could see her life being mapped out for her in Robert McTeer global domination mode, and it made her panic. Nights of troubled sleep had been Jasmine's norm for too long now and she was ready to seriously question her choices and her future choices. It was time to change.

'You can't just give up on a career can you?' asked Jasmine, concern and worry throughout her voice.

'Of course you can sweetie,' replied Jasmine's best friend and lover, Alice.

'But I've spent years doing this job Alice. Look at what I have built up with Alistair.'

It was a statement of fact. Alistair had given Jasmine more and more responsibility, as impressed by her skills and eye as he was with her matter of fact nature, her honesty and integrity, and her down to earth way of dealing with people and business. He had been around a very long time and knew that Jasmine was quite different to the norm in the fashion world.

'Jasmine, Alistair McKay will go on and on with or without you.'

'Well, don't spare my feelings!' laughed Jasmine.

'Babe, you know we both know Alistair thinks the world of you. He's built the London shop around you, but it's your life. We know you're not happy.'

'It's just that Dad has placed such trust in me. I mean I should be committed to this shouldn't I? After all who else gets offered the chance to have their own designs.'

Alice let the words sit between them for a while, allowing a beautiful piece of Mahler's Symphony Number 5 to float across their apartment and put Jasmine's words into some sort of context. Alice had long since put up with anything to do with Robert, a man who she had to meet rarely and to whom she had taken an instant and deep dislike to the first moment she had met him. To her mind he had treated his daughter with a severe lack of love, of time and of care. These were all crimes to her and crimes to which Robert never seemed to pay. He would speak to Jasmine infrequently and see her even less and yet, when he wanted her, Jasmine would be there, dutiful and caring. It broke her heart to see it, but she knew that to step in to the middle of this and offer too strong an opinion would only hurt Jasmine. Her precious and beloved girlfriend would need to see this for herself. It was the only way to deliverance.

'Robert will get over it.'

'Will he?'

'Well, you know him best. He got over us didn't he?'

Jasmine let that go. She thought Robert would never get over his daughter being a lesbian and didn't think this was the right time to tell Alice that. She had let herself, and Alice, believe Robert had accepted them. Had he ever done that really? He certainly didn't talk about it and when Jasmine raised the subject, he would quickly change the subject and move on to other matters.

'Does your career in fashion really matter that much to him?' asked Alice, seeing Jasmine's discomfort and eager to keep her on the subject of her future career. As she asked the question, Alice walked over to Jasmine who was sat in the window seat over looking the Cornwall Gardens large square. It was something she did often from their 4<sup>th</sup> floor apartment, which they had rented since their second year at college. Alice sat down beside Jasmine and took her hand.

'Jasmine, you are the most caring person I know. You bring light into peoples lives. You are special and I love you.'

Jasmine looked into her lovers eyes and smiled. If it hadn't been for Alice she didn't know how she would have coped with all the dark days in looking after her parents, a father who needed nobody and a mother who needed more than anyone. They had taken up so much of her time and brain. Jasmine lent forward and squeezed Alice's hand.

'You build me up too much.'

'Never too much Jas, never too much.'

The sounds of the road below them carried on the workings of a typically busy south London afternoon.

'Dad will only ever want brilliance. He likes things to stand out and make a mark that screams look at me.'

'You do stand out!' declared Alice vehemently.

'Not like he would like. I never have. It's just not me. You know that. I think he is so excited about me now because he has found something, within me, which he can take and have a young McTeer stand out in the fashion world so that he can tell people all about his daughters labels and shops and the rest of it.'

Alice bristled at that. She was very angry indeed but was still trying to keep a lid on it.

'Do you want that?' she managed to ask.

'Of course not!' replied Jasmine quickly and with absolute clarity.

'So, why keep worrying yourself about what you can never be?'

Alice stroked the back of Jasmine's hair.

'I wish I could be like Edie, full of brilliance and talent and absolute confidence.'

Edith Jeffers was the artist daughter and second child of Angus and Maddie. Robert had paid particular attention to her rise as a painter and talked of her often. Jasmine loved Edie and they were very close, but the relationship between the two of them and Robert's involvement was not something that made their friendship easy. Robert used the highflying artist Edith to try and build a fire in his own daughter. Had it not been for the fact the Edith and Jasmine were very close friends, a friendship built over many years of love and care, Jasmine would have had justified reason to hate the very sound of her name.

'Do you really?' asked Alice, knowing the reality to be the opposite.

'Oh you know I don't. Well, I do. I mean, I don't but I do.'

'You can't be who you are not Jas. You just can't. You can chase that rainbow for the rest of your life but you will not be happy.'

Jasmine looked at Alice, her strong dark eyes giving her strength.

'I know Alice, I know.'

'Well that's good isn't it! Right there, that's a breakthrough!'

'Is it?' asked Jasmine, doubting the words yet hoping them to be true.

'Yes! You know when I was on the course with you back at University in that shocking first year?'

'Yes, of course. Unforgettable.'

'And I hated it the course, truly, absolutely despised it.'

Jasmine laughed. She had spent many a tearful night with her best friend. Indeed one tearful night had led to a kiss that had led to their relationship beginning in earnest.

'You were never quite suited to fashion,' offered Jasmine tactfully. The truth was that Alice had no feel for it at all. She had chosen the course on a whim and miraculously fooled everyone at interview. The reality of the day-to-day course soon hit home and caused the young Alice to have to deal with a lot of stress. She just found the whole thing too pompous, seeing the lecturers of the course as too full of their own jumped up self-importance. Where the rest of the students saw much to rejoice in, Alice just found statements that needed challenging and she did just that time and time again.

'Exactly! But what it did do was focus my mind on what I was good at.'

Alice had stood out in class from the first day they had arrived in lectures, as she was the one that asked the questions, so many questions! By the time the second term had arrived she was called into a series of special meetings to help her see that her constant challenging of the various lecturers theories was putting other peoples learning at risk. Alice called the Year Head, an amiable man with many accolades behind him, a prehistoric dictator who wouldn't have been out of place in Stalin's Russia, and promptly resigned from the course, swapping immediately to media studies at the London School of Economics.

'I've always been good at being a busy body! It's what comes naturally to me. Of course I'd like to paint the next 'Mona Lisa' or write the next 'To Kill a Mocking Bird' but that's not going to happen. What is happening is that I'm a damn good journalist. Period.'

Jasmine knew all this to be true.

'What do you think I could do?' Jasmine asked, frailty and doubt in her voice.

'What do you want to do?' asked Alice, pleased to be talking about Jasmine taking her future into her own hands.

'Well, and this may sound silly, probably even wet, but what I would like to do is to care for people.'

'Yes?'

'I have always wanted to do more, give more, be more, you know?'

'Not really,' replied Alice who had long since seen this unique beauty in Jasmine and known it to be something she did not have, 'but I know you do.'

'It's just that what I do now, it just seems, well you know....'

'That it doesn't matter enough? That it is superfluous?'

'Yes. That's it, in a nutshell!'

Jasmine stood and walked over to the bookcases on the far wall. She returned with a dictionary, turning as she did so to the s section.

'Superfluous. Redundant, needless, unnecessary and non-essential! Well that's it. That's me out of there! I can't keep doing it.'

'Well you mustn't!'

The two girls laughed together.

'OK, well this is what I have been thinking,' a seriousness descending upon Jasmine as she opened up her thoughts to her girlfriend, 'You know we have quite a bit of savings.'

'You have quite a bit of savings.'

'No Alice, we have!'

Jasmine had never spent much of her money other than on necessities. She had been able to save a lot of money and this had been added on to from sizeable inheritances that she had come to her from both sets of grandparents.

'Well, you know I have always talked about being a nurse,' continued Jasmine. Alice's heart jumped. Was Jasmine really going to make the decision to actually follow her heart?

'Well, I want to train to be a nurse, specifically a nurse that looks after children. I've been on to the Royal College of Nursing web site and it will be several years of training, but I can do it!'

As Jasmine talked her eyes were alive. This was something she was clearly very excited about.

'Yes,' screamed Alice, delight surging through her cry, 'that's wonderful, truly superb news!'

Jasmine smiled. She knew Alice would be pleased.

'I could study right here in London at the Florence Nightingale School of Nursing. It' a 3 year course and starts in October. There's some open days coming up and I can go and see if I like it and if they like me.'

'Oh they'll like you alright.'

Jasmine smiled, accepting the confidence of Alice but not yet believing it herself.

'And October gives me time to tell everyone, allow Alistair to make other arrangements.'

Alice was so excited she felt she would burst. Jasmine was actually going to break free and follow her heart.

'But, there's the obvious problems,' added Jasmine, her face dropping as she did so and her joy taking a backward step.

'I thought there might be. What are they?'

'Well firstly I won't be earning any money.'

'And?'

'Well, that's where the savings come in.'

'Oh Jasmine, you do make me laugh. We will be fine. You know I earn far too much money. I will cover as much as I can and if we need to dip into savings then fair enough.'

'No Alice, that's not fair. This is my dream and I'm going to pay for it.'

Alice smiled. The same strong-minded girl that she had met 12 years earlier now sat before her. She loved her then and she loved her even more now.

'Let me look after us too Jas. This is a relationship! The two of us?'

Jasmine nodded, knowing that her desire to please sometimes bordered onto the need to control. She saw herself in her father when she was like this and that was enough for her to accept Alice's offer.

'OK.'

The two girls embraced and held the moment for awhile, each girl breathing in the scent of the other, comforted by the heartbeat they could feel and the love with which it beat.

'And there's one more thing that bothers me.'

Alice knew the answer to this before she even asked.

'What's that darling?'

'How will I tell Dad?'

Alice took a deep breath and inwardly counted to 10. How do you tell your best friend and lover that it is best they never ever see or speak to their father again?

'I'm sure he will understand,' said Alice, sounding totally convinced of something she did not believe in at all.

'You know he won't.'

Jasmine knew how Alice felt about Robert because on everything else she had a strong opinion that she never held back on letting anyone and everyone here. On Robert she was always non- offensive and in being so, Jasmine knew she was protecting her.

'He might surprise you?' offered Alice, forcing encouragement into her voice.

'He might!' replied Jasmine, forcing encouragement into her voice too!

'How often have you thought about nursing Jas?'

'Every day for over 2 years. Truth is I have always thought about it, even as a young girl. It's what I should have done. I know that now.'

'Well there's your answer. It's your future too. Shall we go out and celebrate?'

'Celebrate what?'

'Your new career in nursing!'

'Oh Alice, it's a long way off yet.'

'Well some of it is, yes. But the journey has to start so let's drink to that.'

'OK! Yes, that would be lovely. The Queens Arms?'

'Where else!'

2 months later and the decision was cemented with Jasmine's acceptance onto the nursing course she had chosen, and Alistair McKay reluctantly accepting the future without Jasmine.

'I always knew you'd leave me Jasmine, but I didn't

know you were going to go all Florence Nightingale on me! You're Dad told me he was going to make you a designer superstar.'

Jasmine flushed.

'When?'

'Oh at some fashion show I saw him at. He had some young pretty thing on his arm.'

Alistair laughed at this. He had always ribbed Jasmine about her father who he found mildly offensive on the grounds that he simply did not like him.

'Thanks for that,' replied Jasmine.

'You're welcome. Look, it's just that you know you're good enough and connected enough to be a massive success in fashion. There's real money there too Jas for you and Alice. This decision of nursing is, well it's interesting, that's all.'

Alistair raised his eyebrows at Jasmine, asking her in one look whether or not she realised she was throwing away a glitzy career.

'Alistair, you know me. You know all about me. Why, in any part of my life, would I be happy being in the limelight?'

Alistair nodded seeing the truth in that. He had helped coach Jasmine out of intense shyness and extreme low self-confidence. He had helped her see that what she had was beautiful and that others would want that, but he also knew that often for Jasmine many aspects of being in the limelight made her feel intensely uncomfortable.

'Dad shared with you his dream Alistair. It has never been mine. Nursing is.'

'Dealing with sick people?'

'Yes.'

'Wow!'

'You are funny Alistair.'

Alistair smiled. He knew he was self centred and highly self focussed and that the very thought of doing something

285

for others as a living without much in return in the form of cash was not for him.

'OK. Fair enough. I have no doubt your grace will touch many people and when I am sick I hope to God that you are able to nurse me because you are, my sweetie, a very precious person to me.'

'Thank you darling!'

The two of them hugged. They had known many years of business together and had grown very close.

'You are a sweet and generous man Alistair McKay.'

'No I'm not, although I know you think I am and for that I feel better with myself and my life. You must always see me Jasmine, keep me sweet and generous.'

'I will. We can do soup kitchen runs together.'

'OK. We will!'

'You wouldn't?'

'I will. I promise.'

Jasmine kissed Alistair on both cheeks, held his face in her hands and gave him a huge bright smile.

'My god you're happy aren't you! Jas, I'm so pleased for you. Go and be a great success at being you.'

'Thank you. Well, I must dash. I am meeting Dad for dinner to share with him the great news! Do you think I should let him have his dinner first before telling him?'

'Might I suggest you leave it until after you've parted and you text him with the news? I suppose you are meeting him at McDonalds as always?'

'You know, you really are too sarcastic young man!' Greasy Joe's actually!'

15 minutes later and Jasmine walked through the entrance lobby at 150 Piccadilly and made her way to the restaurant, recognising as she did so two of Robert's clearly on show security guards keeping watch by the door. Robert had for many years had a driver who was clearly more than just a driver, but of late security seemed to have been picked up.

Robert had called them a 'necessary evil' when she had asked him why on earth he needed so many of them and for them to be so obvious. Taylor had laughed when Jasmine first told him of the increased security measures calling his father The Godfather. Jasmine had not found it funny at all. It scared her immensely and made her times with her father even more fraught.

Robert had already arrived and was sat right in the far corner by one of the windows under the protection of its elegant drapes. He always chose this position, being in prime of place to observe the people who entered the restaurant and for them to observe him. He was forever the showman.

'Hello darling!' gushed Robert, rising to meet her and kissing her on both cheeks.

'Hello Dad,' replied Jasmine, touched by the affection and feeling quite giddy by the burden of what she was about to tell him.

They both sat down.

'How are you?' asked Robert, nodding over to the headwaiter to come and take a drinks order.

'Oh, fine Dad thank you. And you?'

'Great! Just great. Ah, here's Blake.'

'Hello Sir. How is the day suiting you sir?'

'Fine Blake, just fine.'

'Miss McTeer,' nodded Blake to Jasmine. He had worked at the Ritz all his life and had held the position of Head Waiter for the last 8 years. He knew the McTeer's very well indeed, ensuring they got everything they needed. 'An absolute pleasure as always maam.'

'Hello Blake. Nice to see you.'

'You too Miss.'

'And how's that wife of yours, Sarah, how is she?' asked Robert, genuine concern in his voice. 'Last time I was here you were missing! They told me your wife had taken ill.'

'Well I wish they had not troubled you with that sir. That is personal and not something you need to be burdened with.'

'Nonsense Blake. Don't be silly. Now, tell me honestly, how is she?'

'Well, thank you for asking, first of all. She is in truth very ill Sir. She's in and out of hospital and now she's waiting for an appointment to come up with another consultant. They can't seem to get to the bottom of it.'

Robert reached into his jacket and took out a card.

'Blake, first thing tomorrow I want you to ring this number. Ask for Alison and she will be expecting your call. We will have your dear wife in front of a senior consultant before the week is out. No cost to you at all Blake so don't go worrying about a thing.'

Blake's mouth was open but no words would come out as a state of shock at the gesture stopped him momentarily in his tracks.

'Now come on old man,' added Robert, 'no need to say a word. It's the least I can do. You've been very good to me over the years.'

'Sir, I couldn't possibly....'

'Yes you can and you will. The cost is not a problem for me, but your not being here to look after me is! Let's say no more about it. Now drinks! Have you got any of the Saint Emilion left?'

Blake gathered himself together.

'Right. Thank you so much Mr McTeer. I really don't have the words to...'

Robert held up his hand, a big kind smile on his face.

'The Saint Emilion?'

'Yes we do. One in particular?'

'Yes indeed. Chateau Fombrauge vintage 2000 for me, and for you Jasmine?'

'Oh, water's fine.'

'Nonsense my girl! Have some wine. You like a glass of

chardonnay don't you. Blake, what have you got that's expensive?'

'Dad!'

'Well come on now. I'm here with my beautiful daughter and if I want to buy you an extravagantly priced drink then I will!'

Jasmine smiled awkwardly. She always struggled with Robert being so full of himself. It was so unlike how she was and had ever been. And yet also she admired the confidence of the man, the way he held himself so strongly out to people and spoke with such an air of absolute authority. It seemed that nothing could trouble him and this was a quality she wished she had for herself. Further the little act that had just played out in front of her with its almost Dickensian quality of generous giving that changed a life was quite wonderful.

'Well Sir,' offered Blake after allowing the two McTeer's to have their little conversation, 'we have a wonderful Chardonnay from the Far Niente Estate.'

'That's the Napa Valley isn't it Blake?' asked Robert, already knowing the answer but keen as ever to impress whoever he was talking to.

'Yes it is Sir! You really do have a wonderful knowledge of your wine.'

Jasmine now cringed inside. Watching her Dad have people fall all over him had long since become a bore and a turn into a sideshow that she found embarrassing.

'Well, I've picked up quite a bit from my travels and a good wine remembered is a treasure isn't it. A bottle please.'

'A bottle!' asked Jasmine, knowing that at most she would have two small glasses.

Robert smiled.

'Don't you worry my girl. I will finish what you leave.'

Robert winked at Blake, who almost bowed and left them to choose their food order.

As Robert busied himself with the menu, Jasmine

considered him. He was looking good for an older man and clearly remained on top form. His hair was still dark and glossy, his temples greying slightly yet his skin very bright and softly tanned. He was carrying little weight and looked very fit and healthy.

She thought again of the kind help she had just observed being given to Blake's wife and she felt a wave of tenderness for her father.

'That was very nice Dad.'

'What was sweetheart?' asked Robert nonchalantly as he looked over the top of his menu at his daughter.

'Helping out Blake and his wife of course.'

'Oh, that. It's nothing really is it?'

Jasmine pulled a confused face.

'I mean, it's an easy thing to do and the right thing to do. Blake has been very good to me, to all of us, over the years.'

'Well, yes he has, of course. He's lovely but ultimately he is just doing his job Dad, and I'm sure you have rewarded him accordingly.'

'Yes. But even so it remains the right thing to do if you are able to do it and that's very important indeed in this world.'

'And that's why,' and as she spoke she willed herself to just go through with it, 'I need to do the right thing Dad.'

Robert placed his menu down and gave his daughter his full attention. She had told him on the phone there was something that she needed to tell him and here it was, about to come out. He smiled at Jasmine with a warmth he genuinely felt. In his daughter he saw a kindness and a care that he would never have. He knew where it had come from and he was grateful to his parents for this gift. He waited for Jasmine to speak.

'Well, it's fashion you see, I can't go on with it any longer.'

Jasmine looked at Robert, who simply kept the same face of warmth towards her.

'It isn't really me. It was never really me.'

'You're exceptionally good at it. You have an eye for it Jasmine,' said Robert, keeping his voice level and his smile fair.

'Yes, maybe so, but I don't have the heart for it. I want to do what I have a heart for.'

'And that is?' asked Robert, trying to make his voice remain even and caring.

'Nursing. I want to be a nurse, a nurse dealing with children.'

Robert considered his words. Jasmine walking away from what her education had gotten her, and turning her back on her own labels was one thing; but going into the obscurity of nursing was quite another.

'Baby, I know you are a wonderful person. God knows I know that! I am very, very proud of you, but, and I only say this for you own good, nursing! What is there in nursing apart from long hours of back breaking work for no recognition and hardly any reward.'

Jasmine leaned over the table, touching Robert's hand.

'Simply this Dad, the reward of helping people who need me for that, and that alone.'

And that was it, these words the difference between father and daughter, the difference between Robert and his parents. Jasmine, despite having all the choices before her that the world could offer because of the status of her father and the money that he had, simply wanted to choose a job that had no real relation to money or privilege. That could well be the definition of irony he thought.

Robert looked at his daughter and simply nodded his head.

'I see the same look in your eyes that I saw in Taylor's back in Seville when I went to see him. You are not me and I need to stop trying to make you so. You go your own way. You will make a wonderful nurse.'

Jasmine's eyes immediately filled up with tears that fell

gently down her cheeks. Her father's extraordinary kindness and understanding had been the last thing she had expected to hear.

'Oh Dad, that's so sweet! I was so worried having to tell you this, knowing your plans for me. I thought you would be so angry, such hard work. You have so changed.'

'I have?'

'Yes! This conversation would have taken years before, years of arguing and getting nowhere.'

'And I would have won wouldn't I?'

'Yes, you would. You're too strong for me Daddy. Why so different now?'

Blake arrived with the drinks and as the formalities were completed Robert looked around the room taking in the rich and famous eating their food, enjoying the special ambience of the Ritz restaurant. Stunning frescos covered the ceilings and walls, gold lights adorning the room, opulence clear for all who wanted it and he knew he wanted it. He had always wanted it.

'Thank you Blake. That's perfect.'

'And to eat Madam?'

'Salad Nicoise please Blake.'

'And for your main course?'

'No, the salad as my main course please. Dad, you have a starter.'

'I will! Foie gras please Blake and I'll have the sauté of scallop with ravioli for my main course.'

'An excellent choice Sir!'

'Thank you.'

Robert waited for Blake to leave them.

'This is me Jasmine. This world. It's what I wanted more than all else and it's what I have. I don't hide that and you know me very well. I wanted you two to have the same world and, when I was younger and angrier, I was determined you would have it. I have spent a lifetime successfully imposing my will on people and at work I

292

fully intend to continue doing exactly that, but for you two, no more. Although in a strange way you are doing the same as me.'

'The same as you!' asked Jasmine in a horrified voice.

'No need to use that voice Jasmine.'

'Yes, sorry, that was a little extreme wasn't it!'

'I mean you have both made your intention clear to me despite knowing that I wanted something different for you both. That takes strength of character too and I respect that. My business relies on people rolling over. I have come to realise that my family does not!'

Jasmine allowed her fathers words to sweep over her, each one almost washing away the years of hurt and anguish spent trying to please him. If only Alice could be here now to hear all of this. She would be so pleased when she heard all about what Robert had said. It would take some convincing to make her believe it had actually happened of course!

'Wow! Well, I am thrilled Dad, really pleased. I know this is not what you wanted for me.'

'No. I can't lie to you, it isn't. You could have had whatever you wanted.'

'Well that's the point. That's why I'm going into nursing.'

'Touché! Maybe one day you will come back to fashion after a few years of dealing with the sickly and smelly!'

Robert could not resist offering this tantalising view of nursing.

'Maybe,' replied Jasmine, knowing it was not going to happen, but eager to let her Dad have a little victory.

'So what happens next?' asked Robert, pleased with impressing his daughter and proving the character flaws she had assumed were not there. He had changed. Cassie, his third wife, had helped him change. The fact that she was 6 years younger than Jasmine had helped him get a fresh glimpse of the needs of his children. He thought about saying this to Jasmine but managed to suppress the words. The children had struggled with the arrival of Cassie who had absolutely no time for them whatsoever. They had met her infrequently and every time he had been embarrassed by her behaviour towards them. Jasmine deserved this reaction today because every time she had met Cassie she had returned rudeness with dignity. The problem for Robert was that he was besotted by the new sexy and ravishingly young lady in his life. From the very moment he had seen her on a friends yacht in the South of France, he had desired her and chased her. And now she was Mrs McTeer the third and waiting for him upstairs. No doubt she would be wonderfully naked and moist. Life really was wonderful.

'I start in October. I am working with Alistair up until then giving him plenty of time to replace me.'

'He'll never do that!' replied Robert with panache.

'Oh he will,' responded Jasmine without any regret whatsoever. She was simply being practical.

'And what does Alice think?' asked Robert, keen to include the lesbian lover in the conversation by way of further showing his new good character traits. He would never understand his daughters choices but he wanted to appear understanding at least. In fact he liked Alice far more than he knew she liked him. He very much admired Alice Hughes and her work. She was a journalist of the utmost integrity for getting to the truth and she had developed an enviable and fearless reputation. The fact that he was Jasmine's father saved him from her direct attention and for that he was more than keen for the two of them to live together for as long as possible.

'She's thrilled,' replied Jasmine, absolutely amazed that unprompted her father had asked about her girlfriend and her opinion.

'Thrilled?'

'She knows I've been putting off this decision for years.'

'Does she indeed. Well good for Alice. How's the lefty Guardian treating her?'

'She's fine, thank you for asking. Complains about it of course and actually enjoys every minute of it!'

'Ah the beauty of the British workforce!'

As he spoke Robert pulled out his chequebook and opened it.

'Now then, if you're going to be without money, let me give you some. Let's see, you were earning how much? Forty, Fifty K?'

'Dad! I don't need your money!'

'Of course you do darling. We all need money. You can't expect Alice to support you both on some two bit reporter salary.'

'She does very well actually.'

'What, on the salary of a left wing paper! That's almost scandalous in itself! Those left wing Trotskyites should be content in getting their wages in food rations. What is wrong with this world my dear daughter? '

Jasmine smiled at that. Her dad's politics were very traditional and very right wing. He was being quite funny. Everything was going so well! Maybe, she thought, this is actually a dream.

'Dad, please put the chequebook away. I am fine.'

Robert looked carefully at his daughter, considering her for any sign of worry or concerns. None were present. He replaced the chequebook in his jacket pocket.

'OK. But assure me that should you ever need anything,'

'That I will let you know!'

'Yes?'

'Yes.'

And with that Robert's starter arrived.

# Chapter 20

# Angus

1st July 2023. Thoresby Hall, Nottinghamshire, England

How old do you have to be to realise you simply cannot help someone anymore? Where do you draw the line and accept that a person not only does not want to be helped, but has never wanted to be helped in the first place? When do you stop feeling responsible for someone who you have called your closest friend and step away? How do you come to terms in your own mind in turning away from what you have seen to be hideous and wrong and yet have done nothing really to stop it happening? How do you accept that your own life has benefited from the crumbling of others, that you have accepted your step ahead as a result of another's downfall? How do you sleep at night when others can no longer sleep at all?

These questions had occurred over and over again in Angus' mind ever since Robert began to get involved in land and property in the 80's and in turn involve Angus. Back then he had initially dismissed it all, assumed it would be something Robert would have to work through before eventually returning to his studies and getting himself a 'proper' career. How wrong he had been. Robert, from the moment he had met Ronald Jones, had bought into the dream and had never looked back.

That Robert, carefree and fun filled Robbie that went off to Sheffield University, could become the man he became, was still something of a mystery to Angus. This was primarily because whenever they were together, and still to this day when they met, Robert and he got on so well. Not as though nothing had ever changed, as though they were still sat on his parents second floor roof looking across the Edinburgh roof tops out towards the Firth of Forth, but still very well. Something from their childhood days was still between them and that was special. Angus knew that he was the one soul; the one connection with Robert's past, that Robert had and needed. He realised he was Robert's thread to another life, a lighter life, a life without big decisions and power and the dirt that had all too readily come with it, and Robert McTeer had well and truly embraced it, rolled around in the dirt of it like a pig in muck.

There was no doubt that the loss of Robert's mother, Francesca Marinetti, in 1992 at a time when he was already turning away from this much needed stability, was a major factor in his friends life. It was though at that moment he went into another stratosphere of building a business realm that was already big and had since become beyond huge. Robert had been driven before. In those moments after Francesca's death he had become possessed. The fact that within 2 years his father, William, had alarmingly disappeared, assumed suicide off the dangerous Godrevy Cornish coastline, had only added to the force with which Robert worked. He had become an animal and no one got in his way, at least not for long.

Angus remembered the time around the loss of Francesca and William only too well. The hurt had stayed with him too, grief lay upon grief. Francesca's early death had been a tragedy and Angus partly blamed himself that he had not seen how vulnerable William was when he had met him at Port Isaac. Could he have seen, should he have seen, that William was close to suicide? Maddie assured him they could have done no more and pointed out they had done far more than the son who had, in her eyes, betrayed his mother by cutting off from his father. Angus reluctantly agreed with her. Robert was a man who concentrated on himself to the exclusion of all others.

Early on Robert had passed all his legal matters through Angus and this had continued. As Robert's issues got bigger, so Angus found himself facing ever-increasing mountains of work, cases that in turn made Angus a very wealthy man. Within 10 years of working in law, Angus had bought out the old partners who owned his firm, and he had assumed overall control of Burns & Co. He had shown a burst of ruthlessness himself that he had learnt from Robert and evidenced at that point that some of Robert's thirst for power had become his own. As Jones Ltd grew to become an international brand associated with immense wealth management, so Burns & Co had grown from a humble Nottingham practice to an international law firm based in 5 cities in the UK and 15 more worldwide. Angus, as a result, had become wealthy beyond his wildest dreams with all the potential to match Robert's thirst for power, but this was never really Angus. He was never the same as Robert despite his friend's attempts to mould him thus.

Angus sort to balance his choices by using his wealth for good. Firstly his commitment personally and financially to his family was huge. He gave them all the choices that money could buy and Edith and Charles had benefited so much from this. By giving them his time he had stayed close to them too. They were lovely children, not spoilt, but appreciative of their background and kind with it. Secondly Angus did all he could to give away money to social causes the world over. He never shouted about this.

He did it all privately. It was his gratitude to life for his good fortune and, indeed, he saw it as his duty.

No such duty had followed Robert. Any good cause he involved himself in he made sure that the world knew about it. In turn the world recognised Robert as a leader in social conscience, a key patron of the arts, an inspiration in finding new ways to fight the tough issues of the world. The Robert McTeer Foundation was one of the leading charitable trusts in the world, leading the way on philanthropy and receiving media coverage the world over. It made Robert an international star and he loved every bit of it. Confidence had never been an issue for Robert and, in the world he created around him, The Foundation gave him a perfect platform to shine. It had grown to a huge level built on unbelievably generous donations from the many people Robert's life touched. The Foundation fund raising events were the ultimate social invite and Robert used them unashamedly to gather money for his great contribution to human kind.

The animal that was behind all of this was not to be seen in public display. Only the unlucky got to see the real Robert McTeer and they never got to tell anyone else about it.

After all these years Angus had accepted the inevitability of the relationship, that he, Angus, would play second fiddle to Robert's unending virtuoso performances. The simple truth was that people would see the end result and Robert basking in that glory, whilst much of the real work done by Angus and his team, and indeed Alison and her team, would remain unseen.

As a friend too Angus had learnt to be extremely patient. Whilst their paths crossed all the time through business, Robert was rarely available for his friend. Often Angus would have to wait for months before Robert would turn to his oldest friend to have some social time. Calls, emails and texts would often remain unreturned. And yet when he did get in touch, when he saw Angus, he would act as though only a day had passed since they had last been together. Robert would waltz in and out of people's lives like this for all his life. He was oblivious to other peoples needs. He ran on a charm offensive that seemed to never run out. If he made a mistake he charmed his way out of it. Such a personality meant it was difficult to tell him where you felt he could do things differently. He had made the decision, whether consciously or by fear, to surround himself by sycophants. That was Robert. You accepted Robert if you wanted to stay involved with Robert.

And yet here, on the 1st of July 2023, Angus found himself waiting for Robert having decided this would be the last time he would ever see him. He had dreaded this conversation for years, if not decades, yet the fact that he had procrastinated had meant his life had suffered badly. He had allowed himself to be carried along by Robert's wave with his many plans and whilst his career and wealth had clearly flourished as a result, his personal life had fallen apart. In business Angus had long since chosen the path of least resistance with Robert. He had known from pretty much the off that Robert would do questionable things to get the job done. As the years had gone on the inner circle of Burns & Co spent their whole time ensuring that Robert was washed from the dark sins his companies committed to the clean image on view. Behind what Angus did know, he also knew there were many, many dark secrets that Robert had left unspoken. Hadn't William himself, Robert's wonderful father, told Angus as much all those years earlier? Angus knew he was tainted, indeed haunted, by not acting, by not challenging his friend, by accepting the rewards of a life that he now despised. He was disgusted with himself, with the despicable art of inaction.

Angus's wife Maddie, the one and only love of his life, had stopped waiting for her 'old' Angus to return and had simply one day left him. It was a desperate moment 6 years previously when he had returned home from yet another business meeting in New York only to find Maddie had gone and in her place left a note standing easily against the teapot in the kitchen.

*'Angus, enough is enough. I am too tired of constantly trying to be more than an afterthought to you. No more.'*

At this Angus had burst into tears, long uncontrollable sobs that seemed to wrench out the very insides of him. Maddie was the centre of his life. He loved her with every part of his being and yet he had been unable to separate the needs of his career with the needs of his life.

*'I've left you Angus. Maybe not forever, but certainly for now. You are a special man, but you have lost your way. I have come to see that I cannot help you anymore by being with you. My hope is that I can help you by giving you time on your own. You will always be my love Angus. Don't cry too hard. Your, Maddie XX'*

Of course Angus had cried too hard and he fell into a pit of self-deprecation and despair. He felt his children too now regarded him with inevitable pity and whenever he was with them he felt their eyes studying him with sympathy, siding as they did so, or so he thought, with Maddie. He didn't blame them. He agreed with them!

Angus had just turned 60 and as he waited to 'celebrate' the same milestone with Robert he knew he needed in the years he had left, to get some of himself back and to get Maddie back. He deserved that. They deserved that! Ejecting Robert from his life today would be another step towards getting Maddie back and in her eyes, he knew, the most important step of showing that he, Angus, could truly change.

The two men had arranged to meet at Thoresby Hall,

one of the old celebrated stately homes that had escaped the Reclamation Movement and the Laws that had followed. Many properties had been forcibly converted into apartments, apartments that had then been bought mainly at a massive premium, but a premium that bought respite from crowded towns and cities. Some Stately Homes, such as Thoresby, had escaped the purge as their owners were fortunate to be blessed with enough money to pay the private members club levy. The fee bought sanctuary for themselves and those who were lucky enough to have enough money to pay their fees and join them. Such privileges were easy to men like Robert and Angus.

'Hello Angus!' called Robert jovially as he arrived and made his way through the members lounge to the specially chosen private corner Angus had seated himself in. It always took Robert a long time to cross any room, as inevitably he had to shake the hands of the many who always sort to touch the hand of a great man.

Angus stood to greet his old and best friend and the two, as they always did, embraced. In his heart, Angus wept. This was always going to be the hardest moment of his life. Now he must face it.

'Good to see you old man!' declared Robert, clearly full of himself and as happy as Angus had seen him for a long time.

'Indeed,' replied Angus with guilt in his heart, 'you too. Happy birthday!'

'Ah! Thank you. Who'd have thought it eh! All those years ago, you and I in Leith, and now a lifetime has passed us by. But what a life Angus, what a life!'

Angus called over a waiter and two glasses of the 30-year-old Glenmorangie were ordered.

'Yes Robbie, it's been eventful.'

'Aye, that it has. And still plenty more to go for you and I, though another 60 years might be pushing it!'

'Really?'

'Well, maybe, with modern science and pretty young things, we can manage another 20 or so at the top of our game.'

Angus laughed.

'You are so funny Robbie. I don't think you will ever stop.'

'Of course not. Neither will you. Why should we?'

The drinks arrived and both men pushed their glasses together, toasted one another, and then sat back in their luxurious leather chairs inhaling the perfection of an ancient single malt, before luxuriously letting it slip into their mouths and ease into their blood streams.

'Cassie well Robbie?' asked Angus, keen to let some small talk delay what must follow.

'Yea, she's great. Playing tennis at the club today with people her own age!'

'As long as she plays with you later?'

They both smiled. Cassie was Robert's third wife and was aged 28. She was beautiful and 6 years younger than Robert's first child and petulant with it. Robert was besotted.

'Have you seen your two lately?' enquired Robert, his eyes wide and bright, his face open and his smile as inviting as a June summers day.

'Yes, well I say yes. Charles is doing fine at the Bank but he's very busy. Major reorganisation with the Iranian takeover. They came over last weekend for dinner with the kids. To be honest he's fed up with the way the bank works.'

'Why?'

'Well, you know what the last 20 years have been like. Near bankruptcy, Government bailouts, client anger, profits rebuilt, public backlash. Christ Robbie, they seem to have to wash all their dirty laundry in public nowadays.'

'Yes, but even so, he has an outstanding job and an even more outstanding future no doubt.'

'I know, I've told him the same, but do you know what he said? He said the Bank are just too profit orientated and their client facing promises are at best failing and in all probability bare faced lies.'

'Hang on, are you telling me we have a banker with a conscience? That's a first!'

'Well you know Charles.'

'Too honest for his own good.'

'I meant he's his own man,' answered Angus abruptly. Why did Robert have to try and see himself in every one?

'Yes he is,' offered Robert backtracking and aware of Angus being a little sensitive. 'His family all well then?'

'Yes, thank you. They are. It was lovely to see the kids. They are so beautiful and look so like little Charles!'

'Oh great! Granddad Angus. Who would have thought it! That's two now isn't it?' added Robert, aware that his friend was on edge and assuming he was fretting about Maddie in some way or other.

'Yes. Liberty and Isadora.'

'Good names. So they are up to their quota with this new law! Bloody Hell Angus, regulating the number of children. Whatever's next?'

'Needs must I guess.'

'Good old Angus, always the sensible one.'

'Someone has to be,' replied Angus gravely.

'Indeed. And Edith?'

'Edith, well, you know Edith.'

'She is remarkable. Her work continues to be amazing.'

'Well, you should know, you have bought most of it!'

Robert was Edith's key patron. He had supported her gift since she was a girl.

'Indeed. She was on top form at the opening last week, played an absolute blinder. Maddie was there of course.'

'I know. I felt it best that I stayed away,' replied Angus, sheepishly.

'Ridiculous Angus. Edith is your daughter too. She loves you. She wanted you there.'

'Did she? How do you know?'

Angus was sinking as they discussed his family. For many years now he had felt them slowly grow away from him, pretty much as soon as Maddie decided she could no longer cope with his depression and long hours at work. As she had moved out and left him in tatters, the children, who had become adults, seemed to move on away from him too. Maddie was always the bohemian one that they more easily related to, the one who understood them and stayed close to them. Angus sometimes considered that he had been simply the other one who had brought in lots of money into the family coffers. He felt like a man who had been doing his duty, a man who was alone with no hope of breaking out of the walls of his life, the walls he had built and now found imprisoned him. Such a man was always destined to fail, and fail he had.

'Angus, you just know a daughter will always love her dad. It's obvious.'

'It fucking isn't and you know it.'

The expletive surprised them both. Robert was not used to this. Angus was there for him, never angry with him. Clearly Angus was very worked up.

'Steady on old man.'

'Well what do you know about looking after your own children,' asked Angus, holding Robert's amazed gaze as he did so.

Robert looked closely at Angus. This was not the birthday drink he had been expecting. Still his old friend looked the worse for wear so he would try to be diplomatic.

'Look, I don't know. You know that. I've been a rubbish father save the fact that I could have been worse!'

Angus gave Robert a dirty look and Robert decided to let that pass too. His friend was really beginning to worry him.

305

'But I do know you care for Edith and Charles too in a most extraordinary way. You're special and they know it. We all know it.'

'Robbie,' Angus fixed Robert's eyes, 'I'm tired.'

Robert did not really need this. He had several urgent calls to return and concentration for them would be key. He often found these meetings with Angus were best served if they concentrated on remembering some of the good times and got on with their lives. Angus had an annoying tendency sometimes to concentrate on the negative aspects of their life. It really was a bore and he had not called in at Thoresby for a heart to heart. Still, Angus was his oldest friend. He would have to grin and bear it for a while longer yet.

'Angus, we're all tired. I've just caught you up and together we are becoming old buggers. We are, by the very nature of the time of our life, tired.'

'You're not tired,' responded Angus immediately.

'What?'

'You're not tired Robbie. You ride on the tide of enthusiasm every moment of every day.'

'Well, yes, I do have a sunny disposition.'

'Sunny disposition! You have much more than that Robbie. You always have.'

There was a pause. Robert adjusted his tie. Angus took a sub conscious deep breath.

'Robbie, I know we are meeting to have lunch and, well, you know, to celebrate our birthdays, but I can't.'

Robert was slightly distracted by a pretty young waitress who was helping some people choose from the menu in the restaurant. What sort of a body was waiting under that uniform he wondered.

'Mmm, You can't what Angus?'

'Be your friend anymore Robbie.'

The words hung in the air like cigar smoke. They settled around them whilst they filtered through their heads and sunk into their day.

'Angus? What?'

'It's over Robbie, you and me, it's over.'

'Over? What are we? Lovers? What the hell are you on about?'

Now that this was happening Angus felt a strange calmness begin to fall around him, comfort him and fill him with confidence to keep going up. This was something he had been waiting for over many years and now the words just came.

'It's funny Robbie but in a way lovers is what we have been. Seeing each other when we could, or more to the point when you could. I have been at your side through pretty much every deal you have struck, every poor sucker you have tied down to your deals, and I have put aside all professional conscience to ensure you got everything your heart desired.'

Robert was feeling a nasty headache coming on. This was unexpected, Angus telling him where to get off! Angus, his confidant, his back up, his rock.

'Angus, hold on. Am I missing something? It's the 60 year old thing yea? You are having one of your attacks, one of your black days?'

'No Robbie, this is a good day. A good fucking day! A day we should have had 30 plus years ago when I should have told you to just fuck off then. Instead I meekly opened my life to turn a blind eye to every corrupt thing you did and in turn I corrupted myself. I covered your tracks, I made you water tight.'

'And I made you wealthy!'

Robert had raised his voice at this point causing a few people to turn over towards them and stare. Robert for once forgot about decorum. He no longer cared who was listening or watching. This conversation was on a roll and it needed to run through.

'You did Robbie, that you did. You didn't make me happy though.'

'Happy Angus, happy? We have laughed through nights from here to Tokyo. We have experienced life that most people will only ever dream of.'

'We have, I know we have, but at some point I should have got off the ride Robbie. I should have said I was losing my mind in supporting you, in blindly turning every corner regardless of what I knew to be wrong.'

'Wrong? What is wrong Angus? We live in a corrupt world where every little fucker looks to make their way at the expense of someone else. We have simply done the same, but with immense skill and finesse and we've come out rather well have we not? How can we have been wrong?'

'You know why.'

Angus was speaking calmly now. His voice was clear and precise.

'Why?'

'We have taken what was not ours to take.'

'Angus in every war there are casualties. It is simply a matter of life.'

'Of your life.'

'Of our life Angus.'

Angus considered this.

'Yes Robbie, of our life.'

They waited. A time to catch their breath from a conversation Angus had been saving up for 30 years and one that Robert had never expected.

'I've had enough Robbie. No more for me. I'm out. I hope to win the heart of my beloved Maddie back. God I've missed her.'

'Oh right! I see. This is about Maddie is it?'

Robert spoke with anger in his voice now, anger at the scheming little bitch who had been a thorn in his side from the moment he had met her, the woman who he had put up with for the sake of his oldest friend.

'Yes, it is, and don't you dare turn your anger on her

now, here. You know she is my life and that I have been lost without her. You know this! You see this is about me too. I lost myself.'

Robert simply shook his head in wonderment. How dare Angus speak to him like this, to expect, no assume, that he could do so. As Robert tried to think through his response to shoot Angus down, his friend simply carried on talking. Why wouldn't he just shut up, stop talking!

'I resigned last night Robbie. I sold the business last night to the young bucks who worship you and your money. You can mould them even more into your image Robbie. It will be better for you, don't you see? You don't need me anymore.'

'Resigned! You've resigned!' shouted Robert, igniting the stares of those around them before gathering himself and lowering his voice again. 'Are you mad? You want to walk away from a fucking money making machine? It's our life. No Angus, you can't do this to me. You are my man.'

'That's the truth of it,' replied Angus, his voice continuing to be level and calm, 'right there. I am your man and that is how you see me and it's how others see me. You know it's how Maddie sees me. It's almost definitely how I have seen me.'

'No, no Angus, not my man,' spluttered Robert, aware he had said very much the wrong thing despite it being obviously the truth, 'I meant that you are my back up, my…'

'Fall guy. I am your excuse, your conscience clearer. The man who wipes your arse so you don't have to look at the crap you have spewed out. I make you able to feel better about the awful things that you have done and that you do. I can't do it anymore. I won't do it anymore. I'm done with it all.'

'You can't!' replied Robert almost childlishly.

'I have.'

'I won't let you.'

'You can't stop me.'

'I can.'

Silence. The air settles. Time seems to stand still. Breathing is forgotten.

'Well Robbie, there's the truth clearly spoken. That, in that clear statement, is where we are at, where we have been at for all these years. We both know you can stop me in the same way you have stopped many people before. Ask yourself the question though Robbie. Do you really want to do that to me? Do you Robbie?'

Robert was now feeling sick. He loved Angus. He could not really remember life without him and he certainly could not imagine a future without him. Angus knew a lot about how Robert had built Jones Ltd into a massive international concern, how he had painstakingly removed all obstacles barring his progress from the limiting Ronald Jones to the governments who opposed his takeovers. Angus knew a lot, far too much in fact, though by no means everything. If Angus knew everything there was no way they would be sat across from each other now, no way in fact that Angus would have allowed him to stay in his life and that of his family.

'Now Angus, I want you to think very carefully about what you are saying. You know I have built what I have built around you.'

'And?'

'Well, I simply cannot allow you to just stop.'

'I have stopped.'

'You have my confidence.'

'And you have mine. Are you worried about me Robert, about what I might say?'

An awkward pause sat between them.

'Should I be?'

'If that's how you feel then maybe you should.'

Robert sat back in his high backed leather chair. He

knew he could argue all day about this, about the semantics of who owed what to whom. Clearly though, for now, Angus had no doubt prepared over a long period to say what was said and he was obviously not set for discussing it any further for now. His face was set like flint and that was never a good sign when one was trying to do a deal.

'Look Angus, let's have a week, yes? Why don't you take a break eh? Go on holiday. Get over to your French chateau. Chill a little. I can get you some company out there to take your mind off things.'

'Robbie, I don't want your fucking company. I want Maddie back. I want my children back. I want my sanity back. I want my life back Robbie, my own fucking life! We have to leave each other alone, here and now. If I don't walk away from you now, and I mean now, I will spend the rest of what years I have got left, lost, and I won't do that. I can't do that anymore. Is that clear enough for you?'

Angus was still speaking in a calm and collected manner and Robert was aware of this. This had taken some careful thought. Who had got to his old friend, who had stirred up this disloyalty? He stood up and offered Angus his hand.

'Well, not the birthday celebration I had imagined Angus. I will give you time.'

Angus stood up too and took Robert's hand.

'Robbie, I love you. I truly, truly love you. I have always loved you. You have been, for better and worse, my best friend. I sincerely hope you find your peace. I will not see you again. Take care.'

And with that Angus turned and began to walk away leaving Robert angry and confused.

'Angus,' he called as his friend reached the door of the lounge, 'wait!'

He did not wait. He was gone.

Chapter 21

# Edith

Autumn 2031. London, England

'If you don't get here on time that's fine. Just remember you have to be here for the opening.'

'I can't Edie.'

'Dad, of course you can. You miss too much of what I do and you simply can't miss this. You have to be there, you hear me Daddy, you have to be there!'

Talking to her Dad on the phone was not the easiest of tasks. Angus was a kind, dear man, who she loved dearly, but at some point he had decided he was not needed and trying to bring him back had been almost impossible. She loved him too much to not keep trying.

'Dad, when did you last come to an opening night?'

'Well, let me see now,' Angus waited, pretending to work out the last time, whilst knowing perfectly well it had been at the Tate St Ives back in the Autumn of 2023. It had been in his first autumn of freedom from all that his life had been.

The problem for Angus was in going to any opening night there would be an almost certain appearance of Robert. He attended every opening night of Edith's shows unless he was away, the St Ives show being one such occurrence. Robert was Edith's greatest benefactor, a major support and in many ways Edith's mentor. The relationship between them went back to her childhood and Angus had no problem with it other than the fact that he knew the darkness that Robert kept hidden. Angus knew that this was never on show to Edith and the relationship was now too far-gone, too long in place, to rip it away. Edith loved Robert. Angus in turn was very close to Taylor and Jasmine and saw them whenever he could. It was not the children's fault that he and Robert had fallen apart. However the thought of facing Robert was simply one that he could not possibly deal with. Being in the same room would mean they would have to talk, and Angus had made too much progress, moved forward too much in his life, to risk a conversation with Robert bringing it all crashing down.

Since the fateful meeting at Thoresby Hall on Robert's 60th birthday, the two had only spoken briefly. Several of these times were in the few weeks and months afterwards when Robert would call Angus and the call was taken by accident. Angus remained rooted to his decision and kept conversations short yet firm. Robert in turn had finally seemed to accept Angus's decision and just stepped away. Robert's pride would ensure he would now stop trying to build bridges and for that Angus was thankful. There was always the worry that Robert would fear betrayal from Angus, that his friend might betray many of his dark deeds by laying them out bare and in so doing smash his carefully built and hugely popular public persona. However that would have meant the end of Angus' reputation too, the end of Burns & Co and the end of Jones Ltd. Both in their own minds had reached this conclusion knowing that neither would risk such an outcome. And so an unspoken truce of silence had been taken.

'I think it would be when I came to your opening night

at the Tate in St Ives and I was, of course, the proudest father in the world Edie.'

Edith smiled widely at that, her eyes misting with tears at the thought of her proud father in St Ives all those years earlier.

'You see Papa, that's what I'm talking about. I miss you.'

Now it was Angus's eyes turn to sting with emotion and, as he held the phone close to his right ear, so close so that he could feel like Edith was there with him, a tear rolled down the outside of his cheek and fell to the floor.

'You do?' he asked without confidence. Despite all the years of putting things 'right' with his family, Angus was still not sure of his place in his children's hearts, that in some way he felt they humoured him and that in reality he got in their way, cramped their style.

Now Edith became a little angry. Angus needed to snap out of this. She needed him and he needed her and it was time to get this put right.

'Of course I do! Why do you ask such things Dad? It's me, your Edie! Of course I need you and want you to be part of my important nights.'

'Edie, I, I'm sorry. It's just the faint mumblings of an old man.'

'You're not an old man,' replied Edith with a little impatience in her voice.

'I am,' retorted Angus defiantly.

'You are not! Don't be silly. Come on Daddy, take control! Be the young man that you are! Repeat this mantra every day, 'I am not an old man!''

A smile glanced across both their faces.

'OK. I am not an old man, I am not an old man, I am not an old man! I see what we are doing here. If I repeat it enough it becomes true!'

'Sort of.'

Now they were both laughing and Edith knew the battle was turning her way.

'Will you come Dad? Will you please come? Please.'

'Look, I will come in a week or so, as I always do. You know, when all the fuss has died down. You don't want an old man, sorry an old man in denial, getting in your way, cramping your style. Let's meet up in a few weeks. We can have our usual coffee on the terrace followed by one of our delightful lunches down at Fabio's. We can share chocolate ice cream as a special treat.'

'Dad, this is not usual. It's my opening night in the Tate Retro and it's the most important show of my life and you need to be there. I need you to be there. This show Dad, it's all about everything, you know, start to finish of me to date.'

'Yes, I know. I do know, seriously I do. I read the amazing article in The Observer. You are wonderful and I am so unbelievably proud. I'm sorry, I don't mean to minimise the value of the show and I know how big this is, a real honour.'

'Don't say sorry Dad! You are always in apologising mode as though apologising for a lifetime. Why?' continued Edith, sensing his thoughts, 'Do you think you get in my way, that somehow I would rather squeeze you in after the event like an afterthought? Dad, you are one of the main reasons for the art I have. You Dad!'

'Sorry.'

'You are a treasure, not a burden!'

'I am a treasure, not a burden,' repeated Angus. 'Another mantra for me to use! What an exciting day this is becoming.'

Edith smiled and took a deep breath. Her Dad was always assuming a lack of his own self- importance, seeing grey instead of white. As a child she had called him Eeyore, a nickname that she thought she would remind him of if he carried on.

315

'Look Dad. This is showing 20 years of my work Dad, 20 years! This is not an ordinary show.'

'Yes, I know.'

'And of my 20 years, no my 41 years, you are one of the two most important people in my life.'

'Me and Harry?'

'Harry?'

'Harry Potter! You know how much you loved him. Until of course he went and grew up and did that naked show on the West End!'

'Oh I loved him more then Dad. Now stop it and listen. As you know everyone is there. Mum tells me you were not even going to come to London with her!'

'Well, I…'

'Dad! I don't want to give you a choice, I need you there.'

Edith was being very definite, much more so than usual. Angus felt himself being backed into a corner.

'Your mum's train tickets are already booked.'

'Book yours too.'

'Now you know I'm not good at that sort of thing. I'll probably end up in Penzance!'

'I'll do it then.'

'Right. Well the room's just booked in Maddie's name.'

'It's a double. You can be her surprise mystery lover for the night.'

Angus smiled at that.

'And who will water my plants?' he asked pathetically.

'Your neighbours.'

'They're very strange people Edith.'

'So are you!'

They were enjoying this banter with Edith feeling she was at last winning.

'Edith.'

'Yes Dad?'

'You know the main reason why I cannot come.'

Edith frowned into the phone. Why her uncle Robert and her Dad were still not speaking was a mystery to everyone, although it did appear to have led to her mother and father getting back together which was clearly wonderful. Neither of her parents would talk about it. Robert simply told Edith that Angus needed time, although he could not be too specific about time away from what, as clearly, in Edith's view, he did not know what the root cause of the problem was either.

'Dad. I can't choose between you. You brought me up to love you both. I will not make one of you not come for the other one.'

'Edie, I don't want that either! I know Robert has been a tremendous support for you and he loves you and your work dearly. I understand his need to be there and that he should be there.'

'Thank you. That means a lot. You still have to come though. This time, absolutely this time, you have to come.'

Angus took a deep sigh. He began to take his wall down. He knew he would be going. She wouldn't ask like this unless she needed him there. That was enough. It was time to move on.

'Oh Edie, why do you ask this of me?'

'Because I have some new work too.'

'Isn't a retrospective looking back?'

'Yes. That's why it includes a new painting of you.'

As she put down her antiquated mobile phone that she refused to replace on the principal of the joke that was human consumption and waste, Edith looked out of her long drawing room windows, down across the Cornish blue slated terrace, and over to the garden area with its beautiful trees and plants. She was lucky to have them, lucky to have been able to afford such space in a much over crowded city. From her garden she found enormous inspiration. It stilled her and helped her take this into her studio, which was attached to the back of the house and where she painted for hour after hour, wave after wave.

Her approach had pretty much not changed since she had begun painting more seriously in her later years at the Minster School at Southwell. She painted what she saw by almost photographic reproduction. Clear, crisp interpretation capturing the view on large canvases, normally several metres tall and wide. The effect was stunning, stopping people in their tracks. Edith was mainly known by the public for painting modern landscapes, some peaceful, some not. She often included people, though rarely were they the focal point but rather part of the overall piece. Edith had travelled the world to catch her inspiration. She had seen the barren deserts that now stretched across the world's landscape, taking millions of lives as they did so. She had faced the storms off the Americas and the increasing catastrophic effects of hurricanes and severe cyclonic windstorms. She had narrowly missed a fatal and tragic tsunami off the Indian Ocean, arriving 2 days after the event and catching the devastation in probably her most famous painting. Edith purposely placed herself in the eye of the storm so that the reality of what she felt, the all consuming truth of what she witnessed, would come through on to her canvas and to the eyes of those who would see her work.

Her realism in approach was praised and copied now. It was funny because when she had looked to progress with her painting during various interviews for high calibre university places, she had felt a general reluctance to support her style and Edith, being Edith, had decided she could do without negativity towards her work. She had talked to Uncle Robert, who had always been a great admirer of what she did, and he had sponsored her through one of the annual Jones Ltd foundation grants. He immediately set her up in an old barn in Totley, Sheffield, and just up the road from where he lived. Robert told her to simply paint for however long it took to sharpen her craft without pressure or interruption. The barn, with its big huge opening room and tall white walls, was perfect for her to work in.

The barn was ideally placed on the outskirts of the Peak District allowing her to drive into the peaks in her old battered Defender and spend hours upon hours photographing and filming what inspired her. She would then bring the images back to the barn and leave them on a continual loop on playback on one of the large white wall allowing images to enter her brain and often coming back out with a definite structure that she then painted. She would use this way of finding and defining her ideas throughout her career.

Angus and Maddie had been delighted with Robert's kindness and support, and in turn were highly supportive of their daughter too. Maddie would regularly bring up home cooked food from the family home in Southwell and spend long weekends with her daughter, the two of them taking long walks in the wilds of the moors and returning to make soups, breads and cakes together. Angus would come occasionally too when he could leave work, although this was infrequent and usually saw Maddie admonishing him for letting his life slip away to his career. Angus would receive the words from Maddie like a wounded dog, his big kind eyes asking for pardon and love, which both ladies gave him whilst feeding him the fruits of their labour.

Happy times at Totley saw her build a portfolio and, through Roberts contacts in the art world, most of whom knew him through a combination of Francesca's work and Robert's patronage, she opened her first exhibition at Sheffield's White Horse Gallery in the Autumn of 2011, aged just 21. Robert had insisted that the exhibition had to be in Sheffield telling her that it would be hilarious to see the art world come to her, and not her go to them. Robert had set in motion a marketing storm with a buzz firewall spreading the word of this young, audacious and new talent who had been hidden away in the Peak District for years. They came in numbers and Edith Jeffers was an instant hit.

20 years later and here she was on the brink of a huge show at the magnificent Tate Retro. It was an exhibition to show her journey, the times she had challenged society with reflections of injustice and hate, the times she had soothed society with images of reflection and hope, and the times she had left society to look deep into the heart of one of her pictures and ask as many questions as she had asked when she painted the piece.

And yet her newest painting had, in many ways, been her biggest challenge. Firstly it was to a great extent a portrait and this was a diversion for her. She didn't do portraits considering them too selfish a piece to do, too focussed on an individual. For the subject matter, though, and the fact that it was the Retro Show, this was one diversion she felt she needed to take. The painting had asked her to lay out on canvas an image, yes, but also to allow that image to become a true reflection of the person of whom it was painted. How to dress him, where to place him and how to have him look was her biggest challenge.

Edith had thought long and hard about all these things over several months, having made her mind up as soon as the Tate approached her about doing the show, that her retrospective should include a picture of her Daddy, Angus. She did so because she knew her father had suffered self-doubt beyond all. She knew he had often seen himself as a failure to Maddie, that his wife had managed very successfully to juggle a fabulous career with being a wonderful parent and that he had not. She also saw him constantly feel under the shadow of Uncle Robert, a weight that had finally been broken but only by the two men falling out. How much must all of that hurt and still hurt?

Edith knew that Angus had seen his role to the family as primarily financial provider, but had not seen himself as able to give much more and yet he had.

Things had not been made easier as Maddie had moved out and somehow Angus took it upon himself to see this as his fault alone and that his children were solely on the side of their mother and pulling away from him. Maybe the relationship lines had faltered for awhile as Charles and Edith tried to come to terms with a break up that they had never thought on the cards, but never had Edith, or Charles, pulled away. Always she had tried to build bridges and kept the relationship with Angus alive. When the bombshell of her Dad falling out with Robert had arrived it was an added complication as Edith was very close to the both. The fact that within 3 months her Mum had moved back in with Angus suggested there was more to this than she would probably ever know. None of the three of them would talk about it in depth but the rekindling of her parents relationship was soothing to her, particularly because she knew Angus would be able to find his peace much more easily with Maddie at his side.

She thought of her Dad and heard him apologising. Apologising for not being there, for missing an event, for not being cooler, for not being what he felt everyone wanted, for not being someone else. In short she knew Angus felt inadequate compared to most, and this so hurt her to see. In fact his sincerity in accepting his shortcoming was precious. In her experience most people hid their failures behind their successes. Not her Dad. She adored him. She had never been short of a shoulder to snuggle into and it was this warmth she wanted to catch in her painting. Edith loved him so very much and she wanted him to know this afresh by seeing himself at the heart of her big show.

After Maddie and Angus got back together, Edith felt that she had begun to get through to Angus and he in turn, having amazingly stepped away from his work which had been a huge chunk of his life, seemed to find more confidence.

This painting was her summary of what Angus meant to her. In the end she had decided to use an old photograph she had of him taken at their Southwell home. She had caught it with her new digital camera that her parents had bought her for her 16th birthday. Angus had just arrived home into the early evening of a warm June summers day. Maddie had shouted from the kitchen to go and sit at the garden table with some wine that was already breathing on the dining room table, and wait for dinner, which was nearly ready. He had taken the bottle of red wine and made his way out on to the terrace with his glass and, on reaching the table, poured himself a large helping. As he slipped back into his chair, having drunk half of his glass immediately, Edith had stepped on to the terrace and simply photographed her father.

The moment captured showed a man beginning to relax after a hard days work, his jacket over the back of his chair, his shirt sleeves rolled up and his top button undone, his striped tie pulled down and away from his neck. He was looking directly at the camera, or Edith to be precise, with a proud smile on his face, as he loved his daughter so very much and seeing her always produced this smile. It was as though you could physically see the world and all its problems escaping from his shoulders. This was her abiding memory of Angus and she knew that in that moment a combination of being home, solace, wine and the sight of her had come together to give perfect release. This was what she had caught in her photograph and what she had now transcribed on to her painting. This was her gift to him and this was the glorious reason that her father would attend her opening night and the walls with uncle Robert could maybe finally begin to come down.

Maddie and Angus walked into the Retro bar, helping themselves to the sparkling wine and canapés on offer, and through out on to the Thames facing terrace. It was a stunning early autumnal evening, pleasantly warm allowing you to breathe in the London skyline without fighting the oppressive heat of the summer. The view was breathtaking with its mix of the treasured gems from St Paul's to the still magnificent Gherkin. There had been so much change in London over the last 50 years but so much had been preserved too. Angus thought that was London's biggest achievement, keeping the old at the side of the new and, in particular, not allowing the new to overcome and overtake. To their right, by Tower Bridge, stood the breathtaking and wonderful Shard Tower, which stretched higher than any other building in Britain. Bathed in glass, that was its beauty but also its energy supply, it seemed to catch the light of the capital.

'Isn't this wonderful!' mused Angus, a happy and contented Angus.

'Yes it is,' replied a very happy Maddie, so thrilled to be out with her husband for her daughters big show.

'How do you feel Angus?' asked Maddie, pride running through her body.

'I feel,' Angus looked at his wife, the woman he had met when he was 19 years old doing his law degree at Oxford University, the woman who he had loved from the moment he saw her, and the woman who was the reason he viewed his future with optimism, 'I feel very happy. I feel very lucky. Edith has, well you know.'

'What Angus?' asked Maddie, encouraging Angus to speak from his heart.

'She has reminded me how much I mean to her and that makes me very happy indeed!'

'So you should Angus be!' Maddie couldn't help but allow a big grin take over her face. She loved Angus very much, though he annoyed her in equal measure with his many foibles that were ultimately what made him endearing yet also hard work. Angus had phoned her as he had left Thoresby Hall back in the summer of 2023. He had been so honest on the phone and that had really taken her aback. She had assumed he would falter and go back on his decision but as the days turned into weeks and months it became clear he really had followed his heart and bravely made a new start. That autumn had seen Edith exhibiting at Tate St Ives and Maddie had asked Angus if he would like to go with her. Robert could not be at the event for some reason or other and Angus had jumped at the invitation like an excited puppy. They had not looked back since with their relationship growing almost daily without the anger and upset of having to balance Robert and Burns & Co within their marriage.

Maddie cradled her husband's right cheek in her left hand.

'She has made us very proud indeed and shown you just what you mean to her, to us. You're very loved you know.'

She looked at Angus, tears welling in his eyes,

'If you must cry my lovely, then please do, but you might want to wait until after you have spoken to him.'

The two of them looked to where Maddie had just nodded. There, alone on a near hidden corner table, was the huddled figure of Robert McTeer. He had a bottle of something or other on the table with a glass in one hand and his head in the other. This was not a Robert that people saw, certainly not in public like this. Something was clearly wrong.

'Do you want to leave Angus? It's fine if you do. We've managed to avoid him all night and you've been wonderful.'

'Maybe he avoided us?'

'Yes, maybe he did,' Maddie admitted, suspecting that was the truth of it, though not really wishing to give Robert the credit for it.

'Look Angus, I don't think he has seen us, although looking at him I don't think he would be noticing much at all at the moment. Very peculiar for him? Anyway let's go shall we. We've had a wonderful evening.'

Angus looked at Robert. Still unmistakeable after all these years. A larger than life character with the charisma to build so much and the power of presence to crush too. Seeing him looking more than worse for wear, Angus felt enormous compassion sweep over him.

'No Maddie, it's fine. Are you alright if I go and see him?'

'Yes. Of course. I'm coming with you to check him out first though Angus.'

Angus smiled. Everything felt easier with his girl beside him again.

Maddie walked towards Robert with Angus behind her counting his heartbeat hard as it rose in anticipation of something he had thought to never repeat.

'Good evening Robert,' declared Maddie in a friendly yet firm tone.

As Robert looked up at Maddie and behind her the oncoming Angus, she saw the tears in his eyes and the obvious signs of drink related stupor.

'Ah Maddie and my best friend Angus! How good it is to see you both. Please, take a seat.'

Maddie stood her ground as Angus arrived at her side and stood in silence beside her.

'How are you Robert?' she asked, a strength in her voice that underlined a woman who had never pandered to the man before her.

Robert looked out to the Thames, boats making their way up and down, fulfilling their errands and pleasures, the lights of the city by the Thames reflecting as though there were actually lights in the river itself.

'Not so good as it happens. You?'

'We are very well, thank you. A wonderful night!'

'Yes. Your daughter has surpassed herself! Quite wonderful.'

Robert looked over Maddie's shoulder and nodded to his old best friend, the friend that was his last link to the innocence of his past, and the friend that when he had left him cut off this link and left him alone within his terrible dark world. Angus, in turn, nodded back and then, without thinking, stepped forward and sat down. He turned back to Maddie, surprise and concern written all over her face.

'It's OK Maddie, Robbie and I will chat for a while,' Angus turned back to Robert, 'if that's good for you Robbie?'

Robert nodded enthusiastically in agreement.

'Well if you're sure Angus?' asked Maddie, giving him the chance to step away from the man who she held solely responsible for the stress and anxiety that had taken over her husband's life. In truth in Robert she saw the man that she had such mixed feelings about because as much as he had worked, and she felt used, her husband to the limit, he had showered her daughter with such acts of kindness and inspiration that it was to a very large extent his inspiration and doing that she had got to this point, this night.

'I'm sure sweetheart,' replied Angus softly, tenderly.

'No, I'm happy to stay too!' said Maddie, forcing the offer as she did not wish to have to talk to Robert for any length of time.

'No dear. It's fine, really it's fine,' replied Angus feeling surprisingly calm now that he was sat with Robert after all these years. 'Why don't you go and see if Harry has arrived?'

'Harry?'

'You know, Edie's boyfriend.'

'Harry was ejected from the scene 6 months ago dear.'

'Oh dear. Ejected you say,' smiled Angus, delighted to see he was as out of the family news loop as ever. 'What about seeing if dear Charles has arrived? Oh and ask them to change this infernal noise which they will no doubt be calling music.'

That brought a smile to Robert's face.

'I think you will find it is what the young people today are listening to my dear,' replied Maddie who was also smiling, pleased to see the old grumpy Angus shining through despite the fact he was sat with Robert. 'Charles told me it is the opposite of the drum and bass he used to listen to. They call it Wind and Sea music, or to the initiated, WAS.'

Maddie offered this observation with a grin, pleased with her grasp on modern culture, a grasp that Angus had never even had on his own culture.

'My God Maddie, have you been out clubbing with them as well?' asked Robert, seeming a little upset to be usurped in his knowledge on something new.

Maddie leant down and kissed Angus on his cheek. She straightened up and turned to Robert.

'You're finally beginning to look your age Robert.'

'Thank you for that Maddie. Kind as ever. Science can't stop the inevitable, and my god I've tried.'

And he had. Robert had paid for just about every piece of anti-ageing treatment he could get. He had long since begun to follow his father's balding process and had immediately ensured it would not affect him. His teeth had remained pristine and white. His face too had kept a younger mans look with all sorts of cosmetic work repeated over many years. At the age of 68 Robert had achieved his aim of looking years younger but it was clear, on this warm late September night, that time was finally catching up with him, though whether by way of the natural order of things or by neglect on Robert's part was not clear. His eyes looked heavy with tight lines folding across his upper cheeks and into his temples, his hair showing signs of grey that were usually never on show. His chin too was carrying weight. It was all so unlike Robert.

Angus, on the other hand, never seemed to grow older from the look he had reached at middle age. He had never been too bothered about his appearance reasoning that he would neither better nor worsen his lot by being unduly concerned. He was not blessed with looks or an athletic body. Rather his medium height matched his medium looks that meant he was never going to draw attention to himself in a fashion show! By the time he had turned 30 he was following his father's hair pattern and losing his hair. By the time he reached the age of 40 he was already looking 50. And yet, as he had reached this age he kept this look and had not changed much since. When he turned 50 he discovered running and in fact this pastime had maintained a relatively healthy and trim body since.

'Well, it's good to see you Robert,' said Maddie as she addressed them both before leaving them. 'It's been a long time and I am pleased it has been on this night of all nights. She wouldn't be here without you.'

Robert smiled, genuinely touched by what Maddie had said.

'That's kind of you Maddie, and appreciated. The fact is she is your child and the two of you helped make her what she is. I simply aided the process.'

'Oh you did much more than that. You know you did. We all know you did. I know I come across hard on you Robert and we all know why, but I want you to know how much I appreciate your love and care for Edith. This is your night too Robert.'

Robert just looked up at Maddie, words for once failing him. To experience someone being so magnanimous when he deserved something probably quite opposite from Maddie was very sweet and unexpected.

'So, that's that then. I shall leave the two of you to chat. Be good, the pair of you, especially you Robert.'

Robert looked somewhat crestfallen at that. He had never been able to control Maddie; she was always her own woman and never won over by his plentiful charms over the years. He once tried to seduce her when they were on holiday together and Angus had fallen to sleep after a bottle or two of French wine and not only had Maddie refused him, but she had laughed at him. She had never told Angus this, knowing it would hurt him beyond all, but it had added to the fuel of disgust she had for his best friend. Robert had in turn often dismissed Maddie as a frightened woman unable to cope with what life could really give her. When Angus had walked out on him he had realised she was a formidable lady who had taken away from him one of the two most valuable people in his life. It was a good job she hardly knew Alison!

'You look after my husband, you hear?'

Robert half laughed.

'What do you think I'm going to do? Throw him off the balcony?'

'I'd rather you didn't old boy,' ventured Angus in an attempt to bring the conversation back to the kind words of a few moments before and nodding at Maddie as he did so.

Maddie looked at the two of them one final time, leant forward and kissed Angus on the cheek again, and then stepped away and disappeared into the crowd.

The two men were left and silence sat before them like an actual two-way door waiting to be pushed by the man who would speak first. Two awkward minutes passed and then, slowly at first, Robert's shoulders started to rise and fall as grief rose in him and tears fell. Angus, feeling like an observer in a dream he now found himself in, waited. What the hell was happening?

Time passed. People looked past Robert and Angus, paying them little attention. It was the younger peoples time now and the two old men in the corner were of no consequence to them. Time was inexorably moving on.

'Have you a tissue?' asked Robert, his words choked out as he struggled to overcome his emotions.

Angus felt in his pocket and handed over a handkerchief to Robert.

'Robbie,' against his preferred route of silence, Angus reached out to his old friend, 'I regret we could not stay friends.'

'Aye, well you did the right thing.'

'I did?' replied Angus, confused to hear his old friend give in so easily.

'Yes. You know you did. You got Maddie back.'

'Yes. I got Maddie back,' replied Angus neutrally as what else was there to say?

They waited, their first conversation in years filling the air.

'Cassie's gone.'

'Oh. I'm sorry.'

'Don't be. She was a vicious cow anyway.'

Angus winced at that, his old friend as cutting as ever.

'So you'd had enough?' Angus asked, assuming the same old Robert needing to move on to the next young thing.

'Yes!' a pause waited and then, 'well no, actually. She left me.'

'She left you?' Angus replied, staggered by the thought of it.

'I know. Ironic isn't it. I spend my life leaving people and then, as age hits me, they leave me.'

'When?'

'Today. As I left the house she handed me the papers.'

'Papers?'

'Yes, papers. She had thought it through and taken some serious divorce advice.'

'But you're protected Robbie, you know that don't you.'

Angus had looked after Robert for many years making him water tight in private and business cases the world over. This was something he had continued to do. Of course Burns & Co had some very bright people working there but

330

Angus was as smart as the best and therefore best placed to make sure Robert in his personal capacity was protected. In the sale of Burns & Co, Angus had insisted on keeping a stake in the business and this was something the buyers were delighted to do. They had done so to maintain the knowledge of the man and the connections of the man, in particular of course Robert Jones Ltd. It was a wise move. As a result Angus had stayed briefed on major clients and he knew that Robert had nothing to worry about other than losing a small part of an enormous wealth pot.

'I know, but we both know what lawyers are good at.'

'Yours are better.'

Robert nodded at that.

'You made sure they were. I know you still do.'

Angus caught Robert's eye and in that moment a look of care and interest in one another, feelings that had never gone away, was happily noted.

'Was it a surprise?' asked Angus, happy that Robert knew he had never left him entirely.

'That she's grown balls enough to leave me?'

The old anger was still there and a shot of panic rose through Angus's body. He thought about what may happen to Cassie. Robert looked at Angus, reading his mind as he did so.

'Don't worry my old friend. No more from me. Cassie can leave me. She can take what she wants. I am done.'

'You are done? Done with what.'

The chatter of the party filled the night. Canapés and delicacies mixed with expensive drinks as laughter both false and real reached out and took a hold. The beat of the music nestled the gathering clans and lulled them with an intoxicating mix of rhythm and score. Life was full and overflowing. Opportunity was alive.

'I am done with my life Angus. Done with fixing my world as it has chosen to now fix me.'

And with those words Angus understood what had

happened. Medical science had achieved great breakthroughs but when illness decided to override and overcome age, there was nothing to be done.

Robert had seen his consultant for the devastating news two weeks earlier. For several years now he had been fighting the cancer that was at war with his body. Only Alison knew, supportive and loyal as ever. There had been successes for Robert along the way, not least of which when he had been given the all clear early on when they thought they had caught the cancer in its infancy and the explosive powers of the Angelica drug had taken effect. Sadly though it transpired that they had not been in time after all. The disease had come back and was now irreversible. The doctor had said that he could keep fighting, that with the advances in medicine he could buy himself 1 or maybe 2 more years. Robert told him he had no intention of fighting it anymore.

As he left the hospital that day he felt almost relieved. He had been avoiding looking sickness in its face for too long now, thinking he could fight it and win and then turn his back on it as though it had never held any power over him. With the inevitability of his death settled, he felt different, found himself accepting the cancer, not like a poison, but rather like a part of his body he accepted he needed to live with. Gradually it was eating him alive and he would be overcome by it and die. For Robert he saw the cancer as doing a job he had been unable to do for as it would kill him it would also kill the guilt and blackness that had filled his quiet hours nearly all his life.

He looked Angus in the eyes and through reddened eyes a look of clear fear from what was before him shone out.

'Runaway stomach cancer. I've got maybe 6 months maximum left Angus, probably much less.'

Angus held his gaze. It was the least he could do. Warmth touched Robert as his friend's kindness reached out to him. He knew he deserved no such thing.

'That's dreadful.'

'I know.'

'I…'

Robert smiled, his face notably thin, his lips dry and cracked.

'It's no less than I deserve Angus, we both know that.'

Angus let that sit between them for awhile.

'Does Cassie know?'

'No.'

'Will you tell her?'

Robert smiled.

'No. She can have a share of my estate now, leaving me to give the rest of it to who the hell I like.'

Angus nodded.

'And Alison?'

'She knows. You know she knows everything.'

'Everything?' asked Angus, bravely.

'She always has Angus. Right from the off. Everything.'

The thought of Alison and the enormous trust Robert had clearly placed in her over years touched Angus.

'And how has she taken the news?'

'Badly, very badly. But, you know her. She is very able to cope with anything I throw at her. She continues to run the company like she was in her 20's. Such energy!'

'She won't retire.'

As Angus said this he thought 'neither will she walk away like I did.' He felt a little guilt stab at his heart.

'No, she won't,' replied Robert proudly.

Robert again let his gaze fall across the river. The old Robert would have been looking into the party, looking for an opportunity to devour some pretty young woman or impress a connection or two. Not tonight. Robert was clearly struggling to hold his concentration together.

Angus waited, letting time pass between them, time that had been stolen from them by the pressures of their lives. He saw Robert wince a little and saw him slide his hand down to his stomach and rub a pain as though rubbing could ever make this cancer go away. God this was painful. Painful to watch and painful to know Robert had been carrying so much on his own when he, Angus, could and should have been there for him.

'I'm sorry Robbie, I really am.'

'Hey, we've all got to die.'

'No, I am sorry that I've not been there for you, to support you through all this. I should have been.'

'Well I can't say at times I haven't thought exactly the same my old friend,'

Angus' face visibly dropped at this.

'But, and it's a big but Angus, you were right.'

'I was not!'

'You know you were. Maddie did the right thing. She made you face your demons. I've always loved you Angus, always. I just lost my way, quite a lot actually. It was easy to manage you. I deserved being managed by you instead.'

Angus thought about apologising again, telling Robert to not be silly, but as he let the words fall into his head, he knew Robert was right. He lifted his glass,

'To an end to management!'

The two of them saluted one another, happy to be putting the past behind them.

'It's ironic isn't it?' said Robert after another pause, but this time an easy pause as peace settled upon them.

'What is?'

'That we find a cure for cancer and yet it fights back and still kills like a barbarian from the past. Your mum dead to cancer. Alan, dead to cancer. Fucking hell Angus, it really is the most amazing thing that we can fly a man to Mars but we cannot cure our people of this plague.'

Robert looked into his glass, gently swirling the single malt around and around as though reading some fortune within it.

'I miss her,' he said, simply.

'Cassie?'

'Mum.'

And there was the problem. A light that had shone so perfectly into his life had gone out all too soon. A light that could have touched and changed his darkness had disappeared allowing the depths of anarchy to deepen still further within his already tortured soul. For so many an inspiration, for Robert a fix for his life, Francesca had been cruelly taken away. Here were two older men, time moving them towards the end of their act, still mourning the lady who had died nearly 40 years before and who had never really left them.

'I hope there's no heaven and hell, or at least if there is that I go to hell,' said Robert, breaking the spell the very mention her name had created.

'You do! Why?'

'Because she will be in heaven.'

'And?'

'And I must never see her again.'

'Robbie!' declared Angus, his face showing the amazement that his voice had expressed.

'She has disowned me Angus, and I could not bear to face her.'

Angus felt a mix of sorrow and confusion. Somehow he had known he would have to meet Robert again, knew that this night would eventually need to happen. Here before him the mighty Robert McTeer sat, a broken man. Maddie was right too; he was finally beginning to look his age. Whether that was illness or time, or both, he could not tell. It was clear though that Robert was gradually breaking down.

'Look Robbie, I don't know how desperate you feel now but I can guess it's pretty bad. Many people love you Robbie. My daughter is testament to the good you have done. They say that death often focuses the mind on thinking back to what could have been different, but please remember all that you have done that has been good. It really is a balance Robbie. Your Foundation is living proof of the enormous good you have done, kindness that would not have been possible without you.'

Robert was looking down into his drink, his normally well-groomed hair falling down across his face. He heard his friends soothing words and he felt better for them. It was so good to have Angus with him. Looking back he had realised that it had always been Angus who had lifted him and brought him back to a happy place, to sweet memories of carefree times. However there was to be no hiding away from the truth. He looked up.

'I loved my mum, really loved her. I remember following her around Edinburgh, gallery after gallery, and café to café. I would have walked anywhere with her then but,' and as he spoke he seemed lost in a trance, 'I left her. I grew up and away from her, and Dad too. I closed a door on their love and decided I didn't need them. I have been a fool Angus. Do you remember being in Naples?'

'Yes, of course. Sorting out that Sorrento deal. We talked about Jasmine lots, you remember, she had just decided to go into nursing.'

'That's right. Something else I argued against and was once again proven wrong!'

Angus let the words of his friend flow. He had never seen Robert like this in his whole life. The voice of death was clearly admonishing him.

'Well, you and I went for a walk one night and I didn't tell you but I was looking for something.'

Angus offered raised eyebrows.

'Mum left journals Angus, lots and lots of journals covering her whole life. I'm leaving them to Taylor. You'll see he gets them won't you?'

'Of course.'

'Thank you. In the early ones she talks a lot of Naples,

the place where she was born, where she lived, and where she found her true love. Dad.'

'I thought William went to her in Florence?'

'He did, but only after her aunt and uncle took her in when her family, and her family home, was destroyed by a bomb.'

'Really! A tragic start. I had no idea.'

'Well I didn't really. I mean, I knew the story of them meeting, but not the connection between Naples and Florence.'

'So where were we going in Naples?'

'To find her,' replied Robert in a matter of fact voice.

'Find her?'

'Yes. I knew vaguely where her café was, that is, had been.'

'What was it called?'

'La Libreria.'

'Ah, William's love of books!'

'Indeed.'

Robert winced again as another spasm of pain from his now constant companion took him out of his stride.

'Robbie, let's leave it for now shall we? Continue another day?' offered Angus as he saw Robert unable to hide the discomfort from his illness.

'Continue another day! Angus comes back!' The relief and joy in Robert's voice was very sweet and Angus simply smiled in return. 'Are we to have another day?'

'Do you want one?'

Robert smiled, a broad grin for the first time on this night, for the first time in many nights, filling his face.

'If you would be kind enough Angus, of course I do.'

'It will be my pleasure Robbie. Now, shall we refrain for now?'

'No, I'm OK for a little while more. Let me tell you this bit.'

'Alright, if you're sure.'

'You see, the point is, we walked to where the café was and I, and well I felt nothing.'

'Well?'

'Well, that's the point. It was then I knew she had left me.'

Angus thought about correcting his friend and offering fresh hope, but he knew Robert would have been through this in his own mind a thousand times.

'Time can be cruel Robbie,' he simply offered, 'and our mistakes can cost us dearly.'

'Yes, they can.'

The night air was growing cooler and Robert was beginning to look very uncomfortable.

'Angus, tonight has been wonderful, hasn't it? Edith has been so incredibly talented and so generous with her talent. This show is very special and crowned with her piece of you, of you Angus! I hope that makes you very proud, puts you in the safe and blessed knowledge that she loves you so, that she has always loved you so.'

Angus smiled warmly. It was all true and all so very precious. Robert continued,

'Thank you for tonight. It has meant so much to me. Let me say sorry to you once again.'

'Robbie, I was a grown man, I made my own decisions.'

Robert smiled. They both knew that if he had said to Angus to jump off a train he would have probably done it. The apology was made and that was enough. They both recognised the feeling, the truth in their words.

'And I have done such fearful things in my life, many of which you are either aware of or have guessed me guilty. I suspect you have spent as much time in denial as I have!'

They reflected on this statement and knew it to be true. Angus knew better than anyone that Robert could be harsh and without mercy and whilst he had never seen any of the actual crimes committed, he saw the outcomes when deals that were blocked became unblocked, when people who were unhelpful became more than helpful. He even saw when some people disappeared and doors had suddenly opened. This was Angus' eternal shame and it washed over him again as they spoke.

'So, in my final months, I will be a sad and desperate man my friend. I have surrounded myself with a nursing team and I will die alone.'

'But Robert!'

'No! This is my wish Angus and please, if there are any feelings of kindness you have left towards me, please do not seek to change my mind on this. Please tell my children as they contact you, and they will contact you, that I am not to be seen.'

'But they will come anyway!'

'Yes, but I won't be there. I travel to Switzerland within the next month and I will die in a place of secret. Thereafter I will be flown home and my children will be able to say their goodbyes then.'

'Are you sure this is what you want Robbie?'

'Yes Angus, I am sure. I have had a few years to think about this you know.'

Angus again felt a shot of pity as he thought of Robert fighting his illness alone.

'And Angus, I need to ask you one last favour.'

'If it is something I can do, I will do it.'

'You are my executor, as you know. I never changed that.'

'And I never asked to change it.'

The men let the love within this statement touch them both. They were reminded again that despite everything, they had never truly left one another.

'I know. Look, despite all that has passed, will you still please fulfil this role?' asked a clearly exhausted Robert.

'I will Robbie, of course I will! I will remain here for you to the last.'

Tears filled Robert's eyes. This was more than he could have hoped for.

'We need to redraft and remove Cassie of course. Other than that there are no changes to what you already know.'

'Does Alison know of the wills full details?'

'Some of it, but not all.'

'And your ashes as before?'

'Yes of course, the same. Let me free on Ashover Hill.'

Chapter 22

# The Gift

July 2034. Florence, Italy

As Jasmine allowed the gentle motion of the train to move through her body and soothe her, she thought about her father, Robert. The last few years had been so difficult and losing him had been a blow she had not seen coming, at least not for many more years. She had only known he was gravely ill because dear Uncle Angus had rung her and Taylor to tell them. It was too late then to see him. He had hidden himself in some private nest in Switzerland and would not take visitors or calls. He was determined that to the last appearances would be everything. She had gotten him to exchange emails and a tenderness and regret came through these, feelings that had been so rarely on show in his lifetime coming to the fore as he reached his death. That day came on the 28th of March 2032 as, aged 68; Robert's body gave up its fight. Jasmine and Taylor chose to have a very small and private cremation service with only the very close invited. Afterwards they made their way to Ashover Hill and cast his ashes, as Robert had requested, from the same spot that Robert had stood when he let free his mother, Francesca. This simple act had brought many tears with Jasmine and Taylor supported by their partners, Alice and Charlie. Angus and Maddie too were there with Edith and Charles, as well as Alison who completed the small group.

After much pressure the family gave it's blessing to a civic celebration of his life which took place on the 1st of July to coincide with what would have been his 69th birthday. The service had taken place in the beautiful Sheffield Cathedral and the building was absolutely full as well as being surrounded by the worlds watching media. There was no doubting that Robert had touched many people in his life and had left quite a legacy, which was precisely the conundrum that his children faced. Their father was clearly an amazing figure who had spent such time devoted to the development of people and projects around the world, work that had placed Robert McTeer on the world map, but also work that had changed the lives of tens of thousands of people and probably many more. The flipside for Jasmine and Taylor was that Robert had spent so little time on them, his own children. It was a circle that would never be joined, a series of thoughts that they could make no sense of. Both Jasmine and Taylor had each other and it was this bond, this extremely strong bond that had kept them through their childhood years and followed them into adulthood. It was this that allowed them to rely on what they did know, namely that their love was real and true and if nothing else, Robert had given them the gift of life to know this love. His later years had seen a thaw in the relationship between father and children, though any time they had was always rushed and at Robert's timetable.

After the small group had left Ashover Hill on that day, they had made their way to Milhaven House in Ashover, the place where all those years earlier Robert had thrown his 26th birthday party where a proud expectant mother, Emily McTeer, had stroked her stomach and felt the warmth of her baby inside her. This baby was to be Jasmine.

The party arrived at Milhaven House and retired to a room set aside for them for the reading of the will. Angus, as sole executor, had presided over events. As they took their seats neither Jasmine or Taylor had any idea as to whether they would have been left anything or not. As they had in life, they had no expectation when relating anything to their father.

'Right, all comfortable?' asked Angus, looking over his reading glasses and out to the small group in front of him.

'Give it to us Uncle Angus,' said Taylor, his sun kissed face holding a cheeky smile. 'Confirm what I know will be coming, that the estate has been spent but that he's left us enough for a party!'

Charlie squeezed his hand and Jasmine offered him a warm smile.

Angus nodded.

'Not quite young man! In fact I think there are quite a few surprises to come out now so please be prepared for few shocks and some big numbers. In fact Taylor your father has left a huge estate, an estate that you all knew about but could not know for sure the values or his intentions.'

'No we didn't! Cards close to his chest as ever.' Taylor again, the two whiskies that Angus had given him now having their effect. Charlie squeezed his hand even harder and Jasmine now didn't offer a smile. Taylor took the hint.

'Sorry, interruptions over. Please, Uncle Angus, my lips are sealed! Zip! No more. Carry on!'

'Thank you Taylor, that's very good of you. I will. As I said your father left a huge estate, which on my workings with his team of accountants, means he has left net assets to his private estate in excess of nine hundred and fifty million pounds. This is in fact a much slimmed down version of the overall estate, many hundreds of millions, figures of enormous value, having already been placed into the Foundation after years of careful tax planning coupled with, of course, Robert's unwavering commitment to the Foundation. You will find we will talk a lot about the Foundation today.'

The room was silent now. Taylor's mouth was wide open as he heard a figure he had never heard before. Jasmine, across from him on another sofa with Alice, felt her heart beating way too fast. Angus continued.

'And it was his desired wish that much of this net estate be used for the good of as many of the causes he committed himself to in his lifetime as possible.'

Jasmine immediately felt better when she heard this. She had no expectation of anything from Robert and actually found money quite repulsive. It scared her.

'And so the main Trust, the Robert McTeer Foundation, is set to be the main beneficiary of this estate with the amount of five hundred million pounds going to the charity on one condition.'

Angus stopped reading and looked out to the people in front of him. To his right sat Maddie and Edith, hands held as they looked to him. How times have changed, Angus thought to himself, that here we are, together as a beautifully united family, but with Robert's business as the focal point! He smiled at that. Robert would have done to.

Charles sat by their side looking decidedly like his father and this made Angus very proud indeed. Charles had gone into banking and reached so far up the corporate career ladder only to then feel uncomfortable with the choices of his employer and ultimately uncomfortable with his own choice to be there. At the age 39 he had one day just given it all up. He had found it increasingly difficult to marry up the finance targets of the bank he slaved for with the needs of ordinary people. And so, having seen the effects of a lifetime of work related strain on his father, Charles had bravely stepped away. To his sisters great delight he had sold all he held dear to move into a barge moored on The Thames. Robert had received the news with the same confusion he received the news of Jasmine's conversion to becoming a nurse, sending a note to Maddie and Angus to say how sorry he was. Maddie had laughed long and hard at that. Angus hadn't known whether to laugh or not.

There in front of him sat Taylor and Charlotte. What a wonderful couple they were. Their two young boys, Eduardo and Cesc, had stayed behind in Seville with friends. It was so good to see them again, the last time having been when Maddie and he had called in on them two summers previously in Seville. Café Ana was an established and thriving business, true to the reasons they had set it up in the first place. It remained a focal point of life in Calle Del Betis, and Angus and Maddie had been fascinated by the people and the life that this young English couple were leading. In fact they seemed as much Spanish now as they seemed English, a fact underlined by the Spanish names they had given their boys, names that recognised their Spanish citizenship but also Taylor's love of a certain North London Football club and some heroes that he had worshipped as a younger man.

And then to his left sat Jasmine and her partner, Alice. She was a delightful girl, Jasmine, so unlike Robert that unless you knew different you would have never placed them as at all related. Nursing had been her calling. Angus remembered Robert telling him the news of her new career choice as though relating a death of someone. Angus had laughed at his friend, telling him that there was never a more obvious choice for her and that it would make her very happy indeed. Robert had muttered something under his breath about prospects and a career thrown away, but over time he had come to not only accept her choice, but to admire it. Angus had often thought it was bravado talk when Robert would tell an audience of the work his very own daughter did in the backwaters of the world helping the sick and the dieing. Angus heard the words and knew how much they would embarrass Jasmine and all that she stood for, and he feared that Robert was using his own daughter for his own publicity. And yet now, with what he was about to read, it seemed Robert was not at all making up words he did not believe for a public that he needed and always wanted to impress. Angus now believed that Robert had actually come to realise that Jasmine had done something remarkable in her own way and that it had impressed him enormously. What other conclusion could there be? What was clear was that Jasmine would need after this day Alice's support more than ever.

And finally there was Alison, solid and dependable Alison. She had been at Robert's side throughout his whole business life, this being pretty much their whole adult life. Angus had never been able to break through to her, never able to get past the necessities of business, which always clouded nearly all the conversations he had ever had with her. He knew Robert had broken past this and that he and Alison were very, very close. On many occasions Robert had privately confided in Angus that Alison was the wife he had never formally had. She was his true support and his true confidant, the person to whom he could most trust, the one of whom he had never doubted. The accolade was huge as Robert made it his business to trust as few people as he possibly could. Alison had been able to get through this impenetrable wall. Whether they actually had more of a relationship in terms of sex, Angus had no idea. Alison had always been a very beautiful woman and Angus knew only too well Robert's weakness for that. She was a tough character though and she did not go out of her way to ever make friends. Angus's relationship with her was testimony to that. He wondered if she knew all that was in the will, knew just how much Robert really thought of her.

Angus took off his glasses, placed the will down on the table in front of him, and smiled.

'Do you know that Robert and I were best friends since

we were wee spotty lads in Edinburgh. Obviously I was the spotty one! Even then Robert seemed to be able to surmount most things put before him. God those days seem like another lifetime and yet, even now, I can close my eyes and be there with Robbie, on the flat roof behind the house, seagulls overhead and us overlooking the most beautiful city in the world.'

'I didn't know you could see Seville from there Uncle Angus!' offered Taylor to much hilarity across the room. Angus laughed too.

'Once, when we were both just 14, I saved his life.'

That stopped the laughter. Angus waited, allowing the words to enter the room and be fully digested. There was only silence now as he told a story that only Maddie knew. He had considered it his duty to tell the tale and make the memory of a Robert that the room would have not known, real for them. The choice of this story was an easy one to make, a distant memory lodged in history between Robert and himself, a fact that had he failed to save Robert the people in the room would not be sat before him at all.

'We were on top of the house on the flat roof out the back when Robert decided to go walkabout. It all happened so quickly really. One moment he was teasing me about some girl or other when the next he had slipped and there it could all have ended. But it didn't. He got lucky, or I should say he made his own luck by flinging out his hands to catch himself on the edge of the roof as his short life no doubt flashed before him. Even then he would have gone, his fingers unable to hold his weight, but then, in an instant that all happened so fast, there I was, pulling him back on to the roof, saving his life. You know, that story pretty much sums up Robert's life. No matter what seemed to come his way, he got lucky, and invariably in some shape or other I, or one of you, or one of the many people around him, were there to help him too. And yet,' and as he spoke his voice choked slightly and tears came into his eyes, 'he was clearly a man that we all knew to be possessed by all sorts of demons. He had the Devil on one shoulder and God on the other and yet I don't think he was ever really aware of this, not too often anyway. Maybe in the end things got a little clearer for him. It was a dynamic that made him pretty special, but that left not too much for us. But he loved us, everyone one of us, in his own way. This is the truth and I can only speak the truth on this day of all days. I share this story to underline a man we loved and who has left these instructions that I am about to read.'

Angus cleared his throat and took a sip of water. He placed his glasses back on and went on with the will's instructions.

'To go back to the will then, the condition is simply this. He wishes you, Jasmine, to head up the Foundation and do with it whatsoever you will.'

As Angus spoke the colour drained from Jasmine's face. Angus looked up to her and smiled, and went on.

'He places on you no restrictions in anyway, shape or form, as to the direction and decisions you make in running the Foundation. It is yours to do with what you will.'

Jasmine felt the strong arm of support from Alice around her shoulder as Taylor arrived at her side and took her hand, love and a smile written across his face. She looked to Angus.

'No uncle Angus, no! Why? Why me?' she asked.

Angus looked back and nodded, his warm friendly face making her more at ease with what she was hearing.

'You know Jasmine, he saw in you what he never saw in himself. Your humanity is what he was missing and the truth was that he saw the Foundation as missing this too. Do you remember when you told him you were to become a nurse?'

Jasmine nodded, her eyes streaming with tears.

'And do you remember what he said?'

'He said that there was nothing in nursing but long hours of back breaking work for no recognition and hardly any reward.' As she recounted her father's word she felt the chill of him actually being there with her. The rest of the room smiled and nodded, almost hearing Robert speak the words too, words so typical of his viewpoint.

'He did! He told me he'd said that,' smiled Angus, his very voice comforting Jasmine as she looked back to him. 'It made me laugh too. But do you know how proud he was of you, how around the world he would tell the stories of his daughter working long, back breaking hours, for no reward other than that of a smile of a patient with nothing else to give? For awhile, and to be brutally honest with you, I wasn't sure how much he meant it Jasmine, but he meant it alright. Do you know how much is sat in assets within the Foundation?'

Jasmine shook her head.

'Over three billion pounds in cash and investments and double this and more in fixed assets. The point is this. Left to Robert and his board they could never get away from the mentality that it was better to keep than to give. He knew you would be bold enough to break this cycle because you understand the word humanity.'

'But, but, I... Look, I have a job that I am very proud of. I don't want this.'

'He knew you'd say that,' replied Angus.

'Did he indeed. And?' Jasmine asked.

'He said it's fine. Keep doing what you are doing but you, and only you, must over see the Foundation going forward. He insisted you be the lead in the Foundation.'

'And if I refuse?'

'Then the money from the estate earmarked for the Foundation will be split between you and Taylor to do with what you will.'

Jasmine looked at Taylor who's face showed no sign of temptation of the frankly ridiculous sum of money at all. Why would Robert make them take this choice? She looked to Alice, a warm smile returning her gaze.

'So we could have the money and give it away to whoever we wanted,'

'Or spend it on cars! In fact I could buy a football club. The boys would love that! Re-name The Emirates! How very tempting,' offered Taylor.

'And in so doing lose all that has been painstakingly built up over many years within a highly efficient and globally recognised power for good. Keeping these monies within the Fund is a highly tax effective choice savings the estate millions of pounds in inheritance taxes. Further it will be a sum that can further galvanise the many superb people within the foundation to do better,' added Angus, warming to the final task Robert had given him in Switzerland two weeks before his death.

'But I have no experience!' bemoaned Jasmine, wanting deep inside to be able to take the challenge but feeling unable to deal with the responsibility, the burden on her own.

'Yes, he knew you'd say that as well. He said, firstly, that your inexperience makes you perfect. Secondly he knew you would never go for this alone and that's why he has offered two jobs to two people here today.'

An audible gasp seemed to come from the entire room. Angus allowed things to settle down and then continued.

'Has he offered me the charity café?' asked Taylor, lightening the tension in the room as he did so.

'Not quite Taylor, though if you wanted it Jasmine could probably arrange that! No, Robert has specifically stated that he would like Charles and Alice to take senior positions within the organisation, Charles as Finance Director and Alice as Director of Communications.'

Charles sat with his mouth literally wide open, totally bemused and yet exhilarated to be asked to tackle such a huge job as a force for good.

Alice simply shook her head in disbelief. She had called Robert many things in her own head, and never were her thoughts positive. Now she was prepared to consider that maybe he had a heart after all.

'So you see Jasmine,' Angus continued, 'he knew you wouldn't take the role any other way. He knew you would wish to have the people you love and trust around you and that his wishes, made clear here and now, would pave the way for the senior team in the Foundation to accept the changes and embrace them. The Foundation is now yours to do with what you will on your terms.'

Jasmine shook her head in wonderment.

'Well you have to hand it to Dad don't you. He has taken his will reading to become a recruitment drive for his Foundation!'

The room was now alive with chatter and Angus called things to order.

'Alright, let's finish matters here. Robert's share in Jones Ltd is made over to Alison absolutely.'

Angus stole a glance at Alison who nodded her head in acknowledgement. Everyone had assumed this would be the case and Alison's ease of acceptance suggested she had known this too.

'And, if you are agreeable Jasmine after due time for consideration, then the rest of the estate is to be split equally 4 ways, the work having already been done to have Trusts up and running as follows. He leaves the monies to his two children, Jasmine and Taylor, to you Edie, and to you Alison.'

Edith's face dropped.

'No Dad, no! I cannot be the same as Jas and Taylor!'

'Oh sweetheart,' it was Jasmine, her voice calm and assured, 'you can! He knew you would use the money to do what he has encouraged you with all these years. You carry the torch of Francesca and you know what that meant to him, in fact Edie what it means to us all, to all the family. Besides, Taylor and I, well we know how much you meant to him.'

'I don't know what to say,' Edith said, her mother stroking her arm and wondering what to make of it all.

'You can give it all to me!' suggested Taylor causing Edith to turn to him immediately to see how serious he was and to be greeted by a loud laugh.

'Edie,' Taylor offered, realising a little seriousness was needed, 'it was Dad's money to do with whatever he wanted. I'd said to Charlie that I expected nothing and that would have been fine. It's all good Edie, all good, you hear me, all good!'

Edith nodded.

'You know how much Francesca meant to my Dad,' continued Taylor, 'well, it's like Jas says. In you, you continued that. You still continue that.'

'OK Alison?' asked Angus.

Alison sat wiping her eyes. She was dressed very elegantly and had kept herself to herself all day. She knew all present, of course, and was on good terms with them all. She had often played gatekeeper between them and Robert, had seen the children born and grow up. There had never been any doubt that Robert would take care of her through his will, indeed all those years earlier when Ronald had still been around, Robert and Alison had come to an agreement to this affect. Still, here and now, Robert had delivered his true love for her and the emptiness she felt welled up inside her. He had been her one true love throughout her life. She did not know how she would cope without him.

'Yes, I'm OK,' replied Alison, 'just a little overwhelmed actually.'

'We all are,' said Jasmine, keen to make Alison feel at ease, and walking over to her to take her hand and sit by her side.

'And,' continued Angus, 'he has asked me to read out this note.'

The room went quiet and Angus opened a sealed

envelope, unopened, unseen and unread by anyone until this moment. He unfolded the one page of A4 writing paper and read.

'Hello! Sorry I couldn't be with you but this is one journey I have had to make alone. I don't have much to say so please bear with me.'

Angus took a sip of water and continued.

'To Jasmine and Taylor I would like to say that I have been a poor excuse for a father and I am very sorry for this. You have suffered for my life and this has been one of the great regrets of my life. I hope that you know that you have been loved and that you have always been in my thoughts. As I have gotten older I have come to realise that your life choices have been wonderful, and whilst I have not understood most of them at the time, I have come to realise you were right to follow your own dreams. I am proud of you both and love you both.'

Jasmine allowed tears to fall down her cheeks yet again. Charlie stroked Taylor's hand as he just stared straight ahead.

'To Edith, I know this will come as a shock to you. The gift I have left you is as much about your work and the need for it to go on and be braver and bolder, as it is about you carrying the torch that my mother, Francesca, lit all those years ago. Your work has kept her memory alive in me and that has been more important, more precious than you could ever imagine. She was my everything and when I lost her I thought nothing could touch me again. Your work touched me. Thank you.'

Edith smiled. She knew only too well how art moved people, giving many a sense of a world they often missed. It gave breathing space. It had given Robert breathing space.

'To Alison, I have loved you all my life. We have had a relationship based not on marriage and the formalities that the world looks for, but rather on a simple truth of trust.

We have trusted one another through all and everything over a lifetime. You have always been at my side and my life has been richer for it. I have asked you to support me when others could not and you have never let me down. My Alison, my sweet and strong Alison.'

Alison's face was closed to emotion now. She had heard the words and again simply nodded acceptance of them.

Angus took another sip of water and swallowed hard as he saw his own name last on the list.

'And to my oldest and best friend Angus.'

At this Angus placed the paper down and wiped away his own tears. There was a pause as Angus continued to cry and the room waited. Taylor then stepped forward and walked over to Angus, placing his hand on his shoulder, and then continued to read the note.

'You have been my rock. You have kept me from going insane. You have saved my life on too many occasions for you to ever know. I have caused you immense pain and I am truly sorry. You are an exceptional man, a man I could never have been. I see that now. I love you my friend.'

Taylor stood at the side of the man who was more his father in almost every sense than Robert had ever been. Angus lifted his own hand and patted that of Taylor's, which still rested on the older man's shoulder.

'Thank you Taylor, please sit down. There's one more thing.'

Taylor returned to his seat and to his wife Charlotte, who looked at him with immense love and affection. As he sat down Angus threw him a set of car keys.

'Recognise it?'

Taylor looked at it. He recognised them immediately.

'No! You're kidding right? Really?'

Angus smiled. He had just thrown him the key to a top of the range 2010 shining black Porsche Boxster.

'He bought it back the day after you'd gone. He's kept it ever since. His way of black humour I guess!'

'Where is it?'

'Outside.'

And here, 2 years on, Jasmine was on her way to meet Taylor, Charlotte and the boys to find something 'exciting' in Florence. Taylor had said it was a treasure hunt and would not elaborate more except to say she could not miss it as it was family gold dust. Taylor, from being a child, had always had a look of excitement and lived life as though a new surprise would await him around every corner. There was no mistaking his glowing exuberance around whatever it was he had discovered this time.

She had not been to Florence since a trip with Alice in their early 20's. They had such happy memories of a city bathed in sunshine and beauty. Alice sat across from her now, lost in a book as always. Her long dark fringe hung down the side of her face, occasionally falling too far forward and needing to be whisked back. 44 years old! How had they both reached such an age! Jasmine just smiled, her love for Alice being the most complete thing she had ever known in her life. She loved her completely. Alice caught her looking and offered her a blown kiss, which Jasmine pretended to catch and placed against her heart.

Over the last 2 years Alice had been so important in helping her with the Foundation. It was a task for which Jasmine had no confidence whatsoever, but what she did have confidence in was Alice and Charles and this was Robert's masterstroke. Jasmine had placed them immediately in control of the daily running of the Foundation, working closely with those already there, but with a new emphasis on ensuring all funds worked toward the goals of care and assistance, and not investment and profit as had been a large foundation stone in the old organisation.

Charles had been only too eager to start straightaway,

but Alice needed some assurances that she would be able to walk away if it was not for her. Jasmine had given her these assurances and Alice had not looked back, leading the Foundation with a fresh vision and vigour that would have even impressed the old leader.

Charles had been absolutely brilliant, taking to the Head of Finance role of the Foundation with relish. He took a literal axe to as much as he could from day one, chopping out any waste he could find and making the organisation as lean as it could be. As he did so, Alice took the message of a strong Foundation ready for the next generation out into the world and ensured the fund raising continued at pace.

Over the course of 2 short years they had trebled the amount of monies given into chosen areas, areas too that had doubled in number. Robert's Foundation had been good at helping out in areas that the world could see. It had not been good at getting involved in the hidden world of poverty and degradation. Jasmine saw to it that this was their most important area for new assistance. The people who they helped would be their witness, not the press.

The train pulled into the busy station of Santa Maria Novella at Florence so much of it looking as it had done since it was built 100 years previously, and as it had looked 82 years earlier when a certain young man from England had arrived to meet his sweetheart.

The two women alighted to find an as ever grinning Taylor waiting for them.

'Hey Jas!' shouted Taylor as his sister and Alice walked up the platform towards him.

They met in a flurry of hugs and smiles.

'It's good to see you baby brother!' said Jasmine placing her arm through his as they left the platform and walked into the heart of the station thoroughfare.

'It's good to see you too sis and you too Alice. It's been

too long and you my dear sister are too busy.'

'I keep telling her,' said Alice who had been saying the same thing to her ever since she had known her. Jasmine knew very well how to give time to most things apart from herself.

'I'm enjoying myself,' replied Jasmine truthfully to them both, joy filling her up being surrounded by her two favourite people in the world.

'Well that's good!' said Taylor, proud of the work his sister continued to do, 'but a break is good too Jas.'

'And that's why I'm here!' she replied.

'It is, so it is!' accepted Taylor.

'And why are we here?' asked Alice, desperately keen to know the surprise.

'Ah yes, this must be killing the reporter in you eh?' teased Taylor, 'All in good time Alice! Now, this way.'

They walked out into the hot Florentine sunshine, hailed a taxi and got in.

'River Hotel per favore,' Taylor informed the taxi driver.

'The River Hotel near the Arno?' asked Jasmine, amazed by the memory that had flooded back. Alice and her had enjoyed the views over coffee at the hotel 20 years previously. Staying there was luxury far beyond them at that time, but calling in for coffees had been within their budget.

'Yes indeed, by the beautiful and magnificent Arno.'

'How delicious! cried Alice, 'just where I would have chosen.'

'Have you been to Florence before?' asked Taylor sensing she had.

'Yes, with Jasmine.'

'Sorry, of course! I remember it well. The weekend when you both got down to it.'

Jasmine hit Taylor's arm. Taylor and Alice laughed.

'It was. It was pretty something,' said Alice with a delicious smile across her face.

'At it all hours were you eh?' asked Taylor, delighting in his sister's reddened face.

'Not quite the same energy now though Taylor,' smiled Jasmine, determined to embarrass her brother back.

'Quality Jas, not quantity. At least that's my excuse. And did you stay by The Arno then?'

'You're joking,' replied Alice, 'we had no money then. We actually stayed by the station. It was very lively and totally invigorating. Florence is lovely.'

'Yes it is,' said Taylor, equally entranced by a city that was not only beautiful, but that also had a family secret to unveil.

The taxi weaved its way from the station at Santa Maria Novella and through a plethora of back streets, the driver using his horn to encourage the many mopeds that remained a strong facet of Italian street life to get out of the way. It was late morning and Florence was busy.

'So come on Taylor, why are we here?' asked Jasmine, a question her brother had avoided and refused to answer since he had first called her all those months previously.

'Why do you think?' he asked with a cheeky glint in his eye.

Jasmine smiled. She had thought through many possibilities including her grandparents who had lived here many, many years before. In the end though she just kept coming back to Robert.

'Dad I assume.'

'No, not Dad.' Taylor was grinning now. His sister had not guessed. How wonderful!

'You need to go back further,' he offered by way of helpful assistance.

'Further?' asked Jasmine, knowing already the answer.

'Yes, further.'

'William and Francesca then.'

'Indeed.'

'But why?' wondered Jasmine.

'Because of a happy and delicious memory that may probably prove to be a wild goose chase but could be a wonderful find,' replied Taylor mysteriously.

'Now I'm really intrigued,' said Alice, who had come along to support Jasmine and not known what to expect other than a wonderful break in a city she had loved and couldn't wait to get back to.

The taxi dropped down Via Guiseppe Verdi towards the Piazza Santa Croce.

'You see when Dad came to see me in Seville all those years ago, he told me he would give me Francesca's journals.'

Jasmine's eyes lit up. She knew quite lot about her grandparents as all who had known William and Francesca seemed to have some story or other that they had of them. They were people who were in love and who left an impression, indeed Francesca's paintings were now some of the most celebrated paintings the world over. Robert had told Jasmine that his mother would have been mortified by the prices her pieces were sold for. It had touched her that her father, who was infatuated by money, saw that his own mother was so different. He had loved her so and her art meant the world to him. He had kept so much himself despite the fact that selling it would have meant huge money. When William had died, Robert had given the pieces of Francesca's that his father had to Taylor and Jasmine. That too had touched her enormously.

'So when I sold the Porsche for the second time,'

'You sold it!' exclaimed Alice, amazed that Taylor had sold something that had obviously been some connection between father and son.

'Of course I did! What was I going to do with a car like that? If I had not sold it, Charlie would have done it for me. You know she can't stand trophies of any kind.'

'Apart from you,' offered Jasmine mischievously.

'Well yes, of course. Apart from me! I am her token

trophy! Well, anyway, just as I was clearing it out I found the journals. Dad had left all the journals in the boot of the car. I think the whole thing was his little joke.'

'How fantastic!' said Alice, impressed by the care taken by Robert to leave something so special in a unique way for his son.

The taxi waited, stuck in traffic that the many laws of traffic control were supposed to have ruled out. Trying to get Italians away from their vehicles was proving a difficult puzzle to solve. They had created icons of automobiles and were finding it hard to give them up so easily for energy efficient public transport, despite the fact that as they all sat in traffic, the electric trams moved along without obstruction.

'And for the last 2 years I've been reading them!'

'2 years!' gasped Alice and Jasmine almost at the same time.

'Yep, 2 fascinating years.'

'Why didn't you tell me?' asked an amazed Jasmine.

'All in good time sis! A nice surprise is always a good thing isn't it? Guess how many there are.'

'22?' offered Jasmine.

'128.'

'128!!!!' shouted Jasmine, causing the taxi driver to look in his mirror and offer a frown.

'Yes, 128 amazing, handwritten and illustrated of course, and all extremely personal journals of Francesca Marinetti. They are full of gold dust. They cover everything from her time in Naples where she was born, through to when she thought Granddad was dead, to his arrival in Florence and to Dad and Edinburgh and, well you know, everything.'

'Wow! They must be worth a fortune!' Alice said the words and then felt embarrassed by them, her face reddening. 'I'm so sorry, I didn't mean that. Of course you wouldn't want to sell them!'

The taxi was now moving at last and moving down the Via Dei Benci towards the Lungarno Della Zecca Veccia and their hotel.

'I have thought about it.'

'Have you?' asked Jasmine, surprise in her voice.

'Well I am human Jas! Of course I heard Granddad's voice and I knew where they needed to go.'

'To the National Galleries of Scotland!' asked Jasmine, sensing her brother's thoughts before he could even say them. It had been with pride and joy that they had heard the story from both Angus and Robert over the years about how William had given so much of Francesca's work away to the Galleries, much to the happiness of Angus and the annoyance of their father.

'Indeed. I have set it up for you to hand them over after you have had all the time you need to read them yourself. I've arranged it on a 5 year rolling lease with any ownership to only go back to The Foundation should the charities need ever be that desperate that you would need to sell them.'

'Wow. That's fabulous. Give me a hug.'

Taylor leant over to his sister and they hugged. As he nuzzled his nose in her long dark hair around her neck he could have been pretty much any age. This position had comforted him on many occasions. As they hugged, Alice rested her arm across Taylor's arm that rested around the top of Jasmine's back. The relationship of brother and sister was special and had kept them both from serious harm, harm that Robert had wrought across their lives throughout their upbringing.

The taxi at last arrived outside The River Hotel and they stepped out into the day that was now getting quite warm.

'You have thirty minutes to get changed and meet us all in reception. No time, unless you are very quick, for monkey business!'

Jasmine tutted and Alice smiled.

'Charlie and the boys are so very excited about you two coming over. Cesc particularly is beside himself! Seems to think you mentioned a new Arsenal shirt on the phone.'

'Well, I couldn't resist it!' said Jasmine.

'Thirty minutes?' asked Alice who had been imagining a nice sleep in a cool Florentine hotel room that would hopefully open out into a shady inner courtyard full of flowers and shutters and painted walls.

'Yes, thirty minutes! I have right now a lunch feast on the way, a feast that was last tasted 82 years ago in the Boboli Gardens and that is where we are going to go and taste it again.'

One hour later and the party of 6 were sat on picnic blankets under a set of cypress trees eating a picnic prepared by a friend of the hotelier. They were dining on a banquet made entirely of the ingredients described by Francesca in her 8th journal in the May of 1952 when her love had made his way back from England to meet up with her in Florence. She had written down the contents of the picnic in minute detail and Taylor had therefore had no trouble in having it recreated for them now all these years on. After all it was all local to Florence and the traditions still lived on strongly.

They sat in a spot that Taylor could not be sure was the same spot that his grandparents had sat in all those years earlier, but the view that stretched out over Florence, a city virtually unchanged over centuries, seemed to match that which Francesca had described. It was quite hot now, but the trees were doing their job of shading them beautifully.

As they finished up the picnic having enjoyed Tuscan flatbread, luxuriously mixed extra virgin olive oil, a typical Tuscan meat plate mixed with classic salads, Taylor began to tell his audience why they were in the Gardens.

'You mean you don't even know Charlie?' asked

Jasmine, the 14 year-old Cesc leaning into her side as she stroked his long blonde hair behind his neck.

'Not even me Jas,' laughed Charlie, 'he has been a man on a mission and has guarded this secret for a very long time.'

'You see, I first read about what we are all here for about 18 months ago, but this is the first time we could all get here!' said Taylor, setting the scene for what was about to follow.

'OK Dad,' Eduardo entered the fray, the patience of a 17 year old wearing thin, 'we are all very pleased for you, you know, for the journey you've been on and all.' He had heard this phrase of 'being on a journey' on a football programme recently and he quite liked it. 'But please, for the love of all that is human, please tell us why we are here.'

The party laughed a lot at this summing up. Jasmine had heard Eduardo speak but it could easily have been a young Taylor. The two were so alike.

'Thank you son. I like your style. I will get on to that now. You see this is the spot, ish, sort of, where Francesca and William had their picnic 82 years ago, a picnic that we have virtually just copied.'

'And are we going next to where they had dinner?' asked Eduardo to general amusement.

'And,' continued Taylor, ignoring the sarcasm of his oldest son, 'this is where they chatted and shared their deepest dreams, dreams that they had thought they would never find together once they lost each other in Naples in the second world war. You see, they had thought their futures to be separate, and yet here they began to again believe in their joint future. If it hadn't have been for here, then it would not have been the start of us! No Granddad Robert, no Jasmine and Taylor and no Eduardo and Cesc!

'Bravo Francesca!' said Alice, raising her glass to the group, who joined her in the toast.

Taylor, who was enjoying himself immensely, continued.

'Francesca describes this day in great detail because this day burned in her life, crucially I guess because it included the time when she and William found a new depth to their love. You see after they had eaten, they talked and talked some more and then they made love.'

'Here?' asked Eduardo in dismay, feeling adolescent discomfort at the mention of sex in the company of adults.

'Well not on this spot, obviously! They would have been arrested! They made love near here. Francesca in this journal describes the spot.' At this point Taylor produced a battered looking tan leather book, wrapped together by long pieces of leather that bound around the journal and held it all together. He began to open the pages to where he had placed a bookmark to the sheet that contained the directions.

'So let me get this straight,' asked Alice, laughing as she did so, 'you've brought us here today, including your two young and impressionable sons, to see the spot where your grandparents first got it on?'

Taylor found the place in the journal, looked up and laughed. He looked at his watch. It was 2.00pm.

'Follow me!' he cried, turning to walk up the gardens and causing the group to quickly get up, gather their belongings as rapidly as they could, and fall in behind him.

'Can't you get him to slow down?' Alice asked Charlie.

'Do you think I could get him to do anything given the journey he is on?' laughed Charlie. 'I can't tell you how excited he has been about this.'

'It is all pretty amazing isn't it?' agreed Alice, 'I mean here, all these years on, we are reliving something that started it all.'

'Yes we are!' said Charlie, throwing the last remnants of the picnic into a large bag.

'In your own time!' shouted Taylor in jovial fashion from higher up on a grassy bank. Charlie gave him a gentle look.

'Sorry!' said Taylor suitably reprimanded.

They walked in what was now very hot sunshine up the gardens and on towards the formal walled garden at the top of the hill. As they did so Taylor shouted out a commentary on the Boboli.

'What you see before you is pretty much what Florentines saw for the first time when these gardens were opened to the public for the first time back in 1766! Imagine the excitement!'

'What? Seeing all these plants followed by more plants and, oh joy of joy, more plants!' offered Eduardo, causing his younger brother to laugh so much that it caused him to get hiccups.

'It's the only real open bit of extensive greenery for the whole of Florence, and what a space it is,' continued Taylor who was very much leading the group like a tour guide.

Encouraged to do so by Taylor, the whole group turned at this point and looked at the unbelievably clear and expansive view set before them. Florence looked magnificent.

'It's beautiful isn't it?' he asked to everyone and no one in particular. Even the boys, their teenage years distracting them from most that life had to offer them, were taken with the view before them.

'Camille Corot painted this view in 1834 and it's pretty much still the same today. How many more places can you say that of eh?'

'Camille Corot!' laughed Charlie. 'Did you make that up?'

'No I did not!' replied Taylor in mock indignation. 'I may have picked up the odd fact in Francesca's journal!'

'You should consider doing tour guides professionally!' suggested Alice.

'Indeed I should! Is there money in it? Come on, follow me!'

They dropped along white pebble tracks, the wonderful sound of running water, a soothing feature of the Boboli Gardens elaborate irrigation system, all around them. Here they walked past elegant statues that stood tall and watched these British tourists walk their paths, just as they had watched William and Francesca all those years earlier.

The paths felt far fresher with shade and a slight breeze to help. Finally they came to the magnificent fountain island, still looking incredibly beautiful despite the fact that Giovanni de Bologna statue of Oceanus had first been placed there hundreds of years previously.

'OK. Here we are!' declared Taylor as though he had just led them to the top of Everest.

The group stopped and looked at their guide not knowing what was to happen next and not seeing anything that particularly screamed out what it was they were actually looking for.

'What are we here for Dad?' asked Cesc, tired from the walk but young enough to remain excited by the possibility of a treasure to be found.

'Well son, we are here for a memory. I hope we can find a message that was left for us by your great grandparents how many years ago?'

'82!' replied Cesc proudly as Taylor rubbed his hand through his son's curly tight hair.

'And this message is here?' asked Jasmine.

'Yes it is. It is here! At least I hope it is here.'

Now there was a hush amongst them as they fell in behind Taylor once more as he made his way across the island, past the fountain, and then turned left, walking towards a small statue of Venus. At this point he stopped.

'OK, do I have a volunteer?'

5 hands were raised and Cesc was chosen.

'Why Cesc?' asked Eduardo, now fully involved in matters.

'Because I reckon he would be about the same size as Francesca.'

'Oh,' responded Eduardo with a confused expression that was matched by everyone else.

'Now then Cesc, I want you to walk 20 paces for me, away from me and following the outside of the path.'

'20?'

'Yes, just 20 normal steps.'

'OK.'

Cesc began to pace out the steps and as he did so the others counted out loud and followed. After 20 steps he stopped, Taylor arriving at his side.

'Right, turn right and count five paces in.'

Cesc looked to his right and saw the path turn into plants and looked back his father.

'You want me to walk into the plants?'

'Yes.'

'I'd normally get into trouble for that sort of thing,' replied Cesc with concern in his voice.

'Yes you would.'

'Taylor?' asked Charlie, aware that her son walking into the Boboli shrubbery was probably not the done thing and any watching park keepers would have much to say to them about the intrusion.

'It's OK baby,' replied Taylor with reassurance in his voice. 'There's no one around. Just us mad Brits in the heat of the sun!'

Charlie gave Taylor a confused look, not knowing where he was going with this.

'It will just take a few minutes. It'll be fine, honestly.'

'OK,' Charlie replied.

'Right son, off you go.'

'And if I ruin my trainers?' asked Cesc, concerned about his new and far too white Etnie's.

'I will clean them.'

'But if I ruin them?'

Taylor now gave Cesc a look of encouragement to get on with things.

Cesc took the hint. He liked this game anyway! He stepped into the plants as instructed and counted out 5 steps and then stopped.

'What are we looking for?' asked Jasmine, entranced by the spell she felt under.

Taylor looked at her and just smiled. He looked around the island and saw it was all still very quiet. Only a few fellow tourists were brave enough to be in this heat. Taylor stepped in to join his son and produced from his bag a small spade.

'Taylor!' exclaimed Charlie, 'we'll get arrested.'

'Yes, I know this looks bad. Just form a wall in front of us and try to look casual. Look as though we are having an in depth discussion on Venus.'

'Or football?' asked Eduardo.

'Indeed! Do lots of pointing! Look involved!' offered Taylor helpfully, a mischievous grin written across his face.

They did as asked and Taylor began to dig. Within a few minutes he had dug a small yet wide hole. What was he digging for? He was digging for family history gold dust, a secret message buried in an empty wine bottle by two young lovers towards the start of their journey into a life that they hoped would be full of love, excitement and passion. The fact was that this could be a stupid chase for something that had been moved years ago, a stray item found by accident and simply discarded. Equally the place they had decided to dig at could be so easily wrong. For all he knew he could have misread the pages and they could even be in the wrong part of the garden!

As he dug more earth out of the ground, and sweat fell from his brow, he felt hope begin to leave him. What if Francesca had paced this out all in very short steps or very long steps? What if she had remembered it all differently and written down things that did not match what she had actually done?

As Taylor's heart fell heavy, and the exertions of the day after months of preparation and hope began to take their toll on him, he looked up at Cesc who returned his look with wide and excited eyes. That was all the encouragement Taylor needed. He returned to digging. Three more, four more, five more mounds of earth were lifted until his small spade suddenly hit what he had been looking for. Two more minutes now of careful digging and he had it in his hands. As he rubbed the bottle clean he could see a note. Yes, this was it! He knew it. Within moments the hole was re-filled, and this party of secret excavators left the scene and, laughing as they went, ran into the trees behind.

'OK,' said Taylor, holding the soil covered bottle high before them, 'this, amazingly, I hope is it! The note left secretly from our grandparents 82 years ago and discovered by our fine search party here today!'

He pulled out the cork allowing the air of a bygone age to escape. He then got out of his pocket a small set of tweezers.

'Are they mine?' asked Charlie, knowing the answer already. Taylor nodded solemnly as he continued with the crucial part of the mission.

He lifted the bottle upside down allowing the note inside to fall to the top. Carefully he got hold of the note and pulled it out slowly. As he did so the wind caught it and released it from the hold of the tweezers. Charlie watched as time seemed to slow and the message floated in the breeze as it fell through the air. And then there was Taylor, his sweet hand dropping to retrieve it from the soft ground on to which it had fallen.

There on the note, written by William, was a simple truth. That he loved Francesca and that she loved him, and that their love was for all time, forever. There too were the words from a poem.

*'She walks in beauty,*
*like the night of cloudless climes and starry skies;*
*and all that's best of dark and bright*
*meet in her aspect and her eyes.'*

Chapter 23

# The End

June 1994. Port Isaac, Cornwall, England

William parked up his car at the top of the hill and locked it carefully. Not that he need have taken the care. There was next to no crime in Port Isaac. The local paper was beyond upset on the previous week when someone had doodled all over the phone directory in one of the public phone booths. The story had made William chuckle. If only the level of crime was so extreme across the UK! He had come from city life with all its hustle and selfish mentality, into the sweet and secure isolation of the haven of Port Isaac. He felt very blessed to have found his place to rest after his loss.

He had enjoyed a wonderful day having driven down to Godrevy Head to enjoy one of his favourite views across the bay, past the fabulous white washed lighthouse and over to the sun blessed St Ives. William loved this spot. He had sat for hours lost in the sounds and sights of the bay, a bay that he had enjoyed with Francesca and Robert on several holidays through the years. In fact less than 2 years earlier he had sat here with Francesca, the two of them enjoying precious moments as they dined out on a picnic lunch. He felt her with him now. Her warmth touching his cheek, her body resting in his arms. The truth was that she had never left him. He felt her with him every moment of every day.

There in front of him was Godrevy lighthouse, a place that had always stood out to William and filled him with inspiration. It stood on its own island 300 yards off Godrevy Point, with waves that were invariably mad washing between the two. Trinity House Lighthouse, its official name, was built to protect sailors from the submerged reef, which stretched for a mile across the eastern approach to St Ives Bay. It had been responsible for many a sea calamity and eventually the lighthouse had been built to protect more from death. William had read that the lighthouse reached an impressive 26 metres tall and that it's light reached over 12 miles at night. It was a beacon of hope for sailors and passengers alike, and it had the same affect of uplifting William's spirit whenever he saw it. Somehow it made him feel stronger, more able to face what was before him. The lighthouse with its history and longevity gave quiet to his soul and connected him, in some way, to the earth around him.

William had enjoyed a long lazy picnic and the view that took in the darkly clad surfers to his left as they caught the flying waves that spun them high into the air. They were like sea birds playing with gravity, their wet suits keeping them warm and allowing them to spend hours in this dance.

He then walked north along the coast for a few miles, enjoying the pleasant day and taking in the azure enriched views out to a sea that met the beautiful heathland that this part of the coast was famous for. William had his binoculars with him and sat for a few hours high up on the coast looking out at many types of gulls and other seabirds. The variety was extraordinary. He spent a lot of time looking down too at the grey seals as they spent such energy getting on and off the cove below him. As they did so they barked their extraordinary messages to one another and their voices made William laugh a lot. It was wonderful, all so wonderful.

Eventually as the sun disappeared behind dangerous looking and dark clouds, William made his way back to the National Trust Car Park and drove north to his home at Port Isaac. It was already well into the evening and William felt the exertions of the day creep into his bones as a cold north easterly wind that had just begun to blow made him happy to have reached the warmth of his trusted VW polo.

It was late and quite dark as he eventually made his way down the lane to his cottage. The cloud had now arrived in force and had totally covered the sky as he had driven back up to the North Cornwall coastline. Now, with no moon and stars to help him, William had walked slowly from his car aided only by a distant streetlight. As he rounded the bend to turn down his little lane to the front gate of his cottage, it became almost black. Once again he had forgotten to leave the outside light on and once again the lane lamp was out. Reminding himself that he must contact the local council to mend the blasted light, William fumbled with his gate latch, mumbling to himself as he did so, and then walked down the short path to his front door. It was then that he became aware of steps behind him. His heart rate seemed to double immediately as he realised to his right, by the door, there was another figure waiting for him.

'We've been waiting for you all evening old man. It is time for you to be quiet.'

'Is this a dagger which I see before me,
The handle toward my hand? Come, let me clutch thee:
I have thee not, and yet I see thee still.
Art thou not, fatal vision, sensible
To feeling as to sight? Or art thou but
A dagger of the mind, a false creation,
Proceeding from the heat-oppressed brain?
I see thee yet, in form as palpable
As this which now I draw.
Thou marshall'st me the way that I way going,
And such an instrument I was to use.
Mine eyes are made the fools o'th'other senses,
Or else worth all the rest. I see thee still,
And on thy blade and dudgeon gouts of blood,
Which was not so before. There's no such thing:
It is the bloody business which informs
Thus to mine eyes. Nor o'er the one halfworld
Nature seems dead, and wicked dreams abuse
The curtained sleep: witchcraft celebrates
Pale Hecate's off'rings: and withered murder,
Alarumed by his sentinel the wolf,
Whose howl's his watch, thus with his stealthy pace,
With Tarquin's ravishing strides, towards his design
Moves like a ghost.-Thou sure and firm-set earth,
Hear not my steps which way they walk, for fear
Thy very stones prate of my whereabout
And take the present horror from the time
Which now suits with it.-Whilst I threat, he lives:
Words to the heat of deeds too cold breath gives.
I go, and it done: the bell invites me.
Hear it not Duncan, for it is a knell
That summons thee to heaven or to hell.'

Macbeth
Act 2 Scene 1